INFERNO

INFERNO

Patrícia Melo

Translated by Clifford E. Landers

BLOOMSBURY

First published in Brazil as *Inferno*
by Companhia das Letras, 2000

First published in Great Britain in 2002
This paperback edition published 2003

Copyright © 2000 by Patrícia Melo

Translation copyright © 2002 by Clifford E. Landers

The moral right of the author and
translator has been asserted

Bloomsbury Publishing Plc, 38 Soho Square,
London WID 3HB

A CIP catalogue record for this book is
available from the British Library

ISBN 0 7475 6159 1

10 9 8 7 6 5 4 3

All papers used by Bloomsbury Publishing are natural, recyclable
products made from wood grown in well-managed forests.
The manufacturing processes conform to the
environmental regulations of the country of origin.

Typeset by Palimpsest Book Production Limited,
Polmont, Stirlingshire
Printed in Great Britain by
Clays Ltd, St Ives plc

I

SUN, LICE, SCAMS, GOOD people, *pagode* music, rags, flies,
television, funk, loan sharks, sun, plastic, storms, junk, sun,
garbage, and con men infest the area. The boy climbing the
hillside is José Luís Reis, known as Kingie. Except for Kingie,
no one there is a José, Luís, Pedro, Antônio, Joaquim, Maria, or
Sebastiana. They are Giseles, Alexises, Karinas, Washingtons,
Christians, Vans, Dianas, Klebers, and Eltons, names picked up
from soap operas, television programs, from the international
jet set, from magazines at nail parlors, and from the imported
products that invade the favela.

Climbing. Dirt streets. Eleven years old, the boy Kingie. A
kite in his hands. Orange shorts. A little girl waves at the
cinematographer's camera. Television news crews are a common
sight in the favela. The girl says she knows how to samba. And
she does. She thrusts her rear toward the camera, wiggles her
hips, sensually. Two skinny boys, at the door of Onofre's bar,
mock the girl. They suck on a mango. The fat girl wants to
shake it, they say, just look at the fat girl. They guffaw. She
calls them meddling pieces of crap and goes on shimmying. She
smiles at Kingie. The boys ask the cameraman if they can do a
rap number. Yes. The mango is thrown away. Piles of garbage.
Go ahead, says the cameraman. Buzzards. Dogs. *I wanna be a
metamorphosis/ A metamorphosis that walks/ I rather be that than
listen to your talk/ Metamorphosis/ Talk about this, talk about that/
Time for me to blow this habitat/ Metamorphosis!*

This is Raul, says the cameraman, and Kingie follows them,
moving faster. During their walk up the hill, maids smile
at him, children pass by, people going to work. Hi, Kingie,

bricklayers greet him, children, dogs, electricians, hi, hands wave, barking, dogs, nannies and data-entry workers, dogs, plumbers, gigolos, doormen, car thieves, children, they smile, girls at windows, parking attendants, muggers, seamstresses, they smile, gunrunners, the place is chaotic, children, laments, it's noisy, disorderly, jammed, dirty, and colorful. Kingie makes his way through it all, being especially wary of the dogs that cross his path.

From above can be seen numerous parabolic antennas and asbestos roofs. Low-flying planes. Garbage. Dogs defecating in the underbrush. Trains. Two-story buildings. Public phones, lines of people. A strong wind blows. Kingie leans against the guard rail at the observation point and gets his kite ready. He has never understood why the kids from Berimbau fly kites for fun. What beauty is there in a kite in the sky? None. Just the colors. What was pretty was seeing a vulture fly. If he were going to play, he'd choose something else, running a key over the green nap of the sofa, an old piece of junk his mother's employer had stuck in their house, vrooom, he simulated ignition and carried elegant passengers from the Hotel Nacional, vrooom, Leblon, Copacabana, Ipanema, Barra, shopping centers, purchases, vrooom, Avenida Atlântica, beaches, perfume, women with their legs crossed, lips, vrooom, black silk, white women, high heels, why had they closed down the Hotel Nacional? And if he shut his eyes and accelerated, vrooom, the car would enter a deserted thoroughfare and everything would whiz by him, vroom, the white of the sand by the sea, the blue, the green, the gray of the sea, racing, the gray of the sky, racing, he avoided the poles that appeared before him, vroom, fled his house, vroom, his mother, his bed, fleeing the beatings and the long nights, vroom, vroom, and if he accelerated even faster, after many curves he would find at the end of a tunnel, blocking the road, a tall man with the chest of a professional swimmer. Hi, I'm your father, said the man, getting into the car. Continue. They continued, friends. He always imagined his father as white, despite having seen many times in the only two photos he had stolen from his mother that his father was black, very black. Handsome, his father.

Just, decent, honest, his father, the black one, not the one in the dream. Every time, his father explained that what they said about him was a lie, the stories that he had gone out to buy beer and had never come back. Dirty slanders. The cirrhosis was a slander, the binges, the beatings, the lovers, slanders and more slanders. The encounters with his father didn't occur only when he was on the sofa, driving, but also when he tossed sleeplessly in bed, and vroom, he was a taxi driver. But he didn't like meeting his father that way. It was better when his father was waiting for him at the door to the house. Let's go to McDonald's. Let's go to the movies. Let's have some popcorn. Let's visit Bahia. Let's hunt wasps. It was easy to become owner of a fleet of wasps if you followed his father's instructions: capture them on rainy days, in puddles, pull out their stingers, tie them onto strings and watch them fly, enslaved. Another thing that his father taught him, in the dreams, was to use the broom as a microphone and to repeat words he heard on television: deficit, treasury bonds, real estate market, bank loans, exchange rate. The people on television, almost all of them, were greatly loved by Kingie.

But Kingie was not there at the top of Berimbau hill to play. He was a professional observer. And he liked to observe, not this way, from the heights, the complex, the entire favela, the shacks, the crowds. He liked details. A lady's foot, on the bus, the calluses, the clean or dirty toenails, long, painted, ravaged by fungus, the toes sticking out from sandals, the heels, he could never understand why minutiae, deformities, and disproportion attracted him so, very fat women, or very thin ones, very black, very kinky hair, Kingie couldn't take his eyes off certain kinds of ugliness: the folds of fat of the morbidly obese, the look of bonhomie of mongoloids, cellulite at the beaches, sweat on upper lips, quadriplegics, the maimed, cripples, they all caught Kingie's gaze in the same dizzying way as the beauty of Suzana, his neighbor. Somebody's going to smack you one in the street, Carolaine, his older sister, would say. Stop looking, don't stare at people, she would say when they were on the bus, at the beach, or anywhere with lots of people. Later, when he became Reader's friend, he found out that in France people used the time on

3

public transportation to read. Reader thought the Europeans' habit of reading was great. Just imagine, reading, reading all the time. On the subway. In cafés. Kingie couldn't understand his attitude. He always believed the most interesting thing in the world was men and women. More attractive than books and scenery. The women. He always felt spatially disoriented because he never paid attention to the street, routes, signs, references. He just watched people. The women. The men. The children. And the dogs. And that was precisely his job, to watch. The marijuana smokers were the easiest to recognize, calm, careless, quite different from the cokeheads, who were tense and only slightly less rushed than the users of crack and other hard drugs, addicts who showed up at the drug site in distress, upset, hyperactive, as if they worked at the stock exchange. A junkie's got a hard life, said Miltão, the drug boss in the Berimbau favela and boyfriend of Suzana, who was beautiful to die for. He steals, Miltão would say, he sells any piece of trash he can find at home and runs over here to get straight, it's real crap, the life of a junkie. And if he's hooked on heroin, much worse. Because the guy feels a delicious sensation like he's coming down a roller coaster, that first time, and later he shoots up to keep from shaking and sweating and shitting the bed. It's hell. All this blah-blah-blah, Miltão said, is just so you'll understand: don't get mixed up with drugs, kid. Never. If you want to be a real trafficker, stay away from crack, grass, powder, and all that good stuff we sell here.

It didn't matter in the least if the person ascending the hill was white, black, an addict, a journalist, a charity worker, or some high-society type slumming, the order was simple and clear: the traffickers must know everything about anyone who entered the favela. Be suspicious of everybody, Miltão said, even the tourist groups in rented jeeps who pay to see the sewers and the poverty. They come here, they've got to be checked. And if the guy can't put two and two together, as far as I'm concerned he's fucked, Miltão cautioned. There was a code that controlled the kites' movement in the sky. When children like Kingie suddenly disappeared from their observation points and

4

the kites vanished from the horizon, the traffickers knew exactly what to do.

That morning, Kingie made himself comfortable at the observation point and after two boring hours of work, watching the entrance to the favela, the movement, the alleyways, the antennas, the rooftops, the people, Vintão, of the residents' association, Rosa Maria, the hooker, Dedé and Preta, the washerwomen, the customers, Negão sitting at the door of his shack, selling cocaine, the soldiers, Suzana's mother arriving, Suzana leaving, Suzana, Suzana, Suzana, prettier day by day, the children running, Suzana and her delightful laugh, Kingie felt very sleepy, Suzana, laughter, the boy's eyes were closing against his will. Fighting off sleep, he took from his pocket a piece of paper, tore it in two, drew a grid on each half, numbered rows and columns and drew battleships, submarines, and destroyers on them. He played Naval Battle, taking the role of both players, one of them himself, the other his father. And even having as his opponent his father, whom he loved so much despite not knowing him, despite the horrible things his mother said about him, drunkard, bum, no-good, womanizer, Kingie couldn't help cheating, quickly sinking his father's warships one by one. He made an effort to cheat on behalf of the other I, the father-I, but he soon discovered that there is a primary I inside our Is, an I concerned only with its own interests, self-indulgent, an I that cheats, conquers, and doesn't notice the arrival of the police.

When Kingie heard the shots, it was already too late. It did no good to signal. Goddamn. He reeled in the kite, indecisive, should he go back home? Should he plunge into the labyrinth, taking the chance of getting caught in the crossfire? He finally hid in the water tank. He ducked his head and came to the surface. Pa ra pa pa pa ra. Goddamn. Kingie had heard that some of the lookouts could recognize combat weapons just from their sound, American AR-15s, South Korean Daewoos, Russian AK-47s, guns that shot fifteen rounds a second and cost as much as seven thousand dollars and didn't just kill the enemy but ripped him to shreds. But Kingie knew nothing about guns. Not at that time. He dived again, darkness. Surfaced, pa pa pa ra ra, darkness, pa pa ra pa pa pa, all very fast, the helicopter left, the worst part came afterward, a long silence, a nothing, not even the barking of dogs. Water up to his nose. That's the worst part, Miltão would say, in war nothing is worse than silence. It may be a truce, there's a good chance it's a truce, the trafficker said, but there's an equal chance of somebody taking a bullet in the carotid, of nothingness, bang, and death. Diving. Goddamn. Silence, silence, silence. Nothing else happened. Kingie didn't leave the water tank even when he was sure the police had withdrawn. What would Miltão say? How had he not seen the police? What about his mother? Why are you all wet, José Luís? His mother's cold voice, her impassive gaze. Where have you been, José Luís? Slap, slap. Tell me, you idiot. His mother liked to hit him in the face, on the cheeks, tell me, boy, before I take you apart, and slap, slap, you little fool, I'll teach you, slap. Kingie knew that after the lengthy sequence of blows his mother always calmed down and plopped in front of the TV, that was the only reason she beat him, to be able to watch her soaps in peace. What did it matter if he did poorly in school? Who didn't? Who cared about it? Who knew how to read? Or write? The beatings had nothing to do with that, or with Miltão, though she sang the same tune every day. If you take up with Miltão I'll kill you, she repeated the phrase so many times, I'll kill you, with such force that it ended up putting the idea in Kingie's head and he went to see Miltão to ask for a job. Even today he can remember perfectly how everything happened. It was right after a beating. He took a friend's kite and waited for Miltão to show up at Suzana's house. And while the two were kissing at the gate, Kingie ran back and forth with the kite in his hand. Miltão didn't even look. Nor Suzana. Then Kingie had a better idea. He stopped in front of the couple and began to shout and tear the kite, ripping the paper into pieces, breaking the frame and throwing everything onto the ground, shouting the entire time. Miltão liked what he saw. He laughed. Crazy kid. You want to work for me? That's how it began. After all, it was his mother's idea. Because of his mother's beatings, I'll kill you, I'll kill you if you throw yourself in with those outlaws.

Slap. After the whippings, Kingie felt as if he had swallowed a wad of sadness, a wad that wedged in his esophagus, between his throat and chest, slap. Go ahead and beat me, he thought, beat me, you can beat on me, and in time the wad broke up, slap, and Kingie came not to feel anything, never again, slap. It was nothing but flesh being hit. Beat me, he thought, go ahead, it doesn't hurt, goddamn it.

Here's the kite, they said. A familiar voice. Kingie ducked underwater and was immediately yanked up by the hair. Hey there, lucky, said Look At That, want to go for a swim? Look At That had that nickname because he was always fascinated by electronic equipment. He would say 'look at that' about any piece of junk that whistled or lit up. Look at that blender, look at that clock, look at that revolver, and Miltão started calling him Look At That. Look At That dunked Kingie so many times that the boy fainted.

When he came to, he was in a stuffy room without windows, a team poster of Vasco da Gama on the wall. The other four lookouts were there also, Vavá, Loro, Bisnaga, and Luizão, all sitting on the floor, their clothes torn and their eyes wide with fear. Vasco da Gama. If someday he met his real father, he'd invite him to go to a Vasco da Gama–Flamengo game. Television playing. Jaú and Look At That with their eyes glued to the set. A soap. Gabi is bad news, the actors were saying, she's capable of anything. How did Gabi find out about the safe? She's no good. I'm afraid of Gabi, Ângela. An entire episode saying that, that Gabi was bad news. Goddamn. Kingie shut his eyes, his mother was probably watching the soap too. In all the houses on the hillside, the television on, the actresses' voices, romantic music, then the commercials, buy this, buy that, the music, the buttocks, the beer, the special sales, the newscasts, the misfortunes, Kingie felt a certain relief at that familiar sound, the sound of the TV always gave him a sense of peace and family. So you're awake, huh, kid? Look At That asked.

Miltão came in during the commercials. Turn off the TV, he told Jaú. Fuckers, he said, looking at the boys. Shitass fuckers. We lost Melão because of you five stinking shitass fuckers. I've got five stinking shitass fuckers idiot asshole pieces of shit working for me. Five blind stinking pieces of shit. Imbeciles. C'mere, dumbass. You imbeciles. You ought to be killed. Fucker. You first, Kingie. The rest of you line up. And I thought you had a future, you of all people, Kingie, I thought you could put two and two together. He always said that, Miltão. Two and two together. Assholes. C'mere, asshole. Kingie approached him. Miltão took a .38 revolver from his belt, placed the gun barrel against the palm of the boy's hand and fired.

2

PAVÃO PAVÃOZINHO: MACHINE GUNS, rifles, and grenades, thirty men. Abacates: forty men, AR-15s and AK-47s. Maria Penha: leader Creudão, fifty men, imported arms. Baiana: ninety men, pistols, rifles, leader Feinho. Salvação and Tucano: two favelas, eighty men, automatic rifles, leader Zé Boléu. Rato Molhado and Jacarezinho: 120 men. Kingie was at the home of Bidê, general secretary of the drug site at the Berimbau favela, waiting to talk to him. He liked memorizing the names of favelas, with their leaders and their weapons and their armies. He always carried around a map of the drug traffic in his pocket, from a magazine his mother had brought from the home of the woman she worked for. The headline, in red letters imitating drops of blood, read War in Rio. The city in flames. Shootouts. Tanks. Photos of young boys with their faces hidden by T-shirts, and weapons. Shit. They just loved that kind of photo, the journalists. He'd seen a photographer ask one of Miltão's boys to strike a pose. Raise the weapon, the photographer said. A 9mm pistol. Kingie sitting, swinging his legs, memorizing. Alemão complex, fourteen favelas. Leader? He had difficulty memorizing names. Difficulty reading. Acari complex. Shit. Numbers. Juramento.

Bidê was on the phone, his feet on the desk, shorts, no shirt, the fan blowing straight into his face. Heh heh heh, his laugh sounded artificial, heh heh, so they want to come up the hill, do they? he asked, showing no sign of concern. Do they? Invading's no sweat, heh heh heh, it's easy to start cracking skulls, kick in doors and arrest people, kid's stuff, heh heh heh, the problem comes later, heh heh heh, that's the hard part, heh heh, so you think that's what they want? You know how it is, man, there's no way out of here. Getting out of here's for experts. Heh heh heh. Rocinha, Kingie memorizing, rifles, heh heh heh, Bidê's laughter distracted the boy. Won't those guys ever learn? asked the secretary of the site. An ugly smile, full of holes. Broken. People shouldn't laugh so much. He, Kingie, didn't laugh without a reason. He didn't laugh at all. Shit. He didn't like to laugh. Heh heh. An Israeli Uzi submachine gun on the desk, Bidê stroked the weapon as if it were a cat. They're going to get it, Bidê said on the phone, they're going to eat lead, man, heh heh heh, lead. For sure. My man. The rear bridge, memorizing, sales of fifty-eight kilos a month. Heh heh.

A young woman came in carrying a shopping bag, Bidê gestured for her to wait. Heh heh heh. The rear bridge, fifty-eight kilos, leader Denão, major weapons? In the favela everybody carries bags, thought Kingie. The bus stops are full of shopping bags. And moving around inside the bus, worse still, shopping bags everywhere, bags from the supermarket, fancy boutiques in Ipanema and Leblon, electronics stores, import houses, every type of shopping bag. Poor people don't throw away shopping bags. A blue house, said Bidê, tell me more, man, where're you talking from, is it safe? I know, man. A blue house. I'll show them a blue house, man.

The girl waiting, her shopping bag at her feet, plastic sandals. At first Kingie didn't see the bruises on the woman's face. 'Lowest prices anywhere' was printed on the shopping bag. A swollen eye, a cut over the eyebrow.

Bidê hung up the phone and smiled. Heh heh. You can talk now, lady. The girl quickly poured out her suffering to the secretary, saying she couldn't take it any longer, her husband Waldeci, Waldeci had gone too far. Waldeci always beat her when he drank, but never in front of the children. Waldeci used to be a good father, *used to be*, she said, he isn't anymore. Since he's been out of work Waldeci is like a mad dog. Waldeci drinks like a fish and then he beats me, even in front of the kids, you see this bruise here? That's Waldeci. This one here? Waldeci. The one on my leg? All Waldeci. She didn't care if her husband busted up the house, she was used to it, let him tear it up, poor guy, let him rip everything apart, but destroy her Roberto Carlos records? The only thing I have in life is Roberto's music.

Kingie felt bad sitting there listening to the woman's tragic story; he concentrated on the papers in his hand, the Dendê favela, he heard Bidê advise her, Cidade de Deus, tell her to leave, Nova Holanda, Pára-Pedro, not to say anything to her husband, the Andaraí favela, I guarantee, Bidê said, you won't be getting any more beatings.

When they were alone, Bidê asked if Kingie was feeling better, referring to the wound in his hand, still bandaged. Heh heh heh. Kingie said yes. It's like a hospital around here. Heh heh. Knock knock knock, Bidê rapped his knuckles on the wall and Bidezinho, his brother, came in at once, heh heh heh, I talked to the cop, Bidê said, heh heh heh. Bidezinho listened to what his brother had to say, some scumbag had phoned the police and told them that a house with a blue door would be getting in a large shipment of cocaine. They laughed, both of them, heh heh, identical laughs. They called, huh? A blue house? It was said that Bidê and Bidezinho were twins, but Kingie couldn't see the resemblance, only their laughs were the same, heh heh heh. Bring the kid his pay. And in a minute the bills appeared on the desk. Here it is, you can go, and keep your eyes open. Heh heh heh. The phone rang, Hello, talk to me, Miltão, some heavy shit's coming down on Friday.

Kingie picked up the four fifties and left. Bright sun. It was his first salary. Rosa Maria, the hooker, passed him. Hi, love. She called everybody 'love'. Swaying up the hill, Rosa Maria, tight skirt, wide hips. Four fifties in his hand. His mother's wages was six fifties. A much tougher job. Alzira is stupid, he'd heard his mother's employer say, when he was very small. He'd had a high fever and Alzira had been forced to take him with her to work. I try to teach her, Dona Juliana told someone in the living room, a friend, who listened in amusement, I teach her but it does no good, Alzira is the dumbest person I've ever seen in my life, ask her to say the word 'broccoli'. Ask her to set the table, just see what she does with the silverware. Asparagus is espargus. I'm going to buy espargus, Dona Juliana. And arugula? Laughter. Espargus is hilarious. Laughter. Arugula is aruge. If I depend on that wretched woman I'm dead. 'Espargus'. A complete idiot. She's dumb, she's cunning, she's slow, that's Alzira. So much humiliation for just half a dozen fifties. Thinking about facts like that hurt Kingie. Shit. Take a stand, Alzira. His mother came into Dona Juliana's living room and replied in kind, You think I'm stupid? Well, I think you're fat and useless, doing nothing but eating junk and drinking artificial sweeteners, stuffing yourself with chocolate and cheating on your husband. I hear the stupidities you say on the telephone, Dona Juliana, always giggling with Mr Fernando, the fitness instructor, I know all about the meetings, and whack, this slap's so you'll learn to treat human beings better. That was his mother's attitude. In his dream. In reality, his mother didn't take a stand. She fixed her gaze on the sink full of dirty dishes and listened to Dona Juliana laugh at her, a 'bumpkin', a 'hick', 'dumbbell', and other similar descriptions. Maybe that's why Kingie's father had deserted the family. His father was cool. Intelligent. Tough. A manager. Proper. A businessman. He imposed respect. There are limits to everything, he said, in dreams. Actually, it hadn't been exactly in the dream, Kingie had seen a man on television saying in a forceful way, Enough, there are limits, there are limits to everything. And his father came to talk that way, in the dreams. Enough. Stop. Limits. To everything. When it came to humiliation his mother knew no limit. She descended into hell for her six fifties.

Dona Juliana was the type of woman Kingie often saw in Leblon, as well as in cars, at traffic lights, driving Mercedes and BMWs and Lincolns, neither fat nor thin, squeezed into pants a size too small, effusive women who do a lot of dieting and working out, wear bangs and frost their hair, paint their nails gold, are zealous mothers and yell at Alziras when they're in a bad mood. Kingie, from his bed, separated by a plywood board from the double bed where his mother slept with his sister, could hear the two talking. Stuffy nights, rain. His mother's voice, confiding, lamenting, I can't stand it, I can't take it anymore, daughter, the shouting in my head. All because I stained something. Burned something. Ruined something. Didn't get everything done. Just because I forgot. Just because I don't know. Six fifties. Dona Juliana's children, a couple of teenagers. The boy was nice, Otavinho. So quiet he could come and go without anyone noticing. The daughter was just like her mother, puffed up and a shouter. Marcelinha. Another one with bangs. José Luís descending the hillside, hands in pockets, blue sky, he could feel in his fingers the texture of the bills he was carrying. Very good. Shit. Children, dogs. Onofre's bar, a samba on the radio. The Pentecostal church, its doors closed for good. Miltão had expelled the preacher. Anybody who puts fear into 'my citizens' gets fucked, the trafficker had explained. Here, God has to make allowances, and a priest can't come on too strong. We have businesses on the hill. We work and we make money. That sin stuff can't hurt me, Miltão would say. Kingie, descending. And thinking about many things. Dona Juliana yelling, how could his mother stand it? It's no use, my dear, I've already taught the woman how to make a codfish risotto, rosemary salmon, orange duck, but she cooks like a monkey, what can I do? His mother constantly crying over the humiliations she suffered, complaining to Carolaine, his sister. And Kingie hearing it all. Descending. Things like that were very bad for the boy. Discontent. The desire to lie down and sleep. Hi, Kingie, people liked him, especially the ladies who asked him for favors. Can you carry this bag for me? Tell Créo the gas truck's here. Buy me a pack of Hollywoods, no filter. Créo, the gas truck's here. No filter, please. Kingie had a hard time saying no, he did the favors as he descended the hill, it cost nothing. The boy's pure gold, they told his mother. Such a good boy, that José Luís.

At the bus stop he took the bills from his pocket, looked at them, put them away. He'd buy a new pair of sneakers. He'd always wanted Airwalk sneakers, to take a step and feel the poof, poof, the softness. What if he gave the money to his mother? No. And he also wanted a cap with Nike on it, black. His mother could trade in the TV. Or buy a washing machine. How much did a washing machine cost? No. As he was getting on the bus he saw Suzana arrive, in a taxi. She smiled, waving automatically, as always, automatic Suzana. Kingie hoped she wouldn't expect a smile in return, he didn't know how to smile like that, Hi, he felt awkward, ciao.

On the bus, he didn't want to look at anyone. Four fifties in his pocket, he felt the contact with them, crisp, new paper. So different from Alzira's greasy, crumpled money. His mother had received a wallet from Suzana at Christmas, but she hadn't given up the habit of wadding the bills into her damp hands, furry, stinking bills. Kingie didn't like that. He'd buy a colored T-shirt.

The city through the bus window, factories, housing projects, warehouses, businesses, lots, garages, more warehouses; it was some time before the buildings appeared, buildings, buildings, stores, and the sea, sea, sea, lots of people running, bicycles, skates, people walking, ice cream, coconut water, and health. Kingie got off the bus in Leblon. Four fifties. He stopped in front of the building where his mother worked, on General Artigas, looked at the doorman. He would never be a doorman. A dumb life. *Sitting with a wide-open mouthful of teeth*, the song was right. Anybody who saw Miltão walking around Berimbau could tell the difference. The same with Bidê. Heh heh heh. Cars and imported watches, women, gold bracelets, that was good, but not the best part. The best part was the way Miltão acted. There was a bit of everything in his shack, you name it, gold, VCRs, dollars, imported rugs, anything, Suzana swore to him. But what impressed Kingie was the way Miltão looked at people. Bossing them around. I'm in charge. I do things. I'm the man. He'd show Dona Juliana a thing or two, in Berimbau.

Kingie moved along the *calçadão*, the walkway along the beach, thought about buying an ice cream, changed his mind. Sneakers. Changed his mind. The cap. Changed his mind. He wandered around, bought nothing, went back to the walkway, so many people at the beach. Guys playing volleyball, a group of nannies talking, babies, a pleasant breeze. Rio de Janeiro really was a pretty city.

He lay down on the sand, the sky, hands in his pockets, truly pretty, grasping the fifties. Tightly. And he slept. He awoke stunned, the cars, the motor scooters, the people returning home. He was hungry, a rare thing. He was never hungry.

At home, he found his mother leaning over the stove. I'm making beans, she said, smiling. Where were you? So sad, his mother. At Grandma's. Beans. He lay down in bed. Is Grandma OK? He felt he was about to fall asleep. Grandma's fine. Making an effort, he got up, put the fifties beneath Alzira's pillow. He returned to bed. He wanted to sleep.

3

THE TELEVISION WAS ON. Water running down the drain, dirty dishes, glasses, her hands wet. Alzira's hands were always wet. There was no time to wipe them. She would dry them, sweep, get them wet in the bucket, dry and wash, sink, bidet, water, cleaning, clothes to wash, dishes, to rinse and then dry, at home, at work, her hands always in water. A pot on the stove. Fingertips wrinkled, reddish. She had bought a cream at the drugstore, wasted money, she had concluded later, her hands were still rough, red, hands cooked in cold water. Wash clothes, hang them up, there were many things Alzira wanted to do before going to bed. Order was very important. Cleanliness, she'd always been very clean. Orderliness. The trash could stay outside. In the street. She removed the pressure cooker from the flame and stuck it under the faucet. Sssssssss. I don't have money, but I'm clean. Good-looking beans, smelling nice. The house all straightened up. Cooked hand. Swollen. The skin on the back of the hands was delicate like a baby's, but the palm looked like a beat-up piece of old plastic. She threw oil into the pot, minced garlic, slices of onion, bay leaves, sautéed the beans. Caroline didn't know how to cook. Good thing. Caroline wouldn't be a maid. Or the wife of some bum. She'd work in an office. Mr Rodrigo had gotten her into a computer course. Free. Dirty clothes, she took them to the wash tub. Caroline, elementary school behind her, plus a computer course, the girl was nothing but a source of pride, Alzira even softened her voice when she spoke to her daughter, a mistake actually, softening up, she should be more strict with Caroline, tell her to stop that business of wanting to be a model. Silly little

16

girl. All the girls in the favela wanted to be blondes, models, television hosts. You know how they choose children's show hosts, Carolaine? For their ass, daughter. She scrubbed the clothes, slapped them against the tub, wrung them. Is that true, they're chosen for their ass and not for their ability? And another thing, Carolaine should know once and for all, she'd never be a model. She knew how life was, and things simply don't happen for us, Alzira said. She went to the door. They never work out, good things. Carolaine hadn't come back yet from her computer class. Bad things happened all the time. Young girls getting raped. Girls pregnant. Girls involved with the drug traffickers. The worst thing in the world was to have a female in the house. A virgin. She swept the living room, the bathroom. It was hell being a woman. Men were a bunch of animals. She got the bucket of water and a damp mop, ran it over the floor. She liked the smell of cleanness. Fourteen years old, get pregnant and you're out on the street, she'd said. No end to the dust. I'm not bringing up anyone's child. It's the street. When it doesn't rain, the dust is even worse. Unpaved streets. I do everything for you, Carolaine. I arrange for a free computer course for you, I'll find some way to buy you a computer, I do everything, computer, wait, you'll have one, but if you get pregnant, I swear . . . She crossed the yard and went into the bathroom. I swear I'll kill myself if you get pregnant. Stop it, Mother, stop saying that, Carolaine complained, stop saying I'm going to get pregnant. But I really will kill myself, Alzira declared. I swear it. And she continued on the same note. She gave orders. Study. No foolishness. José Luís should at least finish fourth grade. It was better not to have children, ever. Only if you married a good man. Yes, she regretted it. Better not to have any. Nine-fifteen. Carolaine's class ended at seven, ten minutes to get to the bus stop, plus forty minutes on the bus, ten till eight, half an hour waiting at the stop, eight-twenty; the calculations always left Alzira distressed.

José Luís, your sister is late, she told the boy, who was sleeping in his clothes, the pillow over his head. He didn't move. Dirty, he didn't bathe, sloppy kid. Don't you want something to eat, José

Luís? I made beans. Kingie turned his head away. He hadn't even taken off his flip-flops.

Carolaine arrived at ten-fifteen. Do you know what time it is? The girl kissed her mother, collapsed onto the sofa. Ten-fifteen, Mother, took off her shoes, Mother, let's not fight. It was easy to placate Alzira. The students had gotten out late because the teacher had decided to give a make-up class. We're learning to work with Word. Operating system. DOS. Windows. Alzira liked hearing those words. That's English for 'janela', Mother, no point explaining it, you wouldn't understand.

They ate the beans in a bowl, with a spoon, sitting on the green velveteen sofa, beside the sink. Both barefoot. Carolaine made lemonade.

After dinner, Alzira went to hang the clothes by the fence, behind the house. Nice breeze, cool. She hoped it wouldn't rain. She always thought about putting out a mat and sleeping there, because of the heat. She'd never done it. She never did the things she liked. Everything should be planned ahead of time, order, organization, and Alzira couldn't manage to program her leisure, to go to the beach or sleep in the yard on a summer night. Impossible. It's my temperament, she thought. I was born that way. On Sunday she had woken up late, she had to catch the bus, go to work, clean all of Dona Juliana's silver; she'd already leaped out of bed, upset, when she remembered it was Sunday. She wasn't late. She could stay in bed, sleep till later. Make coffee, drink it slowly, on the sofa, next to her daughter. Maybe go to the beach. She could stay by the gate, chewing the fat with Dirce, Suzana's mother. Did she go to the beach? Did she listen to the radio? No. She worked, she cleaned, washed and ironed clothes the entire day. She couldn't remain idle. She would feel bad. She always had a cloth in her hand, cleaning. Temperament.

Clothes hung up, dishes washed, the house clean, beans ready for the next day, everything as it should be. Alzira took off her green dress, put on a clean T-shirt, brushed her teeth, in the bathroom outside, and got into bed. Carolaine was already asleep. She smelled smoke in her daughter's hair and nudged her. Carolaine, have you been smoking? Mother, please. If you have been, you'd better confess. Don't you lie, Carolaine. All right, Mother, that's enough. I'm not going to pay for vices. OK, Mother. She remembered Francisco, vices. Francisco, the wretch. Every time she thought of him, although lately that was happening less and less frequently, she would murmur, Wretch, cretin, no-good. At first, it was worse, Son of a bitch, she used to think. She couldn't avoid dirty words when the image of her husband came into her mind. The curses used to emerge from her lips like flowers in springtime. Now it was different. There was no more hate. Over time, hate dries up, Alzira concluded. It lasted three years, the rage. Afterward it rotted away. Became nothing. Son of a bitch. He'd die soon, for sure. Let him die soon. Him and his ruined liver. God, I regret so much having sinned. Forgiveness. Three Our Fathers. Three Hail Marys. Three acts of contrition. Amen. The weariness only came at that moment. She would say amen and the fatigue would descend upon her, like a building she'd seen collapse the past summer, it rained so hard, plop, went the building, from top to bottom, all its weight on Alzira, the tiredness, every brick. Her legs ached. Her arms throbbed. Her head felt heavy. Tomorrow: pay the light bill. She would ask for a voucher, tomorrow. Tomorrow, she would start on the living-room windows, Dona Juliana said they were filthy, the windows. How many months, Alzira, since you cleaned those windows? You're like that, Alzira, if I don't say anything, go clean things, you don't clean them, you don't take the initiative, use your head, Alzira. Go clean them. At first Alzira was hurt by the things Dona Juliana said. Use alcohol. Then she learned. Scrub it well. That was just Dona Juliana's way. Disinfect, Alzira. It was Dona Juliana's technique. She would mistreat her help then regret it. Would you like to try this chocolate, Alzirinha? You can leave early today, Alzira. What would I do without you, Alzira? I'm back, Alzirinha. She rolled over in bed onto her stomach, laughing, Alzirinha, and it was then that she felt it. To the touch it seemed like money. She turned on the light. It was money. Four bills. New. She nudged Carolaine. Was it you, Carolaine, who put this money here? Huh? the girl grumbled, half asleep. Huh? This money, was it you? Uhn, no, Mother, uhn, what money, Mother? Let me sleep.

Kingie in an open field, sun, sitting on the sand, saw a troop of horses on the horizon, colored uniforms, the troop coming toward him. Swords. There's a war going on, someone had told him, and we're losing. We have horses, tanks, soldiers, bombs, and we're going to lose. Kingie didn't know where the winners were, he just heard their voices. Them, the winners. Uniforms, gold buttons, the troop approaching, the enemy troop, trotting, in the sand. Where are my soldiers? The troop approached. Nearer. The sounds of the horses. They're going to kill me. They're going to shoot. War. Hooves on sand. Sun. His mother's voice, Wake up, wake up, not yet understanding what she wanted. There were horses, still. The money. I want to know about this money, she said, his mother, this money under my pillow. I dreamed about horses, the boy thought. Whose money is this? Where'd you get it? It's for you, he replied. Who gave it to you? Kingie was slow to answer, he needed a few seconds to think. I'm working, he said. Maybe it might be a good idea to suggest that his mother buy a washing machine or an iron, but he said nothing. Who for? Who are you working for? Kingie saw it in his mother's eyes. Shit. Before she beat him his mother would show it in her eyes. Who are you working for, boy? He didn't answer. Alzira grabbed her son's hand and ripped away the gauze covering the wound. Are you running around with those outlaws, José Luís? She looked at the wound. I knew it, she said. Answer me. With those drug dealers? I kill myself to send you to school, boy. Alzira had promised she wouldn't strike her son anymore, promised herself, but this was too much, out of control, her hand raised, powerfully, no one could hold it back, the deceiving boy, not even she herself, the hand's owner, the hand acted by itself, knowing the path, stupid boy, and struck. Talk, boy, there was no need to talk, and it was better not to talk, now, there's no excuse for stupidity, he needed to be whipped, blows to the head, the cheeks, he didn't even go to school anymore, the stupid boy. Miltão and those other no-goods who died at twenty, whap, she felt a fierce desire to injure the boy, batter him, and she hit, idiot, hit, and he didn't complain, doesn't it hurt? You have to suffer to learn your lesson.

When she left the house, the money in her hand, the boy was lying on the floor, with Carolaine standing over him, crying.

She walked quickly down the alleyways without the least hesitation. Her body felt strong, full of energy. May God be with me, she thought, and her feet trod the stones, holes, puddles, climbing, the empty alleys, potheads sitting around, she knew the smell of marijuana, Rosa Maria coming out of her house, silvery skirt. You all right, saint-lady? A prostitute, is that any way to greet someone? Saint-lady. She didn't even reply, lady, I'm a decent woman, she thought, silver skirt, my God, don't let José Luís become an outlaw, or a bum like his father. He'd taken after his father. Yes. Would she have to pay twice? She climbed the narrow streets, the taste of hate in her mouth, Mr Onofre closing his bar. Everything OK, Dona Alzira? Everything ruined, falling apart, rotten, but we mustn't go around talking about what happens in our own home. Everything's peaceful, Mr Onofre.

An armed youth tried to prevent her from entering the drug site. They were selling cocaine to the customers as they arrived. Any problem, Dona Alzira? She said she wanted to speak to Miltão. Go ahead, he said. My business is with Miltão. The youth took her several yards away and handed her over to another soldier. It's Kingie's mother, he said.

Alzira was taken to a hut close to where Preta, her washer-woman friend, lived. The soldiers went in, Wait here. She waited for over fifteen minutes until Bidê showed up. Bidê, pleased to meet you, let's go inside. You're the boy's mother, aren't you? Kingie. A good boy. Alzira refused to enter. She just wanted to speak to Miltão. He's on his way, he's already been told.

It took Miltão half an hour to appear, accompanied by seven soldiers. Let's go inside, Miltão said. Alzira preferred to remain outside. I won't talk out here. Come in.

They went inside. Sat down. Miltão, Alzira said, looking at

her hands, I know your mother and I was friends at church with your father. Only then did Alzira notice there was blood on her fingers. I used to hold you in my lap. In the name of the departed, your father, I've come here to ask you for something. In the name of Jesus. She placed the fifties on the desk. Here it is. Leave my boy out of this.

4

BEEF LIVER. OXTAIL. HOOF. Chuck. Loin. Zino's butcher's shop was across from the bus stop, from which could be seen a gigantic sign, yellow and red, with a drawing of a smiling cow, its body divided by dotted lines, loin, shoulder, flank, all the parts identified. Next to it, the list of prices. A refrigerator truck parked at the sidewalk, two men got out, opened the doors, and began to unload the bloody pieces, taking them inside the establishment.

There was always a lot of confusion and noise at the entrance to the favela, along Avenida Epitácio Pessoa. Cars were forced to slow down to avoid running over the crowd, which elbowed its way along the narrow stone sidewalks and the only paved street on the hillside. Within a short walk any type of product or service could be had. Besides the butcher's shop there was an automatic teller machine, an auto mechanic's, several boutiques, a pharmacy, hardware stores, electricians, street vendors' stalls, a fitness center, most of which operated illegally. At that hour, the buses discharged, at their final stop, residents returning from work.

Kingie, sitting on the bench in the bus shelter, didn't look at anyone. He was looking at the butcher's shop, absorbed, and at his own lap, the bloody meat, his aching legs, arms, bruises, he hoped no one would notice his swollen face, the wounds above his eyes. He, who always liked remaining invisible in the crowd, to observe freely whatever he felt like, was now the object of curiosity for passersby. He hated the way they stared at him. As if he were a festering boil, a beggar sleeping on the sidewalk, an epileptic having a fit during Sunday Mass.

Was that the way he watched people? Indiscreetly, laying his eyes on others' pain? Never. You and your curiosity, Carolaine said. No. Kingie wasn't some vulgar observer, a rubbernecker, he had technique, skill, knew how to play the innocent when he saw he was bothering someone. In such situations, the boy would lock his gaze on the infinite, like an idiot or a thinker, and concentrate on his peripheral vision, recording everything. You have to learn how to deal with Mother, Carolaine had said, after the beating. Run when she's about to hit you. Run. Why don't you run? You have legs, don't you? The problem was that his legs simply wouldn't move. Run. They were rooted to the ground, petrified. Run away from her. I'm leaving, Kingie had said. Shit. He felt paralyzed during the beatings. Are you in with Miltão? his sister asked. I want to find my father, the boy replied. You want some advice? the girl insisted. Don't tell Ma everything you do. She's nervous. Make up a few little lies. Do like me, she said. Lie. You remember our father? José Luís asked. For heaven's sake, why don't you stop asking about our father? Our father is small. Weak. Short. It had been disappointing to hear his sister's reply. Shit. His father could only be tall. Very tall. He'd never thought of him as short. Very tall. Shit. It wasn't possible to judge his father's size from the photos José Luís had stolen from Alzira, two crummy photos, a birthday party, his father behind the table, behind other people, just his face, serious. In the other photo, his father was cut in half by the frame. Even so, Kingie imagined him tall, muscular, strong as a boxer. And where was his father? I want to go live with him. Carolaine didn't know a thing. What's his profession? Bum, Carolaine had answered. Run. Small and weak. Kingie didn't believe his sister. Run, get away, weak, when she's about to hit you. Small, his father. Carolaine didn't know a thing. Run, get out of the house. Disappear.

It took Suzana a long time to arrive at the favela. She got out of the taxi, two shopping bags in her arms. Kingie left the bus shelter and rushed to help her. He felt shy when the girl took his cheeks between her hands, kindly, asking what had happened. Suzana, pretty, wavy hair, tight bell-bottom pants, her navel showing, red high heels, eighteen years old. She and Kingie walked slowly. What happened? Heavy shopping bags. When he was younger, Kingie loved watching television at Suzana's house, in the afternoon, eating condensed milk out of the can, with a spoon, on the sofa, and often, when the boy was being beaten, Suzana would burst into Alzira's house, breathless, and grab the boy away from his mother and take him to her house. Your mother, she said, gee, your mother is a real pain. And what about Carolaine? Why doesn't she do something?

At Suzana's house, they went straight into the bathroom. Jars and bottles on the shelf over the sink, perfumes, creams, lipsticks, Suzana was vain. Cotton, peroxide. Close your eyes, I'll clean you up. I'm going to talk to your mother one last time, she said. She's got to stop beating you. Where's Carolaine? I want you to do me a favor, Kingie answered. I want you to take me to Miltão. Wow, she said. You really are stubborn.

Kingie had already tried to talk to Miltão. In the morning, he had been through the entire favela looking for the trafficker. He'd stopped by his house, his office, waited for two hours in the square, beside the public telephone, in the hope he'd show up at Onofre's bar. The streets were crowded that afternoon. Miltão's men everywhere, carrying heavy weapons. Paint your door blue, said the voice over the loudspeaker in the square. The paint's here. Pitch in. Everything blue. Can after can of paint being taken from Onofre's bar. Don't you want some, Kingie?

Before looking for Suzana, Kingie had spoken with Bidê. Want some advice? the secretary had said. There's no Miltão, no half-Miltão, no Miltão of any kind, so beat it. You're out, Bidê had said. Heh heh heh. Get lost.

Now only Suzana could help him. Are you, Suzana, are you going to help me or not?

That night, Miltão had prepared a dinner to celebrate the escape of three comrades from the state prison. How's things, Suzana? Seventeen soldiers were guarding access to the spot. Hi, Suzana, they said, smiling at seeing her with Kingie in tow. Music. On the bare concrete of the school courtyard, a project abandoned by the government, people were dancing. How's it going, brother, they said, shaking hands, come on over, man.

Suzana crossed the space, with Kingie behind her, the smell of meat permeated the area, Beretta machine guns, they drank beer from the can, talked, Korean rifles, ate chicken. What's up, brother, how about some beer? Kingie paid attention to the weapons, still unable to recognize them, Uzis, AK-47s, you had to speak loudly to be heard. What do you want to drink? I want a beer, Kingie said.

Suzana left him sitting on the low wall surrounding the spot and came back with a glass of grape Fanta. You can't drink alcohol, she said, I'll be right back, stay here. The atmosphere was one of euphoria. Kingie suspected they were plotting something, the traffickers, and that made him even more unhappy. He didn't feel a part of it, get out, run, a rotten sensation in his chest, run, the words that came to his mind were 'dog crap', 'small', 'weak', and 'little piece of shit'. Actually, he'd never felt himself to be a member of the group, not even when he was the gang's lookout. He didn't walk like them. He didn't use weapons. Or slang. Shit. He didn't know about their plans, nor did he take part in their training. You're out, Bidê had said. Beat it. He put down the soft drink, got a beer, and moved away, always watching Suzana's movements in the distance.

That was the night he met Reader. The youth came up to him, smoking, his fingers stained from nicotine, asking if Kingie had noticed the doors of the shacks. No, he hadn't. You will tonight, he said. He pointed to the three recent escapees, the stars of the party. Armed. They support us, Reader said. I never worry about that type of problem, he said, lighting another cigarette. Kingie didn't understand what he meant by 'that type of problem', or any of the rest of the conversation. Notice the excitement? Reader asked. Yes, he noticed it, but he'd spent the day in a daze, his head throbbing, his arms, his legs, he felt pains in his abdomen, in his joints, he couldn't manage to think about anything. He hadn't noticed the blue doors and didn't even feel like asking why they were handing out paint at Onofre's bar. He wanted to talk to Miltão, that's all. He wanted his interlocutor to vanish, as quickly as possible. Reader was not in the least concerned with appearing indiscreet, he looked at Kingie's bruised face like a merchant interested in a product, attentive, direct. The only thing missing is for him to ask the price, thought Kingie, irritated.

Miltão, in one corner of the courtyard, was chatting with his friends. His hand around Suzana's waist. Miltão's easy swagger, gesturing, laughing, Suzana twice signaling Kingie to wait. Take it easy, she said. Shit. Take it easy.

Reader said he'd read in a book that Bill Clinton had a lot more difficulty taking control of a Texas bunker full of crazy visionaries than he'd had invading Haiti. Cool, said Kingie, avoiding looking at Reader, wanting to get out of there, not knowing what to say, why that dumb talk about Haiti? He didn't know what Haiti was. What did this man want who never stopped lighting cigarettes and filling the air with smoke? After some beating around the bush, Reader asked who had done that to him. Who beat you? Kingie didn't reply. Don't let anybody do that, he said. Was it your father? Kingie closed his eyes in a show of impatience. All right, Reader said, excuse me if I'm meddling. It's just that I can't stand that sort of thing. How old are you? Ten, I'd say. No one, whoever it is, your father, your teacher, whoever the devil it is, no one can do that. I speak from personal experience. Kingie looked for Suzana with his eyes. She gestured to him. Take it easy. And you know what's worse? Reader continued. We get used to being beaten on, man. I'm telling you. Soon you'll think it normal to catch a whipping. Yeah. It sounds crazy, but it's the truth. It hurts at first, but later you don't even feel the pain anymore. And if you goof up, you're going to think you deserve the punishment. It's true. And that's not the most disgusting part. The most disgusting part is that the son of a bitch who lays his hand on you also learns to like it. Yes sir. It's good to hit someone. It relieves the guy's tension, you understand? I know this shit. All the time I see you wandering around, all fucked up. It's not the first time. Every week, to tell the truth. I keep wondering who the scumbag is that did it to you. I'll bet every cent I have in my pocket that it's your father.

Is it your father? Come on, you can talk. No, answered Kingie unwillingly, it's not my father. Reader looked around, thinking that he didn't want to admit it. Silence. He took a piece of paper from his pocket, wrote an address. Come see me if you need to.

Miltão arrived soon afterward, he and Suzana, holding hands. Suzana whispered something in her boyfriend's ear and left. Many years later, Kingie would still remember that night, the things that Miltão had said, trying to seem kind and fair, like a dedicated father, but merely being cruel and unfeeling like any other trafficker in Rio de Janeiro. Thin, slight of build, his face covered with hematomas, a hole in his hand, Kingie pleaded to be allowed to stay in the drug trade, told Miltão he didn't want to go home again, shit, all that was missing was for him to get on his knees and beg. He would do anything, steal, to hell with his mother, he didn't want to go home again, he'd sleep in the street if necessary. No, no, no was all Miltão said. What would he do, then? Go study, Miltão said. School, he didn't want anything to do with school, shit. He hadn't been back to the third grade for six months now. Six months? Go back to school, Miltão said. He didn't understand a damn thing the teacher said, for shit's sake. Had Miltão gone to school by any chance? No one wanted to know about school. Not him either. He wanted to work. But not as a shoeshine boy or carrying packages at some outdoor market or as a squeegee boy, as Miltão suggested. He didn't want that. Impossible, Miltão replied, and you ought to thank me. It's not a good life, the one we're in. You want to die young? Yes, answered Kingie, I want a gun, I want to work. Miltão put his hand on the boy's head, paternally, smiled, and said, It's not going to happen. Shit. Kingie felt a terrible sensation, hatred, a wound exploding and tearing holes in his body, spreading in all directions, his legs, his arms, and especially in his mouth. What about my money? he asked. The trafficker stuck his hand in his pocket, took out a wad of bills, peeled off four fifties. Don't tell your mother, he said, handing him the money.

On the way back, Kingie noted that the majority of the shacks now had blue doors, as Reader had said. He found his grandmother, Cândida, on the porch of her house, painting the doorjambs. They gave us the paint, she said. I thought that was a nice thing to do. Let me paint it for you, Grandma. Can I sleep here?

5

HEAVY LATE-NIGHT RAINS. The street lights had been shattered that afternoon. Total darkness. Only a few lights could be seen at the very top of the favela. Miltão had thought of everything.

A Chevrolet station wagon inched its way up the Papagaios hillside, in front of Zino's butcher's shop, slowly climbing, its motor laboring. Immediately, twenty-four policemen, with shields, armored cars, and heavy weaponry, came out of nowhere like a pack of feral dogs, surrounding the area, blocking access to the favela. Machine guns opened the way. The soldiers advanced and were received by gunfire from Miltão's men. José Bezerra, the commander of the operation, was killed in the first minutes of combat, torn apart by a grenade. The driver of the station wagon was beaten and his vehicle destroyed. The motor was taken apart, the seats removed from the interior, nothing was found. The rain flooded the narrow streets, the mud was increasing, which was good for the traffickers. The soldiers opened fire, broke into shacks, woke families, struck the poor, and sloshed through the mud. Thirty people were arrested, all of them without exception released the following day, as there was nothing to link them to the drug trade. Stories of police abuse, beatings, blows with gun butts, wooden bats pummeling defenseless backs, battering from billy clubs, kicks, and electric shocks, like those of the driver of the Chevrolet, a mechanic for Que-Jóia Electronics, were heard at every bar, public phone, lunch stand, bakery, gate, and porch in the favela, as always happened after invasions. Children played at collecting bullets from the ground and from the plaster walls of shacks. The police hadn't found the 'house with the blue door' or the shipment of fifty kilos of cocaine that had arrived in a Chevrolet, according to the informer who had triggered the raid. The door of every shack, and every gate, wherever one looked, was painted blue. In places it could be seen that the paint was still wet, and cans and brushes were scattered throughout the favela's alleyways. The guys didn't have a chance, commented Miltão the following day, guffawing, easy, easy, it was as easy as taking candy from a baby, he said. The mechanic got his part for having done his job right, taking a beating and keeping his mouth shut. Look At That hadn't acted in good faith with the guy, failing to explain the plan completely. Drive your Chevy up the hill at four o'clock, slow, and go to your place. The guy had tried to back out of the deal, but traffickers don't take no for an answer.

The group was prepared for the raid. Days earlier, an informant had phoned to alert them. Paint that piece of shit purple, Miltão had said when he learned the police had raided one of his sites. Change storage areas. Change days. Change cars. Miltão was chewing gum, cleaning his weapon, less worried about the attack than about police informers. The police you can see. We shoot at them and kill them. But what about traitors? Someone on the inside, someone nearby, giving the cops details on the car that would make the drop, the location of the storage site – that worried him. It wasn't the first time there'd been a leak. We're going to change the setup, Miltão said. They were all at the trafficker's house, on a stuffy Tuesday, the sky darkening, thundering. Reader, when he heard the conversation, made a counterproposal. Reader was all the time saying that they had to put an end to that stupid business of criminalization of drugs, kept repeating to friends passages from a book he'd just read on the subject: Is marijuana bad for you? Then what about boxing? And mountain climbing? And speeding? Why don't they outlaw all of them? Why not outlaw obesity, which kills millions worldwide? We don't want people to fuck themselves but we permit cigarettes and alcohol. That makes as much sense as handing a loaded .38 to a suicide. We smoke till we die from cancer. We drink till we die from cirrhosis. Tobacco and alcohol are what kill. It's hypocrisy. I can allow for such a policy in the United States, with all those puritans, those sixteen-year-old hillbillies from Ohio with their I Love Jesus T-shirts, but here? Our daughters learn very early from television that what matters in this world is blonde hair and a tight ass. That's all. And we can't smoke grass? Or snort cocaine? It's all hypocrisy, he said. Alcohol, OK; tobacco, OK. We can stuff ourselves with pills to stop eating, pills that make us shit all day, more and more pills, pills to wake up, to go to sleep, we're addicted, as I've already said, to TV, food, sex, and lithium, but marijuana and cocaine are forbidden because they're habit-forming. Habit-forming? Doesn't anybody read the research, the statistics? The idiots. They're stupid. It's not me saying that, it's qualified scholars. People who know things and publish books on the subject. We'll be the next Cosa Nostra. That's all.

Nobody paid any mind to Reader's theories, or to the books he endlessly quoted; the others were usually on the phone while Reader discoursed, or leafing through comic books, cleaning their guns, farting, chewing their nails, or else endlessly spouting nonsense. When they make it legal, they said, here's how it'll be, you go to the drugstore and buy a kilo of weed, Los Pablitos brand, with a drawing of a skull, they laughed, finding it humorous, Los Fodidos, La Bolivia, La Colombia, Los Cucarachos Blancos, they laughed, they couldn't care less whether it was legal or not, Los Diegos, they didn't understand, taxes, Los Juans, violence, the ignorant kill themselves and don't even understand what's happening to them, thought Reader. He was used to being made fun of, but that afternoon, when he suggested something different they paid attention. The police are going to show up looking for the shack with a blue door, right, Miltão? Well, let's show it to them. Listen, Miltão, I read the Bible a lot, there's a certain passage. You know who Moses was, don't you? They more or less knew. A friend of God's. A saint. God told Moses, Reader said, to kill a lamb and have the Hebrews mark the door of their houses with the animal's blood. That's in the Bible, he said. The Hebrews did it, and that night God killed the firstborn child of the Egyptians. I don't understand shit about that, replied Miltão, chewing his gum. The problem was the words 'Hebrews' and 'firstborn'. Reader explained everything again. We'll paint the door of all the houses blue, and by doing that you'll be saying to them, we're bigger than you are, we're to be feared, we're indestructible. We have the blood of the lamb of God on our doors, understand? Hand out paint. Miltão liked the idea, though not for the same reason as Reader. Paint everything blue? Cool! We'll fuck with their heads. They'll be in deep shit. And that's what they did. Heh heh, Bidê also approved of the plan. They'll see. In their phone conversations they stuck with the existing scheme, although those involved in the operation were aware of the new unloading route, the new car, the new day.

Reader was amused to learn later that Miltão had dubbed the operation 'Moses Joins the Gang'.

The next morning, when he went out to get some clothes at his mother's house, Kingie felt the same excitement as the day before. Miltão's still laughing, someone said in Onofre's bar. Can't you just picture the look on the cops' faces? Everything blue. It was in the Bible. And how about when it started raining? That downpour, and their boots slipping all over the place. In the Bible. Heh heh heh, Bidê was buying cigarettes. Everything blue. That's what happens. They didn't speak of the dead. After the shooting stopped, the cries of desperate mothers was a common sound. Poor folk perched on top of walls, in search of news. But that day there was no mention of deaths, only wounded.

Narrow streets, unpaved, full of holes, puddles, chickens, automobile hulks, and low-flying planes overhead on their way to Galeão airport. Skinny people. Kingie walking, observing. Fat women. In the favela, the children are very thin and the adolescents are plump. The women are obese and the men all have paunches. It's the rule. Kingie was walking slowly, looking around, feeling tired. That night, he had painted the doorjambs of his grandmother's house, and with the leftover paint he had also done the windows and columns on the porch. At three a.m., still not sleepy, he painted the tires in the yard, used as a support for the table where his grandmother Cândida laid out the samba school costumes on sunny days to embroider them. And as he slathered blue on everything, he recalled Miltão's words and became irritated. Go back to school. He wouldn't go back. He'd made a deal with his grandmother, he'd go back to school. In return, he'd live with her, help with the embroidering, with delivering the work and buying materials, sequins, beads, bugles. He'd do everything, embroider. He wouldn't stammer at the effeminate men who came to his grandmother's place, Mag-*nif*-i-cent, so lux-*u*-ri-ous, said the artists who created the costumes. I want feathers, Cândida, I want gold, I want volume, dear lady, dimension, color, they said, gesturing with their hands and mouths, that blue is horrid, a-bom-i-na-ble, just the sight of that melancholy blue makes me positively ill, gasping for breath, Cândida, melancholy, and they would sit down and laugh and cry, because they were unhappy people, the Carnival revelers. He left me, Cândida, they would say, whispering, I gave him this, I gave him that, I did this, I did that, and they would cry, affectedly, I'm crushed, Cândida, Kingie listening to it all, crushed, dear lady, feeling like laughing at what the men said, at the clothes they wore, dyed hair, pathetic, but he promised that from that day on he wouldn't laugh again. I don't care if they're queer, Cândida said, they're my customers. Kingie would be nice to her customers, he would sew, cook, get breakfast, clean the living room, pick up the sequins scattered on the floor, do everything. But, he had told his grandmother, he wouldn't go back to school. He didn't like school. O K, I'll go back to school, he had told his grandmother. Promised. Painting till three in the morning and thinking about Miltão. And Suzana. So pretty, Suzana. Her white teeth, smiling. Everything blue. When he laid his head on the pillow, the digital clock read 3:52. The shooting began shortly afterward. He and his grandmother listening to the gunfire, clasping each other's hands. Rainfall. Afterward, when all was quiet, they did what everyone did on such occasions: they opened the windows a crack, peeped out, then went outside and leaned against the gate and talked to the neighbors. They didn't go back to sleep. Now I know why they were offering free paint, his grandmother said, when she was informed of what had happened. A smart guy, that Miltão. Cândida spoke of the trafficker in an admiring tone, and that tone, throughout the favela, blue paint and an admiring tone, was precisely what was poisoning the boy's blood as he walked the streets the next morning. Kingie was irritated; it wasn't lack of sleep that affected him but Miltão. Miltão had done away with his job and his future, that night and the ones to follow, October, November, December, he wouldn't have anything to do except wander around, seeing everything, thinking about nothing. He wouldn't go back to school. He's on his way to school, his grandmother had told Alzira when she showed up, terrified, looking for the boy. He didn't even let me know, Mother, he didn't even let me know he was here. He doesn't care about anything, Mother. I didn't sleep a wink; I'm going to have to work all day without a minute's sleep. Ten people are coming to Dona Juliana's for lunch. It's Dona Juliana's birthday. And me without getting a minute's sleep, Mother. His mother's weeping voice, coming from the bedroom. You know the hardest part, Mother? The hardest part is you can't crack open your child's skull and pour good things inside. That's the hardest part. They put a hole in his hand, did you see it? A good thing I have Carolaine, Mother. They're so different, Mother. Carolaine is a good girl. She's studying computers. That little loafer takes after his father. A bum just like his father. I look at him, Mother, and I see that no-account in front of me. Clear as can be. His eyes are exactly the same. His mouth. I tell you, Mother, it's my punishment.

Kingie knew no one was at home. He'd chosen a time when both of them were out, his mother working, Carolaine at her computer class. He moved unhurriedly, his eyes open. Everyone was impressed by Miltão. See what he did? He painted the houses. Killed a cop. Everything blue. Did you see the newspapers? The headline read: Another policeman killed in the drug wars. This leg in the photo here is mine, Kingie. See my shoe? Look at Dona Rosa Maria here in the paper, someone said. That's my leg. Miltão is evil, they said. Miltão

35

must be on cloud nine, he loved it when kids came running up to him. Just look at the sewers, the day-care centers, look what I've done. A vain man. Even Rosa Maria was pleased with Miltão, showing everybody the newspaper depicting a boy from the favela with cupped hands full of bullet casings. Behind him, a pair of legs, someone sitting in the gutter, the upper part of her body cropped out. It was Rosa Maria. I saw them take the picture. They even interviewed me. What's it say here, Kingie? Read it to me. Do they mention me? Kingie didn't like reading. I'm on Miltão's side and won't tell them a thing, said Rosa Maria, holding the newspaper. Look at my shoe. Miltão would come parading by later, Kingie knew. To receive praise. But whenever anyone complained of lack of sewers, lack of day-care centers, of criminality, Miltão would explode. We do everything we can and they still complain. It's that thy-kingdom-here-on-earth way of life, you know the bit? They want a house, food, laundry service. I do what's possible. If there's a way to improve things, we improve them. Look at the pipes. The culverts. Used to be the shit just flowed right through here, in the open. Look at the sewers. We built sewers. We bought notebooks for the children. Erasers. Rulers. We gave them a day-care center. If somebody dies, we bury them and pay all the expenses. We provide the widow with a pension if she's not a whore. And yet they complain. If they don't like it here they can move out.

Kingie approached the house, its windows closed. Suzana's house was also shut. Suzana was working behind the counter at a cosmetics store. Smelling better all the time. Carolaine at her computer class. Everybody working but him. Miltão was a son of a bitch. A real son of a bitch. As soon as he closed the door behind him, he heard sounds coming from the bedroom, something creaking, someone moaning. He held his breath so as not to make any noise, whenever he was afraid he held his breath, got a knife from the kitchen and quickly pulled open the curtain to his mother's bedroom. Carolaine was naked on the bed, on all fours. Kingie didn't even see who the young man behind her was, he turned his back and left. José Luís, his sister shouted. On his way out, the boy grabbed two T-shirts from the clothesline, some socks, a pair of pants. José Luís, Carolaine opened the window, putting on her clothes, I want to talk to you, she said. Kingie slammed the gate and headed toward his grandmother's house. He thought about going back and breaking the man's face. Who was that man? He didn't go back. To hell with his sister. The birdbrain. All that time spent in front of the mirror, hypnotized, dancing, turning around, sideways, from the front, poses, lipstick, dancing, nothing else. And now she was taking it in the ass.

A city truck was blocking the way to the sports area. Kingie crawled under the truck, feeling the heat coming up from the ground. He saw two of Miltão's bodyguards, talking. Tinted sunglasses, a great stereo system, he'd never have those cool things. Hey, wait, Carolaine shouted, following him, barefoot and out of breath. Kingie stopped, watching his sister crawl out from under the truck, just as he had done minutes earlier. A woman passed by hurriedly, carrying her child in her arms, furious. You're little and you don't understand yet, his sister said. The gas truck started its engine and for a few seconds Kingie couldn't hear a word that Carolaine said. What'd you say? He's my boyfriend, we're going to get married. I know. Getting married. Burning sun. Yeah, get married. Have kids. Live somewhere else. A different district. Buy a car. Get a washing machine. Have a better life. Or do you want me to be a maid like our mother? You want them to scream at me, call me stupid? Get paid shit? You want me to fuck myself for good? I'm sorry, José Luís, but I'm not going to fuck myself like her. Burning sun. You want my opinion? Dealing is better, Miltão is better. Much better. That's right, go back to Miltão. Be somebody. Get a machine gun and let them see it. Boys arriving at the drug site, a short line, buyers, runners, dial-a-drug, no waiting. I just want to ask you for one thing. Don't say anything to Ma.

Kingie didn't reply. He turned his back and continued on his way, crossing the sports area. Want to play, Kingie? He didn't. Ahead, Miltão's men, armed with automatic pistols, were taking the customers' orders. Wrap, crystal, or smoke? one of them asked when Kingie approached. Everything, he said. Cash up front, the soldier said. Kingie thought they wouldn't have change for a fifty. But they did. We even make change for American money, the traffickers said, laughing.

6

DING DING, DING DONG ding ding, dong dong ding ding, sang
the children in the background, clapping, while Kingie waited
at the sports field, sitting with his back against a lamppost. It was
a pleasant day, an agreeable temperature, he felt good, neither
sleepy nor hungry nor lazy, dirty feet but his father wouldn't
care. The red car stopped on the other side of the field, honked,
Kingie ran over, got in, Hi, father. Hi, son, what would you like
to do? I want to go swimming. They went to a building in
Leblon. Look, son, we have a playground, you want to play? A
pool. Plopf, into the water, they jumped around, swam. We have
a rec room too, we have gardens, and the beach is nearby.

They talked about football, his father lying on his back,
smoking, eating peanuts, drinking beer. A lot of players are
injured, how can we hope to win? We have to take the game
to the opponent. They swam. A team that hits, that attacks, he
said. They dived. We have to change the players' positions. Hit
harder. That fullback. Attack and mark. That halfback. That
idiot of a coach. And we lost that fullback. He went to Botafogo.
They dived and swam. They bathed with Phebo soap, a brand
that Kingie loved, there was always Phebo in the bathroom at
Dona Juliana's house, and dried flowers, a delicious sweetish
smell, and small hand towels for visitors, with lace, and soft
toilet paper. They played in the playground. A playground and
pool were Alzira's dream. Alzira on the sidewalk, Sunday, an
old newspaper in her hand, enchanted by the photos and floor
plans of the dwellings. Look at this one, Carolaine. Just look.
Three bedrooms. A pool. Playground. A party room. I bought a
lottery ticket, she said. If I win! A playground and a party room.

And a pool. And they could all go to hell, why even think about them, his mother, his mother's dreams, pool and playground, about any of the others, to hell with them, when he could stay with his father, eat in restaurants. Which restaurant do you want to go to, son? They ate at the Mar Manso, a sidewalk table, turnovers, codfish fritters, and ice cream. The problem was appetite, he never had an appetite. They walked slowly, the breeze pleasant. A sidewalk festival. Women in halter tops, running, skating, ponytails, girls practically naked, in bikinis, sand on their bodies, girlfriends, girls burning off pounds, walking, fast steps, girls, playing volleyball, soccer, women, beach paddleball, a lot of energy, bikes, shorts, bikinis, sun, legs, feet, small bracelets around their ankles, his father also enjoyed admiring the women at the beach. You've got to meet Suzana, father. Father. Is Suzana your girlfriend? Yeah. He liked saying 'my girlfriend'. A pretty word, 'girlfriend'. Me. 'Sweetheart', what a weaselly word. You. 'Woman' and 'wife', horrible. 'The Boss', he'd never call his girlfriend boss. Even after they were married. Suzana would be his girlfriend. His father spoke of a woman who worked at the office. Very pretty. A typist. A secretary. Love. Switchboard operator. Want some ice cream? I'd rather have coconut water. And suddenly, a strong wind, the window flapping. Kingie opened his eyes, saw his grandmother's room, Jesus Christ on the wall, thorns, got up to close the window, lightheaded. Children playing outside, near the already broken sewer, clapping their hands and singing. Three o'clock, the days were like that, solvents, glue, airplane dope, ether, thinner, crack, close your eyes, feel that good thing, good thoughts, on your grandmother's bed when she went out shopping, or spread out on the sports field, or in abandoned cars, under the burning sun, anywhere they'd leave him alone. Sometimes when his grandmother was at home, sewing, Kingie would dash off to Onofre's bar. A pool table, a blue countertop in the rear. Above it, a shelf decorated with plastic flowers and an image of Our Lady and a sign: 'My family is like yours, it appreciates respect.' But Onofre's family never worked in the bar. Only Onofre. Hi, Kingie, waved the passersby. Dogs. He always hid when he saw his sister Carolaine hurrying toward the bus stop, or his mother returning from work, always wearing the same tight pink blouse, a present from Dona Juliana. She was always getting things from Dona Juliana. Discards. Take it to the children. Garbage. They'll like it. These worn-out sneakers. These faded T-shirts. What about these boots with holes in them? Things his mother happily brought home. Of course we want them. We need them. So it's a little tight, what's the problem? Put this on. And don't complain. Be grateful to God. His lack of interest in God, in fact, had arisen precisely from that attitude of his mother's, in every adverse situation, hunger, lack of money, cold, poverty. Be grateful to God, she would say. Shit. Be grateful to God for the holes in the roof. For the crappy shoes. For the torn clothing. For the lack of meat. Be grateful to God. He was never grateful. Never.

Rosa Maria, radiant, going out for the night. I found me a gringo boyfriend, Kingie, he doesn't speak a word of Portuguese, only German, and you know that we still manage to communicate? I understand everything, Kingie, it's incredible how man was made for talking and communicating. All those *rrr*s, *raus*, *raum*, I don't understand the words but I know, I sense that he's saying something pretty about love, we understand each other, Kingie. Hi, Kingie, Reader always with books under his arm, a cigarette in his hand, in the company of big women. Kingie, I'm going to tell you since you're here, I'm going to tell you, Reader really likes a big 175-pound broad, Onofre told him. Big and fat. You already know about those things, don't you? he asked in a conspiratorial tone, making obscene gestures in reference to intercourse. Huh? You already done it? Fucking. Women. Cunts. Delicious pussies, huh? Nice and wet. Mmmm. Sucking. Reader loves to stand in a bank line, Kingie, a line at the hospital, the Welfare Office, lines like that. He hangs around watching the women clerks, the tellers, the girls behind the counter, and when he sees a fat one, young and pudgy, black or white, most of them black, when he meets a girl who's never had a boyfriend, a single woman who's never seen a good prick, the needy type, Reader goes to town. He feeds them a line and right away they're at his shack, fornicating. Reader, Onofre said, leaning over the table, close to Kingie's ear, Reader's a lard-fucker. It seems that fat women are great in bed. Really spectacular. The earth moves. Can you believe that, Kingie? They'll even screw on top of the stove, I've heard. A hot stove. That's what the neighbors say, Reader keeps his mouth shut. He's a son of a bitch, that Reader. I've even given him free beer, once got the guy drunk as a skunk and nothing, not a word about the black women. Only fat ones. With me, the only fat woman for me is the old lady, Onofre would repeat. I'm an ass man. A nice round ass to grab hold of, that's what's good. But it has to be a clean ass. I wouldn't go near Rosa Maria's ass. Too many foreigners've been there. I take good care of my cock. You gotta see the look on those women's faces, Kingie, Reader's fatties, when they come by here in the morning on their way home. You'd think they'd seen Jesus Christ.

That was Onofre's favorite topic. Pussies. Wet ones. Round asses. Really firm breasts. Kingie liked him. It was relaxing to smoke some crack and then go to Onofre's to hang out. On one occasion, Onofre told him that Kingie's father was a good man. Really? Yes, a good person, your father. Kingie had showered him with questions, but Onofre couldn't answer any of them. Was he tall? Average. What did he do? I don't remember. Did he drink a lot? I don't remember. His father went away a long time ago. Forgetful, Onofre. It was good to stay there at the bar. An average father. In reality, anywhere was pleasant as long as he had crack in him. Crack was bad, he had realized that a short time after starting to use it, and not having crack was a horror, and crack every day a living hell, and everything could get even worse if he didn't have crack. Before getting hooked, and after Miltão let him go from his job, he'd felt so devastated, but even before all that, forever, there was a hollow in his heart, an enormous hole, several of them, and absences, a diffuse melancholy, he would wake up in the middle of the night, his arms and legs aching from the beating his mother had given him, and to overcome insomnia would imagine his frail body being run over by a truck on the Avenida Brasil. Crash. Dead on the asphalt. At the wake. His mother crying in despair.

Onofre crying. His grandmother. Carolaine. Suzana. And when they all arrived at the cemetery, that was the worse part, Kingie always hated thinking that he'd have to be alone, disintegrating under the ground, dust, he would skip that part, worms, and go back to the wake, dust, he spent many a night at the wake for his own body. With the drugs, some part of that ceased, Kingie began to experience a new sensation, heat in the chest, everything fit together inside, crack, harmoniously, 'the key in the lock', that's what they'd said, the right key, the right lock, an open door. Crack. He would still wake up in the middle of the night, desperate, but when he took drugs he felt a kind of love, the sun, the beach, he thought, nature, the sun, photosynthesis, the thing that makes plants grow, the sea, everything is perfect, life, very good, only man is a piece of shit, Miltão's a piece of shit, a cocksucker, he'd wake up in the middle of the night and think that Miltão wasn't worth a damn, he didn't deserve Suzana, that outlaw pig, he didn't deserve weapons, prestige, he didn't deserve shit. The disgusting pig. He never forgot the first time he smoked marijuana, he'd arrived at his grandmother's house with his eyes red, his mouth dry, and that nice sensation, turned on the TV. Someday, he thought, I'm going to kill Miltão. I'll have my men. I'm going to kill. I'll grow up. He saw many colors that afternoon, feeling that something very important was waiting to be discovered, a truth, a talent, a fact, he went to the gate several times, waiting, expecting the turnabout, the change, the fact, how much longer would he have to live like that?

Cândida, her eyes fastened on brocades and ruffles, didn't notice anything happening to her grandson. The new year was approaching and preparations for Carnival were the priority. How was class? she asked, without lifting her gaze from the dancer dressed in araucaria or brazilwood, the samba school's theme was the Amazon rainforest, mother of all. How was class? she inquired, when José Luís arrived for lunch after a morning wandering the streets, smoking, snorting, his notebook in hand, dirty and without a single word written in it, nothing, roaming around, playing marbles at the rec courtyard or sleeping in the shade. Kingie spent on drugs any money he made in the streets, cleaning windshields at traffic lights, keeping an eye on cars outside movie theaters, or merely selling at outdoor markets the jackfruits that fell in his grandmother's backyard. Whatever came in was rapidly transformed into drugs. Lying in the soft beach sand, high on grass, dreaming about his father, being somebody, not nobody, Suzana, thinking. Shit. He liked the disorder of his thoughts, the humor, the laughter, and especially the dreams. His father. Shit. Cocaine was different, he felt useful, an executive, competent, lively, with ideas, felt as strong as cement, iron, solid, carrying things they gave him, the train of costumes. That's right, child, Cândida, that grandson of yours is an absolute *dar*-ling, said the designer. Go buy more beads. José Luís did whatever they told him. He was never tired, or sleepy, sometimes the hollow in his chest would grow, as holes grow after rain, mud, pieces being eaten away and carried off by the water.

In the street the boys showed him other things. Hey, blood, take a paregoric, take Demerol, it's good, man, take Algarfan, Apetivit, wow, take Binelli drops. Take Cobavital, Periatim, Periavita. Glue, thinner, benzene, ether, do crack. They improvised a pipe from a yogurt container and smoked. The first time, Kingie felt nothing. More crack. The third time, boom, he exploded, in two seconds the world became bearable and filled with brilliant colors.

His money problems dated from that day. He sold his grandmother's blender to buy crack. The silver crucifix. Two new bath towels. T-shirts. A turquoise water lily turban for the Bahian wing at Carnival. Part of his routine was to search the house looking for anything of value to trade for crystals of crack.

One desperate afternoon he saw, on top of the wardrobe, among the knick-knacks, the Mangueira trophy. Cândida had lived in Mangueira and had sewn for the favela's samba school for almost ten years.

He grabbed the trophy and departed quickly, fearful of running into his grandmother along the way. As soon as he left the house, he heard a familiar voice. Hi, Kingie, what's happening, man? You disappeared. Reader approaching him, grasping his

arm. Kingie hated people touching him, no embraces, no hand-
shakes, no kisses on the cheek, any type of contact bothered him,
crack, he kept going, and Reader began mouthing absurdities:
'Behold happiness. It fills a teaspoon, happiness with all its
ecstasy, all its infantility.' What was that about? Teaspoons?
Why was Reader always dredging up conversations about Haiti,
Clinton, and now spoonfuls of happiness? It's poetry, Reader
explained. Good poetry. My favorite poet, to tell the truth. Are
you wasted? Kingie didn't reply, continued walking, the trophy
from Mangueira under his arm, Reader behind him. What're
you planning to do with that trophy? Nothing. Cool trophy, let
me see it. Kingie hated that kind of invasive behavior. Reader
inspected the trophy, fingering it as if he were blind. Yeah,
he said, the great Mangueira, the winner, that's what it is,
whose trophy is it? Mine. Yours it isn't, you weren't even born
when Mangueira won this trophy, look at the date here. Kingie
grabbed the statuette back and turned his back, increasing his
pace. Reader could go fuck himself, the goddamn lard-fucker,
he should drown in rolls of fat. Where are you living? Reader
asked, still following him. Hold up, listen, kid. You moved,
didn't you? I don't see you looking beat up anymore. So you
moved. And now I only see you strung out. Man, you're going
to fuck yourself up in no time, no time at all. Yeah, I know.

Kingie stopped and they stood facing each other for several
moments, Reader smoking, sweating, hair uncombed. What's
the problem? You're not my father, Kingie said. I know that,
replied Reader, I know it very well. And if you ask me why
I'm here wasting my precious time on you, I don't have an
answer. I could be reading Machado de Assis. Get a life,
man. Do something. I ought to let you fuck yourself like
all the others. I see you with the street kids, the grifters, the
delinquents, bums, idlers, at first you had something, the look
of intelligence, a posture. Now, lugging that trophy, you're just
an imbecile. And you think things are going to end there? They
aren't. It's like the song says, You think you've lost everything
but there's always more to lose. And you will. I shouldn't say
anything. Go. Go get rid of the trophy. Snort it all. Leave.

Kingie turned his back and left; he got two pieces of crack for the trophy. It's not worth even one, the dealer said, you just got lucky, brother, 'cause I'm crazy about Mangueira, man. The real thing. Cool.

When he got home, his grandmother was watching her soaps. Go take a shower, she said. Put on some clean clothes. Sit down, we're ready to eat. Beans on the plate. Do you like pepper? The mere smell of food turned the boy's stomach. *The National News*. It is estimated that ninety people have disappeared. Rains. Landslides. The exchange rate, inflation, a poll reveals that Brazilians are concerned about violence. Cândida got up, turned off the TV. Eat, son, she said, sitting down. You need nourishment. And listen to what your old grandmother's about to say. What did you do with my trophy? You sold it, didn't you? Kingie lowered his head. You don't have to answer, José Luís. You sold the trophy to buy drugs. You sold the blender too, I suppose. And the silver crucifix that belonged to your grandfather, the best stonemason on the hill, who built this house and the house where you were born, you sold the crucifix given me by that saint of a man. You sold it and bought drugs. I went to your school today. I know you don't go there. They didn't even know who you were. You dropped out a long time ago, they told me. Are the beans all right? Eh? Not hungry, are you? Sure you don't want any more?

His grandmother took away the plates. There was no hostility in her behavior, none whatsoever, always generous, calm, patting the boy's head. I made some guava dessert too. Want some? Kingie felt a coldness in his body, trembling. The beans hadn't agreed with him, his stomach burned. He lay down on the sofa. He wanted to apologize to his grandmother. He would get the trophy back. There must be a way. Son, get your things, I'm taking you back to your mother's. At first Kingie didn't understand what was happening. Grandma, he said, and started to cry, don't do it, I promise I'll stop, I promise I'll study, I promise, I promise, he walked around the living room, stepping on costumes, as quick as a poisoned dog, suffering, feeling pains. It's no good, José Luís, I'm taking you to your mother's, she's the one to raise you, not me, it's her, it's her, I'm too old, stop, stop hugging me, child, get up off your knees, stop crying, let go of me. Kingie wouldn't release her, Cândida pushed him away forcefully, the boy fell to the floor, and from the floor he said, Grandma, I hate my mother. Don't ever say that again in my presence, José Luís. Get up. Kingie couldn't move, weak and crying. What he felt was hatred. Only at that moment did he realize it. Rage. Come here. His grandmother helped him to get up. She carried him to the bed. I don't want to, Grandma, I don't want to go back to her house. The two embraced, Kingie wouldn't stop crying. We'll see, boy. We'll see how you behave from now on.

7

OVERCAST. THE SOUND OF thunder. Nine a.m. A dark sky, readying for a storm. Red traffic light. Maria Emília, on her way to the hairdresser, was mugged by a young boy who threatened her with a piece of broken glass. Minutes later, Simone, a secretary at a multinational, was putting on lipstick, looking at herself in the rearview mirror, when an urchin appeared out of nowhere, threatening, with a piece of broken glass in his hand. If you yell, you're dead. Ana, a law student. Hand over the bag, the boy said, hand over the bag, and stay calm. Broken glass in his hand. Amélia, fifty-four, was telling her son on the telephone how she had been robbed that morning. I didn't have anything in my purse, fortunately, son. All he got was my watch. What I'd like to do, said Simone, discussing the mugging with her girlfriend at the office, what I'd like to do is take one of those kids and beat him, beat him, give him a beating that would leave the little bastard a mass of raw flesh. This is a holdup, said the boy to Angélica, eighteen, a hysterical girl who had just returned from a vacation in the US. Broken glass in his hand. I arrive from Miami and the first time I'm in my car I'm held up. That's Brazil for you, she said. None of the victims reported it to the police.

Kingie worked alone, though there were always street kids suggesting partnerships. They were never any help, and they carried risks for the victims since, unlike Kingie, they only mugged when they were high on drugs. To get me revved up, they said. Revved up. What's happening, brother? They admired Kingie's competence, and he was invited to steal tape-players, hold up bakeries, and rob people at ATMs. But Kingie preferred holdups at traffic lights, broken glass in hand, no partners, no problems, which brought in enough to pay for drugs and hamburgers.

It wasn't easy. It was impossible to predict how victims would react, especially women. There was a half-moon scar on his right arm from an impetuous lady who had sunk her teeth into him. Let go of my arm, ma'am, please, ma'am, the light changed, ma'am. A real hassle. Another time, a young woman trapped his fingers in the car's automatic window. He took pride in never having hurt anyone. From the very first time, Kingie had always felt fear. When the light turned red his blood would run cold, piece of glass in his pocket, choose the victim. Most of them, the women, were distracted at the light, retouching their make-up, tuning the radio, or talking on the phone. One woman even went on using her cell phone during the robbery. Carlos, she said, Carlos, you're a son of a bitch. This is a holdup, Kingie threatened, hand over your purse. The woman gave him the purse as if it were the most natural thing in the world. Carlos, don't give me that crap, she continued. All I want is the money, Kingie said, returning everything but the wallet. Carlos, she said, putting the car into first and pulling away, you're the biggest skirt-chaser in Rio de Janeiro.

That Wednesday, Kingie arrived early at Venâncio Flores, a street in the Leblon district leading to the beach. It was the first time he had robbed at that location. A lousy day with a scant take. The light turned red, Kingie approached, the piece of glass in his pocket, and only when he got to the car did he see it was Dona Juliana at the wheel. José Luís? she said, startled. There was a young man beside her, well-built, tanned, wearing athletic clothing. Kingie saw the man's hand on Dona Juliana's knee. The man's hand, quick. What are you doing here? the woman asked. Washing windshields, the boy replied. With no bucket, no sponge, his clothes clean. Looks like we're in for a downpour, eh? Really. Pause. Is your sister well? Yes ma'am. The light's about to change, ciao. Juliana put the car into first and the vehicle joined the flow of traffic, turning to the right onto the avenue. Washing windshields, laughed

Fernando, Juliana's personal trainer, washing windshields when it's about to rain. That's a good one. It's Alzira's son. He saw your hand on my leg, Juliana said, concerned. So? Straight ahead, he said. I turned pale, didn't I, Nando? I'm shaking. He's going to say something to Alzira. Don't get worked up over it, Beauty. Cold sweat. Beauty, that's what Fernando called his students. I'm shaking. That way, Beauty, go slow. Cold sweat. The Barra da Tijuca, straight ahead. Before getting to São Conrado, Juliana stopped the car at one of the many motels in the area, while Fernando looked to both sides in obedience to Juliana's paranoid instructions. Look carefully, is anyone following us? Pay attention. I hate motels. It's OK, Beauty. I'm going inside. I don't believe, Alzira, that he was cleaning windshields, she decided she would say to her servant later. Yes, she would. He was robbing, I'm sure of it. Yes, that's what she'd say. If I were you I wouldn't say anything, suggested Fernando, in the motel. The best thing would be to pretend that nothing happened. No bucket, no sponge, I don't know, maybe it was better to tell Alzira everything, say that her son was probably there to commit robberies. Think about it, Nando. What if the boy made some nasty comment? Alzira, with her son's testimony, would soon put two and two together. In fact, she must already be doing it. Alzira's been saying things. Insinuating. I'm scared. Beauty, come here, everything's going to be all right, said Fernando, in bed, Juliana naked, on her stomach, worried. Nothing like that's going to happen, Beauty. Don't say anything to Alzira, it's better that way. A cigarette. Maybe the boy didn't notice anything. After all, what did he see? Nothing. He saw nothing. A hand on her back, her buttocks, Fernando's strong hands. The two in bed. I adore your body, Fernando said. Juliana had an obsessive temperament, I adore your breasts, she would transform the smallest possibility of catastrophe into a daily nightmare, I like your navel, she would feed her fears, ceaselessly, even as Fernando covered her body with kisses, Juliana's concerns were reduced to a single thought, that everything hung by a thread, they would ruin her life, destroy it, bring it all to an end. Later, at home, she would phone Alice, in tears. Hi, Alicinha. Before she got involved with Fernando Juliana's life was very good. Neither happy nor unhappy, Alice. Now, my friend, I'm a wreck. On, all the time. It was better before. Not that she had such a wonderful marriage, but Rodrigo was a good husband, passionless but good, there was peace, which is nice, harmony, nothing wild, two marvelous children, a tranquil life, peace, peace, peace. Do you know what that is, Alice? Peace. I want peace. You ruined my life, she would tell Fernando. Ruined it. When she was away from him her body swelled from boredom, the foolish little things that everyone said, herself included, so much nonsense, why so much wasted time? She was always tense, unsatisfied, worried, waiting for the phone to ring. She and Fernando burning, the bed catching fire, his hands, a man's hands. Don't fall in love, said Alice, from the beginning. A sad thing, to love without being rich, La Bruyère once said. I read that somewhere, and it's true. A sad thing, Jul. A pure but poor man. Just think, Jul, the two of you living on what he makes teaching his classes. Goodbye to blazers. Goodbye to New York. Goodbye to Paris. London. India. Thailand. Juliana never thought in those terms. Alice was an idiot. Fuck Paris. Fuck blazers. She never worried about the fact that Fernando had no money. Fuck them all. When she imagined the future, she thought of the two of them walking calmly, somewhere, anywhere, by the beach, with no husband, no children, even in China, with no need to be home at a certain time. Fernando and Jul in a restaurant. Introducing him to friends. Nando, handsome, funny, healthy, sincere. The lovable things he said. The years he worked as a salesman. The public high school. His family's sacrifice so he could go to college and study physical education. Honest. Hard-working. Sincere. But even so, he'd fucked up her life. Yes, fucked it up. The torment of love. Sleeping poorly. Her thoughts wandering. The crying and suffering. The euphoria and the depression. Suffering. This restlessness of love will be the end of me. Waiting for phone calls, creating opportunities to call her lover, the waiting for their meetings, surviving weekends, the long nights. Where can Fernando be? Yes, because Fernando was handsome and single. And there were Saturdays and Sundays, and every week-night, with all those available and easy women. That wasn't the only way that Fernando had ruined her life. The willing, calm, laughing Jul, lively, sometimes irritable, shrewd, bitchy at home, fatter, more gluttonous, that Jul had simply ceased to exist. The new Juliana was neurotic, tense, a motel habitué, a purchaser of lingerie, with no sense of humor and hooked on nicotine.

Let's go, she said, getting out of bed. Come here, Beauty, it's still early. No, she answered, let's leave, I'm desperate. Juliana wanted to get home before Alzira left.

The sound of thunder. A dark sky. After running into Juliana, Kingie decided not to pull any holdups that morning. It was raining. He'd been lucky. Thunder. He'd once seen an excellent film on TV, 'even if it was in black and white,' and he'd never forgotten the scene with the gypsy woman, in a bar, reading cards and a drunk coming up to her and asking her to read his future. You've used up your future, she said. You've used it up. There is no future. Every time something good happened in Kingie's life, anything that make him think about luck, favorable stars, good fortune, whatever it was, a card game with his sister, dominoes or pool with Onofre, each time he experienced that sensation of having been rewarded, he stopped whatever he was doing. In his holdups, when everything went well, with no screams or hysterics, if he stole a gold chain, some tens, that was enough. Even when he felt safe enough to continue, he didn't. You've used up your quota of luck, he would tell himself, and stop. No future. When he ran into Dona Juliana he had the same sensation. He could have been caught red-handed and he wasn't. He'd been lucky. The sound of thunder. Enough of that, he thought. Thunder and lightning. Kingie walked along Ataulfo de Paiva, he liked the rain, lightning. That's it for today, he thought, the dark sky, he was always dreaming about flying in a plane, seeing the storm, heavy clouds, dark, going into them, he liked seeing the lightning, the water wetting his body, it was good, his T-shirt soaked, his feet in the puddles, it was good. Kingie walked, feeling good. Nothing to worry him. Everything under control. Rain. And he'd been lucky. The bad times are behind me, he thought. After the fight with his grandmother he'd promised he'd go back to school next year. It's October already, he'd said, it won't be long. Very good, son. He would work carrying bundles in the outdoor markets downtown. He would help his grandmother. How nice, son. He'd also promised to stay away from drugs. And he had. Rain. How many blocks to McDonald's? Three. Two weeks without drugs. Yes. Walking. Those were difficult days. Always in a state of panic, suffering insomnia, the shakes. He dragged himself everywhere, wretched, in the outdoor markets, frightened, pains throughout his body, pushing carts filled with vegetables, taking abuse and feeling nausea at the fish smell that permeated the streets. Without drugs. He hated markets.

Downtown was hectic that morning, rain, automobile horns, cars braking, pulling out, heavy traffic at intersections. Kingie stopped at the light, beside a shoeshine boy. He had also shined shoes, in Praça Quinze. Horrible. No drugs and shining shoes, every day. His grandmother's idea. Go shine shoes. The owner of the boxes oriented the shoeshine boys' work. Don't waste polish, he said, be nice to customers and tell them a sad story if you want good tips. After speaking to the boys and handing out the boxes, the man would sit at a concrete table under the trees and read the newspapers he had bought at the corner newsstand. Methodically, he would place the first section in front of him with as much pleasure as if he were preparing to eat a pizza. Folding the paper, he would line up the edges. I never saw anybody so crazy about shit, thought Kingie. Fuck. Eat the goddamn paper. The light changed, a car stopped at the pedestrian crosswalk. Watch the crosswalk, a lady complained to the driver, who pretended not to hear. Kingie crossed the street in a run, thinking about the old man who owned the boxes. He was always complaining, the old man, reading aloud the news items that annoyed him. Look at this insult, he said. The money the politicians make. That gang of thieves in the government. Crooks. And he would repeat the same stories three, four times. A gang of thieves. Curs. Those were bad times. At the day's end Kingie would return home, his hands blackened, raging, debilitated, and if his grandmother was in front of the television, sewing, he would feel an immense unhappiness, a sadness that began at his navel and overpowered everything. Hand me those feathers, dear. The sequins. Come here and talk to your grandma. Tell me everything, dear. How did it go? A constant irritation, he would gnaw his arms in bed, unable to sleep.

The rain slackened. Kingie stopped before the window of a beauty salon, looking at the ads. Brown hair. Wella. McDonald's was right there. He wouldn't trade Suzana for any of those women in the photos. A piece of crap, life without drugs, he went on walking. Now everything was all right. Bad times, those. Shining shoes and sweating. Suffering. Carrying things. Trembling. The suffering had ended the day when, returning on the bus, he met a young man by the name of Fake, reflective glasses, shaved head, beret. I was going to be Conan but I found out there was already a Conan out there. I want to be unique, brother. Sitting next to him, on the bus, Fake placed on Kingie's head the earphones of the Walkman he was carrying and music filled the boy's ears, *Jorge enlisted in the cavalry*, It's good rap, man, *he's happy he's not in the infantry*. Lots of good stuff, man. Listen to this one. Hardcore again, he said, know what they're talking about? Gunpowder. The fashion world. Assassinations. Behavior. Coke. Revolution. Politics. Hip-hop opened my eyes to those things. Understanding. Awareness. I'm who I am, brother, thanks to hip-hop. I'm black. I'm black and I want my share. I'm going to be a famous rapper. Coca-Cola contract, just you wait. Money. We blacks are powerful. I'm going to be rich. Fake took Kingie to the radio station in the favela. I'm the DJ of our cable radio. Brand new electronic equipment. I'm Miltão's bud. In Kingie's view that was Fake's only shortcoming, his friendship with Miltão. It's the black brotherhood, man. Are you the one who plays the music over the loudspeakers in the square? Kingie asked. Fake, in the flesh, the man himself. You like the sound? Kingie loved it. From Onofre's bar he would always hear rhythmic music, da da da, and the lyrics, mixed with the drugs, yeh yeh yeh yeh yeh in his brain, were pure poison, he knew snatches of some of the verses: *I'm the worm that's gonna make you well, words, the mongrel system / down from the hill, to invade the city / to kill*, the words jumbled in Kingie's head, *I don't feel nothing / the gun at his head / at the light*, the verses jumbled in Kingie's head and, strangely, those things, said in just that way, created in the boy the desire to be that thing, to belong to their group, the blacks, to be black too. You're light-skinned, said Fake. Mulatto. There's lots of brothers your color who say they're white. You're black too. Be black. At the studio, a shack painted red, with posters of entertainers, American blacks in dark glasses and extravagant clothes, tacked up everywhere, they listened to a great deal of music. That was the day Kingie went back to smoking crack. He became Fake's friend, started frequenting the studio on a daily basis, with Fake always offering him drugs. More crack. I also supply the TV people, he said. Crack. The cameramen. The cable men. One of these days I'll take you to see a soap being filmed. Very good stuff, crack. Lots of great women. Fake always provided a drug of some kind, crack, cocaine, marijuana. He liked Kingie. I know the artists. Crack's a great thing, he said. Isn't it a great thing? Go ahead and smoke, Kingie. Smoke. Snort. Help yourself. And give me a hand carrying these records. And snort. And smoke. And listen to this sound. Help yourself. In the days that followed, Kingie didn't feel right using his friend's drugs. He decided to go back to mugging. Goodbye markets, shoe polish, grandmother. He wouldn't be a shoeshine boy. Or a porter. They could all go to hell. Let everything blow up. It wasn't hard starting to rob. Shining shoes had been the hard thing. Pushing carts at the market. Sweating. Working like a dog. Robbing was easy. Gold chains, hubcaps, watches, the fences bought anything.

The sound of thunder. The take for the day: one watch and some small change. If it weren't for Dona Juliana, at the traffic light, he could have made more. McDonald's, finally. Kingie went in, his clothes drenched, Dona Juliana, who would've thought it? Three people in line ahead of him. Dona Juliana and her lover at the light, he could only be the lover, that muscular guy. He'd heard his mother talk about it to Carolaine. One Happy Lunch, please. Cheeseburger, no pickles, with ketchup and fries, two Cokes, and a Quarter Pounder with cheese. You know, Carolaine, I think Dona Juliana is very brazen with her trainer.

Kingie on the bus, on his way home, eating a burger, the city there outside, the sea packed with shit. They say. They've polluted everything. A gray sea, on rainy days. When he got off the bus in front of Zino's butcher shop, the rain had stopped. A full stomach. He belched. He crossed the street, stepping in the puddles that formed on the cement, children playing. At the drug site, he bought three rocks. He was dying to have a smoke and listen to the blacks singing in Fake's studio, songs that Kingie loved. Walking and thinking. The rocks in his pocket. Maybe, if Fake allowed it, Kingie could be part of the group that Fake was putting together. Compose raps. Change his life. He felt it quite clearly: his life was going to change. Something was about to happen. He'd even said as much to Fake. But what? his friend asked. What's going to happen? Something, Kingie said.

The studio door was padlocked. Two o'clock. Fake spent the night at funk dances, Dance Columba, Black Fantastic, and was hard to wake the next day. Kingie played pool with Onofre to kill some time. Waited. He sat on one of the barstools and watched the people going by. More rain. He and Onofre. Bidê stretching, shirtless, in the doorway of his house. The same people. Things. The same life as always. The same old crap, said Onofre, agreeing. The novelty was Carolaine, who came in smelling good, just having taken a bath. Hi, Zé Luís, I was looking for you. They sat, drank Coca-Cola, chatted. Ah, you're waiting for Fake. I know Fake. Carolaine also hung out at funk dances. Sometimes. Me and my boyfriend, she said, looking coyly at her brother. We go there. Kingie had tried to go to one of the dances but he was turned away because he was so small. It's really good, Carolaine said. Inside, it's all dark, there's flashing lights in the ceiling, and if you like smacking people you can have a good time. Don't tell that to Mother. I'm not into funk. My boyfriend's the one who likes it. My fiancé. Don't tell Mother. Fiancé. You have to be fast. Kicking, punching, it's fast. Otherwise they'll get you. It's cool. Smacking people. But you know, Kingie, I came to tell you that Sunday's your birthday. Kingie didn't remember. Twelve years old. You silly boy, you forgot your own birthday? Mother's going to make you a cake. Yeah, I'll bet, muttered Kingie. What? Nothing, he replied. Forget it. At home, the cake. Are you coming or not? I don't know, said the boy. Gosh, Zé Luís, Mother likes you so much. Gosh. Suzana's going to be there too. For heaven's sake. Mother's got a surprise for you. A surprise? Kingie immediately thought about his father. What kind of surprise? I can't tell you, his sister replied. You'll like it. His father was going to Alzira's house, that had to be the surprise, thought Kingie. What time? At night, eight o'clock. It's agreed then. I'm on my way, said the girl. Want more Coke, Carolaine? asked Onofre. No, I have to go. She left. Kingie remained behind in the door of the bar. The surprise could only be his father. Three o'clock. His sister going down the hillside. Onofre beside him. I been noticing, Kingie, isn't Carolaine putting on weight? Huh? She used to be so thin. Carolaine's putting on weight, I noticed. Kingie wasn't even listening to what Onofre was saying. What surprise could his mother be preparing for him? It could only be his father.

8

SHOUTING AND RUNNING. ROCKS thrown. Windows shattering. Gunshots. Kill. Grab. Crash. There, you son of a bitch. Get out. Clubs, rocks. The noise outside woke Kingie, he leaped from bed and went looking for his grandmother. In the street, people were perched atop gates and walls, hurling stones and pieces of wood at the police, who fled, revolvers and grenades in hand, with a throng of favela residents at their heels. Cândida, standing on a crate, was holding a colander full of stones gathered from the yard. Get some rotten fruit, Zé Luís.

As the police descended the hill, other residents joined the crowd pursuing them, even those who didn't exactly understand what was going on, like Kingie, excited, screaming, throwing rocks and wood, and cursing. On the avenue, the rebellious mob set fire to a squad car. The police launched grenades, to save face. People fell to the ground, terrified. It was a real drama, said one woman later, when the reporters showed up. Every time the police come up the hill after the drug dealers it's war. They come in hitting anything that moves. Cracking skulls. They hit my son on the head, said another woman, smiling for the photographer. They threatened Zino, the butcher. Poor Zino. The journalists asked about ammunition-making, the reason for the invasion. I don't know anything about ammunition, one young man answered. I'm a worker, with my labor card signed and in order. I took a billy club to the head, that's all I know, and I also know that they threw Osvair on the ground and stomped on his face. Osvair, that saint of a man.

Kingie didn't return home until the journalists left. During his climb he met Fake coming out of Onofre's. He hoped his friend remembered his birthday, he'd said Sunday's my birthday, but Fake was in a hurry. I gotta straighten out a mess, he said. Ciao. Onofre, his ear glued to his portable radio, also didn't remember his birthday.

Sunday, sunny, Kingie liked seeing how people dressed up on Sundays. Their finest clothes. Women going to Mass, their best shoes. Bathed. The best of intentions. Young people and children on their way to the beach, packing the buses. Except Reader. Always disheveled, Reader. Smoking Hollywoods and discoursing on some topic or other. Today's my birthday, said Kingie. Really? Reader asked. Your birthday? Then let's go to my house, I've got a present for you.

The rented room where Reader lived was tiny and suffocating, without windows, books scattered everywhere, piled on the floor, on top of the stove and refrigerator, in the sink, in every cranny. Let me see, said Reader, rummaging through the clutter in search of a special title. A book. I started reading at your age. Kingie regretted accepting the invitation; he wouldn't read the book. He hadn't thought the present would be a book. Shit. Stupid present. He'd thought it would be something better. Choosing a book, hmm, isn't easy, said Reader. Yes, maybe I still have it. *Treasure Island*. Ah, here it is. You're going to like it.

Kingie accepted the book, spiritlessly, the cover, the faded colors, the pages coming loose, a book falling apart. Almost turned to dust, the boy thought. Shit. Read me the first sentence, Reader requested. No way. He didn't like to read, it was dumb, and that sensation of being twisted up in words, tied down by letters, irritated him. Was it your mother who took you out of school? Reader asked. It was her, wasn't it? Suzana told me about your mother. Personal matters, intimacy, Reader was always trying to go too far, asking, probing, sniffing around, which exasperated Kingie. I want to show you something, Reader said, lifting his shirt to reveal several circular scars around his navel and chest. Know what these are? My father. There are worse ones on my feet and legs. If you got beat on a lot, I can guarantee you I had it worse. I know this stuff. We have a thing, Kingie, the two of us. As soon as I moved here, I started watching you at Onofre's bar, and without anybody telling me, I knew. I can recognize it immediately just by looking at a person. Twelve years of abuse gave me real knowledge of the cause. I specialized in that kind of shit. I was lucky, I escaped the worst. Know what my secret was? I never felt sorry for myself. Self-pity, never. There's nothing worse, in my opinion, than self-pity. I keep wondering if you can still be saved.

Kingie listened to Reader without looking at him. Shit. Holding the book. The subject interests me, Reader continued, I read a lot of psychiatric texts. They did a study, look here, he said, showing him a book, this test, it's about drugs but it confirms my theory, a living father, a disappeared father, an absent father, a test, deceased, absent, always absent. All you have to do is answer three simple questions. It's easy. I have to go, said Kingie. Then go, Kingie. I used to be like you. Exactly like you. I pretended it had nothing to do with me. I turned my back on myself. It took me over ten years to realize what I'm trying to tell you now. Anyone who beats a child, whoever it is, is stupid. A piece of shit. They're the pieces of shit, not us. Know what they do to us? They take away our love. They kill our love. And you won't understand that until the time when you truly want to love. Love a woman. There's no cure for it. You're never going to be able to love anything. Not even an animal. You're going to feel inferior, always. An insect. Inadequate, forever. Left out. You'll be as dead as a lump of coal. And it hurts. It's a pain of the soul. You don't understand crap, I know. As long as you go on not understanding, please don't continue fucking up. That's all. Shit, that guy Fake, why are you involved with him? You know who Fake is? You think I don't see you coming out of Fake's studio? You think it's cool to do dope? Cocaine is for scum. And marijuana smokers work at banks, mediocre people. Politicians. Congressmen. Scumbags. Stupid people, you understand that? It's the rabble who snort. Yesterday I saw you snatching a purse. You're going to fuck yourself up but good, man.

Kingie got up. I don't want the book, he said, leaving. At the door he heard Reader say, Happy birthday, loser.

That was a difficult day. He felt distressed, rushed. Loser. A desire to get things done, quickly. And there was nothing to be done. They kill our love, what was that all about? Goddamn fag talk. Such urgency, such agony, for what? There was nothing that needed doing. Not school, not work, nothing. Even his grandmother didn't need help with her embroidering.

Kingie spent the day wrapped in his thoughts, tossing and turning, clenching his body in the bed. To meet his father on his twelfth birthday. He had imagined so many times the encounter between the two, but now it would be different. Reality. The two of them together at his birthday party. Carolaine had been clear about it, Mom has a surprise for you. His father, it could only be that, the surprise. Father. He wouldn't hug his father in front of the others. Shit. In fact, he wouldn't hug his father at all. He wouldn't say anything while there were others around, listening. He wanted to go somewhere with him and talk. Too bad there wasn't a game. The best thing would be to watch the game, silently. Not talking. Rooting for their team. Talking wouldn't serve any purpose. Crying, shouting, throwing it up to him, recriminations, he'd never do that with his father. He would talk about other things. Maybe his father would bring him a present. He'd seen a TV commercial for a videotape about buildings on fire, real-life, tidal waves, earthquakes, everything real, people being rescued at sea, others, dead, floating after a plane crash, a truly harrowing and exciting videotape, they said on TV, he'd like for his father to give him that tape for his birthday. People dying for real.

At six o'clock he took a bath, put on the colorful shorts his grandmother had given him as a present, the T-shirt, and went to Fake's studio. His friend, restless by nature, caught Kingie's attention that afternoon because he seemed more agitated than usual. He bumped into piles of records, looked for the key he'd already found in his pocket. It's from too much work, he explained. Today's my birthday, said Kingie. Your birthday, Fake embraced his friend, wishing him more love. More health, more peace, more drugs, more God, more funk, more father, more money, more everything. Let's go celebrate at Onofre's, he said. He stopped at the door, No, let's stay right here. I've got something for you. A present. Fake bolted the door. He stood on a chair, took down a poster from the wall. This guy's sensational, he said, you know who he is? There was a hole in the wall, behind the poster, Fake stuck his hand in and withdrew a package with a kilo of cocaine. Is that yours? Kingie asked. Yes, I'm working on a deal, answered Fake. Not a word. It's my little scam. The stuff's not pure. It's been cut with a lot of crap, Fake said. This guy's the big shit in pop. Is the door locked? Fake asked. You locked it yourself, Kingie answered. Fake spooned a bit of powder into a plastic bag. Hand me that record there on the table. It's by this guy. Fake replaced the poster on the wall. Somebody gave me an interview that came out in the newspaper about this master, sensational, brother, even back in the stone age this fuckedelic guy was listening to Kraftwerk and saying things like 'I wanna use the groove electronically, find some kind of mix that leads to funk.' And he did. Pure and simple. That's one bitchin' sound. You like it? Without him, you wouldn't even know what rap is. The mother's even sung with James Brown.

Underneath the stereo table were two boxed amplifiers used for parties in the favela. Fake opened one of them and took out several envelopes of sodium bicarbonate, talcum powder, and a sack of marble dust. Let's make some magic, he said. Keep an eye on the door, make sure it's locked.

All the ingredients were mixed together in a plastic bowl, and, Abracadabra, now I have two kilos of powder. While they snorted and packaged the drug in small envelopes, Fake spoke excitedly of his meeting with Gray, who was the friend of a cousin of a rapper talent scout. A pro. Gray's going to open doors for me. I'm not going to spend my life here, listening to rap. I'm going to *do* rap. Create. I want to do a rap that stabs you in the guts, talks about infidelity, lamentations, lowlifes, cries of anguish. At that moment, Kingie realized that he wasn't part of Fake's plans. He would never be asked to join the band. My mother, just think, said Fake, my mother wanted me to be a cop. Think about it, a cop. One day my father said, The police nowadays are only good for robbing and killing. Forget it, Creusa. I want my son to serve the country, my mother would say. She's a little off, my mother. A naïve woman from Bahia, poor thing. She doesn't know about a thing, my mother. But I'm going to serve the country, just like she wanted. Rap's a very serious thing, Fake said. It's a political gesture, brother, you show the crowd the reality of things. War. You denounce. Violence. You criticize. Mud. You show the wounds. Social inequality. That's rap. Loser, why had Reader said that? I'm going to get to meet my father, Kingie said, changing the subject. Really? That's cool. Fathers are important. Mothers are even more, but so are fathers. Fathers are less. You know, José Luís, I'm going to tell you something. Pause. No, no I'm not. I'll tell you tomorrow. Put that powder in your pocket. It's a birthday present.

On the table, which had been brought to the middle of the room, was a cake with condensed-milk icing and chocolate sprinkles, soft drinks, and plastic cups. Alzira, fresh from the shower, kissed her son. Caroaine's getting ready, she said, hugging Cândida, who arrived a little later. Twelve years old, how time flies! Congratulations, son. Take this, she said, handing him a package. Kingie opened it, another pair of shorts. How nice, commented Alzira, when she saw that his grandmother had also given him shorts, now he has two pairs. The surprise is for later, she whispered into the boy's ear.

Suzana arrived soon afterward. I can't stay, she said, I just came to bring you this. It was a picture frame with a photo of Suzana as a little girl, perhaps seven years old, with Kingie on her lap. I found this photograph in my things. Look how tiny you were. You couldn't have been more than six months old. I used to change your diapers. And besides that, another present, a T-shirt with the Rolling Stones tongue on it. For you to wear with your girlfriends. Kingie didn't like that. There were no girlfriends. Shit. Now, Caroaine and Suzana were talking at the gate, Suzana was relating something, excitedly. Now I showed him, she said, I gave him a hard time, I don't want anything to do with him, she said, not with this girl, no way José. Kingie wanted to hear more, was she talking about Miltão? No womanizer for me, but the noise from the TV drowned out the voices, commercials, skirt-chasers don't make it with me, the magician who revealed the tricks, a new treatment for cancer. I told him it's either my way or the highway, the boy in the United States who went to his school and killed eleven of his classmates. Suzana left and Carolaine sat down beside him. Is he coming? asked Kingie. No, he's not coming, I still haven't told Mom anything, the girl answered, thinking her brother's question was about her boyfriend. In an almost inaudible voice, Carolaine explained that her boyfriend was married. To a horrible woman. Two children. But he's going to get a divorce. He told me, he's going to get a divorce and we're going to get married.

Two other neighbors came to the party, acquaintances of his mother's, as well as some children who lived nearby, none of them José Luís's friends; they were just there for the cake. It didn't matter. Soon his father would come in. Kingie felt his heart racing, his father would arrive at any moment.

The television remained on until the moment for singing Happy Birthday. They ate cake, drank soda, Kingie at the door, waiting.

After everyone left, Alzira led the boy to the porch and said, in a ceremonious tone, My son, I'm very happy, I really am. Here's the surprise: I found a job for you. As an office boy. In Mr Rodrigo's office. For a long time, he listened to his mother speaking, without paying attention to the words. He saw Alzira's face, the wrinkles, the excess flesh in her neck, the mouth missing several teeth, the lifeless eyes, the lusterless skin. Shit. He couldn't be fooled that easily. That couldn't be the surprise. A job. As an office boy. He would never be an office boy. Hauling crap back and forth. What about my father? he asked, interrupting his mother's explanation of the advantages of the vouchers for lunch and transportation. Your father? I don't know anything about your father. He must be somewhere or other, bumming around. I thought he was coming, said Kingie. Alzira laughed in a strange way. Your father? That's a good one. In my house? Why would he come? 'Cause it's my birthday, the boy replied. He probably doesn't even know it's your birthday, Alzira laughed again, a scornful smile that caused the boy to react. I don't want to work for Mr Rodrigo, he said. Alzira stood up, there it was again, the raw reality facing her, her dumb son, the idiotic boy. Did you hear that, Mother? she screamed. Me killing myself and this imbecile saying he doesn't want to work in the office. You don't want to be an office boy? I know, you'd rather deal drugs. That's much better. Holding people up. Killing. Are you stupid or what? Can't you see they're giving you a chance? Do you know who the office boys at Mr Rodrigo's are? Boys in the sixth grade. He's giving you a break. You're going to take the job, yes you are. You are. And if you mess up you'll regret it, you'll regret it. I'm not going, Kingie answered, interrupting his mother. He recalled Reader. Loser. Alzira took his reply as a personal insult. She raised her hand, the boy kneeled down and grabbed a rock. They're the pieces of shit, not us. Loser. They take away our love. They kill our love. Oh, so you're going to throw a rock at me? his mother said, her eyes widening. No, he said. Go ahead, stone your mother. You idiot, you imbecile, she screamed, going into the house and collapsing onto the shoulder of her mother, who was watching television. Did you see that, Mother? Why did you tell him about the surprise? Alzira had asked Carolaine the day her daughter told her how she had convinced Kingie to come to the party. It was just a cake, she wasn't going to do anything, the boy didn't deserve it, Alzira had said. A cake, nothing more. But Carolaine had invented that business about a surprise. He wouldn't come, Mother, she'd said, he doesn't like our house. Stated like that, without circumlocution, He doesn't like our house, it had devastated her, destroyed her, and Alzira, feeling herself to blame, had decided to ask her employers for an advance, she'd buy something for the boy, the surprise, a ball, a cart, she wanted so badly for her son to love her, for everything to be all right once and for all, for them to forget the rest, for him to understand the difficulties

65

and be like Carolaine, cooperate, was that so hard? How old is he? Rodrigo asked at breakfast, after hearing the reason his maid had asked for an advance. Twelve. Better than a present, Alzira. Send your son to my office, we're looking for an office boy. He's so young, said Juliana, who was having her breakfast too, twelve, that's very young. That's the way they learn, Rodrigo replied. By working. Alzira had become radiant with happiness. And from that day she had repeated a million times, the surprise, the surprise, making up the lie to herself that her son would go to work and straighten himself out. But God had given her a stupid son. He picked up a rock from the ground, Mother, my own son, and stood there looking at me, you had to see it. He was going to throw that rock at me.

Kingie was still sitting on the porch, listening to Alzira curse and cry in the living room, Cândida and Carolaine, the television set. He thought, Mother, the surprise was that he was going to meet his father. Know what I feel like? Taking him to meet that worm. I swear it. That's what I feel like doing.

Kingie opened the gate and walked down the street. Loser. He felt nothing of the inner pain of which Reader had spoken. It wasn't that, pain. It was an emptiness, inside, in his body. An empty space, a hole. Dripping. Goddamn. He passed by Suzana's house, José Luís, his mother yelled. She was coming toward him rapidly, determined, her purse under her arm, her face. Let's go, it was as if there was nothing human beneath that face, no one, only a nose and mouth and flesh and hatred, let's go, she said, I've decided you're going to meet your father, let's go, you're going to meet your father.

They went to the bus stop, across from Zino's butcher shop, in silence, his mother in front, talking to herself, the boy behind. Loser. They didn't say a word en route. Alzira avoiding looking at her son, pressing her face against the window the entire time. They got off downtown, near Praça Argentina, then walked to the viaduct, silently. Come on. Alzira wandered about the area, searching. Let's go. She'd seen her ex-husband in that same locale, at least ten days ago, when she'd passed there on the bus on her way to Santa Bárbara Hospital. The bum. After so many years. Right in front of her eyes. The animal. And now there he was again, the bum. Unbelievable. Cardboard shacks, beggars, filth. You see that man wrapped in a blanket? That dirty, drunken man there? You see him? He's looking at us. That's your father, Alzira said. You wanted so much to meet him. There he is. Your father.

9

A WASHED-OUT WOMAN, pale hair and skin, faded lips, eyebrows, eyes, everything the same faded color, yellow, the type of woman who was neither ugly nor pretty, small, very serious and graceless. Grace was her name, an unfortunate name; there was nothing in her gestures or expression, no attraction, no grace, but she was a good, proper person who treated Kingie respectfully and cordially. These envelopes, she said, you'll take to the post office. The papers, you make copies. Deliver this ticket to Dona Beatriz, on Barão de Capanema. And when you're Xeroxing, be careful with the order of the pages, they get out of order easily. And, I almost forgot, stop by Mr Rodrigo's house, he forgot to bring his cellphone.

Entering and leaving the Santorini Tourist Agency wasn't easy. There were two heavy steel doors, automatic, one in front of the other, that never opened simultaneously. It was necessary for one of them to be closed for the other to function, and before a visitor passed through them his image was captured by a camera attached to the hallway ceiling. We've been held up twice, Grace explained on his first day at work. Kingie only had access to that part of the agency. In the rear there were more people at work, more heavy doors, more cameras. Our office has several departments, Grace had said, domestic and international tourism, commercial accounts, each division handles something specific, and we don't allow our employees to circulate freely through the departments, in order to avoid congestion.

Kingie would often run into Mr Rodrigo entering or leaving the firm, three-piece suit, clean-shaven, nice, always asking if Grace was treating him well, smiling, That's good, he would say.

Kingie especially liked lunchtime, not because of the food at the luncheonettes in the vicinity, he never was hungry and sold his lunch vouchers, using the money to buy crack and Seven-Up. He also sold anything that could be traded for the drug: staplers, a stack of copy paper, or printer cartridges. The small thefts from the office, which financed his habit, weren't noticed by Grace, and they made the lunch hour a good moment, for seeing people, smoking crack, watching a bunch of girls playing soccer at the beach, the slow-footed, the idiots, all of them looking like suckers. The coach, a gung-ho black guy, yelling, Let's go, Patrícia, let's go, Renata, eye on the ball, shoot at the goal, Renata, go, they didn't shoot, they didn't run, Patrícia was a sly one, blondes who were afraid of the ball. Kingie got a kick out of watching the games.

It wasn't totally disagreeable to catch the bus to make the deliveries, for it allowed Kingie to circulate, see people, which was infinitely better than spending all day between four walls like Grace and the telephone operator Annette, who worked in a tiny plasterboard cubicle, a shoebox equipped with a switchboard and TV gossip magazines.

Therefore, making photocopies, transmitting messages, and performing other small services for a tourism agency wasn't as totally unbearable as the boy had imagined at first. He could quicken his pace, gain time, and afterward have a smoke and wander around at will. But even so, Kingie disliked being an office boy. Every morning, when he squeezed onto a bus packed with doormen and nannies, servants, secretaries, manicurists, on his way to the South Zone, he felt a hollow in his chest, bitterness, all of which improved only after his first morning pipeful in the square near the agency, sssss, the magic potion of power was inhaled through a pipe improvised from a yogurt container, crystals of crack, sssss, burning, sssss, eliminating in the smoke the powerful substance, the nectar, the strength. At the office, he would become irritated at the established hours, the checking up on him, Did you do this? Did you do that? You forgot to stop by the Transportation Department. You got this envelope dirty, go wash your hands. You scrambled these papers. Purchases also irritated him. Buy two boxes of medium-size paper clips. No, those are large, I asked for medium, go back and exchange them. Exchange the folders too, I wanted the ones with elastic, didn't you hear me? José Luís, you don't pay attention. But you didn't mention elastic, Grace. Miss Grace. Yes, I did. Call me Miss Grace. I've been noticing, you don't listen, José Luís. What Kingie detested above all was what he dubbed 'the Mass', when Grace preached about the advantages of an office boy who applies himself and is reliable, of the office boy who does this and that and gets promoted and thus rapidly ascends the staircase of success. Grace took a certain pleasure in that sermon, saying that 'being someone in life', 'getting ahead', 'successful', 'I worked hard', and 'it's necessary to struggle' had the effect of making her more active at work, more efficient, abler. Progress. Success. Grace cited names, related cases. One young boy we hired, a trip to the post office would take him three hours, we let him go, obviously. Fired. Another boy came here just like you, barely literate, and today he's manager of our firm. Adalberto. Kingie liked the way she said 'our firm' as if she were a partner. He laughed at that, to himself, on the bus. We're a mid-sized firm. We're aggressive. We believe in our potential, she said. She shouldn't believe in it, Kingie told Fake, when they met. The woman's going to fall flat on her face. I don't want to be a secretary or the office boy manager. The career perspectives offered daily by Grace made no sense at all to him. And there was the added disadvantage in that job of having his mother on his heels. Mr Rodrigo was expert at forgetting his cellphone at home, his black briefcase, his phone charger, his key, and it was always Kingie who went to get them. Well then? Are you enjoying it, son? Alzira had asked that same question a million times. Are you really enjoying it? His mother in her maid's uniform, her hands wet, washing, her belly against the sink, satisfied. You have to take advantage of it, José Luís. Mr Rodrigo is very nice. Get on Mr Rodrigo's good side. Once, Dona Juliana came into the kitchen at the moment he was saying goodbye to his mother. Hi, José Luís. She was thinner, Dona Juliana. Exercise outfit. She looked at him strangely, Dona Juliana. On another occasion, he'd gone down in the elevator with Dona Juliana's personal trainer. Muscular guy. Hot, huh, man? Good for getting high, the trainer had said. Getting high. He'd also met her children, both of them living it up, easy life, no worries. It's good to be born rich. Kingie made the minimum wage. A pittance. Working eight hours a day to earn that 'piece of crap every month,' as he told Fake. When he was a lookout, he worked less and made more. If he'd been a runner he'd have gotten even more. If he were a soldier at the drug site, more still. How much does a manager at a drug site make? Much more. And if he took over the hillside, he'd have lots of money. If he increased the sales locations, increased the stock of rifles and machine guns, more men and more grenades, he would grow, expand, he'd be fucking rich, practically rich. Eleven kilos of cocaine a month was what Miltão sold. Very little. Miltão, that piece of shit. Rolling in money. And with Suzana to boot. Kingie had seen him at Onofre's, talking his head off, showing the weapon he'd just bought. Mirrored glasses. Asshole. A clip with ninety bullets. How much does Miltão rake in per month, Fake? It was good to chat with Fake. After work he would go to his friend's studio to listen to rap, snort, talk. Fake always had drugs. I'm broadening my plan of action, Fake said, showing him envelopes. Not a word to anyone. Take a look at this. It's the abracadabra system of the miracle of the loaves and fishes. How much do you think Miltão makes, Fake? Miltão, let me see, sniff, about, sniff, I don't know, a pile, sniff, a lot of money. Miltão has a truck, land, houses, rentals. Fake liked Kingie to imitate Grace, Do the frog lady, Zé. That's right, the frog lady, said Kingie, she looked like a white frog, a perfect frog. Look here, José Luís, he said, imitating Grace, I've noticed that your reading leaves something to be desired. To grow, you must study, sniff, study and work hard. And be loyal. Sniff. And not fall behind. And be loyal. And have good manners. And wash your hands. All that's missing, said Kingie, is for her to ask me to bark. Arf arf arf. The two guffawed. She must think that because you're black and a hick you're doing pretty damned good, said Fake, laughing, you're good at that, imitating, you ought to be an actor. I'm not a hick, Kingie stated. Laughter. But you're dark-skinned, you live in the favela, it's the same thing. Once, Fake related, I was watching an American film on TV, the character was Brazilian and named Pablito. Imagine. A Brazilian with a Spanish name. In the United States, anything from Ecuador on down is Pablito. It's the same with Grace, you live in the favela, you're black, that makes you a hick. Come to think of it, that'd make a good rap. Black and a hick.

Kingie thought about money a lot lately. Ever since he'd seen his father, the night of his birthday, barefoot, a blanket over his shoulders, drunk under the viaduct. Go ahead, Alzira had said, talk to him. He's your father. Tell him you always wanted to meet him. Isn't that what you wanted so badly? Go on. Kingie felt his feet glued to the ground, unable to move. See? That's your father. That man reduced to nothing wasn't his father in any way, he was some strange man, not his father, dirty, nothing, fuck, drunk, a beggar. That's your father all right, his mother had assured him, and that band of beggars is his family, bums, they drink and sleep and dirty the city, that's all they do. Why do you think, son, that I didn't want you to meet your father? That's not my father. Yes, it is your father. Yours. That there, that thing you see in front of you, that pile of rags, that human garbage, is walking crap, a piece of shit no good for anything at all. That's your father. He ruined my life, that man. You don't even know a third of it, Zé Luís. The horrible things he did at home. Coming in drunk every day, and my torment would start. He came after me with a knife, when I was still carrying you in my arms, just a little baby. Once, Zé Luís – no, I'm not going to tell you, she said, changing her mind. What good would it do? Go on. He's your father. Don't feel sorry for him, Zé Luís. Don't fool yourself. Your father is a son of a bitch.

Days later, at home, thinking back on that moment, Kingie came to the conclusion that it was the blanket that had given him a negative impression of his father. He'd seen many drunks, dirty and ragged like Francisco. There were dozens of neighbors like that at Onofre's bar, staggering their way down the hill.

The blanket was what made the difference. When his father raised his arms, with the blanket on his shoulders, black wings appeared, an enormous vulture, a hairy, tottering vulture. He had felt so unhappy that night. They had returned home, the two of them, he and his mother, with her weeping on the bus. A repressed crying, sobbing. He felt sorry for his mother. He tried to embrace her, to say something. Forgive me, shit, but all he succeeded in doing was to press his nose against the window and remain there, motionless, listening to Alzira's sobs.

After he began working at Mr Rodrigo's, whenever he had extra time he would go to Praça Argentina to search for his father. He would watch him from a distance. It was common to find him sleeping under the intense noonday sun, pedestrians passing by, feet, crusted filth, rags, wounds. In the early morning he would see him driven away from places, from doorways, the shelter of stores, bank marquees, the police shooing him off, Get out of here, you bum, out. In the afternoon, drinking and asking for money. If he had money he'd take his father off the streets. You think about money a lot, brother, Fake said, my thing is art. Sniff. I only want money so I can set things up. I want to be a performer. I'm not into running from the police or dying at twenty. They all fuck themselves up. I've seen too many fuck themselves up. All of them. Miltão's going to fuck himself too. He's in seventh heaven one day and the next, kerplunk, it's all over. He's gone. My business is art. Rap. Sniff.

Forget that crap. Go to Paris. You deserve it. Greece, the cradle of culture. London. Italy. Spaghetti. You ever been to Bahia? No, never. Nor even to São Paulo. When Kingie thought most about money was the days when there wasn't much work to do and he was forced to sit beside Grace, looking at the posters on the walls, monuments in Paris, islands, food, people laughing and having fun, while he, he and Grace, sat there, without much to do. Why didn't he put an end to all that right away? He felt an enormous urge to say I'm outta here, Grace, and then leave and never come back. He didn't know why he kept coming back. He kept coming back because of his grandmother. A job, a job, the old lady told everybody that José Luís had a steady job. That was the word she used, 'steady', emphasizing it. He was an office boy, José Luís. Big deal, the job. Always broke, without money. Shit.

Grace usually left her wallet in the right-hand drawer of her desk. Go buy a grilled cheese sandwich and guava juice. No, make that watermelon juice. Her hands opening and closing the wallet, money, the wallet being put into and taken out of the drawer, every day, and Kingie always without money, always seeing money, without money, thinking about money, wanting money, Take ten, take twenty, can you cash this check for me? Tens, fifties, here's the change, thank you very much.

Kingie didn't plan anything. It was one of those days without much work. Unbearable heat, the air conditioning out. Grace and he in the office, an overwhelming urge to smoke crack, to get out of there. When Grace went to the ladies' room, he approached her desk. He wasn't going to steal, he wasn't thinking about stealing, he only wanted to see. To touch it. To open the drawer. There wasn't much in the wallet. But behind it, in the back of the drawer, a bundle of new bills. He counted it. Eight hundred bucks. He stuck it in his pocket and left.

10

TWO KILOS OF MEAT. Half a bunch of chopped green onion.
Two cloves of garlic, minced. Two sliced onions. Place on
separate plates in the specified amounts tomato, rinsed rice,
and the seasoned meat. Alzira wanted to have all the ingredients
ready before cooking them, exactly as she saw on the cooking
programs on TV, but it wasn't easy, the phone wouldn't give
her a moment's peace, Mr Fernando calling several times, Clean
the meat, notice that I don't leave a speck of fat, said the hostess,
and Dona Juliana in a bad mood, something awful was about
to happen in the house, she could see that quite clearly, and
Alzira's knives also weren't very good, she had ears and heard
the two of them, the trainer and Dona Juliana, it was going to
end in deep shit, the best thing to do was to be like the three
monkeys, which she'd seen somewhere or other, see no evil,
hear no evil, speak no evil. The knives wouldn't cut, on the TV
programs the ingredients were all separated and organized, they
were dull, the knives, sweet yellow peppers, red bell peppers,
Alzira could hardly get the vegetables cut, they were calling
her at every turn, Where's my black skirt, Alzira? Alzira, the
door, Hi, Mr Rodrigo, you're home early today. Two coffees,
please, in my office. A confused late afternoon, they kept asking
for coffee with artificial sweetener, Alzira was cutting carrots
when Dona Juliana came to tell her, Mr Rodrigo wants to talk
with you, Alzira.

In the living room. Mr Rodrigo on the sofa, legs crossed,
You'd better sit down, Alzira. She preferred to stand, a dishcloth
in her hand, Of course. Something very serious has happened,
Alzira. At that moment, she knew it wasn't necessary for Mr

Rodrigo to tell her anything, she knew, she was waiting for it to happen. She had had a premonition, something awful, something terrible. She had been waiting for it the entire time. And there it was. The tragedy. He stole money, your son. We had been noticing things disappearing from the office, small things. It may have been him. I'm not going to call the police, because he's your son. I'll pay for everything, Alzira stated, I insist on it. He's going to return every cent.

That night, Alzira waited for José Luís at Cândida's house, on the porch, pacing from side to side, impatient at the coming and going of Carnival planners. It was raining hard, but Alzira didn't feel the water on her body, she went to the gate and returned, her clothes soaked, she went to the bus stop and back, first passing by Onofre's, asking. Someone said that Kingie liked to hang out at Fake's shack, over there, right over there, she knocked at the door, a young man with an earring appeared. Can I help you? he said, loud music. Yes, I know Zé Luís, but he hasn't been here today.

In the morning, beside Cândida, who remained at her sewing machine, and Carolaine, Alzira anxiously awaited the arrival of her son. Oh yes, he would see. Stay calm, Mother, Carolaine said. Alzira shouted at the girl, Don't bother me, she was going to smack him, yes, beat him, he would see, a real thrashing, she'd beat some sense into him, she'd give him such a hiding, the shameless good-for-nothing. Stop looking at me, you two. Sometimes, in bed, she regretted the beatings she administered to her son, even cried on certain occasions when she saw the purple bruises on the boy's fragile body, and at those moments she felt herself to be a defeated mother, a failure, but not now, the lowlife, now she understood that she hadn't beaten him enough, beaten, exactly, hit, punched, I feel like grabbing his head and banging it against the wall, Mother, till it breaks. The shame she felt, her son a thief, they said, her damned son, stealing, never, a disgrace, humiliation, the lowlife, she, Alzira, who had a hard time even accepting anything offered to her, had given birth to a thief. She'd rather have given birth to a clubfoot, a retarded child, my God, a retard, her whole life working, cleaning, and scrubbing in other people's houses, enduring hardships, she'd never even taken a pear from the family's refrigerator, her whole life like that, wanting and not being able to, and now, a sneak thief, a lowlife, a robber, oh God.

In the days that followed, Cândida, Carolaine, and Suzana searched the entire favela; no one knew anything about Kingie. We haven't seen him, they said. No, we don't know anything. A scrawny kid with deep-set eyes? No, I don't know. No word.

On Tuesday, Reader went to Alzira's house, with Onofre, ready to help. I know your son, he said, he talked about drugs. Did you know he's doing drugs? No, no, she answered, confused, feeling a weakness in her legs. You're wrong, my son wasn't an addict, isn't an addict, she corrected herself, with less certainty, fearful. Dead, yes, the idea had occurred to her at that moment, her son could be dead now, and I'm to blame, she thought, my son, then said nothing more, listening to Reader tell what he knew. The boy needs help, he stated, crack, she felt crushed by all that, crack, destroyed, how had she never noticed anything different in her own son? Reader advised the family to go to the 17th precinct to report the disappearance. Alzira was so desperate, so repentant, if they found her son she'd promise the Virgin Mary she would never again lay a finger on him, how could she not have noticed? The horrible thing, she told Cândida as she waited to speak to the precinct captain, the horrible thing, Mother, is that I can't even ask where I went wrong, I know where I went wrong, Mother, I know, she said. As the sergeant listened to their story, Alzira could do nothing but cry. Take it easy, lady, Abel, bring the lady here a glass of water.

Kingie wasn't thinking about returning home. He'd been living on the streets for four days, wandering around, money in his pocket, sleeping in public squares and under bridges, smoking, going to the beach, frequenting video arcades, smoking, sleeping anywhere. He bought loads of crystals, he'd never consumed as much as in those days. When it took longer than it should to prepare the pipe, the sensation was horrible, he felt threatened by something, a thing that entered his body to fill it with fear, a kind of invasion, microscopic animals, enemies, piercing his flesh, provoking fear and itching, and, sometimes, the urge to cry and to scream. Two-seven, he thought about calling Fake, two-seven-nine, from the public telephone at Onofre's, if he could just remember the number, he wanted to talk to Fake, maybe his friend could help him, he never memorized numbers, two-seven-five, maybe they'd give him some medicine, two-seven-nine-five, maybe they'd give him some medicine to stop the invasion. He wanted to see Cândida, to rest in his grandmother's arms, but how, if the animals wouldn't stop attacking him, if he was always vomiting and suffering from diarrhea? Goddamn. He couldn't go anywhere. Shitting. Never. Goddamn. Stay. Vomiting. He'd sleep right there. When he closed his eyes, the good images from before, the colors, wouldn't come. He could no longer ride in a car with his father, go to a soccer game, eat hamburgers, that irritated him, ever since he'd met him he'd never again gone out with him, he closed his eyes, the red car appeared, blowing its horn. Hi, father, hi, son, and the driver was him, the beggar, not his father, a blanket over his shoulders, stinking, drinking booze, chasing Kingie's mother with a knife in his hand, Kingie a baby in Alzira's arms, and the vulture flying above them both, trying to kill them, loser, and Kingie hurled himself from the car, waking up, his body aching and someone kicking him in the back, Out, said the policeman, you can't stay here. Shit. Kingie went to the doorway of a supermarket that was about to open, out, the checkout girls arriving, a parked refrigerator truck, move along, the day was beginning, shit, one more day. While he still had the strength, there was always some reserve left in the morning, he walked, went into the video arcades, bought tokens, and passed the time that way, in front of the monitor, playing at lion hunting, killing outlaws, target shooting, blowing up enemies, the problem was the targets, he couldn't hit them, he missed, the lions and the outlaws fled, shit, and to make it worse, the noise coming from the machines made his stomach churn. He joined the beggars and purse snatchers who appeared in his path, he felt good among them, walking with them, nobody cared, including him, he kept quiet, didn't like to talk, felt a dark cloud growing inside his body, a black sphere born in his throat and growing, paralyzing his tongue.

Twice he went to Praça Argentina to see his father. He sat down by him on a bench, the two of them, side by side, his father drunk, Kingie drugged, and watched the street vendors at work, one of them was quite amusing, saying things, singing, they laughed at the man. Crazy guy, his father said, getting up. He didn't have his blanket that day, and Kingie could see how thin his father was.

Saturday night. The yogurt container was cut with a razor blade. Seated on the ground with his legs crossed, Kingie prepared a new pipe. Ahead, three boys and a young girl were observing the parked cars. That one doesn't have it, they said, or that one, the assholes didn't leave anything, they laughed. Kingie only knew the girl's name, Suzana, an ugly thing, skinny. Is your name really Suzana? he asked. Yes, so ugly this Suzana, so different from the real Suzana, his Suzana, the Suzana in bell-bottoms and miniblouses, with her pretty hands and fragrant hair, the Suzana who took him to the beach one day, the two of them sitting on the sand, looking at the sea. What are you going to be when you grow up, Zé Luís? I'm going to be a truck driver. I want to travel. I want to have a clothes boutique, Suzana had said. TV hostess. The pipe didn't turn out well, Kingie picked up another container, cut his finger. Ouch. Now the kids were looking at the tape player in a parked Volkswagen. Kingie lit the crystals, called to the others, crash, the car window was smashed. Want a hit? Kingie shouted, showing the pipe. Crack. Smoke. Run. The group fled, taking with them the stolen tape player, the four of them, ssss, Kingie took a deep drag. Fuck them, he thought, they never refused, the moochers, he inhaled again, felt the power, ahhhhh, something inside him, smiling, or outside, Suzana, the real one, smiling at him, the real Suzana, that was the sensation, he breathed and felt Suzana.

When he raised his eyes, the van had already stopped, police leaping out, boots, those fuckers, those fuckers, they ought to be killed. Two guns pointing in Kingie's direction. They approached dispensing kicks, shouting, hitting people. Shit. They wanted to know where the tape player was. Where are those pieces of shit, the others? José Luís didn't know the street kids, didn't know their names. Just Suzana, her I know. Ah, so you don't know them. Another blow to the ear. Little shits. They searched him. More blows. Little bastards. In the boy's shorts, wrapped in a plastic bag, five hundred and fifty in bills. This is getting better, one of the policemen commented. They split the money among them. Seven crystals of crack. Very good. These little fuckers really get on my nerves, one of the cops said, stashing the crystals in his pocket. OK, put the kid in the van.

At ten in the morning, Kingie was at the Tereza Guimarães Moraes Juvenile Detention Center, his eyes bloodshot, agitated, his blood running cold through his body. They placed him in a small room, took away his clothes, searched him, gave him a pair of slippers and pajamas. There were other boys in the cell. What's happening, blood? They spoke softly. A knife, they said, a .38, some weed, Kingie made no effort to listen. He tried to shut his eyes but knew he wouldn't manage to sleep.

Those eight days were horrible, he could think of nothing but smoking, distressed, banging his fist against the wall, trembling, his gums bleeding, the jailors yelling at him. If you want trouble, we'll see that you get it. Let's go. Make your beds. Fold the blankets, you there, I've got my eye on you. Get your backs against that wall. In the morning they wanted him to attend classes. You can't stay in bed, some old woman said, get up, go brush your teeth, useless, social workers filled out forms and yelled at him, at lunch, Sit down there, we don't allow knives, forks, toothpicks, anything pointed, on your feet, everybody, the stories, the horrible food, disgusting rice, I robbed a supermarket, I killed a baker, I held up a gas station, my father taught me how to pick pockets, and at night more unhappiness, he felt such sadness in his heart, among the other boys, watching television, sadness, the urge to die, he wanted to die, not go home, no father, not even Suzana, he really wanted to die.

On Monday, when he saw Cândida, his grandmother, standing in front of the juvenile judge, signing the surety bond, Kingie felt like a street mongrel. They went home by bus, clasping each other's hand. They shaved your head, she said, but you still look handsome.

When they got off the bus in front of Zino's butcher's shop, Cândida told him that Alzira and Carolaine were waiting for him. Your mother wants very much for you to come home, son, she wants to help you.

The two were waiting for him at the gate. When Carolaine embraced him, Kingie noticed her fuller face. Onofre was right, Carolaine was plumper. Hi, son, said Alzira, her eyes red from crying. The smell of onions on his mother. Her cold hands. Everything's going to be all right, she said, hugging him tightly.

The Support and Therapy Group for Recovery from Substance Abuse. Weekly meetings. Impressive testimonies, bouts of sobbing, lamentations. I started with marijuana. I started with crack. With amphetamines. By the time I discovered my son was doing drugs, the problem was already serious. Speedball is a kind of atomic bomb of drugs, heroin and cocaine mixed together, taking you directly to the top of the abyss. I had the sensation of falling, for hours. My teeth burned. My mother, my father, people would catch on fire right in front of my eyes. I injected it into my jugular. She ran away from the hospital, my daughter, to buy drugs. Look at my veins. I wanted to die. The meetings were weekly, and Alzira felt good getting together with parents and relatives of other addicts. The important thing is to talk. Explain. Dialogue. Set limits, but remember that repression doesn't solve the problem. Only love solves it. Affection. Understanding. Be your son's friend. Give support. Alzira had tried everything. Sometimes, she had the impression that the boy was better, but it was just an impression. José Luís couldn't be by himself for a minute. As soon as they left him alone, he would grab anything, a radio, pots, anything, and trade it for crack at the drug site. He would never come home, they had to go out looking for him, he was always lying in some out-of-the-way spot. Other times, the neighbors, knowing of the situation, would pluck him from the streets, drugged, and take him to Alzira.

It was Suzana's idea to look for Miltão. After all, Alzira, he controls that bunch of boys. The young kids respect Miltão. And besides, Alzira, you don't have that many options.

Miltão received Alzira at Bidê's house one Sunday afternoon, the heavens threatening a violent storm. The radio on, men standing security at the door, nine men, Alzira counted, averting her eyes from the guns. This time, the meeting was different. The woman who months before had come to return the money her son had received working for the traffickers was not the same one who was there to ask for help. Alzira looked older, more weary, and above all, sadder. What do you want me to do? Miltão asked, turning off the radio. Talk to him, Alzira answered. Explain that he's going to die. My son is going to die. I can talk to him, replied Miltão, but I don't know if it'll do any good.

Kingie was in the living room, watching TV, when Miltão came in with Suzana and his mother. The trafficker gestured for the two women to leave. They talked, in reality it was only Miltão who spoke, José Luís listened. A guy does this, a guy does that, but he does what's right, he said. Zelão died. Branco went crazy. Kingie felt like laughing, it was so ridiculous to hear Miltão tell him that drugs killed. But they do kill, brother. People fuck themselves up. I don't use the stuff. Kingie knew that Miltão liked coke and marijuana, that he snorted and smoked. Did you ever see me stoned? No, and you're not going to. I sell the stuff. It's my business. I don't poison myself. Turn off that goddamn TV, I'm talking to you, brother. Kingie turned off the television. If you want to die, Miltão continued, I don't give a shit, but fuck it, what about your mother, man? You're just a kid, you don't have any knowledge of life. That's what I came here to say. Suzana is worried. And your mother. It's no good to crap on your friends. I'll stop, said Kingie, I'll stop doing dope, I swear here and now that I'll never smoke again, or snort, or anything, never again, on one condition.

What? asked Miltão. I go back to work for you. You flipped out, said Miltão, laughing. Way out, guy. Your mother, man. Flipped out. Your mother, did you forget about her? You bust my balls, man. You wear me out. That's the way I am, the boy said. Miltão scratched his head, laughed, and as he did Kingie noticed the gun in his belt. Kingie went to the window. Alzira was talking to Suzana. Mother, he said, come here.

Alzira came in, uncomfortable with the situation, distressed. Mother, José Luís said, starting today I'm working for Miltão. You'll never again see me on drugs.

Alzira sighed, agonized. What more could she do?

STAIRS AND ALLEYWAYS, DESCENDING and ascending, stairs, children crying everywhere, steps, up-and-down, hiding places, stairs, rags on clotheslines, turn to the right, left, go down to go up, climb, steps, descend, roofs and windows, every day Kingie would follow a different route to the highest point of the favela. From there he would observe the movement on the hillside for the traffickers, becoming ever more acquainted with the labyrinth below and the people in it, learning of new alleyways, escape routes, names, Vanessa, Cida, Jorjão, Washington, Dora, Edevaldo, Madeusa, Gisele, Edicréia. He liked it when they waved to him, Hi, Kingie, Fabiane, Lecilda, Wilmor, or when he noticed that by going in here and turning he would come out there. You've got to know every nook, Miltão said, every hole, be like a mouse, that's the advice I give my men, the more like a mouse the better, when you blast the sons of bitches, you got to have the advantage, and the advantage is ours. They know how to come shooting their way in, but getting out, getting away, that's something only we know. Be like a mouse.

He never failed to stop by Onofre's bar to buy cigarettes and drink a Seven-Up. Hi, Kingie, Onofre, rubicund, his hairy arms on the counter, chatting pleasantly with women, telling jokes, offering candy. It's my charm, Onofre said. I offer them free candy, women are serious until they eat the candy and get it all over themselves. I'm crazy about a woman, Kingie, a very refined lady who's wearing my cock to a nub, by all the saints, a killer of a pussy that clamps down on my dick, oh God, she rubs it raw, she devours me, shit, it's good to fuck, the good life is fucking, eating, and sleeping, and here I am selling stuff, eh? You hear about Reader? Who's the girl's that's getting it on with him? Some big smiling, chesty broad? Why the hell doesn't he play straight with me? Huh? The silent type? I've never trusted anybody who doesn't like to talk. How's your sister Carolaine? Everything well with Carolaine? Nothing new with Carolaine, eh?

From up there Kingie had a good view of the main access, across from the butcher's shop, where on Mondays men would unload large bloody pieces of recently slaughtered animals. He could see the entire hillside, an immense, ever expanding gray mass, unfinished, cut in every possible direction by short roads, alleyways, a maze of connections and passageways, with few entrances and exits. Kingie never became distracted, remaining as alert as a watchdog, excited, restless, no crack or marijuana, no powder, ether, chloroform, thinner, nothing, all that was in the past, he'd decided to stop doing drugs and he had stopped. Yes, he'd suffered, but something pushed him onward, determination, perseverance. He had decided that nothing would divert him, nothing, not the sweats, the tremors, the fevers, Kingie had turned his back on what raged inside his body, ignoring vices and desires. You smoke, Miltão had said, you'll have to answer to me, I'll fuck you up the ass, man, I smoke, I snort, I drink because I don't flip out, I tolerate it, I don't go around fucking up. I smoke to eat, it gives me an appetite. I don't like drinking. I drink so I can sleep. And I snort to wake up.

In December, when the rains came, there was no worse assignment in the drug trade than that of lookout. As Bidê said, it's the lookout's job to get wet, heh heh heh. So get wet. The mud descended, holes widened, puddles proliferated, and with each rain it was discovered that it was possible for things to get a little worse.

That day, at the end of his shift, Kingie was told that Miltão was expecting him at the sports court in the abandoned construction site of an elementary school. As Kingie made his way down, his T-shirt wet, his flip-flops slapping in the mud, the hooker Rosa Maria was coming up, smiling, wearing heavy make-up, new clothes, umbrella, black glossy shoes. Know what?

she asked happily. Remember the German guy? The tourist? We're getting married. In Germany. Rosa Maria went on to say that in Germany the government was obliged to provide employment for all citizens, all of them, the cities were clean and orderly, which was very good, Rosa Maria was tired of disorder. Brazilians are too disorganized, 'too much without any basic notion,' Brazilians don't have a goal. Did you know the Germans invented the potato?

Shoot, they yelled at the court. Miltão running, playing with the boys, goal, the little guy scores, shoot, shoot, Kingie leaned against a post, observing. Miltão noticed the boy's presence, waved, goal, Bidê and Look At That were watching the game, laughing, the boys grabbed Miltão's shirt, Miltão got past one opponent, ran, nimble, cunning, before Kingie realized it, he was rooting not merely for Miltão's team but exclusively for Miltão, goal, the words 'fucking bastard' and 'shitass drug dealer' and 'stuck-up piece of crap' didn't come to mind when he thought of Miltão, goal, other words suggested themselves, more positive words, 'strength', 'courage', 'goal', 'leadership', 'balls'. Kingie admired the way Miltão commanded life in the favela, the carrot and the stick, by threatening and by facilitating, by striking terror and by offering help. Miltão was loyal to his men who were in prison, soldiers and site managers who had been 'captured'. A good part of what we make from drugs, Reader had explained one night, goes to the penitentiary, it's what the newspapers like to call organized crime, he continued. You talk about loyalty. That's one opinion. Loyalty and fear. They're scared shitless the inmates will escape and blow their heads off. So anybody that wants to stay alive has to work with the ones who got busted. At least for a time. Tell me something, Kingie. You're a clever type, do you see any organization here? We're small fry. Penny-ante. There's no organization here. It's the Hispanics who're organized, the Asians, people a lot more disciplined and who have international setups, with sensational ways of killing judges and corrupting prosecutors and the police. You know what weapons those guys use? Nuclear power. Yes sir. I'm talking about plutonium and things like that. They run everything: prostitution, money laundering, kidnapping, slot machines, pornography, robbery, forgery, loansharking. It seems that one of those communists even got himself a solid gold sculpture of a Mafioso in Uzbekistan. Now that's organized crime.

Kingie didn't share Reader's ideas. More than anything else in the world, he enjoyed imagining himself as a cog in the wheel, a powerful sphere, a system, a force. And believing that there were many connections. A hierarchy. Codes and laws. Soldiers. Planning. It was good to know that even public health workers needed his clearance before they could go up the hillside for their sanitation campaigns. Traffickers in Rio fire on military barracks, Drug trade moves $250 billion, Drug traffic brings mourning to the favela, said the newspapers about their world, in bold headlines. Onofre always read the news to Kingie. And there was also the style, the money, Hondas, Mitsubishis, hard currency, reflective sunglasses, cellphones, antenna dishes, tracer bullets, funk nights, barbecues, a way of walking, the slang, Suzana, the respect of the residents. Kingie was impressed by all of that.

Let's go, Miltão said after the game. It was already almost five o'clock on a Friday afternoon when they got into the Monza parked in front of Zino's butcher's shop, Look At That at the wheel, Miltão in the front seat, José Luís and Bidê in the back seat. As soon as the car pulled away, Miltão told Kingie he'd ordered the car stolen just for its metallic orange color. I like that color. Kingie felt important because Miltão told him something, orange, he searched for something interesting to say, metallic, but he failed, orange, there was nothing in his head, metallic orange, no response, no idea, he felt like an idiot, whenever he was near Miltão he had nothing to talk about, his head empty, not a word, an idiot. He smiled back shyly. Orange.

Always serious, minding his own business, taciturn, those were exactly the qualities that Miltão valued in Kingie. He never asks questions. Why? You know what? I like that boy. I like him now. He doesn't beat around the bush, he doesn't ask for anything, doesn't complain, doesn't jerk you around, doesn't give me a hard time. He does his job, reliable. And that's how it's gotta be. We're going to baptize the boy. Do you think, Suzana, the trafficker had asked his girlfriend, do you think I can trust the kid? Yes, she answered.

They came to Avenida Brasil in a pouring rain, Look At That watching for the exits. It's further ahead, Miltão said, every time the driver reduced his speed to see the road signs, keep going, it's up ahead, I know the road. Traffic was heavy, many people going up into the mountains. The forecast is for a sunny weekend, the radio said, a cold front heading out to sea, temperature eighty degrees.

A man was waiting for them at the last service station, leaving Rio, a husky black man named Duque. He got into the car, smiling and talkative. Duque could imitate voices. During the trip Miltão kept asking, Do Gringo, do Peroba, Marinho, Preá, Zoba, Voutéir, Ademilson, do Gambá. With each impression, guffaws exploded in the Monza.

It's on me, Miltão told the group as they entered the Brasinha steak house. He explained how all-you-can-eat worked. You put your cards in this thing, he said, referring to a small wooden holder. Red is beef, white's chicken, yellow's sausage, they have everything. Black means you're full. Miltão and his friends chose a table near the television, ordered beer, ate, drank. Duque, a joker, constantly jesting and provoking laughter.

At the end of the dinner, they were joined by another man, Romeu, with an intelligent air about him and shrewd eyes. The great Romeu, joked Miltão, frequently clapping him on the back.

They ordered more drinks, it was a lively night. Kingie made an effort to keep up with the conversation, but a kind of torpor overtook his body from head to foot. He wasn't used to so much meat, so much alcohol, his face flushed, his arms and legs relaxed, the words they were speaking, all of it too fast, kidnappings, weapons, meat, pistols, they shouted, Miltão and Look At That roared, belched, told stories, yelled, and Duque farted, imitating, mimicking. You remember that guy that died, Pitanga? Imitate Pitanga. I don't imitate cadavers, Duque answered. Guffaws. Or fags. It might be catching, ever think about that? More laughter. Only Romeu seemed unamused. A cautious type, an observer, Kingie noted. Shit, he didn't find anything funny, it was strange.

There was one exciting moment, for Kingie at least, when Miltão handed Romeu a bundle of bills, José Luís had never seen so much money. Is that all? Romeu asked. That's a lot, Miltão replied, taking Romeu aside. The two walked to the counter, speaking in low tones, friendly.

On the way back, Miltão, indignant and irate, cursed Romeu with every dirty word he knew. Romeu, a police detective, sold arms and information to the leaders of the drug trade like Miltão. One more little shit trying to get a piece of the action. The goddamn son of a bitch. The shitass. My prices have gone up, Romeu had said. He raised his price, the fucker, you heard him, didn't you, Look At That? The bastard. And that crap about the shipment that came in last week? Huh? You heard it, Look At That. Didn't you? Keep an eye on that guy. He's a devil. He's not going to get anything. The dirty fucker. You see what he was trying to sell me? Worthless junk. I told the bastard: Brother, that piece of crap wouldn't cut through a tin can.

I get out here, Duque said when on the return trip they passed the spot where he'd been picked up hours earlier. Look At That didn't stop.

Kingie felt good, the drinks had relaxed him. It'd be nice, he thought, if Duque imitated other people, maybe that would cheer Miltão up, maybe they could bring back the easygoing climate that had begun the evening. Imitate Onofre, he said into Duque's ear. Duque looked at him disdainfully, Shut up, punk. Don't bust my balls.

Look At That drove for another six miles before turning to the right onto a narrow dirt road. They continued for some minutes, now in silence except for the sound of the motor. Where we going? Duque asked. No answer. The car parked on the deserted road, they all got out, only Duque remained seated, waiting.

Miltão was urinating, looking at the sky. C'mere, kid. Kingie approached awkwardly. Want to take a piss? the trafficker asked. José Luís looked at the sky, there wasn't a single star, only darkness. Are you ready? Miltão said. Ready for what? the boy asked. To kill, the trafficker answered. You're going to kill Duque.

Duque was a police informer, and Romeu had revealed the fact some days before. Miltão had insisted on taking Duque to the steakhouse, fearing that Romeu was mistaken. No doubt at all, it's him all right, Romeu had confirmed when he was alone with Miltão. I'm certain of it. It was him who provided the coordinates for the invasion of the packaging shack.

Miltão explained that no one was forced to do anything. They were going to kill Duque in any case. They would gouge out the traitor's eyes. They'd cut out his tongue. Then they'd set him on fire. That's what they'd do. But Kingie could put a bullet in the man's forehead and resolve the matter more quickly. It was just a favor they were asking. When someone asks a favor, you can do it or not do it. You came for that reason. To say yes or no. You can say, Yes, I can kill that son of a bitch that betrayed us. You can say, No, I don't want to get my hands dirty. Here, a guy has a choice, said Miltão.

Duque was brought from the car. I didn't do anything, he repeated, I swear to God, I swear it, I swear it. There's nothing but scumbags in this world, Miltão said, while Look At That and Bidê tied the informer's hands and feet. The guy was useless, a shitass, you go and give him a job, you help the guy, and what happens? Is he grateful? Does he pay you back? No, he fucks you, he gives up your packaging house. That's all. It's a lie, Duque repeated, sobbing, I swear it, for the love of God, Our Lady, I swear it, Mother, forgive me. One thing I can't stand, Miltão said, is when a shitass coward starts in with that crybaby crap. Duque, you fucker, act like a man.

A sensation of discomfort swept over Kingie when Miltão placed the revolver in his hands. It was the first time he'd ever held a gun. He felt the cold touch of metal on his fingers. There wasn't much to think about. Efficiency. To kill a man. He knew that it would happen, he just didn't imagine that it would be on a day when his stomach was so full.

Kingie took aim at Duque's head and fired. He missed the first shot. It was only then that the boy truly looked at his victim. His eyes were screaming, imploring. Shit. Miltão's men seemed to be amused by it. Beginners are something else, they said. The second shot hit Duque in the cheek, making a hole the size of a tomato. There. The business was done. For several seconds everyone was silent, hearing the muffled sounds of the sobs and gasping of the victim, blood coming from his mouth and ears.

Guts, nerves of steel. I liked that, said Miltão. Real good. It was in this manner that he liked to evaluate the potential of a new member of the group, by executing a traitor. Excellent. Miltão was satisfied. You're baptized, he told the boy as they returned to the car. I like what I saw.

12

I KILLED A MAN, brethren. Hallelujah. And it wasn't for revenge, or in an argument, or anger, or rivalry. Sad to say, and this is the part that condemns me, I killed for money. Hallelujah, God is our father.

A stocky, muscular man, pathetic in his expressions, was relating his tragedy to an audience of the poor, sufferers, abandoned old people, the infirm leaning on crutches, widows, mothers who had lost children, paraplegics in wheelchairs, wives deserted by their husbands, unemployed young people, former alcoholics, ex-prostitutes, all of them residents of the favela, wearing their best clothes.

I remember, ladies and gentlemen, the speaker continued, I remember that as I waited in ambush for the poor devil I was going to murder, I saw the image of Our Lady, hallelujah, I saw, ladies and gentlemen, I was on the porch of a humble house, a worker's house, I saw that tiny statue placed there to protect the family, as is common in many houses that we have around here, I saw, brothers and sisters, the Virgin with her little son in her arms, and immediately I heard the crying of a child, a baby, and at that moment, people, I, holding a revolver in my hand, hallelujah, I didn't realize, O ye faithful, that God was sending me a sign by placing the Virgin directly before my eyes, the baby's crying, I didn't see anything, ye faithful, I didn't notice the divine signals because I was walking side by side with the Devil.

Alzira, sitting in the last row of wooden chairs, at her feet two plastic bags that she had brought from work, listened attentively to the speaker's words. Lately she had begun detouring from her usual homeward route just to pass by the recently inaugurated evangelical temple of the Flock of the Purest Love of Our Lord Jesus Christ. What first caught her attention had been the façade, covered from top to bottom with brown tiles similar to those in Dona Juliana's bathroom. Afterward, on the nights when there were evening services and at festivities, she had begun following the singing and prayers. Several times she'd seen Pastor Walmir, who at that moment was listening tearfully to the testimony of a convert, walking about the church, accompanied by young people. She felt like talking to him, asking him for help. But she lacked the courage. At the end of that afternoon, returning from work, without planning to do so, she had decided to go in. She felt so good there. She recalled the time when she would go with her mother to the Catumbi church and sing the hymns. How good it was. She missed those Sundays, drenched in sunlight, Masses, clean clothes, Sundays with a husband, chicken in the pot, and spaghetti, Alzira and her Sunday-best dress, blue with white polka dots, her, her husband, the children in their arms, going to church together. It wasn't that long ago. How she believed in God in those days. Francisco, her husband, was a fare collector on a bus. A good-looking man, Francisco, happy, hard-working, he would leave home early, You can wait for me. One day he had brought Alzira a necklace of blue beads made of glass. Hallelujah. Why had everything ended the way it did? When Francisco started drinking, Alzira had prayed fervently to Our Lady Aparecida, the Virgin Mary, blessed art thou, and Francisco became an alcoholic, lost his job, all shame, his honor, O Virgin, hear my pleas. Alzira had prayed so hard that she had exhausted all the faith in her heart. Then came the beatings, hallelujah, the threats, I killed, I killed, the other women, the separation, but by then Alzira had given up prayer. She didn't remember the exact moment she'd given up God. Abandoned, simply. She had forgotten God. Now, listening to the desperate words of that man, she felt herself a sinner for saying, years on end, that God had not heard her. It had been she who had stopped praying, who had renounced the Church. Perhaps because at that time she felt such great discomfort when she went to Mass, an uneasiness akin to what she experienced today when she got into Dona Juliana's car, or when she served Mr Rodrigo's guests at the dinner table. But in that small tiled church, Alzira was completely at home. For her, worship of some sort resembled the meetings of the addicts' support group. There was faith, confidence, and human warmth.

When he saw me, ladies and gentlemen, the victim, the speaker said, he asked humbly for me not to kill him. Hallelujah. Oh, how painful it is to remember, my brothers and sisters. I took aim. Oh, so sad. I fired, ye faithful. And his wife came to the door, carrying a baby just like the Virgin, screaming for her husband, the baby terrified. I killed their poor father, an honest man who provided for his family. I killed for money, hallelujah, I sinned, hallelujah.

At that moment, Glory!, wailing swept through the church, the mob weeping, clasping one another's hands, shouting, hallelujah, calling upon God, all of them on their knees. The singing began and even with the voices partially drowned out by the noise from the recreation court, where the samba school was holding its final rehearsals, it lifted Alzira's heart, making her feel something was growing in her soul, Glory, Glory, they sang.

As she left, she thought about speaking with Pastor Walmir. She even took a few steps toward him, her mind made up, then suddenly noticed her clothes, the fact that she hadn't taken a bath, her wrinkled hands, red from so much water and detergent all day long, her hair reeking with the smell of fried food, her mud-encrusted sandals. Alzira wasn't vain. But, without a bath she felt unworthy of addressing that well spoken, nicely dressed man, who was looking at her, smiling, coming toward her, surrounded by the faithful, it was better to leave. Do you want to talk to me, my daughter?

When she knelt and kissed the pastor's hand, Alzira felt a power course through her body, and she burst into tears. Tell me, my child, what is troubling your heart?

Alzira was trembling, the words wouldn't come, only tears and sobbing, and at first she didn't know how to express what hurt her so, everything was unhappiness and despair. Such distress, my daughter, open your heart. It wasn't the work that made Alzira cry, although Dona Juliana was temperamental, certainly, yelled at her, called her stupid. You dumbbell, she would say, your problem, Alzira, is stupidity, but right away Juliana would apologize, weeping, regretful, Alzira, I'm so stressed, my life, Alzira, she'd say, she talked, wanting to tell the real reason for her torment, the lover, Alzira, Fernando, my life is nothing but confusion. Alzira already knew everything but pretended to be unaware. Know what I would do, Mother? Carolaine liked to give Alzira advice. I'd slap her face, Mother. I swear I would. Dumbbell? I'd smack her so hard on the ear the woman would bounce off the wall. To hell with that bitch. Don't say such things, Carolaine. I'll say them, she is a bitch, and I don't like to see you suffer, Mother. You're weak. It wasn't weakness. The truth is that Juliana's attacks of fury no longer affected her, she had become accustomed to the screams, the bad moods, the insults, the lack of respect. It was something else that caused Alzira's suffering, something bigger, much bigger, more important, more serious, more vital, something that took away her sleep, her appetite, and her will to live. What is it, daughter? God is here to help. It was some minutes before she managed to speak.

My son's shirt, pastor, was splattered with blood.

Walmir helped Alzira to her feet, took her to a room in the rear of the church, offered her water. Stay calm. Who is your son? Is he part of Miltão's gang? Tell me everything. What bloodstained shirt is that? Who is your son?

Alzira sat in an orange-colored plastic chair, facing an image of Christ on the cross, and allowed the pastor to grasp her hands. It wasn't easy to speak of these things. These dirty secrets. That her son had almost killed himself from heavy drug use and was now working for the traffickers. That he had begun as a lookout and was now a runner, transporting drugs here and there. That the boy wore chains on his chest and dressed like an outlaw. That he used strange slang and earned good money. That she wouldn't take a penny from her son and that unfortunately her daughter Carolaine didn't share her attitude. And that all that, as bad as it was, she could tolerate. But now he had committed a crime, and although she wasn't sure of anything, had no proof, she knew that it had been something terrible, because she was a mother and mothers know. He had killed. That night, pastor, he came home very late, so tormented, trembling, he ran to the bathroom, avoiding me. He left the water running, thinking I wouldn't hear him, but I heard, pastor. He was moaning in a strange way, it wasn't a lament, it was a horrible sound, he vomited, pastor, vomited, he cried, I had my ear against the bathroom door and heard everything. He came out of there with his eyes red and his face as white as a ghost, then he turned on the TV, just so he wouldn't have to talk to me. I made him a glass of warm milk. Tell your mother, I said, what's going on? I ate too much meat, he replied. The next day, when I went to wash his clothes, I saw the blood.

Alzira went on crying, in the pastor's arms. I accept everything that God sends me, pastor, everything, grief, sickness, poverty, loneliness, death, everything, but that, a murderer, killing a human being, my son, I can't accept that, pastor, there's no way at all I can accept that. I can't accept it.

It was past eight when Alzira left the church, feeling more relieved. There was a strong smell of rain in the air. She bought bread at Onofre's and slowly ascended the hill.

When she entered the house, Alzira found Carolaine in front of the television, barefoot, a can of condensed milk in her hand. Hi, Mother, the soap's about to start. She kissed the girl, taking the condensed milk from her, You'll ruin your dinner. Mother, don't be a drag! Nothing spoiled Carolaine's appetite. She could eat two plates of spaghetti even after devouring a box of chocolates. It was her brother's fault she'd become hooked on chocolate, he was always bringing home packages of sweets.

Alzira scolded the girl for not having prepared the beans and not washing the afternoon dishes, everything piled in the sink, dirty pots, dishes, filthy cups, Carolaine? she called, come here and wash these dishes while I change. She was too tired to do it by herself. How was the computer class? She always asked her daughter the same questions. Did you learn a lot? And Carolaine never gave her the answers she wanted to hear, replying in the most laconic manner possible, interested only in the soap, every night it was that way, Shhh, Mother, Alberto's about to catch Isadora kissing Marcos.

Isadora's with Marcos now? Alzira asked from the bedroom, where she was changing clothes, but doesn't Isadora like Carlos?

When she bent down to look for her slippers under the bed, Alzira saw a small box next to the wall. It was a package of some kind of product. Come look, Mother, Alberto slapped Isadora in the face. What was that doing there? She opened the box, inside were two small vials, one empty, the other containing a colorless liquid. She went back to the living room, What is this, Carolaine?

The girl leaped from the sofa and grabbed the box from Alzira's hands. It's acne medicine, she answered. Don't mess with my things. If it were medicine it wouldn't be hidden, Alzira said, give it to me. She had to use force to take the box back from Carolaine's grasp.

Alzira went into the yard, calling Suzana. Read this for me, she said when the girl came to the fence, a towel wrapped around her head. What's written here? Suzana took the product. She looked at Carolaine. Ask your daughter, she answered. I'm asking you, Suzana. Read it to me. Suzana sighed, agonized. You're going to have to tell her, Carolaine.

Tell me what? Alzira asked. What is it she's going to have to tell me, Suzana? What are the two of you hiding from me? Carolaine ran back into the house, with Alzira behind her. Talk, Carolaine, what happened, daughter?

The girl threw herself onto the sofa, clutching a cushion to her chest. Talk, Carolaine, whatever it is. I need to know.

I'm pregnant, said Carolaine.

Oh my God, Alzira shouted, advancing toward the girl and grabbing her by the hair, I knew this was going to happen.

I gave you so much advice, I warned you so many times, so many times. Let me go, Mother, you're hurting me, let me go, Carolaine said. Alzira pushed the girl into the yard, Out, get out. She locked the kitchen door, Go away, you ingrate, she screamed, crying, closing the windows. Open up, Mother, the girl implored, open the door, don't leave me alone out here, Mommy. Out, Alzira repeated, out, I'm not going to raise any child of yours, I've been working like a horse, like a horse, why did you do this to me, Carolaine?

Alzira sat down on the sofa, crying, aware of her daughter's sobs, outside. You're not even fifteen, she yelled. My God, not even fifteen.

After she calmed down a bit, Alzira changed clothes, got her purse, her mind made up. She opened the door, Carolaine was sitting on the kitchen steps, her head in her hands. Take me to his house, now. What, Mother? whimpered Carolaine, what is it you want? Stop being devious, I want to talk to the father of the child. No, Mother, it won't do any good. Either you take me to him right now, or you'll never set foot in this house again. Get your shoes on.

On the way, Alzira ran ideas through her head. She wouldn't even talk to the boy. She'd talk directly with his parents. Yes, thought Alzira, the parents would have to take responsibility. After all, her daughter was a minor. Didn't they make a child? Let them get married. Let them raise the baby. The child would have a father. A name. They'd get married. End of story.

When they got off the bus, in Jacarepaguá, Carolaine still hadn't succeeded in explaining anything to her mother. They walked slowly, her legs heavy, her arms brushing against her swollen breasts, not knowing how to convince her mother to turn back. They walked two blocks till they came to a row of duplexes. That's where he lives. A decent house, Alzira thought. At least that. A very good house.

At that instant, a man appeared on the porch, accompanied by two young children. That's him, Carolaine said, José Paulo.

A mulatto, husky, over forty. Come on, Juninho, here with Papa, he said. José Paulo was helping the children into the back seat of a VW beetle parked in front of the house, when he saw Carolaine and Alzira on the opposite sidewalk, looking at him, stock-still. It was a desperate moment, the three of them exchanging glances, fearful, with no notion of what would occur the next minute. A woman, pregnant, hurried from the house, Let's go, love, did you get Juninho's diaper? Yes, he said. What's the matter? she asked, noticing the presence of the two women. Nothing, he replied. Nothing. Let's go. They got in the beetle and left. It was all very fast.

An old man, said Alzira, still stunned by the revelation.

Carolaine sat down on the curb and began to cry.

An old man. And married, my God. Married. An old lecher, married, with two children. Does he know about the pregnancy? asked Alzira.

Yes, the girl replied. He won't talk to me anymore. It's no good, Mother.

Oh God. Two children. I can't wait to die and meet Jesus Christ, said Alzira, helping her daughter up from the curb. Let's go, girl.

Silently, they walked hand in hand to the bus stop.

13

WHEE, WHEE, WHEE, WHISTLED the master of the drum corps. Waiting around's a drag, thought Kingie. Unpleasant, shit. José Luís hated to wait. Even there, at the sports court, watching the general rehearsal of the samba school, a glass of beer in his hand and practically naked women swinging their hips before his eyes, Kingie couldn't tolerate waiting for anyone, whoever it was. When he agreed to meet someone, he was punctual. Always. He didn't keep anyone waiting. Never. He'd told Fake a million times not to be late, if he couldn't keep his word, better not to set anything up at all. But Fake was incorrigible. The week before, he'd allowed Kingie to cool his heels for forty-five minutes in front of the Frenesi, a funk club. Easy, brother, Fake had said at the time, relax, I'm in the Latin hip-hop rhythm, and you show up all pissed. You don't even look like you dig funk. Your problem, Zé Luís, is that you're half white. Your white side fucked you up. What's all the hurry, man?

It wasn't any longer the desire to meet his friend and have fun that night that kept him there, waiting impatiently. Now he wanted to see Fake just to let him know how exasperated he was, how unpleasant and nerve-racking it was to waste time waiting, shit, he'd missed a good TV program, *Black Mask*, a film with lots of fighting and punching, or he could have gone to see Kelly, the girl he'd met at Reader's birthday party. My mother's on the night shift at the hospital tonight, Kelly had commented when they bumped into one another at Onofre's. And that meant the two of them could be alone at her house. Kelly wasn't all that sensational, large breasts, she talked too much, but José Luís enjoyed the encounters, they would make popcorn and fool around on the sofa until all hours of the night. It would be fun. Better than staying here doing nothing. All because of Fake. Tonight, Kingie, Fake had said, at the studio, I'm going to introduce you to a knockout girl. A real hunk of woman. One foxy babe.

Whee whee whee. The drum corps wasn't for shit that night. Couldn't anybody see that? Didn't they know what a cadence was, the idiots, and why was the corps master whistling like that if nobody gave a damn about anything? How could they parade at the Sambadrome that way? The entire favela was already singing the samba-enredo, *Our emerald planet,/ you're a splendid fount, you are life, you're the explosion of life*, Kingie only succeeded in memorizing the chorus. He liked Carnival, even felt like being part of the drum corps, but he wouldn't wear those shiny costumes that his grandmother sewed for the revelers, he wouldn't go out dancing drunk and celebrate like the others, especially knowing they were going to lose. They would lose. They lost year after year and were devastated.

What impressed Kingie that night was the appearance of normality in the rehearsal. A tourist who came there and saw the platform of honor where the bosses of the illegal lottery sat with their bodyguards, surrounded by black women with straightened hair and minuscule clothing, would think that everything was advancing full steam ahead. But everything was going very badly. Days before, Kingie had visited his grandmother on her birthday, to give her a new mixer, and Cândida had brought him up to date on the misfortunes. The lottery bosses contributed a pittance, Zé Luís. The time is past. It's gone. Not to mention Miltão. The trafficker had promised and promised and that's all it was, promises. Cândida sewed, complaining. To make things worse, the float of the golden lion tamarin had been ruined by the weekend rains. And Kiko, the favela's Carnival creative director, had discovered he suffered from panic syndrome. Did anybody know what that was? Cândida had asked the assistants around her. Fear of dying, she said, answering her own question. They invented that complicated name for a very simple thing, he's shit-scared. Kiko's problem wasn't any longer just a case of nerves. The man sweated and his eyes bulged, from fear of cashing in his chips. A grown man. Ask me if I think about dying, ha, with all these costumes I have to sew? That's all I need! And no money. That's the question, why work, everybody works, but we get a pittance for making Carnival, that's love, that's love, my son. I give my life to the samba school. Talk to Miltão. Whee whee whee. If the climate at his grandmother's house was one of defeat, there at the rehearsal area, with tourists paying ten dollars to come in and samba, the atmosphere was relaxed, victorious. It was good to hear the powerful voice of the lead singer, a garbage man, at the microphone. He didn't even seem to be that same awkward, inexpressive little man who during the week was second to none when it came to lowering his gaze. He smiled as he sang. He even seemed taller somehow. And not as skinny. Kingie didn't approve of the new standard-bearer. He preferred Suzana. Suzana unfurled the banner like a lady, whirled gracefully, did the steps correctly, light, agile, beautiful Suzana. But Miltão had forbidden his girlfriend to parade that year. There were rumors about them, that they'd been arguing a lot. Jealousy, Onofre said. It's not easy to hold on to a gorgeous woman like that. Suzana is luscious. With all respect. Really sensual. You don't have to look at me like that, Kingie, it's just a comment. Beauty is meant to be admired. José Luís felt like asking Reader if the rumors were true. Reader was there, smoking incessantly. But what if they were? What difference would it make? Suzana always treated him as if they were mother and son. My dear, she would say, hugging him. My, how you've grown. You don't even look like José Luís. Is Miltão treating you well? Eh? If anything's wrong, let me know. Tell me everything. I've spoken with Miltão, I don't want to see you carrying a weapon. No weapons. You're too young. Kingie felt embarrassed when Suzana acted like that in the presence of the traffickers. No. He wouldn't ask Reader anything. Better not to know. Besides which, Kingie was fed up with Reader always spouting rules at him. Every time he got near him, he'd start in on some endless speech or other. He wouldn't let anyone else get a word in edgewise. Better to leave, try to get some sleep. He was in a foul mood that day. It wasn't Fake's fault, or anybody's. A strange sensation. It hadn't been a good idea to go to Duque's house that afternoon. He'd had the man's address in his pocket for days, ever since he killed him. A tumbledown shack much worse than his own. Three small, dirty children, unkempt and hungry. A resigned woman hanging clothes on the line. What the devil did that have to do with him? Now, shit, besides his father, was he going to worry about that washerwoman too? Shit. Why couldn't he forget it? Yes, he had killed, but so what? Duque was a traitor. Whee whee whee. A traitor. And we kill traitors, Miltão said. When somebody goes into this business they should know one thing, if you rat, you die, it's the law, he ratted, he died. Shit. Two-twenty. Time to go to bed.

Kingie was about to leave the area when he spotted Fake coming toward him. Let's go to that funk dance at the Black Rose, he said, want to go? Shit, Fake, now? Shit man, you set something up and, shit, you don't show, shit, a real crappy thing to do, shit!

There was a Volkswagen van waiting for them at the bus stop. Kingie got in the back seat, squeezed in between the usual bunch, shouting, wow, wow, wow, oh, oh, oh, one of them, the one called Jap, kept shouting at passersby in the street. Kingie also liked to yell along the way, especially at the entrance to the clubs, to make an impression, to make his presence felt, as Fake put it, but that night nothing held any appeal for him, including the Black Rose. As soon as they entered the dance area, Fake vanished into the middle of the crowd, singing Do you love me? Kingie felt discouraged, he was so fed up with it all, the dances, the binges, plunging into crowds and pushing forward, getting pushed back, throwing punches and singing, it was stupid, why had he come anyway?

Fake returned with three adolescents and two funk rockers. Hey, bro, Jessica here's got grass, anybody up for it? Fake didn't even wait for an answer but danced his way forward with the group, toward the exit. One of the girls stayed behind with Kingie. She was wearing a white T-shirt with a plastic appliqué, two yellow bears holding hands. Her name was Marta. Thin, with short hair, an inch or so taller than Kingie.

I don't smoke, she said.

Much later, José Luís would still remember that night, the impact that Marta's arrival had on him. In less than a second he had changed his mind about leaving and his mood had improved. He no longer felt depressed, as he had at the beginning of the night. He no longer thought about Duque, or Duque's wife, or Duque's children, or about Kelly, his mother's red eyes, which hadn't stopped crying since she learned of Caroláine's pregnancy. He and Marta stood side by side, observing the movement of the gangs, laughing at the punches thrown by the rockers, from time to time, she would make some comment in his ear. Look at that troglodyte! Did you see that sneaker fly through the air? Kingie felt Marta's mentholated breath against his face, which provoked a hot rush that made him tingle from head to foot. I'm thirsty, she said. Let's go get something to drink, Kingie replied, and as they forced their way through the crowd, they clasped hands. When their fingers intertwined, something completely new happened to Kingie, he felt overcome by euphoria, so many girls, he thought later in bed, he'd known so many, most of them throwaways, all of them forgettable, why was just one person, in the midst of so many others, capable of bringing out that passion? He's strong, Marta would tell her girlfriends the next day, and oh God, how he kisses. He's a great kisser. Oh, oh, Marta would sigh, anxious to love and adore. She's pretty. His eyes are the color of the sea on a rainy day. She's got a nice body. He's funny. She's tall. Oh, what a kiss!

They returned to the dance area and spent the rest of the night holding hands. Marta told him that it was her third funk dance but she didn't like them, she preferred slow music even though she didn't know how to dance. My body's stiff, she said. She was in the seventh grade and helped her father with his business. What does your father do? A merchant, she said. What about you? I'm an office boy. She laughed, half the guys here are office boys. Do you like funk? Yes, he said. What about samba?

Love it. Me too. Rap? Love it. Rock. Almost love it. More or less. She was crazy about American shows and music and was dying to go to a live performance to see the actors up close. He was a 'rabid' fan of the Vasco soccer team, liked watching boxing on television, and was a skateboard whiz. The skateboard lie wasn't the only one he told that night. Kingie had also spoken about his father. About how close they were. Very close. His father was manager of a shipping company. A good position. He'd separated from Kingie's mother and married his secretary, Rosa. Very pretty, Rosa. At first I didn't like my stepmother, you know how it is, because of my mother. She's cool, Rosa. They had lunch together every Sunday. And they'd go skateboarding afterward. Does your father skateboard? asked Marta. Yes, it was him who taught me. I got my first board when I was five. His father used to be a good soccer player too. He'd almost been a professional. A real figure, his father, he wanted Carolaine and him to go live in Flamengo with them, but Kingie felt bad about leaving his mother by herself. Then, later, it was good the way it was, each of them on their own. It was during this pile of lies that José Luís made his move. He didn't know if she'd let him. They were so close, it was impossible to avoid it. Their lips touched, succulent, their tongues sweetened by the sodas, they kissed for a long time, indifferent to the frenetic rhythm of the dance. They were in the corridor leading to the dance floor, blocking the way, some of the people pushed them, but they didn't even notice it. They kissed. The world could blow up.

It was during that burning kiss that someone bellowed in Kingie's ear, Come on, hurry up, they busted Fake. Jap, who'd come in the van with them, was tugging anxiously at Kingie's arm. Don't go away, stay right there, he shouted as he left.

Outside, the Black Rose security guards were trying to separate the crowd of onlookers. Break it up, break it up, they said. While he attempted to push his way through, Kingie could make out a couple of sentences. We were on the other side, the police came by on patrol and saw him on the corner, hiding something. The guy's always selling powder here, one of the security guards said to the other. Serves him right. He's fucked. With great difficulty, Kingie got to the police van parked in front of the entrance. Three youths were being put into the vehicle. Fake was one of them. Tell Miltão, he shouted when he saw Kingie. Tell Miltão.

Kingie went back into the dance area, stunned, he wanted to say goodbye to Marta before leaving. He didn't believe that Fake had been so shit-stupid. Fake wasn't a runner, like him. Or a fool. For some time now, Miltão hadn't wanted Fake working for him. He let Fake go on taking care of the radio but was always on his case. He was constantly asking questions. And Fake knew all that. José Luís himself had told him, when he was promoted to runner. Miltão had said, I know the two of you are friends. Fake is out of this, he had said. At least for now.

Marta wasn't at the agreed-upon spot. He didn't want to leave without speaking with her. He didn't have her address, nothing. How would they meet again? He asked two girls who were chatting nearby if they'd seen a tall girl wearing a T-shirt with small bears on it. They laughed. You can't even see anybody's face, they said. Kingie looked around the dance area carefully, then waited for a few minutes outside the ladies' room. Nothing.

When he left the Black Rose it was already getting light. He was worried about Fake, unhappy, anguish growing in his chest. Damn, why had she disappeared like that?

14

A THOUSAND PROBLEMS IN his head. Miltão unwrapped a piece of candy and put it in his mouth. He hadn't eaten anything the entire day. Fake a traitor. Nothing but problems. And Suzana. Suzana was acting strange lately. That ring on your finger, what is it? Miltão had asked when the two were in bed, after sex, their hands intertwined. I bought it, she'd said. And the next day there was a different version: A girlfriend gave it to me. Did she get it as a gift or did she buy it? An endless quarrel, three weeks arguing because of the ring. A girlfriend, what bullshit, how could he believe a stupid thing like that? It's not easy to lie to someone who's as attentive as a dog. What about Rita? And Valéria? And Cidoca? You think I don't know? Suzana screamed, I'm sick and tired of hearing that you screw every woman in Berimbau. What Rita, what Valéria? Don't change the subject, Suzana, you got the ring and you're getting all balled up trying to explain who the loser is that gave it to you, that's right, baby, so spit it out. Goddamn. Problems. But that could be taken care of later. That fucking ring. First, to business. Look At That had just shown him the result of the search of Fake's studio: 300 grams of cocaine hidden in a hole in the wall. In the lining of the sofa were found vials of bicarbonate of soda, talcum powder, and marble dust. Son-of-a-bitch. Miltão remembered Arnóbio, known as Noble, the former boss of the Berimbau favela. It was with him that he had learned to say 'son-of-a-bitch' that way, separating the syllables, son-of-a-bitch, with his voice hoarse, scratchy, with the mouth full of rage and disgust. It was contagious. Two days with Noble, and everybody was saying 'son-of-a-bitch' just like him.

It was even possible to find out if a guy belonged to Noble's gang merely by the way he pronounced 'son-of-a-bitch'. Fifty, sixty men, an entire battalion saying 'son-of-a-bitch' the same way. And when someone turned his back, Noble began calling him a son-of-a-bitch also, even if he was a friend, an important ally. That's how Noble was. To Noble, who was currently doing time at Padre Moraes penitentiary, everybody was a son-of-a-bitch. As soon as he was sent to prison, Miltão would visit him on Sundays, in Block 7, Sector C, to listen to his advice. Noble had plans to increase the points-of-sale, but they never progressed. The topic was always the same. The sons-of-bitches. The scum. The traitors. The dregs of society. Every Sunday Miltão listened to the same litany. At the time, Noble, sentenced to 117 years in prison, consumed a large part of the money sent him by Miltão on jailors, prostitutes, luxuries, and to pay conniving lawyers. Miltão personally took charge of the trafficker's escape and had spent 'a fortune' because of Noble's whims. I want to walk out the front door, Noble said. I insist on it. And he in fact did. The problem was that Noble didn't have good 'reality testing', as Look At That said. He had been making himself an easy target in the city, strolling around without the slightest concern for the police. And he'd been recaptured. A pile of money down the drain.

Direct contact between the two traffickers had ceased more than a year before, when a warrant for Miltão's arrest had been issued as a result of his appearing in a TV report brandishing a machine gun and making embarrassing statements about the police in Rio. At the time, the state government was studying the possibility of undertaking a 'sanitation action' in the favelas by sending elite troops from the armed forces up the hillsides. Rio de Janeiro is experiencing a civil war, argued the proponents of military occupation. And our enemies have superior firepower, they said, displaying the weapons captured in ever more frequent raids. Just take a look, Urus, an HK-47 rifle, they're well equipped. The truth is that we're at the mercy of the scum of society. The army must control the favelas. The problem in Rio, countered those who rejected the idea of a military invasion, is neither the drug traffic nor drugs themselves, it's social inequality. When you talk about organized crime, the focus should be on the illegal lottery, a politician stated to the press. If the issue is one of doing away with what's corroding public power and corrupting the media, our target is the clandestine lottery.

The hills of Rio with their hooded, heavily armed young men illustrated the debate over army intervention in the war on drugs, an obligatory topic in every important magazine and newspaper in the country. 'We'll blow them away,' Miltão told a TV reporter. The image of Miltão, with an AR-15 in his hands, had been published and glamorized in such a way and so repeatedly that he had become what Reader called 'the symbol of the buffoonery'. To increase the effect of Miltão's statement even further, the trafficker's likeness had been sold to dozens of papers and magazines that reproduced it endlessly under sensationalist headlines: War! says the trafficker. Kingpin of Berimbau favela challenges the authorities. The result of all this confusion was that now Miltão could no longer leave the favela as in the past, for fear of being arrested. Which made not the slightest difference to him. His world was right there, the rest of Rio de Janeiro could go to hell. If it was a drag not to be able to circulate freely in the favela during the daylight hours, at night the hillside was his. And as for not being able to visit Noble in prison, the truth was that Noble was no longer the same person. He'd lost strength. The proof of that was the episode with Fake. Two months earlier, Miltão had sent Look At That to convey his fears to Noble. He was suspicious of the rocker. He'd been hearing things. Noble's answer was short and to the point: Fake is clean. Leave him alone. Now that Fake's betrayal was a proven fact, Miltão chastised himself for listening to Noble's idiotic advice. Just because Noble had played football with Fake his whole life he refused to believe his friend was a son-of-a-bitch. Miltão had had it with all that. He'd lost the opportunity to fuck Fake but good. Pretty soon they'd be saying he couldn't cut it anymore. And that would be the beginning of the end.

Nothing but problems. And on top of everything else, Suzana. Nothing but problems.

The immense building, with dozens of minuscule apartments on every floor, was near the Central do Brasil train station in downtown. Kingie knew the place very well. He took dozens of envelopes daily to the prostitutes, bank employees, pimps, idlers, homosexuals, and students who lived in such tenements. Egg-sized kitchenettes smelling of poverty. There wasn't a single upper-class type among his clientele. Kingie had heard millions of stories about the era when famous personalities, politicians and the upper crust, would snort cocaine from trays at the city's notorious parties and nightclubs. He regretted not having lived in that period. He served only nobodies on their last legs. And with no money, always looking to pay later. Later, tomorrow.

Kingie waited impatiently for the elevator. He wanted to deliver the merchandise as quickly as possible and get back to the favela. Maybe Miltão already had an answer. Miltão had promised to move fast, he would speak with his informants in the police and find out exactly what was what with Fake, then decide on a course of action. Yes, Fake was his best friend. He wanted to help him, put an end to this dispute. It never occurred to him to think that Miltão couldn't solve the problem. They would bribe the police. Everybody has his price, as Bidê said, we buy congressmen, detectives, jailors, so pay the fuckers. Although he was convinced his friend's torment was of his own making, there was another reason for all the agony. He wanted to see Fake as soon as possible to ask about Marta. He was enchanted by her. What a girl! The mere act of speaking her name, Marta, inflamed his heart. My father's going to teach you to skateboard, he'd told her the night before. I'll be embarrassed, she'd replied. Because of my father? The man is sensational. You'll love my father. The wet kisses. Those kisses were completely unlike Kelly's. Sure, it was good to run his hands over Kelly's breasts, roll on the floor, all that fooling around, the bad part was the talk, I'm a virgin, I'm scared to death of getting pregnant. José

Luís hated it when Kelly talked like that, that blah-blah-blah about babies and pregnancy and commitment reminded him of Carolaine and his mother. That makes me go limp, he said, it's a turnoff, Kelly. It's just that I'm scared to death of getting pregnant, she replied. He liked Marta from the start. She didn't smoke. She didn't drink. She didn't say dumb things. And she studied. Tall, slim. The only thing he couldn't understand was why she hadn't waited for him. No doubt Fake would know where to find her. He'd go there. This very day.

Despite not having slept at all the night before, Kingie was up for it, alert. The elevator was taking too long, so he decided to climb the twelve flights of stairs, running. He rang the bell at 1207. The door opened and a powerfully built individual, hair uncombed, wearing nothing but undershorts, answered, still half asleep. Kingie wouldn't have recognized Fernando, the personal trainer for Dona Juliana, the woman his mother worked for, if the young man hadn't become so confused. You, he said, what a coincidence, you here. Good lord. I didn't know. Kingie asked if they could talk inside. He didn't like making deliveries in hallways or in public squares, he was cautious. Never make things easy for the worms, Miltão had taught him. A good runner is one who doesn't get caught, who carries around only a small amount of merchandise, makes the delivery between four walls, and gets the hell out. And that was how Kingie did it. You here, good lord, said Fernando, small world, of course, let's go inside. The living room was full of glasses scattered about, cushions on the floor, a stinking hole, thought Kingie. Fernando said something on the order of the-powder-isn't-for-me, but Kingie didn't even hear it, he was interested only in collecting the dough and getting out of there fast. A woman came out of the bathroom, wrapped in a towel, and went into the bedroom. Kingie recognized her immediately, Alicinha, a blonde with good muscle tone, a close friend of Dona Juliana. They're like sisters, Alzira would say. Neither one does anything without the other. Obviously not. Fernando gave him a check. Please, he asked, don't say anything to Alzira. You know, Juliana, he said, and stopped, searching for words, pathetic.

Kingie agreed to everything, all he wanted was to get away from there. Ten grams of powder. And in his pocket a check from Dona Juliana. He knew the signature. In the period when he was working for Mr Rodrigo he used to make Dona Juliana's payments. The check was from her all right. Alicinha. Damn. Kingie didn't care in the least about them, if they fucked, cheated, and snorted coke on other people's money, what was the problem? Dona Juliana's check. The people were scumbags. Son of a bitch. He thought about the time he worked for Mr Rodrigo. He even remembered the smell of the aftershave lotion he wore. A lemon aroma that entered his nostrils and stuck there, for days. Scumbags.

Miltão didn't call Kingie until the end of the afternoon, when he had information in hand about Clêmio dos Santos, a.k.a. Fake, who had been sent to the São Francisco de Assis Center for the Rehabilitation of Minors. Sit down, Zé Luís. You came here this morning, scared, to tell me that Fake was in jail and needed help. So listen. Know why he was arrested? Because he was carrying twelve envelopes of cocaine. And whose cocaine was it? Mine. The fucker was stealing from me.

Plastic containers and packaging materials were on the table. See that stuff? It was stashed in the studio. Which is also mine. The studio belongs to me. It's my community radio. I pay the guy and he steals from me. That's for shit. Here's the thing, Kingie. You're going to do me a favor. Sunday's visiting day at São Francisco. You go there and tell that motherfucker that if he shows his face here again, he dies. The only reason I don't have him killed there inside is that he's buddies with Noble. Otherwise he'd be dead already. Tell him: I'm just waiting for the fucker to set foot on my territory. That's all, Kingie. I've said what I have to say. I can see you'd like to say something, but let me give you a warning: if you're thinking of defending the bastard, keep your mouth shut. You can go.

I already told you, Kingie, I don't know who this Marta is. I don't know her. Change the subject, brother. Look at this bunch here.

These delinquents. Muggers, every last one of them. They're still in diapers and already doing muggings. It's the in crime, brother, mugging. Everybody's a mugger in this country.

It was Sunday, the detainees were with their families in the courtyard of the São Francisco de Assis Center for the Rehabilitation of Minors. Kingie and Fake, sitting side by side, shielded themselves from the sun reflecting off the cement floor, dazzling them. Fake was upset by what Kingie had told him about Miltão. He'd laughed at first, saying, I doubt he'd take on Noble. Noble will protect me. After a few moments he no longer felt that way. You really think they're going to kill me? he asked. Yes I do, answered Kingie. Brother, I'm in a fix. I swear to God, José Luís, that wasn't my coke. It was a guy who asked me to deliver it, that's all, I just made deliveries. Fake rose, full of energy, saying that Kingie could help him, they had to rectify the situation, they'd talk to Noble, maybe to Reader. We can agree on a fine, I'll pay Miltão some money, how about that? Fake was absolutely certain that would work. Yes, we blacks have to stick up for one another, that's why I love the US, there they have black power because they're united, isn't it ridiculous to kill a brother over ten envelopes? Twelve, corrected Kingie. OK, ten, twelve, what's the difference? The difference is that you've been stealing for some time, Fake, and Miltão knows about it.

What if I confess? asked Fake anxiously. I go there and say, Everything's cool, brother, I was wrong, I stole a few things. How much? Kingie asked. I don't know exactly, I started out by taking a little during the packaging. For how long? José Luís asked. Fake didn't answer. He suddenly realized the seriousness of his situation. Miltão would never forgive him. He was a marked man. They'd do the same to him that had been done to Nói and Raimundo. To Zecão. They would take him to some deserted piece of land and put three bullets in his head. All I wanted was to make my demo tape, Kingie. Remember Ned, that black guy who did some poems inspired by the Fundão massacre? He found a producer for me. It's a very good recording company, and it makes recordings by newcomers. But I have to pay the expenses, you understand? I'm an artist, tell Miltão that. When I have my own band and I'm famous, I'll do free shows for you guys, for life. God, I fucked up royally, brother. What should I do?

In Kingie's opinion, the best thing was to let time go by. Maybe Miltão would calm down. I'll have a talk with him. You promise, brother? I promise. You think it's going to do any good?

When they finally exhausted the subject of Miltão, Kingie mentioned Marta again. Who the hell is this Marta? Kingie explained again. She was with you on Thursday. Marta? I don't know any Marta, I already told you. Sure you do, when you all went outside for a smoke, she decided to stay with me. I don't have any idea who this Marta is. I don't know any Marta. You're bugging me, brother.

Kingie was disappointed when he left the rehabilitation center. He still hadn't slept. He had spent Friday and Saturday at the Black Rose, looking for Marta. For hours, he had remained at the spot where they'd met. Nothing.

Life in the ensuing months consisted of looking for Marta. Even when he delivered the envelopes to the usual customers, Kingie nursed the hope of running into her somewhere or other. And when he would sit beside his father in Praça Argentina, which was more and more frequently, he still paid close attention to the passersby. One day he would find Marta. He visited Fake often, contrary to Miltão's wishes. Know what I miss? Fake asked. Not my shack, not the hip-hop, or anything. I miss the power to just wander around, piss where I feel like it, looking at the sky, that's what I miss. José Luís listened to his friend talk about the government, society, justice. Systems don't fix shit, brother, here the only thing we learn is to steal, squeal, stick it to the other guy, and fuck. Nothing else. This is one fine little training school. Before this, Kingie, I was innocent, now I know how to boost a car, I know that the best method for getting away from the police in a holdup is to shoot some little old lady crossing the street or a student at a bus stop, that's how you stir things up and throw the cops off your trail, I know everything. Kingie listened patiently to his lamentations, only so he could ask one more time: You're sure you don't know Marta?

Although he always made an effort to call up the mental image of the girl before going to sleep, he only succeeded in dreaming about Marta a single time, on September 17. In the middle of the delightful dream he was awakened by his mother, screaming excitedly, Go get a taxi, your sister's about to give birth. That same night Carolaine's son was born. Seven pounds one ounce, mulatto, healthy, a robust boy. What're you naming him? Alzira asked. Caroline, lying in bed at the public hospital, her eyes closed, didn't answer. He's going to be Alas, said Alzira. I think that's a pretty name. Alas José Reis.

15

ALAS TOOK TWO HALTING steps and fell. Did you see that? asked Suzana, who was playing with the tot in the kitchen of Alzira's house. He's just dying to walk, the little darling. Say it, Alas, god-moth-er. Alzira was ironing diapers, then stacking them on the Formica kitchen table. Gah-mah, babbled the baby. Suzana smothered him with kisses, Did you hear? He calls me Gah-mah. It's your godmother, isn't it, you sweet thing? So beautiful. Carolaine, come get these diapers, Alzira requested. Carolaine, on the sofa, was absorbed in reading the TV supplement to the Sunday paper. So cuddly. Godmother's sweetheart. Carolaine, Alzira shouted, did you hear me? I'm reading what's going to happen in the soap, Mother. Isabel's going to find out that André's been with Amélia. Listen, coming chapters: Monday, Antônio Luís overhears Amélia say on the phone that she's sick. Eunice implores Rafael to return to the shipyard. Clarice suffers nausea in an elevator and Marcos becomes suspicious. André hears Isabel tell Clarice about Isabel's illness. Tuesday: Isabel follows André to Amélia's house. Antônio Luís receives a letter from Isabel breaking off the engagement. Rafael prevents Otávio from entering the patriarch's house and says that the magnate Pedro Albuquerque is going to disinherit him. Henriette arrives from Japan, setting the Albuquerque family's nerves on edge.

What's the fun of knowing the chapters ahead of time? inquired Alzira. We ought to stop watching the soaps, Pastor Walmir condemns them, there's nothing but vice and sin on television. That's not what the pastor said, stated Carolaine, without looking up from the newspaper. Walmir thinks that anyone who watches TV all day long ends up being tempted by the Devil. We're not like that, we don't spend all day glued to the TV, we just watch our soaps, what's the harm in that? Everybody watches the soaps, Mother, all of Brazil. Even Mr Rodrigo, agreed Alzira, laughing. The seven o'clock and the eight o'clock. That huge man wolfs down his dinner so he can be in front of the TV as soon as possible. Carolaine went on reading the summary of the week, but Alzira was no longer paying attention. She felt happy at home, ironing clothes with the iron that Dona Juliana had given her a week earlier when she bought a new one. She felt calm, the television on, her stomach stuffed with chicken, spaghetti, and Coca-Cola, Suzana playing with Alas, everyone well. They were living in accord with the teachings of God. And happy. Without much money but with Christ. And fortunate. Alzira had suffered greatly of late, she had been through a bad stretch, but now she was happy. Thanks to the pastor. Yes, if today Alzira enjoyed peace in her life, she owed it to Pastor Walmir. It had been he who had shown her the path of Christ. Christ is at your side, he always said. Within you. How could she have gone so long without Christ? Everything was easier with Christ at hand. Even work. Dona Juliana had stopped yelling at her and calling her a stupid, awkward, incompetent nigger. Christ was the reason for the change. Soon after she had turned to Christ, Alzira found Dona Juliana crying one morning in the living room because of a quarrel on the phone with Fernando. Encouraged by Christ, Alzira said to her in a single breath: You're living in sin and only Christ can save you. That was enough. Her employer now treated her with respect. Thank you very much, Alzira. Please, Alzira. Take this extra change, Alzira. Thanks to Christ. And it was not only at work that things were going well. Carolaine, who had given her so many problems, had undergone a drastic change. She had rejected Alas at first, but now everything was different. With Christ. Thanks to the pastor. Glory be to God! Carolaine had given up her rebellion. She had become religious and now attended worship services daily and accompanied Walmir in many activities. Your daughter just needs guidance, the pastor had said. She's a good girl. A little lamb. Extraordinary, the pastor. True, Carolaine neither worked nor studied, but then who would take care of Alas? And José Luís continued in the company of what Alzira called 'that band of riff-raff'. A thing of Satan, the cur, the devil, the one with horns, the hoofed one, an imp from hell, malignant. But she didn't lose hope. Now that the pastor was a frequent visitor at her house, who could tell? He had managed to make Carolaine into a lamb, why couldn't he bring José Luís into the fold as well? José Luís would be a good servant of Christ. And Kelly, also, another lamb. Alzira approved of the relationship. I think it's good that André finds out about Isabel's illness, said Carolaine. Later they're going to discover the diagnosis was wrong, the lab made a mistake. Did you hear that? Suzana asked, Alas said Gah-mah again. Say it for Suzana, say it. Gah-mah. Alzira watched her grandson with loving eyes. Gah-mah. That boy, she said. It's time for bed, come on, Alas, time for beddy-bye. Gah-mah. Sleep in Grandma's bed. Suzana kissed Alas on the cheek several times. Beautiful little boy, she said, so cuddly, gah-mah's darling, I'm going to miss you so much. What's that about, Suzana? Are you going on a trip? Alzira asked warily. No, the girl replied in a confused manner. You two, Alzira said, taking the baby onto her lap, you two think I'm dumb. But I'm on top of things.

Carolaine went with Suzana to the fence that separated the two yards. The girls embraced at length. We're giving ourselves away, commented Carolaine. That's true, I'd better go, Suzana said goodbye, just look at my eyes, I'm already crying. Take good care of Alas, Carolaine. Be a good mother. And not a word, all right? The two embraced again. Carolaine waited until Suzana went inside, then returned to her house, hearing Alas crying. How that little devil liked to cry. She couldn't stand children crying. It was irritating. If repentance killed – A bawling baby.

Dear Onofre, Germany is an organized country. Everybody works and is healthy. There are many old people like you here, but nobody as ugly, as big a dirty old man, or as tight with money. The snow is nice and white, and Heinrich treats me very well. I have a fur coat made of leopard skin that cost six hundred dollars. I'm very happy, Onofre. I only miss the hot sun, black beans, and *caipirinhas*. In all the rest, everything here is better. The supermarket at the corner of my block is the prettiest thing in the world. It sells everything. Even cars. I live in a house with three bedrooms. The only problem is the language. I don't understand shit, Onofre. Tell all our friends that Rosa Maria is happy. (Tell your wife.) Kisses. Rosa Maria Schoffler.

The postcard had been mailed in Germany, Berlin, and depicted a ski lodge full of colorful, good-looking people. Onofre, after a weekend of showing it to his customers, was talking with Suzana, who had stopped by for cigarettes. Who could have written the card for Rosa Maria? She was illiterate. Or was she? Who would have thought, eh? Rosa Maria married to a Fritz. Actually, it doesn't surprise me. Those Fritzes love a big-assed mulatto woman. They should. Did you ever see anybody less interesting than pale white women? They're pretty when they're teenagers, the freckles, rosy cheeks, but once they hit thirty it's all over. They fall apart, the white women. They turn into sacks of potatoes. And as red as Santa Claus. Everything goes flabby. It's horrible. Our black women are more like rock. Yeah, right here in Brazil. And rounder. There's always a bunch of Fritzes drooling over our black women in Copacabana, isn't that true? I can understand why. But what I can't understand is why a rich foreigner would marry a prostitute with as many miles on her as Rosa Maria, huh? And giving her a fur coat and all? You think there's such a thing as a fur coat for six hundred dollars? Rosa Maria must be jerking me around, the dirty whore. What's the matter with you, Suzana? Cat got your tongue? Where are you going in such a hurry? Where's Miltão?

Suzana paid her bill at Onofre's and quickly descended the dirt road, carefully in order to avoid staining her new shoes, a present from Zequinha Bigode. In the bag on her shoulder, just two dresses, two pairs of panties, and a bra. It was better that way, without a suitcase to arouse Miltão's attention. Here, Zequinha had said, you'll have everything. All you have to do is ask. Clothes, shampoo, barbecue, a cellphone, luxuries, a VCR, just ask. You're going to be my princess. Zequinha wasn't like Miltão. There was no comparison. Refined, well mannered, a high school graduate. She had met Zequinha at the birthday party of a girlfriend in the Marrecos favela. She hadn't liked him at first, finding him brash, with hungry eyes, full of idiotic questions. Hi there, beautiful, you by yourself? You like meat? I didn't give him the time of day, Suzana told her friend. And later, in the weeks that followed, Zequinha wouldn't leave her alone, sending messages every day through the girlfriend. Meet me at the Boi Gordo, Saturday at eight. No way, Suzana said. Conceited, what's he thinking? But when Zequinha sent her that small gold chain with a heart inscribed 'Cleopatra Suzana, I'm in love', that was when Suzana fell. That felt very good. A fine idea. And then came the gold ring. I fell head over heels. Twenty-four-carat, he'd said. You're a very expensive girl. I've spent a fortune on this woman, he said. He was hot. And fun and games in bed. Indefatigable. After she began sleeping with Zequinha, she thought of Miltão as merely 'the fucking machine'. Plug him in and fuck. Not Zequinha. He did everything but pray before sex. He would kneel, amazed at Suzana's perfect body. Beautiful woman, he would say. You're my light. A queen. Princess. Goddess. An angel, he said. You know what you're going to do? he asked. Just set off World War III, that's all, he joked, when the two were in bed.

During Noble's time, the Berimbau and Marrecos favelas were embroiled in combat over drug-distribution locations. When Noble was arrested, Miltão and Zequinha reached an agreement to divide the territory. The difference, Zequinha said, is that I go on growing and Miltão is still a two-bit smalltime drug dealer. Actually, he said, the problem with the trade here in Brazil is simple, it's stupidity. There's no cure for stupidity. Stupidity and progress don't mix. The traffic doesn't advance because of the traffickers, ignorant people, fucked-up bunglers who don't have a pot to piss in. Zequinha Bigode, unlike most of the bosses, hadn't gotten involved with the drug trade because he was one more poor devil with nothing better to do. He was an electronic technician. But it happens, he said, that I wasn't born to be a slave to the system. Or to go hungry. I'm no fool, he said. Today, with forty-two drug sites, he was the leader of the traffic in Marrecos. If he remained in command it was because he had a knack for the business. He knew that investment in corruption was sure and safe. The police got their weekly take, but his business flourished. He enjoyed a comfortable life. He'd bought a good house where he lived with his two teenage daughters and his mother. And he owned two taxis, four trucks, three sheds, seven minivans, and two large pieces of real estate. All in his daughters' names, because he wasn't stupid. His motto was 'With me there's no such thing as maybe.' Now, after seven years as a widower, he had decided to marry Suzana. His daughters disapproved at first, but what could they do? Their father had been adamant: Suzana's coming to live here and that's that. You don't like it? Lump it.

As she descended the hillside, Suzana encountered some of Miltão's soldiers. In front of Zino's butcher's shop was a car waiting for her. She got in and left without looking back. A new life. Thank God.

Know what's going to happen? said Onofre upon being invited to José Luís's party for his fifteenth birthday. They're going to marry you off. I understand the situation. It's marriage all right. Kelly's mother, Yolanda, is like that. A determined woman. She decides you're the husband for Kelly and, bang, you're engaged. Onofre was exaggerating, there wasn't any engagement, much less a wedding, it was just a birthday party. But at her house? asked Onofre. I know Yolanda. They're going to get you married, I'm onto the whole thing. And tell me something, are the two of you already – eh? he asked, slyly. What's she like, huh? If the daughter's anything like the mother, whoo, the mother, I've heard she's hot to trot. Hey, you're turning out worse than Reader, what's your problem with talking, huh? Did you know Reader's screwing Lalá? Must be some kind of vow, to screw Lalá, don't you think? And what about you, you pussy hound? You think I don't see how Kelly's been acting lately? The two of you always at her house, alone? I see everything. José Luís was irritated with Onofre's conversation. Meddling old man. Always butting in. He shouldn't invite him to the party. And if he did marry Kelly, what was wrong with that? He had long ago lost any hope of finding Marta. He had spent all night going from one funk dance to another, and nothing. He still dreamed about Marta, his heart still raced whenever a tall, slim girl with short hair crossed his path, but so what? Marta didn't exist. And there was no one better than Kelly in the favela. At thirteen or fourteen the girls were already showing their asses and looking for trouble, as Reader put it. And they were only interested in armed men. The bigger the weapon, the greater the guy's chances. Doormen, garbage collectors, elevator operators, in a word, honest, normal types, Reader said, don't have a prayer with the women in the favela. Kelly was serious. She liked Kingie. And since the first time they made love, in her mother's bed, Kingie came to respect her more. That night, after sex, the two remained embraced for a long time, quiet, the stereo on. Kingie was almost asleep when he felt something hot on his chest, it was Kelly's tears. Now I'm yours, she had said. It was amazing to hear those little words: I'm yours, to have someone. It was good to fuck Kelly for several reasons, but mainly because she loved him. I love you, I love you, I adore you, she was saying all the time. They went together, the first time, to the gynecologist. Before sex, José Luís always asked her, Did you take the pill? He feared she would get pregnant, he felt responsible for her. And for Yolanda also. An admirable woman. It was much more pleasant to spend time with Yolanda and Kelly than with Alzira and Carolaine. Yolanda treated him with respect, affection, and didn't look at him with recrimination every time he brought a present or offered to pay some bill. Very different from Alzira. That money, Alzira would say, is from the Devil. I won't take it.

Kingie's fifteenth birthday was celebrated on the porch of Kelly's house with a barbecue, samba band, and beer. Besides the family, a few friends were present: Reader, Onofre, Look At That, and Bidê. Kingie proudly showed off his nephew Alas. Alzira made a mistake, said Cândida, his grandmother, the boy, being the great-grandson of who he is, ought to be named Abre Alas. That's a Carnival song, replied Alzira. Alas doesn't have anything to do with Carnival, it's a foreign name. It's like Carolaine. It's English.

Although he had invited Miltão, José Luís didn't expect him to show up at the party. First because, for reasons of security, Miltão avoided leaving his house before nightfall. And, second, for some time now the two of them had barely spoken to each other.

Many things had changed of late. With the crackdown and subsequent drop in sales, Miltão had decided to support a kidnap group to raise fast money. He lent arms, soldiers, and safe houses and took a percentage of the profits. Romeu, the police detective, had suggested it to him. José Luís had been present when the initial negotiations began. I say kidnapping is a good investment, and I can prove it, Romeu had said at one of the meetings. If it's done intelligently. If you're talking about kidnapping bakers, count me out, there's no money in it, answered Miltão. It's a sure thing, Romeu promised. You set up a base, a structure, a system for collecting the ransom, and that's all there is to it. Romeu could never explain how collecting the ransom would work. Are you talking about a garbage truck going around town and picking up the bags of money? asked Reader, laughing. I'm talking about professionalism. What happens nowadays is that the guy decides in the morning to pull a kidnapping that afternoon. He can't do it. It takes planning. Kidnapping is a highly cerebral activity. Think about it, Miltão. We'll make money. It's a sure thing. Lots of money.

After the first kidnapping, Miltão tapped José Luís for a 'less boring job'. You've been a runner for a long while, he said. It's about time you became a soldier. Kingie had been anxiously awaiting that moment. He had always dreamed of being a soldier in the drug traffic. But during the conversation he realized that in reality it was all bullshit, that Miltão only wanted him to keep an eye on the safe houses for the hostages. Shit. That was a job for a dog. A German shepherd. No way, replied Kingie. No fucking way. Why not? the trafficker wanted to know. Because I don't feel like it, he said, in a challenging tone. Ever since he was small, Kingie had only one objective in life: to be a trafficker. He wanted to work with drugs, selling, packaging, transporting, negotiating, making a profit. It had never entered his head to be a car booster, a bank robber, a kidnapper. Never. You're turning down my offer? Yes, answered Kingie. Give it to somebody else. OK, stated Miltão, fine with me, you want to be a runner, you'll be a runner. No sweat.

All the boys who had entered the trade along with Zé Luís were soldiers by now, walking around armed, and some managed sales sites, packaging houses, or warehouses, except for Kingie. Miltão kept him in the same job for over a year as punishment. And treated him with disdain. In the meetings he didn't say hello to him, and to send an indirect message, he would rant about shitass cowards: There's this chickenshit, a delicate flower who can't imagine picking up a piece. He has to be a babysitter. Or maybe a garbage man. There's no place here for chickenshits, he would say every time José Luís was present.

For these reasons, Kingie didn't expect that Miltão would appear at his birthday party. When he saw him come in, wearing surfer shorts and carrying a plastic shopping bag, José Luís forced himself to be hospitable. Hey, man. Glad you could make it. Kelly, bring Miltão here a beer. How's it going, brother? They shook hands in a friendly fashion and exchanged pleasantries, while Alzira, uncomfortable with the trafficker's presence, served cake to the guests. What gall! Explain it to the pastor, Carolaine, explain that I didn't know he was coming. The pastor even tried, twice, to start a conversation with the trafficker. For some time now he had been wanting to meet him. But Miltão, who had already lost some of his men to the temple of the Flock of the Purest Love of Our Lord Jesus Christ, refused to even look at the preacher. He kept his back to him, deliberately. The little twerp better stay out of my way. I'm warning him. Where can we rap? Miltão asked Kingie. José Luís led him to Kelly's room and closed the door. Miltão opened the shopping bag and took out a light automatic rifle stolen from the armed forces. It's your birthday present.

José Luís took the weapon, analyzing it, surprised and happy.

For me? Shit, Miltão. Cool. Shit. I don't know what to say. Shit. It's time we worked out this business between us, said Miltão. Shit, everything's settled. Now you're a soldier. The two shook hands, looking each other in the eyes.

Wednesday night, we're invading Marrecos, Miltão told him, now sure of Kingie's support. You're going to lead five men. I want to stick a grenade up Zequinha's ass, he said. And as for Suzana, I'm bringing that slut back, dead or alive.

Routinely, around two a.m., the owner of the Pétalas Brancas Flower Shop, returning from work, would slow his VW minibus to enter the narrow street leading to the Marrecos favela. That night was no different. The driver, returning home, thought he was about to be held up when he saw his way blocked by a van at the entrance to Avenida Epitácio Pessoa. Twenty men from Miltão's gang, armed and wearing improvised masks, got out. After spreading out on the floor of the bus, they ordered the Japanese man to proceed up the hillside as always. With a gun aimed at his head, the driver made his way into the favela, waving at Zequinha's soldiers on duty at the foot of the hill.

They climbed slowly. When the vehicle stopped in front of a public phone, flares began bursting in the sky. Someone was signaling an invasion of the favela. You Japanese son of a bitch, Miltão shouted, pulling the trigger. The driver's head exploded like a bottle at the firing range.

No one was able to explain the succession of errors that occurred afterward. Theoretically, they were prepared. There was a plan of attack, they were to divide into small groups, advance by four different routes until reaching Zequinha Bigode's house. Don't give it any thought, shoot first and ask questions later, kill them, kill them, we're here to kill. They just mustn't kill Suzana. Suzana's coming back home where she belongs. Alive, you hear me? Miltão had spent the afternoon with his soldiers, trying to draw a map of the labyrinthine streets of the Marrecos favela, but at that moment, amid the shooting and explosions, the men dispersed in all directions.

In reality, neither Miltão nor anyone else had the slightest notion of the layout of Zequinha's defenses. Kingie, who had spent the previous two nights on the soccer field with Look At That, Jaú, Bidê, and eighteen other soldiers recruited for the operation, handling AR-15s, M-16s, HK-47s and learning to use Dutch grenades, saw in the very first minutes of combat that there was no chance of success. They had barely gotten out of the minibus when the shooting began. Jaú fell only five yards from the station wagon, before he could locate the enemies' positions. Kingie felt that the metal-clad bullets were raining from the sky. On the spot, Miltão's soldiers abandoned the war and sought protection individually from the attack.

Kingie crawled toward an opening between the bakery and a mechanic's shop, where he remained the entire time. Bullets ricocheted, shattering windows and ripping holes in the shacks. Jaú, Jaú, someone yelled. Only at that moment, hearing the whistling of bullets past his head, did he understand Reader's position. I'm opposed to the invasion, radically opposed, he had said. We have fewer men than Marrecos, fewer weapons, and they're on the alert. Miltão seemed not to hear. He was looking at the map of the streets, smoking a joint, pensive, occasionally spitting out the marijuana fibers that stuck to his tongue. He's going to get fucked, he said. The bursts of gunfire weren't stopping. José Luís, protected, didn't dare fire a single round for fear of being located and shot. At no time did he think he'd leave the Marrecos hillside alive. He was alone, and at any moment Zequinha's soldiers could execute him. He wasn't afraid. He only felt sad about dying before he could tell his father: I'm your son. Before he could find Marta and say that he loved her and that every time he thought of her it was like an earthquake inside his body.

The firefight lasted two hours. Then total silence. José Luís waited patiently. When morning came, he took advantage of the hubbub of children leaving for school, and the mass of laborers leaving the favela for another day of work, to make his escape. He passed three bodies before making it to the asphalt. They were covered with newspapers, but he recognized them by their sneakers. All of them belonged to his gang.

16

SUNDAY, BRIGHT SUN. THE beach was jammed. Carolaine and Kelly, sitting near the water, were building a sandcastle for Alas.

Iced tea, shouted the vendor, carrying the Styrofoam container on his shoulder. Who wants iced tea? The hubbub of voices came from every side, shouts, conversations, laughter, children's cries, people strolling about, the noise of the waves beating against the rocks of Pepino Beach.

It was Kingie's first free day since the war had begun a month earlier. Rolling a towel into an improvised pillow behind his neck, he lay on his back, eyes closed, feeling the sun and thinking about life. That was the way he made important decisions, quietly, in silence, without listening to anyone's opinion. *You are light,/ la ra la ra ra la la/ you are sun,/ my desire,/ lara ra ra ra*, the girl beside him, a flaccid mulatto in a tiny bikini, was singing the latest hit from the radio, breaking his concentration. Amazing how people can't manage to keep their mouths shut, thought Kingie. They're always talking. José Luís was irritated at the inability of Kelly and Carolaine to remain quiet for even a minute. Shit. The prattling on the bus to the beach had left him dizzy. Nothing but nonsense, shit, this one, that one, the pastor, the soaps, diets, my mother said, a butt of steel, unemployment, wouldn't be a maid if you put a gun to my head, cellulite, babies, boring crap! It was so good to be silent, thinking about this or that, observing. Why are you so quiet? Kelly asked. That really got to him! Even after sex Kelly wanted to talk, What are you thinking, love? Shit, Kelly. Love. Iced tea, Coca-Cola, guaraná, grape Fanta, the vendor announced. With great effort, José Luís distanced himself from the noise around him and concentrated on important questions. His father. He couldn't get his father out of his head. The last time he'd seen him, at Praça Argentina, near the truckers, he'd had the impression that Francisco was waiting for him, and, more moving still, had spruced up for the encounter. Kingie was overcome with affection when he saw him with his hair combed, his torn, wrinkled shirt tucked inside his pants. He had given him a pair of sneakers that same day. Francisco put them on and spent a long time admiring them. Afterward they went to a lunch stand where they had *feijoada*, his father fascinated by his new sneakers, gleaming white, American-made. They were friends now. They sat in the square, talking, Francisco frequently complaining about the delinquents who lived there. They're talking about me, haven't you noticed? He believed the boys were planning to hand him over to the police. He yelled at them, What are you looking at, you fools? You stinking little thieves. Glue sniffers. Purse snatchers.

It hadn't been easy for the two of them to come together. What does this kid who came out of nowhere, being generous, starting conversations, want? thought Francisco suspiciously. With the beggars who lived at the square, he at first referred to José Luís as the patsy, the sucker. Over time, he became friends with the boy, and even enjoyed their meetings. He awaited them impatiently, not only because of the cigarettes, food, and blanket that José Luís gave him, but especially because he felt good when he was with the boy. You're a good person, he'd said on one occasion, when the youth had offered him money. What's your name again? Zé. He always forgot José Luís's name. Such a dumb name, I never can remember it. When he was drunk he was unbearable. He would turn nasty and say things that Kingie didn't understand. Or he would grab a piece of wood and threaten him. You're a cop, he'd say, you're here to pin something on me. When that happened, Kingie would go home frustrated, feeling like giving up. But he didn't. Now that his financial situation had improved, he thought more and more about the possibility of bringing his father to live in

Berimbau. He would rent a room for him. He would take him to Alcoholics Anonymous. He would buy a van for Francisco to do hauling. Hadn't he worked for years as a fare collector? Well, now he would drive. And Carolaine would help him take care of their father. Cleaning the house, cooking, just till things got straightened out. Are you out of your mind? I don't want anything to do with that worthless man, Carolaine had said when her brother broached the subject to her. What's that old man good for? To give us heartache, to make our lives hell. Never. Can't you think about our mother? How unhappy it'd make her? I refuse. No way. Absolutely not. Subject closed.

A beach-paddle ball fell near José Luís, throwing sand onto his belly. Kids. A drag. He got up, saw Carolaine coming toward him carrying her son. Hold Alas for a minute, she said, I'm going to phone Pastor Walmir, I told him I'd stop by the church after lunch. Be right back.

Smiling, Kelly waved at him from the water. José Luís responded without great enthusiasm. He was feeling irritated lately. It wasn't possible to stretch out and enjoy the beach. He simply wasn't able to. Always tense, thinking about things. He recalled Grace, Mr Rodrigo's secretary. She had told him that there were days when she spent so many hours in front of the computer that at night, before falling asleep, no matter how she tried, she couldn't keep from mentally typing the words of her thoughts. With Kingie, during the war, something similar happened. When he would lie down, he felt that his hand was a weapon, and in the darkness of his bedroom he would pick out targets, shooting and killing enemies.

Alas began crying for his grandmother. José Luís picked up a small bucket of sand to amuse him. At that moment, Marta appeared before his eyes, in a blue and green bikini, all tanned and with wet hair. José Luís? she said. Do you remember me? I'm a friend of Fake's. Kingie got up, bewildered, leaving Alas on the beach towel. Something in his body seemed to want to explode, the muscles of his chest inflated. Marta, he said, shit, he'd been looking for Marta for so long, he had scoured every funk dance floor, a lot of time had gone by, shit, so many questions to ask, there she was, finally, Marta, ready to answer, shit, he was still totally mad about the woman, shit, and so what? Alas began to cry. What a cute baby, she said. He's not mine, José Luís replied, afraid that Marta might draw the wrong conclusion. It was urgent to explain that he was free, single, and unencumbered. He was so preoccupied with clarifying the situation once and for all that he paid no attention to the child's screams. He only became aware of what was going on when he heard Kelly's strident voice overpower everything. José Luís, you're standing on Alas's hand, she said. And he was. Shit, I didn't see him. Kelly picked Alas up, examining his fingers. Sorry. Alas's crying was making conversation impossible. Ice is good for that, Marta said. Yeah, Zé, get some ice, Kelly agreed, hurry. The poor little dear.

Upset, Zé Luís went looking for a soft drink vendor, there wasn't one in sight, son of a bitch. He looked everywhere, distressed, ice, completely dazed by what had happened, Marta, there she was, helping Kelly. Where do you live? he would ask her later. Ice. He'd get Marta's telephone number and call her later, when Kelly wasn't around. Dot the *i*s and cross the *t*s. I love you, he'd say. He loved Marta, of that he was absolutely sure. It was love. No vendor in sight, impressive how the fuckers can disappear. Really love. Ice. God, Marta. She simply appeared, suddenly, right before his eyes. Pretty. Shit. Ice. José Luís decided he'd gain time if he went directly to a stand at the sidewalk, and he ran in that direction, the sand and asphalt burning the soles of his feet. He got a few pieces of ice and returned, anguished, shit, from the distance he could see that Marta wasn't there.

Alas was crying on Kelly's lap when José Luís approached. Where's Marta? he asked, handing her the ice. You hurt his little hand, just look. Kingie was looking around like a hunting dog seeking its prey. Poor little baby, Kelly said, you'll be all right. Where'd that girl go who was here? The one with short hair. Take the ice, Zé Luís. Help out. Goddamn it, Kingie screamed, aren't you listening? Where's Marta? I don't have any idea who Marta is, Kelly replied, irritated.

And stop yelling at me. I just hope you didn't break his finger.

José Luís went along the beach like a poisoned rat, scrutinizing every square foot of the sand. Where had she gotten to? He went to the sidewalk, returned, no sign of Marta. Back to the sand. Nothing. In the water, on the sand, the sidewalk, nothing. The sand, nothing.

On the bus ride back, with Alas in his lap and Kelly displaying her hurt feelings, he could only repeat 'goddamn it' over and over. His bad luck was phenomenal. It had to be the evil eye. It couldn't be anything else. He'd looked so hard for Marta, and she'd appeared then, of all days. Goddamn it. Wretched Sunday. He had to cry, the brat, he thought, uncomfortable with the weight of the child, who was sleeping soundly in his arms. Spoiled kid. Without a father to boot, that prick. Carolaine, far away from it all, was stuffing herself with popcorn on the rear seat.

Kelly didn't utter a word on the entire trip back. I'm sorry, Kelly. It's just that Marta owes me money, you don't know how hard it is to get people to pay up. I know. Kelly was in no mood to forgive. In her opinion, ever since he'd become a soldier José Luís was acting very stuck up. Just because he owned weapons and the girls looked at him, he thought he was the greatest. Big deal. Talking to her that way, just because he wanted to collect from somebody? Give me a break. She'd barely gotten a look at that Marta. She struck her as someone who was sly and who'd made Alas more nervous still. She hadn't really paid any attention to her. You going to keep on beating a dead horse? José Luís asked, grabbing her at the gate to her house. Kelly smiled, mollified. You're forgiven.

As he climbed the hillside toward his house, Kingie noticed the police helicopter flying over the favela again. He didn't like that at all. Not a good sign.

Night of tragedy for Berimbau, read the headline of one of Rio de Janeiro's most important dailies. The story related the events of the combat that had taken place during the night, killing five, all belonging to the gang of Milton dos Santos, commonly known as Miltão do Berimbau. There was a photo of José Antônio da Silva, a.k.a. Zequinha Bigode, leader of the invasion that had sewn panic among the Berimbau residents.

All Brazil knew the details of the bloody battles through articles like these and TV coverage, which gave great play to images of bodies hacked to pieces, mutilated, reduced to ashes, clandestine cemeteries, and traffickers striking heroic poses, firing their machine guns into the air.

Everyone in both favelas knew that the real reason for the war was Suzana. But no one dared say anything to reporters. In the interviews, the residents supported their leaders. We're with Zequinha, they said. To us Zequinha is pure gold, one interviewee had stated. Good hearted. He pays for my kidney medicine. I like Miltão, another had declared, because he does everything a mayor ought to do. Criticism, when it appeared, was without focus. I'm used to it, one housewife commented, there's always bodies scattered about, especially on weekends.

On TV you see pictures of Iran, Israel, bombs going off, Onofre had told one journalist, people burned alive, children running through the streets crying, desperate, ten-year-old boys armed to the teeth, people missing a limb, beggars everywhere, blood, hunger, the devil. Here it's the same thing. We have our own Iraq, our Saddam Hussein, our Arabs, our Turkish shit. What's an attack like? Rent a war film, take away the soldiers' boots, take away the fatigues, take away the blond hair and blue eyes, and you've got our war. That's what it's like.

What amazes the public, Reader told José Luís on one of the occasions when they met at Onofre's to drink beer and talk about the war, isn't precisely the war but the shooting back and forth among the authorities. They're running around like a chicken with its head cut off, just read the papers. Ending the drug traffic isn't the responsibility of city government, declared the secretary of public safety. It's the aegis of the state government, claimed the minister of justice. What do you want from us? complained one federal legislator in an interview, we're tied hand and foot. Now, with the law guaranteeing the sanctity of the home and the

Juveniles Protection Act, our work's almost a joke. We can't go after the traffickers in their houses without a search warrant.

The truth, Reader continued, the truth is that there's no discussion of what's really necessary, legalization of drugs. Think about it, Kingie, if it weren't for that shitty law, everything would exist as it does now, the seller, the buyer, except it'd be cash-and-carry, you understand? Like in a pharmacy, everything nice and legal, displayed on shelves, no weapons, no violence. Because if drugs were legal, and it's not me saying it but a very important scholar, he said that if drugs were legal many deaths, many crimes wouldn't occur. With legalization the price of drugs would fall, there wouldn't be as great a demand, that's what the experts say. If they don't legalize, get this: we're going to end up just like the Italian Mafias. The police want to come up here to wipe out the trade. Look at the helicopter. They'll come up, kill a lot of people, arrest others, and what will be the result? Nothing. Absolutely nothing. Others will take their places. Why? Because drugs are lucrative, they're good business. Not to mention the fact that Brazil could be a power. Marijuana could lift Brazil out of the shit it's in, and that's the truth. It's much cheaper to grow marijuana than beans or corn. And unlike sugar cane and soya beans, it can give several crops a year. This isn't second-hand talk, I study a lot. I'll show you my books, Kingie. It's all there, all these ideas.

Miltão's gang suffered many casualties in the invasion from Marrecos. They lost thirteen soldiers. In addition, an enormous quantity of weapons disappeared mysteriously from the depot. Zequinha Bigode took control of two drug sites on the border between the favelas and began sending abusive messages to Miltão. Tell that 'citizen' that with me there's no such thing as maybe. If he's tired of eating lead, we can stop. But if he wants to go on fighting, he's got to send real men to do the job. I don't like killing kids and gutless wonders.

Miltão blamed the pastor for the failure, even if the number of soldiers who had converted to the church of the Flock of the Purest Love of Our Lord Jesus Christ was negligible, a mere eight. Ever since Vivinho, a former mechanic who handled machine guns with great dexterity, had told him that from that moment on he would take orders only from Jesus Christ, Miltão had come to concentrate all his hatred on the pastor. Doing more drugs than normal, his nerves on edge, Miltão would exaggerate every time he mentioned the subject. The preacher's a dummy, he said, to him everything's a sin. Carnival's a sin, fucking's a sin, eating chocolate is a sin, drugs are a sin, but giving money to some scam artist of a preacher, that's not a sin. Neither is fucking the preacher. I know about everything. He's feathering his nest, I see that. He wants to fuck me over, take away my men. I'm warning him, he makes one slip-up and I'll see he's in deep shit. I'll close down that place and grease the skids for the grifter and his women, send him the hell away from here. Your mother's a churchgoer, Zé Luís, tell her. I'll close down that piece of shit.

Miltão's outbursts of rage would occur for any reason at all. The trafficker had become intolerant with his gang and visited injustices on his friends. Reader was his greatest victim. His advice was of no interest to Miltão, who considered him foreboding. Shut up, he said, every time his friend alerted him to some matter. Shut your face. Don't talk crap. It wasn't long before Reader, humiliated, began talking about 'Miltão's successor'. Always in a whisper, looking to both sides. Most of the time his interlocutor was Kingie. You're the only one who can assume command, he said. You've got leadership. You're brave. You're intelligent. You know what you want. With the war, Kingie had become famous in the favela. It had been he who killed Branquelo, Zequinha Bigode's right-hand man. And Hunchback Capixaba. He had also killed the head of a family, a thirty-five-year-old man, victim of a stray bullet. But José Luís didn't know that. He knew only that he was getting more and more powerful, and he could imagine life in the favela once he assumed its leadership. He did not, however, admit that possibility to anyone. I don't want to be boss, he replied to Reader whenever the subject came up. Now that he had become the confident of Miltão, the only one above him in the hierarchy, he would not betray his friend. Yes, Miltão was his friend. He trusted him. He wouldn't stab him in the back. Never. Not ever. What if Miltão died? Yes, if Miltão died it was a different story. But kill Miltão, never. Don't ever say that again, Reader. For your own good.

Miltão opened his eyes and felt his head throbbing in the temples. It was as if the sound of the helicopter were entering directly into his arteries and muscles, churning his stomach. The scene had repeated itself for two days now. So the police wanted to invade, did they? Let 'em. Whatever it took to put an end to the noise of those overflights, the patrols at the foot of the hillside, vans, dogs. It was nerve-racking. Miltão preferred fighting. A thousand times.

Even before his feet hit the floor, the trafficker had already grabbed his Israeli-made machine gun. He went to the window, saw the nine men responsible for his safety. He spotted the plane flying over the shacks. The mental image of the police inside the craft made his blood boil. Sons-of-bitches. Just when he was sleeping like a log, thanks to several joints, the worms woke him up. Miltão knew his situation was critical. There were already eight outstanding warrants on him, four for drug trafficking, one for rape, three for homicide. They wanted to catch him at any cost. The press called Miltão 'one of the biggest traffickers in Rio'. Is that what it says? he had asked Onofre, who kept him informed about everything about him that appeared in the newspaper. I like that. Very good. I'm going to keep that paper as a souvenir, let me have it.

After watching the helicopter's movements for some minutes, Miltão went back to bed, only then seeing the naked girl, asleep, her head beneath the pillow. He didn't remember her name. Nowadays it was like that. He generally sent the girls on their way immediately after sex. When one of them starts in, I tell her right off, see you later, baby. It's fuck and get lost, he told his friends. It was the way he'd found to get even with his former girlfriend, whose name he avoided mentioning. He referred to her as 'the deceased'. The deceased is going to be sorry, he said. The deceased is going to want to come back. She's going to beg, the deceased is, mark my words, Onofre, and when she returns, know what I'm going to do? Not a goddamn thing. The deceased can go fuck herself. Thinking about Suzana hurt him tremendously. The whore.

He opened the refrigerator, took out a Coca-Cola. He woke the girl up, offered her the can of soda. Run along to school, cupcake. He stuck a fifty in her hand. Nowadays he also loved doing that, paying women. Use them and pay them.

After he was alone, he went to the closet and stood there studying his weapons: two M-16 rifles with laser telescopic sights, four clips, two AR-15s. He loaded the rifle and removed a roofing tile from the right-hand corner of the living room. From there he had reasonable visibility and a good firing position. The helicopter was still circling above the shantytown. When the craft swept down, Miltão shot. When they saw him firing, the soldiers sought cover and the gun battle began.

It was a spectacular scene. The helicopter plummeted from the sky and smashed into the ground in a fireball. None of the police on board survived, the newspaper later reported.

Miltão celebrated the victory all day by drinking and taking drugs.

That same morning, both entrances to the favela were taken over. One hundred and fifty soldiers from the Special Operations Battalion, along with shock troops from the military police, climbed the hillside with their dogs and their grenade launchers, exchanging gunfire with the traffickers. Military helicopters attacked from above, launching grenades and opening the way. When they got to the top of the favela, the situation became more difficult. Groups of soldiers swept through the shacks and interrogated the residents, but no one would cooperate. They succeeded only in capturing Bidê and apprehending two kilos of cocaine in the secretary's shack. Two policemen were wounded, one seriously. Miltão managed to get away.

In the days that followed, seventy soldiers from the military police remained on watch at the foot of the hill to prevent new conflicts between the rival gangs. It was this episode that forced a truce between Miltão and Zequinha Bigode.

Now everything's all right, said the residents. The gunfire had ceased.

Kingie moved in with Kelly and avoided going outside, as a precaution. In any case, there was nothing to do. It was necessary to wait for Miltão to make a move, and that wouldn't happen until the police had stopped occupying the favela.

Reader visited him almost every night. The problem is that many died in the battle, he said. They killed Monga. Beco. Mangueira. Yeah, he said, we're dying off. It's an impasse. As long as Miltão's our boss it'll be like this, just dying and having done with it. Get that through your skull, Kingie. To continue the drug traffic here, Miltão has to exit the scene. You want to take his place or not?

Kingie hated that kind of talk. Shit. How many times do I have to repeat it, Reader?

17

UNTIL I WAS ARRESTED I was an almost famous DJ, Fake said. I had my admirers. When I'd come grooving in to some rave with all my stuff around my neck, my dreadlocks and my yellow glasses, it was pure energy. I could really get the people going. There's some funk brothers that just want to play da da da da, like a pile driver, nothing else. Not me. I'm poetic. When the crowd exploded on the dance floor, all frenetic, I would shift the rhythm, jazz-step, groove, slow-dance. My dances had gals from the South Zone, all of them digging the vibe. I was even in the newspaper. One of the papers. So if that Marta chick is saying she knew me, that she's a friend of mine, that could be, she knows who I am, you know? A fan, maybe.

It was ten o'clock on Saturday night. Fake and Kingie were on their way to Cinelândia, kicking cans. Whenever they spoke of Marta, Kingie had the impression that his friend was hiding something. Fake's theorizing intrigued him. He overexplained, invented details, made everything seem logical, believable, acceptable. Which was exactly why Kingie was suspicious. The truth was never simple like that. Most times it was crippled, full of holes. He himself, on various occasions, had had to lie a little to make the truth sound less untrue. I don't understand, continued Fake, how a brother can have it so bad for a girl he hardly knows. I don't understand it. To me, love is something that grows slowly, a kind of sickness that infects you bit by bit, first your prick, then climbing to the chest, the mouth, and finally infecting your brain, until you become a complete asshole. Love, for José Luís, had happened differently. It had fallen out of the sky onto his head, plop, all he could think of was Marta, that's how it had been. He could still recall her smile, her pretty teeth, her wise eyes. And in his mouth was the constant taste of Marta. What a woman.

Next to the iron bars of the Public Promenade, Fake opened his zipper and urinated, looking at the sky. Ah, it's so good to be able to take a piss just anywhere. Since he had gotten out of prison, two days earlier, Fake was always saying that. I don't know why, Kingie, but I get all philosophical when I piss somewhere. I piss and think serious thoughts, that's how I piss, reflecting. It's good.

They crossed the street to see what was showing at the Cine Odeon. A prostitute passed by, in a hurry, click, click, click, arguing with a very thin child who was following her in a resigned manner. I'm not under any obligation, she said. You're not going to wear me down. Click, click, click, the heel of her shoe. Kingie followed them with his eyes. Click, click, click, it's no use trying to explain. The poster at the theater showed a sensual blonde, her hands on her hips. Click, click, click. *Gloria* was the title. The gal's pissed off, Fake commented, admiring the photo of the actress. What a set of legs, just look. Click, click, click. Fake went on gazing at the poster, absorbed. Jesus, a year and a half without seeing a movie. A year and a half without going to a funk dance, without eating a decent meal, a year and a half of life in the trashcan. I'm not resigned to it. Jesus. Come on, Fake, his friend said.

They continued walking, kicking the same can of Coca-Cola, Fake recounting for the hundredth time his life at the Center for the Rehabilitation of Minors. He'd spent four hours of his day sunning himself and the rest of the time doing nothing. 'Absolutely nothing.' Weakening my soul. Fucking my mind. I sunk pretty deep. I came out of there a piece of garbage, ready to steal, mug, rape, and kill. And if you think it was the inmates who taught me, you ought to know that as far as criminality is concerned I learned a lot more from the staff, the administration, the guards. They're past masters when it comes to getting the upper hand and screwing their fellow man. They're there for the business. Everything is business. Business and the soft life. If the guy isn't selling crack or some other crap, he's taking it easy. There was one guy who did nothing all day long but fart. I left with that as my apprenticeship. Going downhill, learning the negative, is the easiest thing in the world. But I'm one feisty nigger. I want to take off. To be a success. I'm artistic, brother. My thing is the stage. Glitter. I'm going to launch my CD, I want to be king of Brazilian hip-hop. I want to be Mr Explosion.

In the bar, drinking beer, Fake insisted that Kingie talk to Miltão about his returning to Berimbau. I slipped up, brother. It was a lapse, Fake said. But it's different now. I have lots of ideas. I want to go back to Berimbau, he said. I want to take charge of our radio. I'm going to organize Miltão's young supporters. Fake was living at home with his mother Creusa, still a young woman, who sold cosmetics door to door. The problem is she married a born-again Christian and I can't stay there anymore. My God is here, said Fake, pointing to the image of James Brown printed on his T-shirt. My God is Mr Dynamite. And their god is the one that lives on the cross. It doesn't work. The two don't go together. You can imagine, brother, how strange it is to have your mother marry some old geezer and all of a sudden he's the head of the household, giving orders, and looking at you like you were evil. It doesn't work. Miltão's got to take me back.

Kingie promised he'd speak to the trafficker. Miltão was an unpredictable guy. It might not be totally impossible to arrange a pardon. It cost nothing to try.

He's out already? Miltão asked, laying out another fat line of cocaine on the glass top. Yeah, answered Kingie. Damned good coke, he said. With the CD remote in his hand, he would punch replay every time 'You're Going to Pay for This', by the group Pagodança came to an end. Cool stereo system. So talk.

Since he had returned to the favela two weeks earlier, Miltão had scarcely slept at all. Every night he would take refuge in a different shack, in the company of girls to whom he offered drugs and alcohol. Willful and irascible, his only amusement was to tune in to the police band on the radio. You chickenshits, he cursed, you trash, closet faggots, you only come here to suck our blood, he said, just come up here now, you pieces of crap. Come on up.

Kingie didn't like what he was seeing. He felt bad when forced to witness such scenes. Miltão had changed greatly of late, there was no denying it. A few days after his return, the trafficker had thrown a barbecue for his friends, mobilizing his soldiers to prepare the party. Zino and two other butchers were obliged to supply the meat, and the booze came from the robbery of a liquor store on Avenida Epitácio Pessoa.

At the end of the night, Miltão insisted that each of the guests take home a case of beer. A doggy bag, he said, guffawing. It was a noisy night, with much wasted ammunition. At every turn, Miltão fired his rifles into the air. Go for fucking broke! he yelled.

When most of the guests had already left, Miltão, drunk, took Bidezinho, the twin brother of Bidê, who was doing time in Padre Moraes, to the upper part of the favela. They sat at the lookout point and gazed at the city, the illuminated Christ statue. They smoked a joint, laughed, and talked nonsense, and after all that, Miltão blew Bidezinho's head off with an Uzi submachine gun. Kingie, Reader, all the managers of the favela witnessed the scene. From now on, he said, that's how it is. I kill my enemies.

The next day, Bidezinho's tongue was found stuck to the door with a kitchen knife. All that violence occurred because there were rumors that Noble had ordered Miltão's death. Some said that Miltão had refused to send money to their comrades imprisoned in Padre Moraes and would be killed for that reason. Others said that Miltão's days were numbered because he was 'weak'. The talk never ceased. There was even speculation about possible successors, Zequinha Bigode or Paredão, from the Marrecos favela. A daily flurry of rumors: Nal said, Duda heard, Micuim's going around saying, they said, it seems that, it's what they're saying. Which is why Miltão had executed Bidezinho, to put an end to the rumor-mongering.

The only stories allowed to circulate were those that Miltão himself passed along. Anybody who talks to a reporter dies.

Anybody who talks to the cops dies. Anybody who does anything stupid after ten at night dies. The next one to die is the preacher. Miltão had an ongoing vendetta against the evangelicals. He had learned the prayer 'Hail Mary, full of grease, the pig is with you,' taken from some book of Reader's, and would repeat it in a loud voice when he crossed paths with a religious type.

Alzira feared for the pastor's life, even more so because Walmir was 'like a father' to Alas. Don't come here anymore, she'd told Walmir the previous Sunday, it's better you don't come up the hill. That Miltão is an evil soul. One day that man is going to wake up and find he has horns and hooves. A devil. A demon, a fiend. The blood of Jesus is life, she repeated, to protect us from Miltão's evil. But Walmir had no fear of the demon. He would go to Alzira's house every Sunday, sometimes during the week as well, often passing close to Miltão's men. How well Walmir and Carolaine got along, it made Alzira happy to see it. Always planning Christ's work. Carolaine, he assured her, has a way with words. In the future she can be a preacher if she stays with it. A ewe. Carolaine had loved the idea. She had taken to reading the Bible aloud to her mother. You know, Mother, Walmir showed me that I belong to God. I'm God's secretary. A ewe. Alzira understood her daughter's words perfectly. She also felt the same way. Jesus' secretary. Dona Juliana, now that she was calmer, would tell her friends, this is Alzira, our secretary. Jesus' secretary, that's what she was. She served Jesus. That was why she was so worried about the pastor. She even asked her son to talk to Miltão.

It wasn't a good idea. Miltão didn't like it. You should stop asking for favors. You're all the time asking for things.

The residents of the favela left their houses only to go to work. When reporters climbed the hill for interviews, they were run off and threatened.

Now we have a law of silence, a curfew, said Reader. And we're collecting taxes from the merchants. I asked Miltão what the reason for the taxes was. Know what he said? Don't bust my balls. That's the only thing he can say these days. Stick it up your ass, you son of a bitch, I'm going to fuck you. That's how he treats me. People are terrified. This isn't going to work. We're nearing the end. Any day, any day now some head honcho from the next favela will show up here with troops and all and we'll all die. You should prepare yourself, Kingie. We have to have a successor. You. I've told you a thousand times. You.

If, on the one hand Kingie showed no inclination to discuss the matter with Reader, he no longer asked him not to talk 'garbage'. He listened attentively, pensive and nervous.

That night, Kingie felt bad because he was once again in Miltão's presence, asking for another favor, that he allow Fake to return.

Here's what you're going to do, Miltão replied. You're going to set up a meeting with that prick. And you're going to put three bullets in his head. That's what. I've been looking to kill that queer for a long time. Now go. Leave, get out of here.

Kingie walked aimlessly through the cramped streets, watching the hungry, mangy mongrel dogs he encountered along the way. Barks. Until that moment he hadn't given serious consideration to Reader's ideas. His feelings in relation to the trafficker had always been paradoxical, bedazzlement and aversion. Dogs rummaged through the garbage, futilely making the rounds, sleeping in the hot sun, Shoo, Kingie said. Miltão was the man who had shot him in the hand and given him a job. Shoo. The man who killed his enemies cruelly and gave free meat to the unemployed. Without Miltão, Kingie might still be carrying inside him the sensation that he was a piece of shit, a nothing. Shoo. Children were standing around two dogs copulating. It's the butcher's bitch, they said. Miltão had given him a position. If he was a respectable soldier today, if he paid his bills, ate well and wore imported sneakers, it was thanks to the trafficker. Yes, he owed a lot to Miltão. But now things were different. It was Fake's life he was asking for.

Things would have to change in Berimbau. Reader was right. Get out of here, dog.

'Onofre, you dirty old man, how about my handwriting? You don't know how nice progress is. In my house, everything is automatic. Microwave, heating, computer, washing machine, everything built-in, white, and working. I don't mind washing, ironing, and cooking for Heinrich. Brazil is very backward. Even the poor people here are better. The poor here are the Turks. But you can't even tell they're poor (or that they're Turks). They all wear good coats and live in houses that make your shack look worse than it really is. And clean. Cleanliness is the best thing about Germany. We don't have that mess you have in Brazil, candy wrappers and ice cream on the ground. The streets are so clean you can eat off the sidewalks. And the dogs don't take a shit just anywhere. Another good thing is parking your car. They have some little machines in the streets, you put in a coin and that's it, no car watcher, nothing. That's the good side. The bad side is that the subway smells of sweat. I can't understand how a people that won the war can't overcome body odor. The women don't shave under their arms. And Heinrich travels a lot. I'm always by myself. I can't manage to learn German. Heinrich hired a Portuguese woman, Dona Augusta, to give me lessons. It's very hard. I think it'd be easier to make a hole in water. Next month we're going to Brazil. Tell my friends that Rosa Maria is on her way. I want to get my fill of *feijoada* and *pagode* music. I'm bringing you a Swiss army knife as a present. A hug from Rosa Maria.'

Onofre was moved by the letter from Rosa Maria. He read it enthusiastically to Kingie and Reader, who were eating turnovers at the counter. A Swiss knife, you believe it? It must be very expensive. Oh, Rosa Maria. She's really something. How much do you suppose a Swiss knife costs? Onofre no longer referred to his friend as 'the hooker'. He spoke of her with pride. Did you see that she has a private tutor? Dona Augusta. I'll bet it's Dona Augusta who writes the postcards. Just look. Such careful, rounded letters. Eat off the ground, can that be true? That Fritz of hers must be filthy rich. I'm happy for Rosa Maria. Look, in this world, with willpower anybody can make it. Oh, Onofre, Reader answered, laughing, enough bullshit, let me talk to Kingie.

Onofre moved away to read the letter to other customers.

I'm going to throw her a party, Rosa Maria deserves it. A Swiss knife. Eat off the ground.

Kingie and Reader went back to their conversation in hushed tones. Yesterday, Reader said, he kicked Tampinha in the ass. I swear. A real hard boot. Imagine that big six-foot-seven black guy getting kicked in the ass. Huh? How long can that go on? We have a delicate matter on our hands. You can't simply say you're not going to kill Fake. Some time ago there was a terrible case here in Berimbau. You were still a kid when Giba moved here. Giba was less than five feet tall, intelligent as hell, and screwed every girl in Berimbau. The guy was a bit crazy, ugly as sin, but he had a tremendous gift of the gab. Women fell all over him. One day, a young girl was found dead in a vacant lot near Onofre's, raped, her eyes gouged out, a horrible thing. She was thirteen, and everybody knew that the girl was chasing after Giba like mad and getting nowhere. Giba never wanted to have anything to do with her. I don't screw little girls, he said. But the entire favela accused Giba when the girl turned up dead, it was all people were talking about, especially because the night before the crime she had gone to Antônio's pool hall after him. And here comes the part that applies to you. Take note of this, Miltão wasn't certain of anything, it was all rumors, hearsay. Even so, he called in Valinho, Giba's brother, and said, You're going to kill Giba. Valinho refused. So Miltão killed them both, Giba and Valinho. And that's not the worst part. Later they discovered the girl's real murderer. It was a neighbor of hers, a hard-working bricklayer, much loved around here. I'm telling you this just to let you know that Miltão doesn't accept anyone refusing his orders. Even someone like you. Here's my opinion: let's arm ourselves. I'll help you. You have my support.

On Monday, Kingie met Fake at the same bar in Cinelândia at nine p.m. He went directly to the subject: Miltão wants me to kill you. Fake started laughing. I can't believe that the son of a bitch thinks I still owe him anything after a year and a half inside. Yes, he does, said Kingie. You're going to have to disappear, and disappear means really disappear. Vanish. If you can, change cities. Go up North, to the Amazon, disappear. As long as Miltão is boss of Berimbau, forget this place exists.

Reader and Biga were present at the meeting. Everything had been planned. Days before, Reader had gone to Miltão to say he suspected that José Luís wasn't going to kill Fake. He suggested that he and Biga witness the execution. At first Miltão had said that he'd kill Fake himself. Reader had agreed immediately. Yes, you have to kill the prick. Great idea. You yourself. You alone. Although it would be more painful if it was his friend who killed him. But your idea's better. You yourself, in person. The leader stomping on a flea. It'll set an example.

Lately this was how Reader succeeded in changing Miltão's opinions. If no one opposed what the trafficker said, the man would soften his stance. I'm not going to get my hands dirty on that piece of shit, he had finally replied, after smoking a joint. Kill the fucker right away.

That Monday, when they returned to Berimbau late at night, in the car driven by Biga, Reader went to offer an account. We put a lot of bullets into the bastard, he told Miltão. We burned the body and dumped it near the Fundão. The buzzards must be having a feast by now. Reader had fantastic details, enough to make Miltão roar with laughter at the scene of Fake crying. He was prepared to tell a story full of cruel details. It hadn't been necessary. Miltão wasn't in the mood for conversation that night. Michele, fifteen years old, in shorts and a cutoff blouse, had just arrived and was sitting on the sofa. The trafficker just wanted to get rid of the guys and be alone with her.

18

ZZZZZZZZZZZZZZZZZZ, THE DEFECTIVE VACUUM cleaner emitted a sharp, penetrating sound that put Alzira into a diabolical trance. After turning it off, she needed to wait a few seconds to understand what the people around her were saying. She heard the words, saw their lips articulating sounds, but it was as if everything were in a foreign language. My breakfast, Alzira, get my breakfast on the table, Mr Rodrigo requested, I'm late. Every Thursday was cleaning day at Dona Juliana's house. Alzira pushed back the furniture, removed the rugs, stripped the living room, doing everything with pleasure, because she enjoyed cleaning. As she worked, she thought about Jesus, and that imparted a great deal of meaning to the act of scrubbing and washing. If the dirt was persistent, better yet, for such was the road to heaven, difficult, scrub, scrub with faith, at the end of the day, her arms and legs aching, she would lie in bed and feel her heart full of Christ, a good kind of tired, of one who had served God. The problem was the interruptions. Coffee, milk, papaya, and bread with butter, here's your breakfast. Mr Rodrigo, in the morning, was always rushing, hurried, spending two hours in the bathroom reading the paper and showering, and then would start yelling around the house, Where's my brown tie? Didn't my suit come back from the cleaners? And before her employer started in with his gripes, Alzira had already faced the first round, getting the children off to school, Alzira, my bread, my tangerine juice, my red sneakers, take this, Alzira, water, come here, Alzira, go up to my room and see if I forgot my pencil. Here's the pencil, Alzira, I found it. Cleaning was squeezed in between the other activities, just like prayer in the lives of certain sheep. And even so, she enjoyed cleaning, better than cooking. When she cooked she couldn't think about anything. The cut vegetables, Dona Juliana's grilled fillet (without a drop of fat, Alzira), Marcelinha's French fries, Mr Rodrigo's rare steak, preparing the food ruined her concentration. But not cleaning. Ciao, Alzira. It was incredible how fast the dirt accumulated. She had cleaned everything last Thursday, and there was the black dust, a dirty world, Alzira soaked the rag in ammonia and scrubbed the glass, imagining that each stain was a sin. Please get me my breakfast, said Dona Juliana, coming into the living room, still in pajamas.

Another interruption. A slice of whole-wheat bread with cottage cheese, half a cup of milk with sweetener and coffee, along with piles of pills for cellulite. What good did it do to have that skimpy little breakfast and then stuff yourself with bread? My problem is carbohydrates, Alzira. I get anxious. I don't care about sweets, she said. That was a lie. She was always picking at other people's plates. Losing and gaining weight, week after week. Like Carolaine. Except that Carolaine only put on weight. She had even outgrown the pants she'd bought after Alas was born. Why that big belly? So young, Carolaine. Yes, Alzira was fat too, but her life was at its end. She had married, had children, and that was that. Why lose weight? But not Carolaine, so young, with a belly like that. She couldn't believe it. Take this bread away, for God's sake, Alzira, said Dona Juliana, the telephone at her ear. I mustn't put on weight. Hello, Fernando please. Pause. What? He didn't go to work? Will you tell him Juliana called? Yes, Juliana. Alzira, more bread. Why did you take away the bread, Alzira? Juliana hung up the phone, concerned. Did Fernando call? No, he hadn't called. If he calls, tell him I'm out. No. I'll talk to him. I'll talk to him, all right, Alzira?

Juliana had noticed that Alzira had been wearing a sour expression the last few days. Maybe she'd heard Rodrigo's cutting remarks. Speak more quietly, Rodrigo. Friends in the living room, and Rodrigo saying, Alzira is proof that God, if he exists, is a son of a bitch: Alzira is ugly, poor, stupid, and ignorant. We adore Alzira, they had said. But she is truly stupid. So stupid that the other day she wrote down a telephone number like this: 555 44 77 333333333, thinking that meant 35 24 27 93.

Yes, Alzira was in a bad mood. Now I treat her like a queen, Juliana had told her friend Alicinha. Alzira knows about Fernando. The way she looks at me, Alicinha, I'm telling you, I'm going to have to get rid of the woman. Fast. But if I fire her, she'll tell Rodrigo everything. I'm sure of it. She asked me for a raise the other day. I gave it to her on the spot. I'm paying her a fortune. Jul, dear, answered Alicinha, in my opinion Alzira doesn't have to say anything about your affair with Mr Gatorade, you're doing it yourself. You're practically sending up flares, dear, that day at Helena's luncheon, I counted, you mentioned your fitness training seven times. It's hard that way; keep your little mouth shut, sweetie. What would Rodrigo's reaction be if he found out? Rodrigo, who was all the time commenting on the fact that so-and-so was having an affair with his secretary? A secretary? How horrible, he said, how lazy can you get, screwing a secretary? Screwing a chauffeur. Screwing an assistant. An intern. How middle class. There was nothing worse, in Rodrigo's eyes, than calling someone or something middle class. A middle-class restaurant. A middle-class guy. He's real middle class, he would say. Careful with Rodrigo, dear. He's not dumb. Well, yes, she needed to mention Fernando less often, but Fernando drove her wild. Alice, he must have somebody else, I can feel it. He's changed. Do you think, Alice, that I'm sagging? Eh? She stood in front of the mirror, lifting her breasts. I don't have a single girlfriend who hasn't had plastic surgery. Look at this cellulite here. I'm doing a ginkgo biloba treatment. I drink six liters of water a day, I run, I work out, massages, and look at me. Cellulite is a curse. It runs in the family. You know, Alicinha, turning forty is the worst thing that can happen to a woman. It's like falling off a cliff. Being forty is a kind of sickness. I lie nowadays. I say I'm thirty-nine. It makes a tremendous difference. Not physically. Men will still go out with a woman who's thirty-nine. Forty, no way. Maybe

Fernando's met some thirty-nine-year-old. Do you think? It used to be, Alice–oh, what good did it do to tell Alice? Alice didn't give a damn. Alice was part of what Americans called 'addicted society'. Her thing is going to parties so she can talk about who was invited, who showed up in the society pages, who's important, who has money. A few days ago, Juliana commented to another girlfriend, a few days ago Alice told me, For my birthday I want an 'A-list' group of people, she read that somewhere and kept repeating 'A-list', how idiotic. In actuality, Juliana didn't feel all that different from Alice, she herself had repeated several times with other friends the expression 'A-list', she'd found it interesting, the problem was, well, since her friend had started classes with Fernando, well, it wasn't good to even think about it. Could it be? Fernando always arrived from Alice's house with a blasé air about him. Do you think, Alice, that he has another woman? Haven't you noticed anything? Nothing. Nothing at all. Shh, lower your voice, Alzira's coming. Have you seen how ill-tempered she's been? Always with that ugly look on her face. That's how she is these days. I've nicknamed her 'Miss Bulldog'.

Alzira wasn't angry about anything. It was her leg that was giving her no peace. Just above the right ankle, a lesion had appeared. She had first noticed it a week earlier. She had put Mercurochrome on it, to no effect. She hadn't hurt herself, of that she was sure. Maybe it was an insect bite. More coffee, Alzira. Thank you. She was always well mannered, Dona Juliana. A well-mannered sinner. Which was better than being a sinner without manners. Vanity was a sin. Fornication was a sin. Adultery was a sin. Gluttony was a sin. Alzira had already attempted to save her employer from the Devil's clutches. She had offered to bring Pastor Walmir for a conversation. I'm Catholic, Dona Juliana had replied. Alzira understood very well the meaning of that kind of response. I don't pay the slightest attention to God, that was what Catholicism was. That was the problem.

The intercom rang. Alzira dragged her ailing leg to the kitchen to answer. My name is Fake, a voice said from the other end, I'm a friend of your son's, I was here with him once, a long time ago, could I speak to you for a minute? She remembered him. Yes, come on up. Another bad seed from Miltão's gang. She didn't want Dona Juliana to see him in the kitchen. How are you, Dona Alzira? asked the youth very politely, when Alzira opened the door. What good were all those manners if he wasn't one with Christ? When the Devil appears, he speaks in soft tones. Could you please give this envelope to Zé Luís? It's important. Very important. Don't forget.

Alzira closed the door and sat down to rest a bit. What was this thing on her leg?

The place was located in the lowest part of Berimbau, behind Zino's butcher's shop. A ten-foot-square shack with a cement floor, no windows, and with asbestos roofing. Not far from the door was a dark open ditch where raw sewage ran. It'll look fine once you paint it, the owner said. The woman, supporting her massive body against the doorframe, went on enumerating the advantages of living at the foot of the hillside. It's near the bus stop, she said. When the shooting starts, it's easy to get away. I saw on television, the woman said, that these days not even the garbage men want to go up the hill for fear of catching a bullet in the forehead. The best thing is to live down here.

Kingie wanted something higher up, near Kelly, who'd promised to help take care of Francisco. But on second thoughts, not having to deal with steep streets every day was an advantage. He closed the deal, paying six months' rent in advance.

Kingie climbed the hill, thinking about future measures. Hi, Dona Zita, he said, greeting the woman sitting in the doorway to her house with a child in her lap. He would buy paint, when he had time, and paint the place himself. How are you, Dona Elza? At the end of the day, children were playing in the streets and the women, at windows and gates, already bathed, were talking with their neighbors while they waited for their husbands or sons to arrive. How are you? A bed, a stove, a television set and refrigerator, he would only buy the basics for his father. Yes, that and a minivan. But only once Francisco gave up drinking.

Good evening, Mr Pedro. Of course he'd stop drinking, his father, and he'd haul freight, there were always people arriving, leaving, getting married, parties, relocations, there was no end to work. Soon his father would be able to buy another vehicle, and then another, they would work together, form a fleet, they would have a company. Good evening, Kingie. Father: businessman. Mother: domestic. They could also buy taxis. And hire drivers. Hi, Zé. His father would run the whole thing. They'd have a secretary. The problem would be how to tell his mother. And Carolaine. Hi. Maybe if he asked Cândida, his grandmother, for help. Cândida wasn't as hostile toward Francisco. Your mother was always very nervous, she'd said on one occasion. I remember one day when your grandfather and I had lunch at her house, you were a baby, Carolaine was a little girl. Your father was watching TV, lunch was on the table, and just because he was a little slow in coming, your mother raised Cain, a silly thing. I said: Alzira, marriage isn't like that. Men don't like to be treated that way. She didn't listen to me. And what happened, happened. She had it coming, thought Kingie.

Some street kids approached noisily. They wanted a new ball for their elementary school. We can't play without a ball. I'll see about it, replied Kingie. Show us your gun, they asked. The children of Berimbau loved to see machine guns. Miltão had gotten them used to it. He was always giving away candy and amusing them by displaying his arsenal. No, José Luís answered. Shoo. Is it an AR-15? they asked. Get out of here. Climbing, lost in thought. What about his father? What would he say to him? I've found a place for you to live. No. Maybe he had to tell him the whole truth. You're my father. I'm José Luís, Alzira's son, Carolaine's brother, Cândida's grandson, I live in Berimbau. He felt great anxiety when he thought about the possibility. It was strange to go up to your own father and say, I'm the son you deserted. 'Deserted', he didn't like the word. It was what Alzira always said, That no-good deserted you two. A degenerate, your father. A shameless womanizer. A disgusting sot. Hi, Dona Cida.

When he entered Kelly's house, the soap opera was on TV.

You, said the actor, are a miserable human being, neurotic. Gustavo was right to marry Gilda, I'm going to destroy you. Kelly? José Luís turned off the set. There was a nice smell in the house. Kelly, I'm here.

He peeled a banana and went into the bedroom. Kelly, in bra and panties, was drying her hair in front of the wardrobe mirror. Hi, Zé, your mother left this for you, she said, pointing to an envelope on the dresser. Kingie looked at Kelly's naked thighs. My mother? He placed his weapon on the chair near the door, then put his arms around Kelly from behind. Umm. I'll read it to you, Kelly continued, opening the envelope: 'Zé, we need to talk. It's urgent. Meet me tonight at 9:30 at McDonald's in the Fashion Mall. Fake.'

Kelly's body gave off the aroma of soap. Zé Luís, with his body, pushed her toward the bed. Kisses. Take off those clothes, she said. What do you think Fake wants with you? José Luís didn't want to think about Fake or anyone at that moment. He had something better to do.

Drawings of colored pennants. 'Great fair of Jesus Christ. The June festival of the Flock of the Purest Love of Our Lord Jesus Christ. June 27, at the Berimbau sports area. Games, fireworks, hot grog, and lots of fun. Don't miss it.' The poster, made with cardboard and felt-tip pen, had been placed on the counter of Onofre's bar by Pastor Walmir. Walmir was telling his friend about the activities that were being prepared, a gymkhana, an egg-and-spoon race. That I want to see, said Onofre. I'm going to enter my old lady in the gymkhana, she's good at those things. Is there going to be a sack race? I can get some burlap, he said.

The festival would be held on a Sunday, and with the money raised they would begin construction of a day-care center at the church of the Flock of the Purest Love of Our Lord Jesus Christ. I'm going, sure, said Onofre. And speaking of money, don't you want to buy a ticket for the raffle of a bicycle? I'm selling them. It's for the barbecue I plan to give for Rosa Maria. Do you know Rosa Maria? My German friend?

At that moment, Miltão, Reader, and two more soldiers from the gang entered the bar. Hi, good people, said Onofre, embarrassed by the situation. What'll it be? A nice cold beer?

Walmir greeted Miltão respectfully. How are you?

Don't talk to me, replied Miltão. And don't look at me either, you hear? You hypocrite. In church he busts my balls, he told Reader, who was leading him to the rear of the bar toward the pool table. Let it go, man, Reader said. Let's play. Miltão knew that Walmir had been condemning his actions in sermons at the church. His own mother, who was also an evangelical, had told him. She suffered from high blood pressure and had felt ill after Sunday's sermon. Did you do all that, son? Did you kill a boy and cut out his tongue? Of course it's a lie, Mother. Do I look like somebody who'd cut out a tongue? Huh? You brought me up, and you believe that? Your son who gives you everything you need, food, pots, blankets, shoes, a house, medicine, think about it, does your son go out and do such things? What else did he say, Mother?

Reader couldn't hold the trafficker back for long. Miltão returned to the counter in a rage, saying loudly, I don't like this talk about a church festival and a day-care center, he said. I wasn't consulted. I didn't approve anything, you hear me, God-clown?

Walmir looked at him with no sign of fear. He said that the idea for the festival and the day-care center had been discussed with Reader and approved by him. Reader doesn't run things, Miltão answered. Reader is a shitass. I'm the boss around here, he said.

Reader lowered his head in embarrassment. Not that anyone expected a reaction from Reader, but to see him humiliated, his head hanging, not saying a word, caused everyone discomfort.

Miltão, said Onofre, hoping to avoid a commotion, today the beer's on the house. Don't give me any grief, Onofre. Since when do I need free beer?

Onofre, concerned, gestured for Walmir to leave quickly. Here's the beer. Who won the game yesterday?

Walmir was already at the door when Miltão grabbed the

poster and tore it to bits. It's decided, he said. No festival. No day-care. You clown.

Walmir's reaction surprised everyone. Only if you kill me, he said. I'm holding the festival, Miltão. I'm going to build the center. And I'll go wherever I want to, even if you continue to threaten me. You don't own the hill. The hill belongs to God.

After saying this, Walmir turned his back and left, not hurrying.

Onofre had to grab Miltão so the trafficker wouldn't draw his weapon. Not here, he said. Not in my bar. Please, Miltão.

Who does he think he is? shouted Miltão. He's disrespectful and he's fucked, he said. Now he's really fucked. He'll see. That little louse is fucked. Finished.

Kingie arrived early for his meeting with Fake. He walked aimlessly around the shopping center, observing the girls strolling by in groups, laughing, joking, navels showing. Now and then he stopped in front of a display window. Everything on sale. Shit.

At 9:15 he went to McDonald's, bought a Coke and waited, sitting at one of the small tables. Beside him, a teenage girl was devouring a Big Mac at an impressive speed. Shit. That one eats. She's probably never seen a dick in her life, José Luís thought, amused. When the girl went to the counter and ordered another Big Mac, José Luís began laughing to himself. Shit, the bitch must weigh over two hundred pounds. And eating like that. And banana cream pie, French fries. Cellulite. Shit. She looked like Carolaine.

What's happening, brother, said Fake, sitting down beside him.

The conversation was an objective one. Fake said that he was now living under Zequinha Bigode's protection. One sensational black guy. Very clever. Human as can be. And competent. He wants to rap with you, brother. And it has nothing to do with your good qualities, Zé. It's Suzana, your fairy godmother, who's behind it all. She rules, that lady. Know what that means? Your time has come, brother. You understanding me? To be king, how about that, huh? Get the idea? That's what it is, brother. If

155

you don't want to be Miltão's errand boy for the rest of your life, now's the time. The man is willing to help you. He wants to set up a meeting. How about it? Aren't you going to say anything? Cat got your tongue? Make up your mind, brother. What do I tell them?

19

THE FATHER TAKES HIS daughter by the hand/ tells the doctor that she's sick,/ she won't eat or go school,/ doesn't sleep or work a lick, sang the accordion player hired by Pastor Walmir to liven up the festival. The stage, despite having been put together hurriedly, enchanted everyone, with its decoration of banners and streamers of colored paper. Two costumed fiddlers provided the rhythm for the celebration. *But the doctor takes him aside,/ says, You have to understand,/ it's just a case of growing pains,/ with no cure known to man.*

There was every type of delicacy in the sixteen stands installed in Berimbau's sports center for the Festival of São João: peanut brittle, green-corn pudding, beef jerky, coconut-covered marshmallows, turnovers, milk candy, macaroons, corn on the cob, hot grog, buns, popcorn, corn cake, tapioca custard, barbecue, fritters, small meat pies. Carolaine, very excited, wearing a colorful calico skirt and a straw hat, was going from side to side inspecting the church personnel and humming *She wants only,/ she thinks only of falling in love.* Can I try the peanut brittle? Crunch. Real good. I know very well what all this appetite means, she thought, stroking her belly. *She wants only,/ she thinks only of falling in love.* She felt happier than ever, crunch crunch crunch. For three days now her life had centered on the festival. *With no cure known to man.* Munch. She had been the one who coordinated the entire production of the food and drink, collecting money and assigning tasks to the forty-seven sheep of the flock of Christ. I just love milk candy, she said, sticking a portion in her mouth, yum. *She wants only.* Yum, very good, yum. It's a lot of work to coordinate everything. I haven't even been able to watch my soaps, she told Kelly, do you know if Felipo Albuquerque kissed Magda? Yes, answered Kelly, and Tarsila fired Irene. And there's more: Marcela Aragão was thrown out of the shipyard. Really? Carolaine asked, good riddance, Marcela's a bitch, oh my dirty mouth, hope Walmir didn't hear me, amen. Where's Kingie? she asked. Over there, Kelly replied.

Kingie was talking to Onofre and Reader at the grog stand. They waved. How's Carolaine? Reader inquired. He hadn't recognized her. Carolaine was very proud of her brother. Without him, the event wouldn't have materialized. It had been Kingie who had succeeded in calming Miltão. To tell the truth, not even José Luís could explain the miracle. That night, after listening to the pleadings of his sister, who had appeared at Kelly's house in tears, distraught, José Luís went to talk to the trafficker, without great hopes of changing the leader's position. Miltão had been snorting a lot recently. Once he was on drugs there was no end to his humiliation of his soldiers. You don't like it? Get the hell out. Fuck you, he said. Fuck up and you'll get a bullet up the ass. Don't ask him for anything, Reader advised. Be careful with him. Yesterday, he reamed out Biga simply because the poor guy forgot to put gas in his car. What a fucker. If he were still a great man, OK, but in reality Miltão is over the hill. A goddamn nothing. Noble, for example, may be crazy, but he never fired on a police helicopter. In his day nobody was mugged here in the favela. And nobody had to pay a toll either. Want my advice? Tell the pastor to go ahead with the festival and fuck it. I want to see Miltão's reaction. Let him burn his bridges with the community. The idiot's not going to cooperate. Know why? Miltão gets some of his greatest kicks from being a prick. That's how he has his fun, by making life hell for others.

In the very first minutes of his talk with the trafficker, even before José Luís could defend the festival, Miltão told him it wasn't necessary to 'bust his balls'. I'm clearing the festival, he said, without further delay. Tell the Bible-thumper that he can pop God's popcorn. That's how Miltão was. Unpredictable.

Without my brother, Carolaine had told the pastor as soon as they learned of the developments, without Zé, that feud of yours would have serious consequences. There was no discord, Walmir had replied. It was he who confronted me. Even so, my love, with or without a feud, without Zé, my dear, the festival would be nothing but a dream, you don't know Miltão. Carolaine, listen, Carolaine, pay attention, you're going to forget yourself and call me 'my love' in front of your mother, Walmir had warned her that day. Oh, damn them all, the girl thought. She was dying to tell the world that she was crazy about Walmir. Even more so now that she was carrying his child. And she hadn't gotten pregnant on purpose. Just the opposite, she had tried to prevent it. She had even consulted a gynecologist, who had prescribed birth control pills. But she forgot to take them. Her head just wasn't good for 'those things'. She would have to tell Walmir that she was pregnant. One thing was certain: the baby would serve to bring a quick solution to the situation. What if they hear you calling me 'love', Carolaine? Walmir had asked that night. What will they think? I don't care what they think about us, she replied. I do, Carolaine. I'm married to Clotilde. Oh lord, the same old story as always, Clotilde, my wife, I'm married, I'm a pastor, what God hath joined together let no man come between. To hell with that blah-blah-blah, Carolaine thought. Besides, you promised to leave Clotilde. Never, Carolaine, never. What I said was that *if* Clotilde were to die someday, a natural death, be it noted, a natural death, we can get married. *If*. I'm a pastor. *If*. A pastor is a role model. A foundation. A point of reference. It had been like that from the beginning, always the same arguments. Carolaine became furious when Walmir started explaining the importance of the pastor for his flock. I'm the one that takes the lead, a creature of God. I'm the arrow. I'm the way. Sometimes Carolaine would go two or three days without speaking to Walmir, to punish him for being married. She didn't know Clotilde. Walmir never brought his wife to church. He would never allow Carolaine to go to the district where he lived. I don't want you to suffer, he said. Why meet Clotilde? You're the one I love, Carolaine. Big deal. He loves me but won't marry me. She couldn't wait to see Walmir's face when she told him about the baby. And Clotilde. What a name. Clotilde is the name of the old-maid aunt in the seven o'clock soap. A tall, skinny woman who's always constipated. That's Clotilde, she would sometimes say, just to irritate him. God hears our words, Carolaine. And what is God doing while you're fucking me, with my clothes on, after the services? Does God close his eyes? Oh, Carolaine, how you martyr me, by exposing my sins in such a cruel fashion. Carolaine liked torturing him when she was angry because of Clotilde. She loved imagining herself revealing to the sheep of Christ, some Saturday night while Walmir was taking his wife and children for pizza, how Walmir had seduced her, right inside the church. There was a small room at the rear, an office, with a cot. It had been there. My God, she told her friend Kelly, in bed the man doesn't even seem like a pastor. He's an animal. Wow. He forgets God completely. Only Kelly knew of the romance. She had sworn 'not to let the cat out of the bag'. But she'd told José Luís everything. Shit. Carolaine is a slut, her brother had said. She loves to fuck up, that fat bitch. Shit. Goddamn it. That stupid woman. I feel like beating the hell out of her. Swear to me, swear you won't fight with her, the poor thing. Shit. Fight, she can go fuck herself, shit. Kelly had also told her mother, Yolanda. The pastor and Carolaine. I knew it. Him with his shirt all buttoned up, he never fooled me. I know womanizers. He has that concentrated way about him, all serious, a man of integrity. But they don't think about anything except their dicks. Screwing the poor girl. Who would've thought it? Did you know, Onofre? Yolanda said later to her friend. About Walmir and Carolaine?

A highly orchestrated festival like that hadn't been held for many years in Berimbau. The children showed up early at the sports area, while the booths were still being assembled. They ran around frantically, trying to help the adults.

Attention, folks, if you want to play bingo, the cards are now being sold by Mr Caju, near the goalpost.

Hi, Mother, said Carolaine to Alzira, who was manning the

green-corn pudding and tapioca custard booth, have you seen Walmir? Alas, with a mustache that Kelly had drawn on him, blue jeans, checkered shirt, and a bandanna around his neck, was playing with an empty pan that his grandmother had given him. I don't know. Caju's looking for him too. He wants the bingo cards. I'm going to look for Walmir, Carolaine said.

On the way to the church, Carolaine, looking at the starry sky and the full moon, felt such a huge sensation of well-being and happiness. She was overcome by the certainty that this was the moment. She would tell of her pregnancy right there, in the church. Of course it wouldn't be easy, but the two of them together, with Christ, would face the situation. If necessary, she herself would talk to Clotilde. The only thing she didn't want to do was tell Alzira. Alzira was so scandalous. So overreacting. She couldn't take the browbeating, the how-hard-life-is and men-are-no-good sermons. Not again. No.

Walmir? Carolaine, when she entered the church, noticed the bingo cards on the floor near the pulpit. Walmir? The lights were on in the small room in the rear. Walmir?

Carolaine slowly approached the door, which was half ajar. When she pushed it open, she saw the pastor lying on the bed on his stomach. The pillow was soaked in blood. The right side of his head was simply not there, and there were pieces of brain even on the wall.

Oh Jesus Christ, screamed Carolaine, kneeling beside the pastor. No. Don't do this to me. Don't leave me alone, Walmir.

With an egg held in the bowl of a spoon clutched between their teeth, men and women were walking rapidly toward the finish line, provoking shouts from the rooting section, Run, run. Children guffawed when the eggs splattered on the ground, Run. And the dogs quickly lapped up the yolks before they were totally absorbed into the soil.

Carolaine made her way haltingly through the crowd around the gymkhanas, the stalls, and the bonfire. Excuse me, out of the way, she said, crying. Carolaine, come see Onofre run like a frog. She didn't hear what they were saying, she could barely see the people in front of her, as if she were walking underwater, her movements slow, her head spinning, the image of her dead lover. Jesus, she said, with your power, don't let him be dead, Jesus, she said, don't abandon me pregnant, even if he were crippled, Walmir, brain-damaged, even without a head she wanted him back, Jesus Christ, who is good, just and powerful, don't leave me without my Walmir. All we're waiting for is the bingo cards, the accordionist announced.

When Carolaine climbed onto the stage, almost no one noticed that her clothes were stained with blood. She took the microphone from the singer's hands, under the curious stares of the residents. Sing, sing, sing, they began to chant, clapping their hands. He's been killed, she attempted to say, her voice failed her. They've killed Pastor Walmir, she said on the second try, between sobs. They put a bullet in his head. Sobs. Over at the church. Sobs.

At first there was a great silence. When the girl's body fell unconscious on the wooden platform, confusion reigned. It was Miltão, someone shouted. The faithful kneeled, crying, praying, asking for justice. Zino, the butcher, climbed onto the platform. Attention. No one wanted to hear him. Listen to the butcher, said the singer. Listen to what he has to say. We're not going to tolerate this kind of thing in our favela, Zino said. We all know who killed our pastor. Yes, screamed the residents, raising their fists. We can't just go home and go to sleep as if nothing had happened. It was Miltão, shouted the residents. We're going to get justice. Yes, they all roared. Vengeance. Justice. What's this crazy suggesting? asked Biga, disturbed at the tumult. If I understood right, answered Reader, he's repeating the advice of an American judge I read somewhere or other and like a lot: 'It's time for us to go home and get our baseball bats.'

Soon, men, women, and children were arming themselves with clubs, knives, and stones, and en masse began scouring the favela looking for Miltão. Several groups of ten and twenty people combed the narrow, winding streets of the hillside, making noise and calling to their windows the few people, most of them elderly, who hadn't gone to the festival. As no one knew for certain the trafficker's address, they wandered about aimlessly. They surrounded and stoned the house of Miltão's sister. They set fire to a drug site.

Miltão wasn't found in any of his hiding places. No one knew anything about him. Someone said he was in Caxias. That's a lie. Murderer.

When they saw the residents taking over the streets, enraged, out of control, resolute, Reader, José Luís, Biga and some other soldiers met outside the favela at a gas station on Avenida Brasil to discuss the matter. There's very little to think about, said Reader. The guy's fucked. I saw a lot going on back there. In the bloodiest Mafia war, I read this in a sensational book, a capo strangled, burned, beheaded, shot, beat, tortured, dissolved in acid, and roasted on a spit several judges, journalists, police chiefs, and a pile of other people who got in his way. I don't think any priests were on the list. None at all. Finito. That's all I have to say. *Fin. Fine.* The end.

Almost everything about Pastor Walmir's life came out at the wake, held at his residence the following morning. The faithful were impressed first by the house in Catumbi, large and luxurious, and by the three cars in the garage. I didn't know he was rich, commented Alzira, observing the bar in one corner of the living room, made of mahogany, with bottles of Scotch whiskey and crystal glasses, the beverages displayed in an impeccable fashion, exactly like in the house of her employer. Look at the rug, she whispered in Carolaine's ear, it's beautiful. Look at the lace curtains. Alzira, who had always admired the pastor blindly, had the sensation that she'd been right upon learning that her mentor was rich. Carolaine, paying no attention to her mother's words, was trying to guess who among those present was Clotilde. And where were the children? Walmir had described to her a graceful little girl with curly hair and a plump little boy with intelligent eyes. The children at the wake were homely, awkward, with kinky hair like Carolaine's. Without curls. Without intelligent eyes. Only crying, sullen people, only mourning and sadness. The kitchen is beautiful,

Alzira told Carolaine after a brief walk through the house. Take a look. The exhaust fan will suck your hair right up. Dona Juliana would love it. He didn't seem rich, she kept repeating. Walmirzinho. He loved my spaghetti. So simple. Like Moses. Moses was a prince, did you know that? Walmir is like Moses, she told everyone. What will become of us without our Moses? How will we cross the Red Sea? Think about it, Carolaine, what a good soul, what other rich man do you know who's a friend of Christ like Walmir?

The coffin, in the center of the living room, had been sealed so his friends would not see the deplorable condition of the cadaver. His head, someone commented, was 'hollowed'. The brain had been blown out. Carolaine, prepared to meet the widow, suffered a crisis of despair when she said hello to Clotilde, a woman of eighty-two, presented as 'Walmir's mother'. You have the same name as the pastor's wife, Carolaine said, confused, choking on the words. No, Walmirzinho wasn't married, the old woman explained. Thank God. No wife, no children to suffer.

Carolaine left Alzira and went outside where she could cry. He wasn't married. Walmir, you lowlife, she said, you lying bastard, you made up a wife just to lead me on, and sobbing, with me pregnant, you scum, and him unmarried. No wife or children to suffer. She felt so wretched. She remembered, not knowing why, Walmir correcting the way she pronounced certain words. You say 'don't have none,' the correct form is 'don't have any,' you say 'pitcher' for 'picture', 'ax' for 'ask', 'seen' for 'saw', we have to correct that. On other occasions, he'd asked her to straighten her kinky hair. Use a gel. Why don't you straighten it? Clotilde straightened hers and it came out fine. Are you going to wear those slippers? he had asked the day of José Luís's birthday. Everyone in the favela wore flip-flops or sneakers, why is he asking? And the way he stared at her as if that were ugly, as if he were different from all the rest, with his black laced shoes. She didn't know why she remembered those episodes. She felt small, betrayed, powerless. Slippers. Why hadn't Walmir simply said he didn't want to get married? A bachelor. And dead. Whatever happens, he would say, I'm on your side. Liar. Curls and intelligent eyes. She was afraid of the future, of being alone. Her belly would grow, a baby would be born, and she was already familiar with that story. Alas had taught her: get fat, give birth, bring up the child. Sad and awful. And then she understood that maybe it was God's punishment. That was it. She had learned something. She had discovered that God didn't care about justice. Once again, she would be the one who would have the baby and suffer the consequences of all the sins committed against her. Lowlife, she repeated.

Upon her return to the living room, her eyes bloodshot and her nose running, she observed two young women weeping copiously around the coffin. Then she noticed another woman, on the sofa, holding her teary face in her hands. A blonde woman was being comforted in the kitchen by friends. I can't accept it, she said, between sobs. And then other memories came into her head, of other young women the pastor helped, of the ladies he had received in the same room in the church where he and Carolaine had sex. I want to have a few words in private with Dona Irene, with Dona Cláudia, oh God, how stupid she'd been, the messages she'd taken down. Tell him that Tânia called, Lúcia, from the post office, what an idiot, always women, lots of women. And everything fit together so perfectly, there was no longer the slightest doubt. I'm a total idiot, thought Carolaine, wiping her eyes. Where did that inclination toward pregnancy and unhappiness come from? The sudden revelation of his countless lovers affected her less than the news that Walmir was single. The lowlife.

At São João Batista cemetery, Alzira pushed through the crowd to get closer to the tomb. I want to see the coffin descend. Oh God, what injustice, to die like an outlaw.

It was a sunny day. Our father who art in heaven, hallowed be thy name. The parasols held high by the throng of the faithful made access to the tomb site even more difficult. Thy will be done, thy kingdom come. I'm pregnant by Walmir, Carolaine whispered in her mother's ear while the women recited the prayer. ·

Alzira fainted. But no one noticed. Several women fainted during the funeral.

As soon as the station wagon's doors were opened by Miltão's soldiers, a strong smell of fresh meat invaded the scene. At first, only the children came up to see what was happening. Free chicken, one of the men explained. A gift from Miltão. You don't have to pay. Take one and go. Free chicken.

From the top of the hill Miltão, who had ordered the chicken stolen from a hypermarket on Epitácio Pessoa to offer to the favela residents, watched the scene through binoculars. When it's time to eat, people clam up, just take a look, everybody's taking the chicken. He laughed loudly.

Reader, who'd been called in for 'a confab', watched the scene in silence. What do you think, Miltão asked, wasn't it a good idea to give out chicken? Tomorrow I'm handing out ground meat. That's so anybody who's pissed at me can see that I'm still the same as I was. Bible-humping sons of bitches. I'm Miltão, the people's friend. I'm boss of Berimbau. Reader, who tried to avoid arousing Miltão's suspicions, agreed with everything. Great. Excellent. Wonderful idea.

Business establishments were in mourning because of Walmir. Many residents were dressed in black, others hung black ribbons in the windows of their shacks.

At every turn Miltão would lay down the binoculars and speak on a cellphone to a girl. How's things, you luscious honey pie? How's that little belly button of yours? The trafficker turned his back on the soldiers and in a cloying, almost infantile tone, poured out his best smooth talk for the girl. Tonight. Yeah? Luscious honey pie. To him, there was no problem in the favela, except for the evangelicals. He wasn't aware that he had lost power and was at risk. Even hearing someone yell Murderer! when he went into Onofre's bar. Even reading 'Down with Miltão' on the walls of the stairways. Even seeing the dispersal of his soldiers. It's all bullshit from the evangelicals. They're against me because I'm against exploitation. I already told my mother, they only care about money. It doesn't have anything to do with God or with Christ. It's all business. All that's missing is a license. I'll fuck those guys in two days. I've ordered Agnaldo to make a list of the assholes who've bothered my family. How am I to blame if somebody killed the preacher? I didn't kill the preacher. Unfortunately. I would've loved to shove a grenade in the fucker's mouth. That shitass Onofre came out with some crap about 'You went too far.' I'll put a bullet in his ass if I hear any more of that drivel. Take a look, he said, picking up the binoculars again. The chicken's all gone, he said, watching the truck through the binoculars. See?

Not far from there, Kingie was waiting for Fake at a bus stop. Kingie had phoned him early that morning to set up a meeting. The time had come to act. Even though he had resisted. When Fake had come to talk to him about Zequinha Bigode's help, he had refused. Shit. You're out of your mind, Reader had said at the time. You know what Zequinha is offering you? A partnership. You're going to be the boss of this ball of shit. You missed your shot at it. Zequinha doesn't give second chances. End of story.

But Kingie, although he disagreed with the acts of stupidity that Miltão was committing, didn't want to be a traitor. No, he'd told Fake that night. I'm out. There's a name for that, Fake had answered: dumb. You're choosing to fuck yourself. Fake had used every argument: Zequinha had told him that Miltão was going to die in any case, Noble had given the order. And when a top dog like that fingers a guy, brother, there's no ifs, ands, or maybes to it. One of these nights somebody'll escape from Padre Moraes and pay Miltão a visit. That's how it'll be. Miltão in bed, fucking some chick. Bang. In the head. If it happened like that, OK. But Kingie wouldn't betray Miltão. Miltão had lifted him out of the mud. It had been Miltão who had seen to his recovery by getting him off drugs. Everything he had he owed to Miltão. Especially in recent times, the trafficker had paid him well.

But after the pastor's death, Kingie had changed his view. Alzira herself had said to him: Do something. Seeing Carolaine crying like that had been horrible.

So that's the story, brother, Fake said, getting off the bus. Let's get something to eat.

They went to a corner lunch stand, ordered turnovers and Coca-Cola. José Luís said he wanted to have a meeting with Zequinha Bigode.

I like what I'm hearing, brother.

Fake went to the pay phone, dialed. He returned and confirmed the meeting. Tonight at nine.

It's a deal.

José Luís had already been up the Marrecos hillside several times, always in the context of war. As a soldier, he knew the entrance well, and the narrow street that led to the bakery was, on those occasions, just one more battle area. In war, the important thing is to locate the target, the enemy, take shelter, find the best angle for attack. That night, however, with stars in the sky and a full moon, going in on a mission of peace, the place seemed completely different to him, very welcoming and organized. Pay phones in several places, ditches for the removal of sewage, lights dotting the entire favela, and good houses. What he liked most was seeing in various spots small signs with street names. A very good idea. José Luís knew that one of the favela dweller's problems, when he looked for a job, was not having an address. This way was better, Rua da Paula, number 5. Problem solved. It was Zequinha's idea, Fake explained, climbing the hill alongside Zé Luís, greeting many of the people he met on the way. Since he had taken over the local radio, the funk rocker had become known to the residents. Zequinha's soldiers, scattered along the route, greeted them warmly. Hey, brother. The man's waiting, they said. Up there. It's not everybody who gets to go up there, explained Fake. Nobody, in fact. Only the top dogs. Suzana really likes you, man.

Zequinha Bigode's house was a fortress, strategically situated in the middle of the poorest shacks in the favela, which afforded him protection. At the door, the two were subjected to a rigorous inspection by the security men. It's always like this,

Fake explained. Even his friends have to be frisked. The two were then led to the living room. Kingie had never imagined such luxury. Shit. A slate floor, colorful rugs, coffee tables with bric-a-brac, shit, velvet sofas. Rich folks, Zé Luís commented in Fake's ear. Miltão really was a piece of crap. Shit. What most impressed him was the amount of imported whiskey on the bar. More than twenty bottles. Real luxury. José Luís tucked in his shirt; the pomposity of the setting made him feel badly dressed. Shit. Tap tap tap, someone was coming down the stairs. José Luís avoiding looking up, waiting with his hands folded in his lap, staring at an arrangement of artificial flowers on a marble-top table. Shit. There she was, beautiful, in shorts, a skimpy blouse, and heels. Shit. So it's you my father's waiting to see? asked Marta, smiling.

20

THE THING IS THIS, Zequinha said categorically, you can kill a merchant that hassles you, or a neighbor who's getting too chummy with some bastard of a cop; and I don't think it's a bad idea to get rid of some gossiping woman if what she says creates problems or loss of personnel. No one approves of killing, naturally, but those of us who want to make money from the sale of drugs can't tolerate people who run red lights. Morally speaking, I accept that certain citizens must be eliminated, Zequinha Bigode continued, cautious, ever alert to the coming-and-going of his daughter in the living room. Martinha, he shouted, go study in your room, I already told you once. In front of him, seated on the red velvet sofa and visibly ill at ease with the luxury of the setting, were Fake and José Luís. Where was I? Zequinha asked. Ah yes, it's no big deal, he continued, to kill a prick, a traitor, some piece of crap, them we kill with no problem. Now then, eliminating a pastor is a much different story. That's going too far. It's placing yourself above God. The pastor is, shall we say, Christ's stand-in on earth, isn't that right? In my opinion, there are people who can't be killed. Priests, for example. Priests and children. We don't kill them. That's anarchy. That's why I'm calm. I'm going to be completely clear: with me there are no maybes. I don't betray. I hate falsity. But it so happens that we're here to talk about the fate of the cur who murdered Berimbau's pastor. Betraying a zero takes away absolutely nothing. Because, when you get right down to it, Miltão fucked everyone. He fucked the evangelicals. He fucked my business. He fucked the community. He fucked Noble, who was an excellent cop-exterminator and a big son of a bitch as well. And all of that because he thinks he's the supreme leader.

It was a long conversation. Zequinha loved to carry on a monologue. He felt important when he used phrases like 'in my personal opinion', 'particularly speaking', and 'the crux of the problem'. What is it, Martinha? Didn't I tell you to stop that roaming around? For heaven's sake, can't I have a conversation in peace?

The girl apologized, claiming she was there merely to pick up the glasses at the request of Suzana, who was in the kitchen preparing some tidbits. I know, I know, her father answered mockingly. Glasses. Curiosity killed the cat, daughter. Get the glasses and clear out. Move, girl. Zequinha winked at Fake and José Luís. That one there, Zequinha confided, loves to overhear my conversations. She's all the time asking to work for me. Can you believe it? She's got guts, that girl, he said proudly. Her birthday's next week. I asked her what she wanted for a present. You know what the little imp said? A Glock pistol. Can you believe it? The three laughed. I almost said: Does it have to have a laser sight too, you silly girl?

Kingie forced himself not to show any interest in the girl, who kept coming and going in the living room, taking her time and opening and closing closet doors and casting glances in their direction. Was it an impression, or had she gestured toward him, designating the rear door to the living room? Confused, he asked permission to use the bathroom. That way, Zequinha said, pointing to a door opposite the one indicated by Marta.

In the lavatory lined with white tiles with flowers in high relief, he observed the reflection of his pallid face in the gold-framed mirror. He had felt an adrenaline overload, tense, ever since he'd seen Marta coming down the stairs in her blue shorts, her hair uncombed. Shit. Fake didn't tell me you were coming too, she'd said. Shit. Marta. He hadn't had time for anything, the questions he wanted to ask, shit, to speak to her, set up a meeting, say everything, I love you, I've been crazy about you since that damned night at the Black Rose, but suddenly, shit, Suzana came into the room, talkative, effusive, Zé dear, how I've missed you, boy, wow, how you've grown. How's Kelly? And Alas? Kingie didn't hear the questions, answered disconcertedly, he could see nothing but Marta, at the foot of the stairs, her bare legs, sandals, her delicate feet exposed. He was so used to seeing ugly feet in the favela, on the bus, at the beach, feet with bunions, calluses, and sores, thick toenails, infested with fungus, even Kelly, who had always been careful, had large, ugly feet with her heels and toes almost spilling out of her sandals, thinking about it, why did women paint their toenails? Marta didn't. Her feet were as pretty as her face, her delicate fingers, her fine, smooth, healthy skin, her clean, trimmed fingernails, shit, José Luís couldn't take his eyes off them. Kelly's fine. Yes, Alas too. Her feet. My mother still works for Dona Juliana, same as always. Alas, yes. To make everything worse, Zequinha came into the living room at precisely the moment that Marta rushed to answer the telephone. It's a pleasure to have in my home a young man who was practically raised by my wife, he'd said solemnly. They shook hands. José Luís couldn't help hearing Marta's words on the telephone. 'Nine o'clock.' 'Me too.' 'Ciao.'

Maybe, José Luís thought, in the bathroom, opening the faucet and splashing cold water on his face, maybe at the other end of the line a boyfriend had made an impassioned declaration of love. Shit. How could Fake have been such a rat? A boyfriend, that's what it had to be. 'Me too' was the reply to 'I love you.' I love you too. Shit. Now he'd missed his chance completely. It was Fake's fault. Maybe she was engaged. A wedding date set.

When José Luís returned to the living room, Suzana had opened a bottle of beer. To cool our heads, she said. Marta wasn't prowling around anymore, nor was Fake there. You know, Zé, she said, offering him a glass, we have to do like the politicians. Build alliances. Suzana sat beside her husband, and they took each other's hand. Where had Fake gotten to? I'm from Berimbau, she said, I have a great interest in what we decide here tonight. Yes, stated Zequinha, even though Suzana lives here, she was born in Berimbau, and I want to live in peace with my wife's birthplace. The couple looked at each other, in love. José Luís wanted to ask about Fake, it bothered him that

172

his friend might be off in some corner with Marta. Shit, that's all I needed. As far as I'm concerned, the matter is already resolved, Zequinha assured them, but it so happens that Miltão keeps on making trouble, the cur. That son of a bitch Fake. I can't even visit my mother, Suzana confessed. Really, the 'Berlin Wall' was the last straw, said Zequinha, referring to the barbed wire that Miltão had ordered installed on the border between the two favelas to prevent residents from crossing freely. Only with my permission, Miltão had decreed. Anybody coming in will be shot.

Where's Fake? Kingie asked. Outside, Suzana answered, this isn't a matter for him. Listen. Since the war started, I always said: Miltão doesn't let things go, he doesn't forget. He's mental. The guy snorts, smokes, drinks, and spends his time coming up with a way to fuck people over, he still plans to kill me, I can't sleep nights because of it. Shit, that's all I need, Fake and Marta together, shit. When Zequinha leaves the house, I shake with fear, I can't sleep, said Suzana. Woman, complained Zequinha, I don't want José Luís to think we're afraid of Miltão, sweetheart. Forgive me, love, but it's fear, she affirmed, and Zé here is like my son, I can tell him. Fear of that piece of garbage, yes sir. I'm shit scared. Outlaws, ghosts, the police, earthquakes, nothing makes me shudder. But crazies do frighten me. Miltão is crazy. Shit, that son of a bitch Fake, if he's got something going with Marta, I don't even want to think about it. I'll kill the guy. Every day I hear the same old thing, Suzana continued, Miltão is fucked, he doesn't have any soldiers, no money, but somehow the man hangs on. How many have we killed in this war? Only Miltão doesn't die. I've thrown away seven cellphones and I can guarantee you the prick knows the number I'm using now. I answer, and he's at the other end of the line, breathing heavy. He used to call to whine. Come back to me, he'd say. He forgave me. He loved me. Of course he loves you, said Zequinha, a gorgeous woman like you, the guy can't accept losing you. No, Zequinha, it's got nothing to do with love, Suzana replied. It has to do with getting kicked in the ass. The guy still hasn't accepted it. Suzana, said her husband affectionately, stay calm, let me talk with Zé, please, angel, everything's going to be all right, my little flower. Love-bunny, treasure, that was how they addressed each other. I just want to ask the two of you for one favor, she said, before leaving the room: settle this shit right away. Put an end to it.

That Fake is a real fucker. Shit.

I can explain, hey, wait, brother, what is this? asked Fake, warding off the punches that José Luís threw at him as they descended the Marrecos hillside. Shit. You said you didn't know any Marta, José Luís said, irritated, pushing his friend. It was almost ten at night, the few people still on the favela's poorly lighted streets looked at the two with curiosity, not knowing whether they were playing or really fighting. Out with it, Fake, you lying SOB, shit. Easy, brother, I'll explain. Can I talk? Easy.

Fake admitted that he had met Marta when Zequinha called him in to ask a favor. The brother was crazy about Suzana and wanted me to take a package to her, he knew I was 'friends' with a friend of Suzana's, you don't know the chick, I had an affair with her. Shit, José Luís interrupted, this topic's starting to smell, you were Zequinha's informant, is that it? Don't diss me, brother. There's no ratting in this story, I never leaked shit to Zequinha, all I did was take some presents to Suzana, nothing else. I'm clean. My thing is rap, funk, soul. I'm out of the war.

In reality, Fake had been working for Zequinha for two years. He received a generous salary for keeping the leader of the Marrecos favela informed about important drug transactions in Berimbau. Even during the time he was in prison, Fake had been working for Zequinha. Each week he would pass along to the trafficker the information that Kingie brought during his visits. Hours later, Fake would regret not having told his friend the complete truth. Yes, he was an informant, he betrayed Miltão, but wasn't José Luís betraying him too? What about Reader? And Biga? Hadn't Miltão himself betrayed Noble? And Noble had killed his predecessor, Josué. And Josué had murdered his best friend, Janjão. They were all traitors. At that moment, however, as they descended the hill, these arguments didn't occur to him. He denied it with such conviction that José Luís believed his story. He spoke about his first meeting with the girl at Zequinha's house, Marta was listening to a cool stereo, our talk became synchronized, we spoke about technotrance, house, groove, techno, acid techno, that's what it was, a real gabfest, we exchanged phone numbers, we went out a few times, just as friends, we never got involved, she enjoyed being at my sound console, at the Fogosa, watching the people dance. Except that one day Zequinha called me, fucking mad. Stay away from Marta, he said. He didn't explain or anything. That was before you met her at the Black Rose. Brother, I've been around, and I don't want hassles with Zequinha. I don't want it and it's not going to happen. That's why I clammed up when you asked about Marta. That's the reason, brother. And if you want my advice, forget her. You're asking for trouble.

The rest of the walk to the bus stop took place in silence. José Luís was confused by all that had happened. There were so many important things to be done, so many things to organize, shit, the talk with Zequinha, everything to be planned, men, weapons, plots, and still he could think about nothing but Marta. Shit.

A car horn sounded, requesting to be allowed through. José Luís stepped aside, opening the way. Zé, someone shouted. He looked, saw Marta getting out of a red Mitsubishi station wagon driven by her older sister, Priscilla. Hi, she said, approaching them. Fake scratched his head, I knew it, brother. You forgot this on the sofa, Marta said, placing a small envelope in José Luís's hands. Ciao.

Later, locked in Kelly's bathroom, Kingie read with difficulty Marta's handwriting: 'Saturday, after 11 p.m., go to Rua Nossa Senhora da Paz, number 1230, apartment 709b. It's important. Kisses. Marta.'

Whatever they say, whatever they think,/ I'm not doing anything, and neither are you, the record spinning on the turntable, at maximum volume, laughter, animated conversations, the atmosphere was festive, exactly as Onofre, the organizer of the *feijoada* in Rosa Maria's honor, had dreamed. Paper-covered tables stood in front of the bar with steaming trays of dried beef, pork sausage, pigs' feet and pigs' tails surrounded by those whom Onofre termed 'people who really matter': Reader, the musicians and the standard-bearer from the Unidos do Berimbau samba school, some merchants, the president of the neighborhood association, and old colleagues from Rosa Maria's former life.

Onofre hadn't left his friend's side since she got out of the taxi that late Saturday afternoon. Rosa Maria looked wonderful. She's even whiter, Onofre thought. C'mere, you dirty old man. They hugged. You old goat, how did your gut manage to get even bigger, huh? Must be a long time since you saw your wee-wee in the shower. Guffaws. More hugs. Let's go on up, the folks are waiting for you.

There was an air of happiness and prosperity to Rosa Maria's arrival. They said she was a countess, a duchess, an ambassador's wife, that she was married to a very important man, a rich German, who satisfied her every desire. No one any longer remembered her past as a prostitute. Look at my shoes, Onofre. I'm wearing Chanel. It's French. Who's that there, Didi? My God, Didi looks like some outlaw. He's in with Miltão, I'll bet. Come here, Didi, she said. Don't touch my *tailleur*, shorty. Take this. Some coins. It's yours to keep, you hear? Oh, she said, looking at the pitiful shacks, the poor children surrounding her, asking for things, none of this has changed at all, Onofre. The same shit as ever.

Heinrich hadn't come to Brazil because of duties in his firm. That was all Rosa Maria said about her husband. To tell the truth, she didn't know much more; communication with Heinrich was very difficult, and to make matters worse, Heinrich was annoyed at his wife's slowness in mastering the new language. Rosa Maria claimed to be trying as hard as possible, with classes daily, but in reality her teacher Augusta, an elderly, extremely lonely Portuguese woman, was really the one profiting from the lessons. Besides having gained a generous friend who taught her to do the samba and to prepare oxtail, her Portuguese was becoming richer and more fluent by the day. She was very curious about the latest slang terms. Now, when something pleased her, whatever it might be, from an apple pie to a luxury car, she would say in her strong continental Portuguese accent, That's *show*.

It's a hard language, Onofre, and the Germans themselves are hard. Nobody likes to kiss. Friendly hugs, showing fondness just isn't their thing. Heinrich was like a piece of wood with me at first. The poor man didn't even know how to caress somebody. It's upbringing. A stiff people. And they don't like blacks, those palefaces, I know that now. They're all the time looking at me out of the corner of their eyes. I don't let it get to me. You know who invented German, Onofre? It was a genius. You know what a verb is? Go, eat, those things. Well, the Germans stick the verb at the end of the sentence, they talk talk talk talk talk and then tack on the verb over in the next county. It gets to be funny. Now I'm not sure if it's the verb or the subject they stick at the end. You know what a subject is? I'm a subject, you're another. You, we, they. I'll have to ask Augusta.

Rosa Maria was staying at the Copacabana Queen. You know why, Onofre? They had it in for me, those snooty doormen, who were all the time shooing me off the sidewalk. You know, Onofre, one of them recognized me. He was an old goat like you who was always giving me a hard time back in the days when I was hooking. I couldn't even look at the hotel, they don't allow whores around there. Or anywhere, for that matter. In the whole world, Onofre, even in Germany, they don't like whores. In 'Yolland', they tell me, they sit in show windows, like pieces of meat in a supermarket freezer. I cried when they told me that. What a humiliation. And in Europe, no less. If it was in Ceará I could understand it. But, getting back to the subject, that old goat of a doorman at the Copacabana Queen, when he saw me all dolled up, having drinks by the pool, sashaying around in Chanel and all the rest, you should have seen his face. At first he didn't understand. A cool black woman, making it in life, guys like that can't stand it, because they're all getting fucked over, making shitty wages and seeing a lousy little future ahead of them. The old goat kept staring at me, staring at me, and finally got up the courage to say, with a sour expression,

I've been following your success, ma'am. And does it hurt, my man? Does my success hurt a lot? My very words. You know, Onofre, it's very good to have a nice house, nice shoes, food in the refrigerator, but the best part of all is to be able to see, every day when I wake up, the pained look on the doormen at the Copacabana Queen.

During the *feijoada*, Rosa Maria was busy listening to the residents. With the exception of Reader (who remained on the alert for movement among Miltão's soldiers), everyone was there mainly to ask for money, money for a day-care facility, for the samba school, medicine, crutches, a roof, food, shoes, wheelchairs, money to build the sewage system, operations for varicose veins and cataracts. But only the Unidos do Berimbau samba school profited from Rosa Maria. After the show, with twenty uniformed drummers and mulatto women dancing, Rosa Maria, drunk by then, pledged a generous donation.

At eleven that night, when everyone had left, Rosa Maria, sitting at the bar, barefoot, was massaging her feet and still talking to Onofre. She was thinking about taking the daughter of a friend to live with her in Germany. Remember Dadá? Her daughter. I'm going to take her. I went by there yesterday. If the girl stays here she'll end up a prostitute, I know that. Not that she wants to be one. But Dadá thinks it's better to be a prostitute than a maid. And deep down, she's right. Look at Alzira, slaving her life away. If she were a whore, maybe she'd suffer less. Or not. I don't know. But I like the girl. She's nice, a pretty little mulatto. Clever as the devil. I don't want her to be a whore. And I also need someone to help me around the house. You know, a girl to do the dishes, some cleaning, do my nails, you know how it is? Germans, Onofre, don't have servants.

The most emotional moment of the night was when Rosa Maria took from her delicate purse a small package the size of a pack of cigarettes. For you. Onofre, choked up almost to the point of tears, opened it. Is it the Swiss knife? he asked, disappointed at the object's size. I thought it was bigger, because of being Swiss and everything, he said. This isn't one of those big knives like they use in the North, Onofre. The advantage is that it's small. Look, it fits in my pocket. Onofre became more excited as Rosa Maria put the knife through its paces. You can pick your teeth, cut and polish your nails, undo screws, open bottles of beer, take out corks, jab the belly of some punk trying to rob you, all with just one tool that fits in the palm of your hand. Are the Swiss that economical? Onofre asked. The Swiss, Onofre, invented the Swiss watch, the one that never loses time. Even though it does no good in Brazil. Over in Europe, nine o'clock means nine o'clock, not ten after nine or nine-thirty, people show up on time, which I have to admit is irritating. Heinrich has a knife just like this one.

Suddenly, after the noise of an explosion, the lights in the bar went off.

Terrified, Rosa Maria threw herself to the ground. Oh my God, she said, I don't want to die without going back to Germany.

Kingie, after blowing up the electric generator and cutting off light to the Berimbau favela, briefed his thirty men to climb the hillside, always with an eye toward the protection provided by the shacks. He separated them into groups of ten, assuming command of one, and putting Biga and Carlito in charge of the other two. Most of the soldiers and weapons had been lent by Zequinha. It was a sophisticated arsenal from South Korea, Germany, and the United States, precise, powerful weapons with plenty of ammunition. As the one responsible for the armaments from the Marrecos favela, Kingie had spent two entire days familiarizing himself with the equipment. The soldiers themselves were top-quality, as José Luís soon discovered. Zequinha had of course given him the best: Ratão, Zé Miguel, Louriva, Black Cat, and Lizard, men who were in the drug trade to make money, professionals, as Reader said. Zequinha's men were experienced, many of them from years in prison, all quite skilled at pulling a trigger.

Reader had helped José Luís greatly in the days preceding the attack. They talked, discussed strategy. In moments of doubt, Reader gave him moral support. Of course you're taking the right position, he said. We have to end this war. Spending more time killing and dying than making money is a terrible thing, as that big Mafia chief put it. The fact is that Miltão was dragging us down into the mud. He likes fighting, killing, creating confusion. And without peace there can be no traffic. Just look, we can't do anything, the police are always camped out here. This way our hands are tied, Reader said. And in any case Miltão is going to die because he's a fool. If he were a reasonable type he would've already gotten the hell out. But Miltão can't see his hand in front of his face. To him, everything is fine, everything is cool. Just yesterday he said to me: I only trust two people, you and Kingie. That proves he's unfit to lead.

It was only Saturday afternoon that José Luís became aware that the invasion would be that night. Zequinha had told him to be on the alert, that the attack would come any day, at the moment he considered most opportune. That was the way Zequinha worked, through surprise, even his allies had little information about his movements. Fake had brought him the word. Today, why today? José Luís had asked, concerned about his meeting with Marta that night. He was disturbed at the thought that they wouldn't see each other and wanted to find some means of communicating with Marta. He even asked Fake for the phone number at Zequinha's house. Brother, I have just three words for you: no fucking way.

That night, climbing the Berimbau hillside under heavy fire, José Luís thought only of Marta. He had waited such a long time for her, he didn't want to die without having known love. He liked thinking of Marta in those terms, his true love. Before her there had been no one. Love. Even Kelly, who was such a friend, so good, generous, honest, a companion, meant nothing compared to Marta. The fact of fighting alongside the men her father had handpicked to support him also gave him a feeling of destiny, the assurance that all had been plotted so that in the end he and Marta would be together and be happy. He wouldn't die.

The combat lasted three hours. His men advanced rapidly, some of them were very familiar with the steep, narrow streets of the Berimbau favela.

Miltão's soldiers surrendered when Kingie's troops reached the top of the hill. There was no resistance. Only Miltão continued firing from the window of one of the rooms of his shack. It was José Luís himself who killed him, and the act gave him neither satisfaction of any kind nor a sense of victory, although his companions resoundingly praised his performance. José Luís upheld the tradition of the great leaders of the Rio de Janeiro drug traffic. He dragged Miltão's body to Onofre's bar, fired his machine gun into the sky, and announced that from that moment on Berimbau was under his command.

Zequinha had prepared everything. The idea of losing the war had never occurred to him. His men were at their posts. As soon as José Luís signaled, vans came to take the bodies away to clandestine cemeteries on the Jacaré road. Thirty armed soldiers occupied strategic positions in the favela, protecting the access points, the homes of Kelly, Alzira, Cândida, and the shack where, theoretically, José Luís would spend the night.

No one celebrated the victory. In reality, the residents didn't exactly comprehend what was going on between the traffickers. Among his old friends, only Reader was there to greet José Luís. It was also Reader who arranged for a car to take him secretly to Nossa Senhora da Paz. It was almost two in the morning. En route, José Luís squeezed the note from Marta in his pocket, with the address where they would meet. He was on the way to happiness, he thought, satisfied. That is, if happiness was still there, waiting for him.

SHIROTA CHEESE. LIVE LACTOBACILLI, fermented milk, fruit pulp yogurt. Dannon pineapple, coconut, and strawberry flavors. Parmalat milk drink, liquid yogurt in a liter bottle. Pasteurized cheese, vitamin-enriched toddy. Tang, shake before using. Cream cheese. Dream Whip. Caramel. Marshmallow. Neapolitan ice cream. Orange juice, 100 percent natural, ready to drink. Chocolate milk. Lite mayonnaise. A loaf of sliced bread. Standing before the refrigerator, José Luís gazed at all the products jamming the shelves. He loved it. His favorite was yogurt. He still remembered the first time he'd seen a container of Dannon, many years before. Alzira had worked as a cleaning lady for a ballet dancer, Renata was her name, a pretty, healthy woman. Renata's refrigerator was always full of cosmetics, fruit, cheese, and yogurt. José Luís had been intrigued by the packaging of the Dannon strawberry yogurt with its pink metallic lid displaying a drawing of the fruit. You can have one, Renata had said when she found him in front of the refrigerator. But Alzira had grabbed it from the boy's hands. No, she'd said, he doesn't want it, and later, out of Renata's presence, had slapped his face. That, Alzira had said, is so you'll learn not to touch other people's things. From that day on, Dannon came to occupy a kind of special category, as did pears, meat, condensed milk, and whipping cream, products that his mother would never buy at the supermarket. When Alzira went shopping, she seemed afraid of the colorful bins, fled from the crackers, the enriched cookies, the malted milk, the powdered chocolate, the cake mixes, and the canned soups that were always appearing in TV commercials. She would only get the basics, rice, beans, oil, flour, noodles, That's stuff for rich people, she answered Carolaine when the girl would ask her to buy something.

Now that he was leader of the Berimbau favela, José Luís kept a brand-new refrigerator in his office, a shed located at the top of the hillside, full of sweets, although he ate only the yogurt. Everything else was devoured by his right-hand man, Fake, Brother, just look at my stomach, and by the men he trusted: Lobo, Negaço, Mário Paula Rodrigues, known as Paula, Cachaça, and Reader. Since I started working in 'the business' ('the business' was how they now referred to the drug traffic), I've been putting on weight, said Negaço, whose only regret was not being able to smoke marijuana anymore as he'd done in the old days, to 'work up an appetite and hit the fridge'. José Luís's men were forbidden to use drugs. They're bad for the health, Reader said.

Fake was José Luís's private secretary. He answered the phone, hired soldiers, made payments, and arranged the secret meetings with his boss's new girlfriend, Marta, daughter of Zequinha Bigode. Actually, when he set up his 'basic team', Kingie had been fearful about his relationship with his friend, for everyone suspected that Fake had been Zequinha's informant, and his behavior vis-à-vis the ethics of trafficking had never been exemplary. Reader had been against including Fake, but José Luís thought it would be easier to control his friend if he were close at hand. You're on thin ice, and if you screw up, shit, man, I personally will fuck you but good, man.

Fake still wore dreadlocks, flashy glasses, piercings and glitter, but he no longer nursed the dream of making a demo tape and becoming famous. Now he was a businessman. Business, he repeated all the time. Money. We're going to make it big. He had given up funk dances but hadn't stopped listening to James Brown ('I'm black and I'm proud') or talking for hours on end about trance, acid techno, and other psychedelic sounds. He had spread the infection to his comrades, Negaço was now humming parts of 'Flesh Tones' and Reader found it amusing when one of them would start regurgitating ideas from one of the fanzines forever scattered around the office, with phrases like 'Rap isn't music, it's movement.'

That morning, José Luís opened a yogurt, coconut flavor. He sat in his chair and gestured for Fake to send in the 'next complaint'. He had already attended to several residents that day. Most of the women were domestics like his mother. They would come in smelling of soap, their clothes clean and their faces etched with suffering, and José Luís, however he tried, could not avoid concentrating on whatever was the worst thing about each person, dandruff, varicose veins, fungal infections, wounds and dark stains on the skin, the feet, shit, the ruined toenails, shit, broken and grotesquely painted, shit, the enamel always old and peeling, red, pink, white, and all of them complaining about the same things, threats, mudslides, desertions, mistreatment, shit, quarrels, insults, conflicts, and especially the robberies. They stole the wash basin, they would say, a towel, a bag of potatoes, a hubcap, a hoe, a bowl, a sandal.

The most serious case of the day had been Maria das Dores. I pay for gas, electricity, the installment on my refrigerator, everything on time, she had said. I pay the water bill, Social Security, the girl's day-care center, I pay everything and don't get behind, but now I'm out of work, how am I going to pay the rent? And the man is a curse, she said, referring to Valdo, the manager of the rental agency, he threatens all the time that he's going to beat me, take away my stove, just think about it, take away a stove. Is it right for them to take away our stove?

José Luís told his men to bring Valdo to the office. Valdo had worked in the traffic in Miltão's day and had been converted by the church of the Flock of the Purest Love of Our Lord Jesus Christ. Now he worked as a rent collector for one of the three local real estate agencies. His reputation as a 'mean man' was much worse than in the time when he had gone around armed and killed Miltão's enemies.

In less than ten minutes, Valdo was standing before José Luís, full of arguments. Those people, those quarrymen, those doormen and nannies, those domestics, the people nowadays are lazy, and that's the truth, any little thing, their employer yells at them or complains about the grub, they ditch the job and I'm the one who gets fucked. These people from the backwoods always manage somehow to get their dried meat and squash, there's never a shortage of that. But they don't pay their rent. The shack is a wreck, Das Dores said, the piece of crap is sinking. You're lying, Dona Das Dores. The woman laughed. That's a good one, she replied, now I'm 'Dona', yesterday I was 'you tramp' and 'you deadbeat'.

How much does Dona Das Dores owe you? José Luís asked. Two months' rent, the man answered. OK. Here it is, said the trafficker, handing him a wad of bills. And, starting today, Das Dores will only resume paying when she finds work. Tell the people at the agency. Understand? And you, Dona Das Dores, start looking for work this very day.

The community's problems were solved in this manner, without argument, and as a result thieves stopped stealing, husbands stopped beating their wives, exploiters stopped exploiting, and Zino, the butcher, stopped selling tainted meat.

The ritual was repeated every Monday. Even before he arrived at the office a line of residents had already formed, waiting to make their complaints. The idea had been Reader's. We need to protect the favela residents, he'd said when José Luís took power. There's only one way to keep the police off our backs: we do their dirty work for them. We keep watch, we enforce the law, we hand out beatings, justice, we kill the unmanageable ones, and we bring order. In plain language, we have to solve the residents' problems ourselves. Or rather, *you* have to, José Luís. You have to take care of these poor fucked-over people. And don't even dream of dogging it. Open your ears and let them pour out all their shit on you. And when you feel like you can't take it anymore, remember those stories I read to you, about that cocaine kingpin who had a private zoo in his house. Or that Italian who gave his friend a solid gold bathtub. And think also about how we work like slaves, distributing the drugs, it's a step toward the next level. But that's another story.

It had also been Reader's idea to train a group specifically for stealing cars, as a way of raising money for the trade. Now things are different, he would tell them during the training sessions, forget everything you learned with Miltão. We're not murderers, thieves, criminals. We're not sons of bitches. We're businessmen. This thing we have here is a business, he told them constantly. So therefore, no one is going to kill or rape.

Zequinha Bigode lent the weapons for the robberies, taking 30 percent of the profit. In the future, Reader said, we'll have our own weapons and our business plan. But for now, we'll do like a fireman climbing a ladder: one step at a time.

A former policeman fenced the stolen cars, paying his suppliers according to the 'market price': nine hundred for domestic-made cars less than a year old, double that amount for imports. With the money, José Luís bought the cocaine and marijuana to stock the fourteen drugs sites he had taken over.

That morning, while he waited for one more resident to come in, José Luís thought with a certain degree of pride that the favela wasn't what it used to be. Shit. The community had taken Miltão's death with equanimity. The next morning, José Luís's soldiers had washed away the bloodstains from the wall of the day-care center, where the executions had taken place, and done whatever they could to erase any signs of combat. At Onofre's, someone had pasted up a new report of Miltão's death. Settling Accounts, the headline read. He deserved it, José Luís's friend said. Good riddance. Everything was going well, except Fake was running behind schedule, and shit, what's the matter, Fake? Goddamn, he's late, said José Luís, looking at his watch. Eleven-fifteen. He was already late for his meeting with Reader. He stood up to get another yogurt from the refrigerator. He wouldn't see anyone else that day, he decided, at the exact moment that his office door opened and Fake came in, with Alzira.

It was the first time mother and son had met since José Luís had taken control of the drug traffic in Berimbau.

O St Expeditus, Alzira had prayed that morning, kneeling before the bed, saint of the hopeless sheep, hear my plea: don't let my son be a good leader for the outlaws. Let him be expelled from the drug traffic, alive. Alzira had been suffering many disappointments lately. I'm eating the Devil's bread, she told Dona Juliana as her employer was having breakfast. The advantage of all this is that when the world comes to an end, I'm not going to spend a thousand years, pardon my language, shitting and pissing fire, as they say around here. I've paid for my sins, thank God. I've worked like a horse. Look at this sore growing. It looks like a flower in spring. Bigger every day. Here's your coffee. It's the sickness. It's Caroline pregnant. Here's your diet cracker.

She hadn't yet had the heart to tell Dona Juliana that her son, the little boy who'd been a messenger in Mr Rodrigo's firm, who'd stolen money from the office, was now the leading outlaw in the Berimbau favela. She was very ashamed of her son. Sweetener, everything's here, anything else? I've been walking a hard road, Dona Juliana, since they killed the pastor. Life is sad without the pastor. Sheep need their shepherd. Alzira was no longer angry at Walmir for getting Caroline pregnant, she believed the stories the girl told her, that the two of them had been planning to marry soon. See the bad luck, Dona Juliana? I'm really suffering. Dying just before the wedding. And this whatever-it-is in my leg to torment me.

Everything she was told would heal her, Alzira had already tried; she had covered the lesion with coffee grounds, sugar, paste from *babosa* leaves, many kinds of ointment, but the ulcer kept growing. You have to go to the doctor, her employer had told her. And put down that bucket. Put down that ladder. Leave early today and get some rest, Alzira. Juliana was in reality thinking about a way of getting rid of her long serving maid. It bothered her the way she treated Fernando, always genteel, smiling in her best 'I-know-all-about-it' manner. You can't imagine how happy Alzira looks when I come home and she says, Mr Fernando called. (Which reminds me, he hasn't called me for a week. Did you know that, Alice, a week?) You'd think he was *her* lover. That makes sense, said Alicinha, laughing. That Gatorade hunk! Who wouldn't want him? Dear, go fuck yourself, and take that chocolate out of my sight, please, why do you always have those damned Swiss chocolates in your house, Alicinha? Look how I've put on weight.

Alzira had no inkling that her employer was getting ready to move against her. She was too busy suffering to notice anything. And though she said that what was wrong was the ulcer on her leg, what in fact tormented her was thinking of her son as leader of the drug trade in Berimbau. She had heard terrible stories in church, told by converted outlaws. And all of them had pointed out the dangers of Satan, a new refrigerator, money, a good house, meat every day, and then he would come in person, Lucifer, the demon, to collect his debt. Alzira had decided to accept nothing that her son offered her. She hadn't accepted it before, 'much less now,' she told Jesus Christ while she washed clothes or scrubbed the floor. She regretted that Carolaine didn't follow her example. Her daughter had ceased to be what Alzira called a 'sheep of Christ'. She didn't read the Bible, didn't pray, and no longer suffered over the church of the Flock of the Purest Love of Our Lord Jesus Christ having closed its doors. She runs around like a rabbit, Alzira thought, always going to shopping centers, wearing shorts, spending all her time with Suzana, another outlaw's wife, and Kelly. Deliver us from sin, O Lord.

That morning, Alzira had left for work late. Near the bus stop she had noticed a parked VW minivan. It hadn't been the car that caught her attention. Who was that shirtless man, the one scratching his belly? Was it possible? No. No way. Never. Merciful God, it *is* him. Yes, it was Francisco. The lowlife. The cur. And in a car, on top of everything. Who had given him the car?

Now, facing her son, Alzira demanded explanations. Yes, it was true. Francisco was living in Berimbau, José Luís explained. Yes, he had brought his father to the favela. He'd given him the minivan so he could make deliveries. For you? Alzira asked. No, Mother, he's going to live off what he makes on his own, José Luís explained.

Alzira, flustered in front of her son, felt that her body was giving out. She thought about asking her son why he had done that, but she realized the reason didn't matter. Nothing mattered. She didn't want to know. Damn them, both of them. To the Devil with them. Because he's my father, José Luís would have answered, with the same simplicity with which he had told the truth to Francisco a month before, on the day he moved in. Francisco had been suspicious when he saw the shack, not thinking himself worthy of all that and not understanding why the youth was so concerned with him. I don't have any money, he'd said. I won't do any dirty work. I'm your son, Kingie had replied. They didn't exchange another word. Francisco went into his new house and lay down, looking at the roof and the solid walls, while José Luís went up the hillside, carrying his new machine gun.

José Luís had taken his father to Alcoholics Anonymous. He had closely watched his struggle to give up the vice. He had seen him admire Carolaine from a distance, lacking the courage to approach her. Seen him take Alas in his arms, overcome with emotion. And now his mother was there, saying unpleasant things. Francisco deserted you and Carolaine. Shit, Mother, listen. I'm not listening to anything, Zé, that leprous cur ruined my life, and you, José Luís, you, you must be on marijuana, smoking marijuana and using those awful things, that has to be it, because a son with his head on straight wouldn't cause his mother such unhappiness. Shit, Mother, shouted José Luís, losing his temper, listen to what I'm going to say, for shit's sake.

Alzira rose with difficulty, her eyes filled with tears. I'm not listening to anything, she said. José Luís rushed to help her. Don't touch me, she said, you're full of sin. I'm not listening to anything. I'm not interested in what you have to say. Not at all. Stay with your father. Stay with drugs. With outlaws. You don't love your mother, she said before leaving.

José Luís thought about shaking Alzira and yelling at her, shit, saying there was nothing wrong with helping his father, goddamn it, living near his father, protecting his father, loving him, but it was as if his body wouldn't obey his orders, remaining motionless in his swivel chair, watching Alzira move away, slowly, heavily, limping toward the door. Her sharp voice had seared into his flesh like a bullet. You don't love your mother, she had said. Goddamn. Like a bullet. Not love his own mother. A terrible sensation of unhappiness rose in his chest. Shit. You don't love your mother, she'd said. The truth was there, as visible and palpable as his new AR-15, capable of firing 800 rounds per minute. It was hard to admit it, but it was the truth. It's very sad not to love your own mother.

Mongrels picked up off the streets, hungry, mangy, and unprotected, and also thoroughbreds bought in kennels, strong, ferocious, fearsome, the offspring of champions, large dogs. José Luís was constantly surrounded by dogs, every time he descended the hill the pack went with him, a kind of court, the excited dogs around their sovereign, and other dogs, from the houses, would join the cortege, beside the residents, who like the dogs flattered and greeted the new leader. A veritable spectacle, said Reader. 'Doggie style,' Negaço called it, amid guffaws. The only thing I don't have is a poodle, José Luís explained to his comrades, I can't look at a poodle without wanting to kick its ass.

That day, as he descended with his dogs, Hi, Anderson, to meet Reader, hi, Gisele, José Luís felt satisfied, up, despite the unpleasantness with his mother. Hi, Christian, he was truly happy, and it had nothing to do with power, hi, Daniel, or with fame, hi, Kleber, or with weapons, hi, hi, it had a simple, fine explanation: Marta. The Saúde de Ferro pharmacy. It had been a month since their first romantic encounter, but Kingie remembered every detail. Hi, Dona Cida. 3 × 4 photos while you wait. It had been in an apartment in Copacabana lent by a girlfriend of Marta's. Guimarães Hydraulics. Hi, Mr Vado. Viagem Azul Auto Mechanics. Want to see something? Marta had asked, putting a piece of bubble gum in her mouth. Pop, pop, pop, she blew enormous bubbles, one after the other, with amazing speed. Nobody's better at this than I am, the girl had said, pop, and shit, it was true, pop. Marta did that very well, and pretty, shit, bubbles, pop, one after the other, pop, pop.

The two were awkward at first, with nothing to talk about. José Luís never felt adequate in such situations, starting a story, conversing. What is it? she asked, laughing, what's wrong with my legs? Take off the sneakers, José Luís requested, and she did so, you have the most beautiful feet in the world, he said. You think so? Yes. Then why don't you kiss my feet? she said, and that's exactly what José Luís did, kissing them and then moving his lips upward, her legs, and then he pulled her to the sofa, kissing her on the mouth, slowly. There were many kisses, promises, before beginning what Marta would later call 'that fantastic fuckfest'. Who was that fat girl with you at the beach? Marta asked when José Luís was putting on his clothes to leave. She didn't let him talk about Kelly. Pop. I don't give a damn about her, Marta said. I'm warning you, I'm jealous. I only want to do this if it's the real thing. If you want to see me again, tell that fat girl that it's over between you. Pop. All over. Today. Marta repeated, all over for Fatso. And one more thing, my father can't know about us. Pop.

You didn't have to tell me you were in love, was Kelly's only comment when José Luís broke off the relationship. The conversation between them had been very sad, Kelly sitting barefoot on the kitchen steps, trying to wipe away the tears before they rolled down her cheeks. Kelly was sensational. And Yolanda too. Both of them. Wonderful. Shit. He felt great affection for both of them, would do anything to keep them from suffering, shit, pay their bills. What do you need, Yolanda? Take this extra money. Meat. A cellphone. A stolen car. Kelly's going to find a good boyfriend, he'd told Yolanda. But not one like you, the woman had replied. What did you expect? Marta asked, in bed, lying naked on top of José Luís. You're the big man in Berimbau. Pop. The leader. The owner. The fat girl wasn't going to be stupid enough to pick a fight with you. There's nothing sensational about it. In fact, I've never met a sensational woman in my life. What you mostly find is lowlifes. José Luís didn't want to fight with Marta. But the truth is that there were lots of sensational women in the world, and Kelly was one of them. After ending the romance, José Luís went on living in Yolanda's house for five more days and was treated very well. Yolanda had helped the trafficker find and rent a new house. And it had been Yolanda who had bought the furniture and set everything up. And Kelly took care of his father on a daily basis, taking him food and doing his laundry. For all these reasons, José Luís didn't like it when Marta referred to Kelly and Yolanda as 'those hussies'. The mother is a procuress, imagine letting her daughter sleep with her boyfriend! But he was so much in love with Marta that he forgave it all, laughed at her jealousy, and pretended to be amused by the terrible nicknames his girlfriend gave Kelly: the fat girl, the sack of potatoes, the Virgin Mary of Berimbau, the local good girl, the walking basket case, and the more they made love, the more his love grew, shit, he was always so hungry for Marta that it was a kind of vice, of hunger, of urgency, two hours away from her and he was incapable of doing anything. Shit. Take off those clothes and lie down with me, she would say when José Luís arrived at the apartment in Copacabana, where they met almost every day. Come. Tell me you're mine. I'm yours. Tell me you'll never again fuck any other woman. Never, not ever, I promise.

I'm going to talk to Zequinha, José Luís said. No way, answered Marta, you'll ruin everything. It took José Luís some time to understand that the powerful trafficker of the Marrecos favela would not accept him as a son-in-law. After all, Zequinha treated him with respect. He's a talent, that boy, he told Suzana. He's a good person. And he doesn't want his name in the papers. Smart, a hundred percent, that boy. No maybe about it. I like the guy, he said all the time. He often called him in to discuss business. José Luís was also very satisfied with Zequinha. He placed great store in anything he said. He's a genius, that Zequinha. Very experienced. The guy's fucking great. He loved being invited for lunch at Marta's house, he felt happy and important at the table, eating Suzana's fabulous *feijoada*, his girlfriend so near, even if he couldn't be alone with her, just being there alongside Zequinha's family, seeing himself part of it, was wonderful. Maybe, he told Marta, maybe your father will accept us as a couple someday. But one Sunday at lunch, José Luís understood everything. I want my daughters to marry solid citizens, Zequinha said, lawyers, engineers, dentists, pediatricians. They have to have a college degree, he said. Here in the favela all you have are traffickers and poor people. Priscilla speaks English like an American. Marta is a whiz at accounting. Am I going to be fool enough to hand my daughters over to these dummies, these nobodies, these shitass losers? No way. And don't give me this talk above love, I've already laid down the law on that. With love, without love, you're marrying a lawyer. Dear, don't talk like that, Suzana scolded. My goddess, my lady, the most beautiful woman in the world, angel of my life, I'm just expressing my ideas. That's how I am. With me there are no maybes.

José Luís was still thinking about Marta when he heard Reader call his name and wave from a car parked in front of Zino's butcher's shop. José Luís spoke with the butcher before getting into the car. He asked him to deliver two kilos of filet mignon to Yolanda's house and two more to his mother's.

Negaço loved telling jokes. It's the one about the black test tub baby, he said. Test tube, corrected Reader. Some scientists, Negaço continued, wanted to create a black in the laboratory. They tried everything, Negaço went on, but no results. Know what conclusion they came to? Blacks are born fucked. Guffaws. That's an old one, said Paula. And you, being so black you're almost purple, commented Fake, shouldn't be telling jokes about blacks. I'm a fucked-over black, said Negaço, laughing, you gotta have fucking, prick and pussy if you want to make a badass black.

José Luís gestured to the waiter at the Sete de Espadas bar, where they were meeting, and ordered more beer for the group. The 'executive encounters', as Reader called them, were always enjoyable. Always in some nearby bar, with plenty of crackling, cassava pudding, dried beef, and beer, José Luís's group would resolve the most pressing issues. But that day there was nothing to discuss. So they let Negaço tell as many jokes as he wanted to, talked about Vasco's latest game, laughed, spoke too loudly, until Murilo, the cop they were waiting for, showed up, bringing the information that José Luís had been anticipating for a week: yes, it was true that the son of the owner of a supermarket chain was being held hostage by a group of kidnappers in Berimbau. This is Romeu's doing, Reader had said days before when he'd heard the rumors. And I'll add this: he's doing it to fuck us. The prick was a buddy of Miltão's. Soon there'll be cops around here. And once you've got cops you'll have informers, and then the war starts all over again. Nip this thing in the bud, Reader had recommended. Kingie had already sent Romeu a message. From all I can tell, it didn't do any good, said the cop. They're still there, the informant assured them, although he didn't know the location of the hiding place. All I know is it's near the reservoir.

José Luís refused to wait till nightfall. He ordered twenty soldiers to comb every square inch of Berimbau that same afternoon. Go through everything. Turn it upside down. I want to find that hiding place. Today.

The soldiers scattered through the favela. Heads will roll, they warned, brandishing their menacing weapons as they searched the residents' houses. Everybody'll catch it. If anybody's sitting on information, threatened Paula, he's fucked but good.

It was an old washerwoman who told them of the hideout: I thought it was something José Luís was doing, she said. That's why I kept quiet. They've been there for days, but they're good people, they don't bother anybody. They just stay in there, nice and quiet, watching TV.

At six p.m. the kidnappers' hideout was surrounded. José Luís and Reader were quickly summoned as soon as the kidnappers were overpowered.

Inside the shack, in a filthy, fetid, room without windows, José Luís found the hostage. He was a youth of less than twenty, his hands and feet tied, his head covered with a hood. Reader thought he would vomit when he entered the place. Goddamn, he said, that Romeu is some human being. I like his style. José Luís united the knots around the hostage's legs, helped him to his feet, and told Negaço to release him near some police station on Avenida Brasil.

Just look at what they gave the poor guy to eat, said Reader, picking up from the floor a plate of crusted beans where a cockroach lay dead. Anybody hungry?

Paula brought out the three men who were taking care of the victim, 'the little angels,' he joked. This one, he said, referring to the tallest of the three, a blond, who didn't raise his gaze from the ground, this one here, they tell me, when the soap opera was over and he didn't have anything else to do, got his kicks scaring the hostage half to death. He would stick his revolver in the guy's kisser and count to three. He'd pretend he was going to pull the trigger. Real nice.

Is that true? José Luís asked, approaching the man.

He didn't answer.

José Luís aimed at the kidnapper's head and fired. The wall behind was covered in blood.

Tell Romeu, he said to the other two terrified youths, that there'll be no more kidnappings here in Berimbau.

When they were leaving, he asked Paula to find a car for him. I'm going to Copacabana, he said.

22

NAME: EVERALDO DOS SANTOS, known as Vivico. Leader of Block 5. Killed Mário Silva and took control of the Saudade favela. Arrested April 7. Name: Zezinho Caolho, for three years ran the drug trade in the Formiga and Boca Pequena favelas. Seven homicides. Arrested in May, in the hospital where he was recovering from appendicitis surgery. Replaced by Geraldo Zacarias, a.k.a. Bife de Chapa. Cremaldo Moreira, alias Crê, specialized in execution of policemen. The list of traffickers incarcerated at Padre Moraes penitentiary was long, and José Luís made a point of learning the names of the leaders before meeting with Noble, the one-time boss of Berimbau.

The visit had been planned for some time, at Reader's suggestion. José Luís had sent Fake, a friend of Noble's, to Padre Moraes the week before to propose the meeting. That story about the Red Commando, Reader had said, is like Santa Claus, believe it if you want to. And those who believe spread it around that they belong to that brotherhood of criminals, which makes a lot of sense. Especially if you're in prison and want to go on selling fifty kilos of cocaine a month and controlling seventy men in your army. You say: I belong to the RC, and nobody knows exactly what the RC is, whether it exists or not, or what the power of that 'organization' is, and that ignorance helps a lot, it creates fear. After all, who are we dealing with? The Red Commando is here, they say, inside the prison, we're outside, we're everywhere, and we can get into your house too. Who wouldn't be afraid? Take good care of our wives, they say, take care of our kids, pay our bail, our grocery bills, our rent, underwrite our escapes. Of course, you can ignore them and everything may turn out all right. But there's also the possibility that you'll end up dead somewhere, and everybody, the press included, will say your death was a 'settling of accounts by the Red Commando,' even though nobody can explain what the RC is. Let's not be foolish enough to expect a manifesto, a structure, an organization from those guys. It's a band of criminals, that's all. The other day Paula got all excited and told me that he'd seen an RC membership card. Bullshit. Imagine the members of the Yakuza, those heavyweights who exploit whorehouses and have a gigantic worldwide white slavery traffic, showing a membership card. Name: Yakisoba-Something-Or-Other, member of the Yakuza, position: manager of the heroin division, how about that? People in Brazil love to make things up. Even Paula comes to me with that story. Anyway, getting back to the subject, what I mean is it's no concern of ours whether there's such a thing as the Red Commando or not, or whether Noble is or isn't part of it. What matters to us is that we need to be on good terms inside Padre Moraes. Because in the future one of us could be there. It's better to secure the bases.

José Luís blindly followed Reader's advice. Actually, nothing was done without his OK or input. Kingie admired his ideas, his erudition. He liked to spend time at Reader's house, books everywhere. Have you read all this? he asked. Two hundred pages a day, minimum, Reader assured him, taking every opportunity to talk about his favorite subject, the decriminalization of drugs. So much nonsense has been said about the subject, he commented. They claimed, for example, that a man on hashish can go around killing anybody who says hello to him. That's so ridiculous it's funny. Marijuana, with rare exceptions, at most transforms a person into a vegetable. I don't smoke grass, I'm against it, but if a guy wants the right to turn into a sack of manure, what's the problem? Why forbid it? This book here says that billions of dollars a year are wasted on crimes that addicts commit to feed their habit. And the prediction for the future is for it to get worse, it says, the more drugs we use, the more crimes we commit. Impressive data. And as for that stuff about legalization stimulating consumption, that's crap, it says. This specialist here, an expert, continued Reader, showing passages underlined in red ink, this expert says that legalization can actually control use. And, as a bonus, reduce crime. I study. I read a lot. Legalization is the only solution. There's no downside to it, especially for us. And the best argument for legalization is what they've already said, that we have to pay in any case. We spend a bundle on the police. So why not legalize it and pay taxes to the government, like the tobacco industry?

What José Luís really enjoyed was, after these conversations, to go around repeating words like 'strategy', 'legalize', or expressions like 'the corruption industry', 'crime cartel', which made a big hit, especially with Zequinha. The only time it was unpleasant was when Reader, when he was in earshot on such occasions, would act like an eager teacher and correct him in front of the others. Shit, let me talk, shit, I'm talking, goddamn. Or when he would launch into questions like, What's that? he'd ask at any moment, you only eat junk, Dannon, what's that? Explain your idea better, what's that you're saying?

Reader always demonstrated great interest in people and thus had won everyone over, especially José Luís's closest female friends. Marta loved him, as did Kelly and Yolanda. But his biggest admirer was Carolaine. Four months pregnant, she was constantly after Reader. Whatever problem or doubt that arose, she would seek him out. He's so intelligent, she said. And he knows how to use the Internet. I'm going to take this cake to Reader. Alzira didn't approve of the friendship. I have the impression, Jesus, that it's that fat girl with glasses who's taking Carolaine away from the Lord, she would say in her prayers. I'm not sure anymore that God is on our side, Carolaine had told her the Sunday before. Holy Virgin Mary, don't talk nonsense, girl.

It had been Reader who prepared José Luís for the meeting with Noble. Say this, say that, don't promise anything, show firmness. Look him in the eye.

Sitting beside José Luís, amid prisoners receiving family visitors, Noble showed little interest in the conversation as long as the topic was the drug trade. He asked few questions and replied laconically. He was now part of a committee whose objective was to make jail, in his words, 'a human place'. When he talked about his new activities, his voice rose and even his posture changed to one more erect and vigorous. Everything here's cleaner, we have cleaning groups now, we take turns cleaning the latrines, the cells, the yard, everything's better. Did you know we consume an average of thirty kilos of rice a day?

Only at the end of the conversation did José Luís broach his proposal, a monthly stipend to be sent by way of Fake. Noble scratched his head. Are you saying you want to give me money? That's good, he said, laughing. The guys are going to like that. Tell me more.

Click. The cover of the metal trunk was opened, revealing a large quantity of weapons, submachine guns, rifles, and shotguns of various makes and calibers. This one here'll penetrate the wall of a safe. Costs fifteen thousand dollars. One of the few differences between this rifle and the Sig-Sauer is the price, it's a steal at five thousand dollars. How much does this one here cost? José Luís asked. Nine hundred and fifty rounds per minute, three thousand dollars, answered Isório, the gunrunner, already on his third shot of the whiskey offered by Zequinha.

Most of the material for sale by Isório was bought in the United States. From there, with forged documents, the arms were shipped to Brazil along with various kinds of electronic merchandise. There was what Isório called a 'special routine for clearing cargo,' a scheme that involved many people, each doing his part, and Isório's role was to take the armaments to the favelas and get the best price for them. Some weapons he bought for a song from gangs that robbed the armed forces. He had even brought Zequinha twenty M3 and M4 grenades. Sure you don't want them, Zequinha? They're a bargain. This was the first time he'd negotiated with José Luís, but what he'd heard from the Marrecos leader couldn't be better: Mark my words, Isório, in a year this boy will be one of your biggest customers, he'd said on the telephone.

Zequinha, sitting beside José Luís, proved to be a true

connoisseur of weapons. Is that the new Glock? he asked. The gunrunner nodded. Look at the finish. Americans are crazy about this weapon, just hold the mother, Zé, twenty-one ounces, it sticks to your hand like a cat that's scared of water, said Isório. Incredible what those guys can make when it comes to technology for killing.

José Luís carefully examined an HK-47 rifle. He likes the Pope weapon, commented Isório. Pope? Zequinha laughed. They tried killing Pope John Paul II with one of those, he explained.

They spent most of the morning analyzing the merchandise. José Luís was very familiar with weapons, but this was the first time he'd bought them for his soldiers. Since Miltão's death, he'd been in a precarious situation, always needing to resort to Zequinha, who lent him the weapons for special operations, at a price, obviously. With weapons, you have to buy a few every month. It's an investment. Nobody loses money on weapons, he said.

José Luís bought three rifles and two submachine guns, and Zequinha got the latest version of the Glock pistol.

After Isório left, Suzana called them to the table. Come have lunch.

Rice, beans, creamed potatoes, sausage, and kale. I love this food, Zequinha said, helping himself. Suzana, my goddess, pass the ketchup, I put ketchup on everything, he said. All the time he was in the dining room, José Luís couldn't keep his eyes off the staircase, hoping that Marta would come down at any moment. Ketchup on noodles, rice, beans, and if I don't watch myself, even ketchup on the ice cream. At that time, Marta should be home from school. I don't like fag food, Zequinha said, stroganoff, soufflé, pizza with pineapple, those weirdo things, can't stand them. When they start getting fancy, I don't like it. I like round steak. What's the matter, love of my life? Zequinha asked Suzana. Aren't you eating anything? I'm not hungry, Suzana replied. Not hungry? I don't know what that's like, continued Zequinha, not to be hungry at lunchtime. I'm hungry at lunchtime and at dinnertime, quite a coincidence, isn't it? Pass the olive oil, flower of my existence. You should eat that sausage, my Cleopatra, I've heard sausage is good brain food.

José Luís wondered if later there might be some way to escape from Zequinha and go up to Marta's room. He imagined her in bed, wearing panties and braless like Friday night when she lied to her father that she was spending the weekend with a girlfriend and showed up at José Luís's house in denim shorts, a leather blazer, and Ray-Ban sunglasses. I'm here to stay, she said, pointing to her backpack. Look what I've got here, she said, dumping the contents of the pack onto the bed: keys, two clean panties, a toothbrush, and surprise, two tickets for Zeca Pagodinho's show. She hummed *I've discovered that I love you too much la ra ra* and began dancing around the living room, pulling José Luís by the arm. For the first time, the couple spent two whole days and two nights together, sleeping in the same bed, having lunch and dinner, a paradise, shit, even when it came time to pee they went together, her sitting on the toilet and him standing at the door, hearing her talking, wonderful, they fucked so much, shit, that Marta got the notion to scratch little crosses in the headboard with a hairpin every time they made love, shit, they missed Zeca Pagodinho's show entirely. What José Luís most liked to remember was Marta showing him her buttocks, two round spheres, well defined. Tell me the truth, do you think I have a pretty ass? My God. Your ass is prettier than the full moon. He recalled Onofre asking: Is it true what they're saying about you and Zequinha's daughter? Oh, good, I thought for a while you'd gone bonkers. Good thing it's a lie. Just as well. Marta's so skinny and awkward she looks like a homeless person. She must weigh 110 pounds at most, I'm good at these things. And what about her ass? I always tell the women who come here and don't want to eat my turnovers: A woman can lose everything except her ass. A woman without an ass is like beer without pretzels. Where's the appeal?

But, in José Luís's opinion, Onofre didn't understand the first thing about asses. He was crazy in love with Marta and thought about using the lunch meeting with his father-in-law to lay his cards on the table once and for all, why not? I want to marry Marta, he'd say, just like that, straight out.

You prefer barbecue or pasta? Zequinha asked for the third time. The fellow's not listening, Suzana. Sorry, replied José Luís, barbecue, sorry. Maybe this was the ideal moment, José Luís thought, to speak the truth, I want to marry Marta, have a family with her. How are the girls? he asked suddenly, interrupting the story Zequinha had begun about his trip to the southern part of Brazil. Why? responded Zequinha, staring at him confrontationally. Sweetheart, said Suzana, what a question? He wants to know about the girls. Love, leave it to me, no maybe, OK? Tell me, Kingie, why are you asking about my daughters? No reason, answered the youth, turning pale. A silence descended over the table. It's manners, Zequinha, said Suzana, Kingie has good manners, that's all. Ah, that's good, my goddess, if it's because of manners, that's very good, I have good manners myself, speaking of which, how's your mother? Good, replied José Luís. Give her my best. It seems she's still suffering from the death of the pastor. Yes, said José Luís, upset at what had just happened. A shame they killed the pastor, he said. Miltão was a real piece of shit.

After lunch, Zequinha offered to go with his friend to the 'Berlin Wall'. That was how the area residents referred to the border zone between the favelas, although there was no longer a fence separating the two hills. I'm going to get my wallet, wait here. As soon as he left the room, Suzana approached. Zequinha's no fool, she said, I saw very clearly how you were looking at the stairs. Watch your step. Be careful.

On the way, Zequinha placed in José Luís's hands the Glock he had just bought. It's yours, he said, a present from a friend. Shit, for me? Thank you. Your father, he later told Marta, giving me a gun like that, shit, it was sensational. Very strange, his girlfriend commented, my father is so tight, he didn't ask for anything in return? No, replied José Luís. Not a thing.

But in reality Zequinha had asked for something: I want to invade the Sambacuim favela. If we win, it's eight more sites.

What about it? Can I count on your support?

It's a deal, José Luís had replied.

OK, said the voice at the other end of the line, you can advance. José Luís turned off the cellphone and gave his men the final signal. If he looked behind, he could see the back of an army barracks, but that was of no concern to José Luís's group. The police never interfered spontaneously in a battle between traffickers, especially when they had no prior information about the leaders and the weapons the outlaws were using.

The invasion wasn't as easy as Zequinha hoped, but neither was it extremely difficult, as Paula and the other soldiers later told their close friends at a barbecue to celebrate the victory. That evening, the Sambacuim leader had been executed at an amusement park in the Baixada Fluminense. Zequinha had set up the ambush. I set the rat trap, he said at the barbecue, bursting with vanity, I set the trap and the rat showed up hungry for cheese. José Luís's role in the war had been to invade the hillside at night and wipe out the trafficker's guards. When there's unity in a group, like the Sambacuim people, Zequinha had explained, it's not enough to get the leader's head. In this case, speaking from personal experience, the thing to have is a revolving machine gun. There's no maybe to it.

The details of the invasion had been worked out beforehand between Zequinha and Reader. Reader had been offended by José Luís's stance in relation to the profits from the operation. I don't understand what you mean by 'I didn't negotiate about that,' Reader commented, if there are eight sites, how many do we get? José Luís replied that this was merely a detail. A trifle. Reader laughed. Fake, he said, call Zequinha and tell him I'm on my way over to work out the 'details'.

The conversation with the trafficker hadn't been an easy one. Zequinha was a very likable sort, but where money was involved he would get nervous. I just asked for help, and now you want to skin me alive, shee. Where's your sense of solidarity? I want help, not partners. I've given a lot of support to you people. It was agreed that of the eight sites to be taken over, two would be for José Luís, and the costs of the operation would be covered by Zequinha's team. Suzana, Zequinha had said after Reader left, I'm going to have problems with that so-and-so. I can feel it in the air. I'm not going to get along with that guy.

The invasion was quick, the enemy retreated, scampering away down the hillside, but at the top there was a true confrontation, with grenades rolling along the pitted streets. But to no avail, as Negaço boasted later. In less than two hours we wiped out the sons of bitches.

The only unpleasant aspect had been the bullet that one of José Luís's soldiers, Valtinho, had taken in the arm from Negaço's own gun. I said, Wait for the signal, when the cellphone rings, you advance, I'll cover you, Negaço related. Except that I didn't give any signal, there were grenades falling close to us. Suddenly I see somebody trying to reach us, and I shot, man. I opened fire. It was Valtinho, damn it. But I didn't find that out till I called Valtinho and he cussed at me. Stop firing, he said.

The episode enlivened the barbecue that night, offered on the rear porch of Zequinha's house. Valtinho, after being treated in the favela, was drinking beer and laughing at Negaço's jokes.

In celebrations like that, Zequinha forbade his daughters or even Suzana to move about the house. Marta watched the activities from behind the blinds of her window. As soon as she saw José Luís arrive, she called his cellphone. Come up to my room, she said. Now.

At his first opportunity, José Luís went inside the house, climbed the stairs, careful not to be seen. In the hallway, a door opened, pop, Marta pulled him inside. Pop, would you be so kind as to explain to me what this is?

It was a bank statement, a certificate of a deposit in the name of Yolanda Moreira, Kelly's mother. Five hundred. Pop. I found this shit in your wallet, which you left in my handbag, said Marta, irritated. Pop. Spit it out.

José Luís sat on the bed. It would be hard for Marta to understand what had occurred. Pop. It had been Caroline, his sister, who had told him. Pop. It had all begun with a dumb comment of his, I want to have a child, he'd said, in an idle conversation with his sister. You almost did already, Carolaine had answered. What the shit are you talking about, girl? Carolaine had tried to change the subject but had finally told the truth, that Kelly, at the time he broke off the relationship, was pregnant, had had an abortion and had almost died. And she didn't say anything, Zé, because she didn't want to upset you. It had been horrible to hear that story. José Luís felt so guilty, and so relieved at the same time, thanks to Kelly, what an extraordinary woman, what a fantastic person, Kelly, shit. Say something, Zé, Marta shouted. Pop. I'm waiting. She had an abortion, José Luís said, stammering, and the phrase provoked such an explosion of rage in Marta that she could barely hear what her boyfriend was trying to explain. You prick, you scumbag, you got that whale pregnant? For shit's sake, love, let me explain. Marta threw a lamp at José Luís's head, kicked him in the shins, scratched his arms, while José Luís begged her to calm down. They'll hear us, he said, trying to get her back in control of herself, but Marta was implacable, pushing him out of the room, slamming the door. Get out of my life, she screamed, sobbing. Marta, goddamn it, open the door. At that moment, Zequinha appeared at the top of the stairs. What are you doing here? he asked. I'm looking for the fucking bathroom, he replied.

Zequinha scratched his head. Motherfucker. He didn't like that in the least. Not in the least. That way, it just wasn't going to work out. I hope I'm wrong, he thought, sighing. Come with me, he said, the bathroom's downstairs.

23

BOOM TICK BOOM TICK boom tick boom, in Onofre's bar, in the streets, tick boom, in the access ways or the upper part of the hill, from any part of the favela, tick boom boom, could be heard the sound of the Unidos do Berimbau samba school, which that Wednesday night, tick boom boom boom, two days before the start of Carnival, was honoring its new sponsor, José Luís Reis. Wearing white pants and a Vasco team shirt, José Luís came into the sports area, accompanied by the men he trusted and by his inseparable mutts Pirosca, Tutu, Jaboti, and Gulliver. Taller, fatter, more talkative, and especially more confident, smiling, dancing, waving at the guests, José Luís showed no resemblance to the shy adolescent who had assumed power six months earlier. Almost seventeen now, he was a leader, in the literal meaning of the term. How's it going, man? Kiko, the Carnival creative director, greeted him, shaking his hand. Kiko had made a point of being there to receive his friend. Yes, after so many arguments, now it could finally be said that they were friends. *It's the world that spins, it's the world that rocks, that rolls*, sang the lead singer in his impressive booming voice. Every year, José Luís was moved when he witnessed how Carnival transformed that man. From March to December, he would see him moving through the favela's streets in the dark-blue uniform of a municipal garbage collector, downcast and listless. But at Carnival time, leading the paraders, the man was the picture of happiness. *Let's hear it for Pelé, for Garrincha, for Tostão*; football was the theme chosen for the samba-enredo. José Luís had received the news with great enthusiasm and had immediately sent Reader to advise the organizers of his desire to cooperate. We're accepting money, Kiko had replied, through José Luís's grandmother Cândida, who was the samba school's seamstress. The guy doesn't know how things work, Grandma. Tell him to come here for dinner tomorrow night.

At that time, 'how things work' was, for José Luís, magnanimously represented by the man who, as Reader had informed him, reinvented the Mafia. Since Reader had told him the story of Lucky Luciano, José Luís's attitude had changed entirely. He didn't want to be just one more favela drug boss. Kingie's ambition was to gain the title of 'the biggest drug dealer in South America.' This magazine, Reader had said, showing him the drawing of the Mafioso illustrating the story, this magazine talks about the magnates of our century. Lucky, I read, is the man who gave the Mafia a new image, more modern, more dynamic. The guy started out as a street kid and ended up a great name in the international economy. It was under him that the Mafia was transformed into a money machine. Those were hard times, Reader continued. The struggle for power gave no quarter, shootings even during breakfast, you know what that's like? Lucky was very clever and knew that violence was bad for business. In those days everyone thought that Al Capone was the big cheese, but to Lucky, Capone was nothing but a violent and unproductive outlaw. Like Miltão, you know? Know what he did? He murdered his own boss and took control of the business, with non-violent methods.

José Luís had been impressed by the similarities between his own story and that of the great Mafioso Salvatore Lucania: he'd also been a street kid, and he'd also killed his boss to put an end to the violence. And everything he'd been doing lately was exactly what Salvatore had done in the Golden Age, according to what Reader had told him: put the house in order. Now, at Reader's suggestion, all the 'structural' team in the traffic used cellphones. In 'production' (a large shack where the boys divided into groups, some cutting the cocaine with marble dust and talc, others separating, weighing, and packaging the drug), everything was computerized. The user would send an e-mail with coded orders, and the drug would be delivered to his residence. This is the beginning of a whole new thing, Reader said. It's been said that capitalism always starts with the undertaking of a lawbreaker, those crazies who mine ore and build railroads and later end up as pillars of the nation's economy. That's more or less what's going to happen to us in the future. What's this 'us' stuff, paleface? asked Zequinha, who was there that day and heard Reader's theories. That's a pile of crap. If they legalize drugs, the winners will be the Philip Morrises of the world, my boy. Forget it. There's no maybe to it. Zequinha has a very narrow vision, Reader had told José Luís later. He can't see the future. Zequinha doesn't take into account, for example, that Brazil is the world's largest channel for the flow of cocaine. Zequinha's ignorant and doesn't know that. Kingie had completely bought into that ideology. At their meetings, the words heard most often were 'professionalize', 'expand', and 'structure'. I get dizzy, commented Negaço, from all those big words. I don't understand shit about that stuff. All that 'discussioning' makes my head spin. José Luís's favorite subject was progress in Berimbau. Peacetime, he repeated constantly, despite the fact that his people hadn't stopped invading drug sites and killing vulnerable leaders. It's been five months since anybody was killed in the favela. We don't kill our wives anymore, he said proudly, we don't beat our children, we don't steal the neighbor's bucket or his propane canister, we don't fight at Onofre's bar. Why? Because we, the businessmen of the trade, are here to bring progress. Peace. Yes, it's true there had been a few squabbles, small stuff, Francisco, José Luís's father, had run over Dona Crecilda's cat, little things, a trifle, and because of that the woman had started saying that Francisco was a drunk. Has anybody here seen my father drunk? Huh, Onofre? No one had. So there. Everything in order. Tell Dona Crecilda to shut her trap.

For José Luís everything was running very well, better than well, great, including his personal life. His romance with Marta was better and better, beyond excellent, superb, everything was going full steam ahead, and the watchword was organization. And the dinner with Kiko had been expressly to expound that idea. Organization. Progress. The future. Expansion. But Kiko, responsible for Berimbau's participation in Carnival for the last twelve years, wanted only the traffickers' money, as what he received from the bosses of the illegal lottery was insufficient. He wouldn't allow any type of interference, and basically that's what José Luís was thinking of, interfering. We don't have any money, José Luís had argued, guided by Reader. What I can do for you, he'd said, is 'structure Carnival'. You don't know the miracles that organization can achieve. José Luís had been impressed when, days earlier, Reader had told him there was no reuse of parade materials. Everything is just thrown away somewhere around the favela, near the football field, and then ends up in the trash. Reader, the trafficker had asked during the dinner, explain our idea to Kiko. Days later, Kiko had already incorporated the entire conversation about recycling of materials and reuse of floats, statues, and decorations.

The truth is that the creative director was enchanted by José Luís, which surprised no one, after all the entire population was fascinated by the new leader. And anyone who wasn't satisfied had resigned himself, accepting him as the boss of Berimbau, 'my hill,' as José Luís customarily referred to the favela. José Luís was well mannered, respectful, attentive. 'He does a lot for the poor,' people said. He fixed my roof. He paid for my child's medicine. He gave me a brand-new tire. He's building a school, up the top there. Although the incentive to construct a school near the new headquarters of the drug traffic could be more the need to use children as a shield against police raids than any desire to meet the residents' needs, José Luís had in fact been bringing various improvements to Berimbau. Around his house there were now sewer pipes. I just love Kingie, said Kiko. Love him to death. Kingie is the one who gives me the least money, that I admit, but to make up for it he's the one giving the most moral support.

The dialog with Kingie had become difficult only when Kiko told him there would be a float to honor Oscar Cox. Who's he? Cox, Kingie, introduced football to Rio de Janeiro, Kiko replied. Really, cool, said the trafficker, I thought football was born here. No, replied Kiko, who researched the themes rigorously, the Chinese played ball even before Jesus Christ was born. Honest? How about that, said José Luís, so this Cox guy was Chinese? No, Cox studied in Europe, and he helped found the Fluminense Football Club. What? said José Luís indignantly. Yes, the first great soccer team of Rio de Janeiro. That was when the confusion began. A fanatical Vasco fan, José Luís vetoed the homage to Cox. Fluminense is a crappy team, he said, I won't allow it. No way. But it's history, argued Kiko, history with a capital H, we can't just skip over the facts. Fuck history, Cox is out, not a chance, damn it. It was Reader who broke the impasse. It's been said, Kiko, that it was Vasco that brought about the redemption of the black man in football. Vasco ended race prejudice in Brazilian football, did you know that? Why don't we have the Bahian wing represent the Vasco fans? How about it, Kingie? We have Cox *and* Vasco, how about it? José Luís agreed with the terms, as long as Vasco came before Cox.

The fact is that José Luís became a kind of owner of the Berimbau Carnival. For any problem that arose, they went to his house (or houses, since José Luís, following the example of residents who made money in Berimbau, had bought the shacks surrounding his own, thus expanding his dwelling) to talk about it. Kingie's the one to see, Kiko would say, go talk to Kingie, and the trafficker would get involved in every issue, even in choosing the area where Cândida would buy sequins and beads. Marta's the one who knows those details, he would usually say. Whenever he could, he brought Marta into the dealings, although his girlfriend knew absolutely nothing about Carnival. Yes, but she's going to study business administration, José Luís argued, proudly.

Goal, the stadium screams, every fan dreams, it's a goal, sang the lead singer, exciting the crowd. Kingie, said Kelly, interrupting his conversation with Kiko, how nice to see you. And it was at the exact moment that they were hugging, he and Kelly, that Zequinha arrived with Suzana and his daughters Marta and Priscilla. And it was also at that moment, without any prior agreement, that Fake stepped between the two and asked if everyone had heard the news, Kingie and Kelly are getting married, he said. Really? Zequinha asked. Great. Excellent, congratulations, said Suzana, embracing Kelly. José Luís couldn't say a word, looked at Marta, distressed, pop, let's circulate, she told Priscilla, ciao, Father, pop. And she disappeared. People continued to congratulate the couple. Since I found this goddess, Zequinha boasted, referring to Suzana, this light, this polished diamond, my life has been paradise. And everyone went on wishing happiness to José Luís, saying good things about marrying and having children. For God's sake, Fake, he said later when his friends had left, what kind of crazy talk was that? Keep your mouth shut and make like a fiancé, brother, I saved your ass, Fake replied. Zequinha came to me, he's pissed, even a blind man can see what you and Marta are doing, what's the matter with you? You trying to fuck yourselves, is that it? What are those clothes? asked José Luís, only then noticing Fake's pleated pants. They're new, his friend replied, you like them, brother? I'm even wearing suits these days. Business. José Luís recalled the pants that Mr Rodrigo wore, the same type of pants, two pleats on each side, relaxed fit, shit, I'm fucking mad, shit, where's Marta? he asked, looking around for his girlfriend. Brother, all I'm going to say is this, Zequinha is the kind of person who's done everything imaginable to his enemies, and I can guarantee you, it's always unexpected. Look at him smiling over there, Fake continued, pointing to the trafficker on the other side of the court, beer in hand, smile at the man. Zé Luís smiled. Marta must be royally pissed, said Zé Luís, dialing his girlfriend's cellphone. This telephone is not in service, said the recorded message, leave your message at the beep. Voice mail, shit.

Boom tick boom tick boom tick boom, at that moment there was a tumult. Call an ambulance, someone yelled. Carolaine, despite being in the ninth month of her pregnancy, had danced all night without stopping and was ill. She sat on the floor, sweating. Call my mother, she asked Suzana.

It took four strong men to get her onto the automobile seat that served as a sofa at the sports area.

Fake went to get a car, and José Luís stayed at his sister's side, calming her. Carolaine kept calling for her mother, whimpering. She had no fear of dying in childbirth or of the baby being born with birth defects. She was crying at the thought of how things would be, the future, the changes. Her life was so good lately. Zé Luís had given her everything, clothes, food, even a new 14″ TV. With remote control and everything. She would go out every afternoon, walking about, knocking around, visiting Reader, Suzana, or else she'd go to the home of her grandmother, Cândida, just to see the dancers trying on their Carnival costumes. She had given up her studies, all that boring stuff, and now she even had a young woman helping her with the cleaning, José Luís's idea. It was great not to have to clean the house. And Alzira didn't even know about it, as the maid only came when Alzira was at work. It was wonderful to have a servant to cook, scrub the floor and wash the dishes and clothes, and thanks to this privilege Carolaine could devote herself to her favorite pastime, watching TV, especially on the hotter days. She would turn on the television and the fan, plop onto the sofa with a box of cream-filled chocolates, and watch movies and reruns of soap operas till she fell asleep. Alas at the day-care center, the house peaceful, Carolaine didn't remember ever before in her life having such tranquility and peace. And now, what would it be like? Breast-feeding, changing diapers, getting up in the middle of the night because of the baby. Deal with it, Carolaine, I'm too old to raise a child, Alzira had said. Who would watch the baby when she went to dances with Reader? Alzira had taken charge of Alas, but her mother had already warned her millions of times that she wouldn't be nanny to another grandchild. Enough. The soft life is over. During the nine months of pregnancy, especially after the pastor's death, Carolaine came to look at her pregnancy in a very simple way: she completely ignored it. She simply didn't think about the matter. She barely glanced at her belly. When Alzira complained, she left the house, shrugged her shoulders, forgot about it. But now, what would happen now?

Call Mother, she asked José Luís again, on their way to the hospital.

*　　*　　*

We will now show, said the TV announcer, how the murderess premeditated every detail of the crime, the night she visited her lover on the pretext of having forgotten her keys.

Alzira, sitting in the armchair in Dona Juliana's bedroom, was watching TV beside her employer, who seemed calmer now. I'm going to warm some milk for you, Alzira said, rising. No, Alzira, thank you, I'm fine, stay here. On the night of the crime, the announcer said, the murderess left work at six o'clock.

Alzira liked that kind of program; it was good for reminding everyone that the Devil was there. Loose in our world. Not as she had imagined him when she was a child, horns, half man, half animal, the Devil was far worse, a man from head to toe, with no outward sign to alert us, very normal, walking among us, speaking, working, mulling over all kinds of things, completely normal. Two days earlier, Dona Juliana had read to her an article in the paper, a statement by the Pope. The Devil has been defeated, the Pope had said, and now the truth was right there before their very eyes. The Pope was wrong. The Devil continued to fight. Walking anonymously amid the multitude. She thought about telling Dona Juliana that, but changed her mind because she seemed calmer and had finally stopped crying, why mention the Devil?

Mr Rodrigo was in São Paulo on business and the children, Marcelinha and Otávio, were away on vacation, the girl at Disney World and the boy studying in London. These were peaceful days, Dona Juliana always on a diet, just something grilled and a salad, the house in order, everything easy. Even the ulcer in her leg had gotten a little better. It hadn't healed but it wasn't an open wound anymore. See how much better it is? she'd asked Dona Juliana. Don't show it to me, Alzira, I hate looking at rotten things. That afternoon, everything was serene, Alzira was changing clothes to go home, having left an arugula salad in the refrigerator for Dona Juliana, the house had that smell of cleanliness, a smell so honest and proper that it calmed Alzira, it was so good, she was about to leave, when her employer suddenly came into the kitchen, crying, and threw herself in Alzira's arms, moaning, sobbing. For the love of Christ, Dona Juliana, what happened? Juliana, when she managed to speak, said the same thing over and over: something horrible, Alzira, horrible, she repeated, choking in her tears. Was it Marcelinha? No, no, sobbed Juliana, not explaining herself clearly, it's nothing like that. Then what was it, woman, for heaven's sake? said Alzira anxiously.

Juliana wouldn't say what had happened, talking about it was too humiliating, not even to that poor illiterate woman had Juliana managed to say what she'd seen with her own eyes, a horror, Fernando and Alice, her best friend, in bed, it had been horrible. And everything had begun so well, a lovely day, she'd had lunch with Lila, who had just returned from Paris, they laughed a lot, Juliana felt good, happy, on her way home, listening to music on the car radio, the sea an olive-green, everything wonderful, when suddenly she had the idea of surprising Fernando. She stopped at a deli, bought French bread, Camembert, and champagne, oh, it was horrible. Fernando's door was unlocked, the living room a mess, and on the armchair, a woman's purse, a fancy purse, in good taste, and oh the horror, why hadn't she turned and left right then? When it comes to ending things, she would tell her psychiatrist the next day, I border on the spectacular. That's my specialty, destroying things. Wiping everything out. I knew I was going to fuck myself, and even so I went inside, opened the door to Fernando's bedroom. It was horrible. Her lover's perfect body, his muscular back, on top of Alicinha. Horrible. Juliana had run down the stairs, that had been the worst part. She hadn't expected anything of Fernando. But Alicinha, yes, she thought that Alicinha, her best friend, would come after her, wrapped in the sheet, even naked, she would come after her. She would ask for forgiveness, perhaps they would cry together. That whore. That traitor. Juliana even slowed her pace to give her friend a chance to find her on the stairs, destroyed. But neither Fernando nor Alicinha came after her. And for the five minutes she sat sobbing in her car, parked next to Fernando's building, neither of them appeared at the window.

Now, finally, after shedding the last of her tears, she felt calmer. Rodrigo, her husband, had called from São Paulo shortly before. Why are you so sad, my love? What happened? I miss the children, she'd replied. Sweetheart, I'll be there tomorrow, be calm. We'll have dinner at that restaurant you like so much.

She felt grateful for Alzira having stayed with her, she wouldn't have been able to get through the night alone. And Alzira found nothing wrong with spending the night at her employer's house. If not for Alas, she would have little desire to go home. It irritated her immensely to run into her ex-husband around there, the bandit, living it up in a minivan, thinking he was the greatest. She wanted to ignore Francisco, but she was always seeking him out with her eyes, trying to catch sight of him, and when she bumped into him in the street, God forgive me, how awful it was to feel such hatred in her heart, a powerful hatred, voracious, that grew and wanted to grow even more, such was the hate that took control of her head and her legs, forcing her to change routes in order to see Francisco and detest him. That was all she did lately, abominate Francisco, she could barely pray, she was constantly cursing the worm, the lowlife, the imbecile, the idiot, coward, drunkard, blast it.

At 11:15 that night, when the phone rang, Alzira was dozing with her head resting on the arm of the chair in Dona Juliana's bedroom. Your second grandson has just been born, said Suzana at the other end of the line.

Alzira asked if Carolaine was all right. Yes, everything's fine, it's a boy, Suzana said, excited, a lovely baby. He's going to be called Junior. Junior Reis.

Alzira hung up the telephone and went back to the bedroom, feeling great sadness in her heart. Another child. Poor Carolaine.

24

'MY DEAR POT-BELLIED dirty old goat, you know that pretty snow you see on television, all white, fluffy, and nice? It's lousy, my friend. Walking in the snow, making snowmen, that's only for TV or postcards. I just came in from the street, thirteen degrees below zero! Frankly, Onofre, I prefer that killer sun. I was shivering like a steer at the slaughterhouse. The snow piles up, melts, and it's shit to walk on the streets packed with dark, frozen mud. Today, for example, I landed on my face and scattered my tomatoes in the dirt.

'At five o'clock people begin soaking up dark beer at bars, and by nine at night there's not a soul in the streets, everybody in the city's gone to sleep drunk. Nobody leaves the house. If they go out, they run to buy their sausage for the day and that's it. Worst of all is the color of the sky, Onofre. From ten in the morning till four in the afternoon it's the same thing, totally overcast, everything gray. That starts in October and doesn't end till March. I'll confess, you old goat, that always joyful Rosa Maria doesn't laugh as much as she used to.

'Still, I'm happy. Jennifer, Dadá's daughter, arrived two weeks ago to live with Heinrich and me. A really nice child. And very clever, she's already saying gutentag. Heinrich likes her. At least I'm not so alone anymore. (She's the one who was very sad last week. Everyone in Unidos do Berimbau wanted her to be the standard-bearer of the samba school, did you know that? Instead she spent Carnival here, shivering . . .)

'I just ate the box of candy that you sent me. Next time, send the brand with the little red heart, it's the best. Can you also send some guava paste? I'll be waiting. Hugs for the whole gang there. And a big kiss for you from Rosa Maria.'

You think, Onofre asked, after reading the letter to Negaço, you think Rosa Maria is going to invite other people to go to Germany? Yeah, answered Negaço, holding a soft drink and watching attentively the movement of the passersby, she's going to invite you, I heard. You know the joke, the trafficker continued, about the guy who gets hit in the face and says to the one who did it, This isn't gonna end here. And the one who punched him says, You're right, it's gonna swell up and turn purple. It's the same thing, Rosa Maria's situation is gonna swell up and turn purple. What're you talking about? asked Onofre indignantly, that's stupid, you can't even carry on a conversation, I'm here talking about something and you come out with an old joke that's got nothing to do with anything. Negaço laughed, I know, he said, soon you're gonna pull out that Swedish knife of yours and run off at the mouth about Rosa Maria. Swiss, corrected Onofre, my knife is Swiss.

Onofre looked at the postcard of a snow-covered Berlin. How much, he asked, do you think a ticket to Germany costs?

Negaço was paying close attention to the boys playing football at the main entrance to the favela. Someone signaled him. I'm leaving, he said.

What's going on, Negaço? Why's everybody so nervous today?

Marta opened the personal refrigerator in the Serenade Motel and took out a chocolate bar. She went back to the bed, lying down and nestling in José Luís's arms. What time is it? he asked. Five-fifteen, she replied. Go on with that. I was enjoying it, he said. You fell asleep, said Marta. I didn't sleep a wink. So what was I saying? You were saying, answered José Luís, that the male explodes. More or less, explained Marta, I was saying that the difference between men and women when they come is that the man explodes and the woman is exploded. Do I explode you? José Luís asked, caressing Marta's stomach. It was true, José Luís had to admit. He exploded. Something deep inside him went off during sex, and before the explosion a powerful force concentrated itself somewhere in his body and suddenly became pure potency, erupting, piercing his viscera, slicing through him from top to bottom like an arrow, shit, it was good.

Marta's mouth tasted of chocolate, her breath was always delicious with the scent of the cinnamon and spearmint chewing gum that she bought by the dozen and carried in her purse and the glove compartment of her car. I'm hooked on gum, she said, pop, and it's your fault, if you didn't kiss me so much I'd chew, pop, less of it. For me, Marta said, when your prick enters my body it's like a knife, it seems there's a ball inside there, a kind of heaven, then suddenly, pop, the knife explodes it. Pop.

How good it was to be at peace with Marta, thought José Luís, and better still when she managed to understand, at least for a few moments, that there was nothing between Kelly and him, no possibility of there being anything. I have as much interest in Kelly, José Luís said, as I do in a piece of cardboard, Kelly doesn't interest me, and I don't want to have anything to do with any woman but you. But she loves you, Marta replied, the fat girl lives on hope. So what? said José Luís. So what? She's a zero, a nothing. Yes, Zé, but it so happens that since Fake made up that song-and-dance about marriage, the fat chick's been looking at me with her I've-got-something-you-want expression. I don't like that. She just wants to help, argued José Luís. The tramp. Pushy bitch. She's so fat she's even got cellulite in her arms. You ought to be glad Kelly's my friend, José Luís said, it shows I'm a nice guy. Pop, Bullshit, that fat broad better watch out for me, I'll wipe her out. Pop.

Marta was very curious about business matters. She was always asking questions, wanting to find out things, giving opinions on this and that, pop, I've got a knack for it. There was one situation in which José Luís had a shipment of cocaine stolen by the police, who got information about the delivery site through a wiretap. It had been Marta's idea to set up a phantom operation over the tapped phone line. That way, José Luís's men killed the three cops involved in the robbery. On another occasion, as José Luís was mulling over the best way to transport arms from one favela to the other, for rental, Marta showed up with a newspaper story about the use of garbage trucks for transporting weapons and drugs. Shit, that's good. In reality, it was a terrible idea. Since the police had already been alerted, the garbage trucks were the subject of raids, leading to José Luís losing a small part of his arsenal. But the negative outcome of the operation did not affect his image of Marta in the least. Shit, the girl's a genius. Does she or doesn't she have a knack for the business, Reader? Reader agreed, mainly because Marta supported him in the idea of establishing direct contact with suppliers, without Zequinha's intervention. My father has to understand that you've grown, she said.

After they made love, they remained in the bed, naked, talking about business. Lately, Marta had been concerned about her stepmother. She looks at me funny, that woman. You know, Zé, she's very ambitious. The idea you have of Suzana, a friend and a great mother, doesn't wash with me. She manipulates my father. The whore. And, now, she's all the time coming to me saying, Careful, careful, who does she think she is?

In the middle of this conversation, José Luís's cellphone started ringing. I'll be there in ten minutes, he said, after Negaço told him 'the artist' had arrived.

Marta was fascinated when she learned that José Luís was on his way to meet a man who made commercials. Real commercials, for television. A publicist, then, she said. Right, a publicist, repeated José Luís, enjoying the new word. Which commercials does he do? José Luís didn't know the answer.

He knew only what Negaço had told him, as his friend had set up the meeting. Days earlier, an old acquaintance, Dunga, a television producer who got his cocaine from the favela, had come looking for Negaço. Dunga had asked Negaço to introduce the American publicist Rick Molzer to José Luís. Rick had come to Brazil to make a soda commercial and wanted to use the favela as the setting. The gringo just wants your OK, Negaço had said. Reader had opposed it. What's in it for us? It's not worth the risk. Pretty soon it'll hit the newspapers. I'm against it.

José Luís was too flattered by the request to pay heed to Reader's warning. Somebody that important, an American, wanting to meet him, asking permission. Television commercials. Shit. Following Zequinha's example, Kingie avoided speaking to reporters. It's strategic, Zequinha said. Fame, in our case, is only good for buying trouble, said Marta's father. But now the situation was different. It was an American, an artist.

For a week, everyone anxiously awaited the meeting. There was the threat of cancellation on Rick Molzer's part, but fortunately everything worked out in the publicist's agenda.

Can I go? Marta asked. It did no good to beg, pop, go down on her knees, as she always did when she wanted to make José Luís crack up laughing. He laughed loudly and said no. He put her in a taxi and left for Berimbau alone, riding his 1200 cc motorcycle.

Seated comfortably in a wine-colored velvet armchair, a glass of Coca-Cola in his hand, Rick Molzer was chatting with Fake and Reader through the intermediary of the producer Dunga, who haltingly translated his questions and the traffickers' answers. With his very short blond hair and wearing a white Hering T-shirt outside his red jeans, the young man was a big disappointment to Fake. They had spoken so often about the man, the American, the artist, that Fake had imagined a different person. He had dressed carefully for the occasion, beige pants, a dress shirt of the same color, coffee-colored shoes and belt, evoking laughter from his friends. Negaço had even said, 'The brother is going white on us,' not that Fake cared about that type of 'ignorant comment'. They're stupid, he told Reader, what I want is to progress, I can't work with drugs and go around dressed like a Christmas tree. I'm black and proud of it. What's my clothes got to do with my color? But, finally, everything had been settled, he'd even cut his hair to receive the American, and now the dude shows up wearing pants that were half-dirty, crummy sneakers, not Nikes or Reeboks, Adidas, nothing, a white guy who looked like some office worker, no suntan, nothing, what was this? To be a white like that, he must not own a yacht, Fake would say later, laughing. In my opinion, Reader would say afterward, as he took José Luís to the 'really important' meeting, in my opinion the American's a fag.

How many people live in Berimbau at present? asked Rick Molzer. Really? That many? Almost the population of a mid-sized American city. The insipid conversation went on until José Luís arrived, an hour late, and the entrance of the boss of the Berimbau drug traffic was, in Rick Molzer's view, spectacular. Motorcycle helmet in hand, machine gun strapped to his body under his denim jacket, laughing, giving orders, at ease, amusing, he could even be part of the commercial, he would later tell his art director.

The conversation lasted for two hours.

I just adore Rio's favelas, he told José Luís. You have such creative solutions. You make fantastic use of materials. I adored those plastic curtains at Onofre's bar. I adored the antennas everywhere. José Luís didn't quite understand what he meant by that, liking those banal things, antennas, plastic, didn't they have antennas in the United States? Translate that, Dunga, I want to know. Yes, we have antennas, replied Rick, laughing, but nothing like what you have here, this explosion of colors, this visual feast, this is absolutely postmodern. And that's why I'm here. I want something new for my clients. Showing young people at a rock concert drinking soda is uncreative. We're going to show a nice-looking dark-skinned girl on a summer day, in the middle of the favela, sweaty, sensual, suddenly she stops, exhausted, and poof, in her hand there magically appears a bottle of soda, which she drinks with pleasure. Then she looks at the camera and says: This is life!, translated Dunga, struggling to keep up with the American's English.

José Luís considered it an excellent idea. This is life! He could suggest two good 'locations' (to use the word that Dunga repeated several times), the one at the vegetable market, where the walls of the houses were all painted blue, and Maurinho's workshop, full of fancy cars. But what I want to show, said Rick, is the favela itself, it's the color, the movement, I adore favelas. That's Rio. It's Brazil. Favela, to me, is where it's at.

It's Brazil itself. I don't want anything prettified, painted blue. I want vibrant reality itself.

The conversation went off down other paths. José Luís, despite Reader's signals, spoke about the traffic, the important relationship between his team and the community, but Rich Molzer wasn't especially interested in the subject. He asked a few questions, Aren't you afraid of dying? Have you ever been arrested? Wounded? What's your favorite weapon? Not paying great attention to the answers because of the atrocious English of Dunga, who was slow to 'find the words'.

To José Luís, the meeting had been more than good. He'd never heard anyone speak 'that kind of English,' and it had struck him as terrific. Out of the ordinary, shit. Tell him, Dunga, that my work here is essential to the community. Although Rick had not reacted effusively to the information about the traffic, José Luís felt very important at that moment, as if he were being filmed, he laughed, smoothed his hair, gestured, always for effect. He wanted the American to like him. A cool campaign, Rick's, he told Reader later. A piece of crap, in my opinion, Reader replied. It's idiotic to show poverty. Did you see how he looked at us? The guy's really dumb. He asked a lot of dumb questions, Reader said. And what about when he wanted to know about our plastic sandals, huh? Goddamn it. You Brazilians like that, he said. Actually, what he meant wasn't you Brazilians but you the poor. You people in the Third World. You, the fucked over, who wear cheap sandals. Why is it, huh? He's stupid, the gringo is stupid. He thinks we're different, something else. Now the Americans have taken to liking the poor. Poor, black, and queer and a lot of guilt, that's the in thing with those guys. The imbecile. Oh shit, commented José Luís, paying no attention to Reader's virulent comments. He should have mentioned the day-care center, shit. He'd forgotten. You think, Reader asked, that American is really interested in what you have to say? The man's here to sell soda, Kingie, he's just one more seller. Don't you know that if he made the commercial in a studio, for example, he'd have to build a pile of contraptions, pay professionals, spend a fortune?

Very clever the idea of using the favela. I know the story. Dirt cheap. You should have charged him more. José Luís didn't even hear Reader's foolishness. Shit. He'd also forgotten to mention the new church that was being built. It was a surprise for his mother, he could have said that, the people need support, and the church is a form of support. He repeated, 'The church is a form of support,' trying to memorize the phrase for the next occasion. He could have talked more, but Reader had set up a very important meeting for that night. A pity.

In wholesale cocaine dealing in Rio de Janeiro, no name was more prominent than that of Zé Gavião. Anyone who saw him calmly sitting in the armchair in his luxurious home could not imagine his dynamism for work. He never dealt with small buyers, and although José Luís increased his amount with each new order, to Gavião he was merely one more 'small fish'. He agreed to see him because he was a friend of Zequinha's, and also because 'the boy won't leave me alone, he never stops pestering me'.

Until that moment, Zequinha had always served as a go-between for the purchases by the Berimbau boss, and it upset him to see José Luís looking to become independent. Today he wants to negotiate his own drugs, he said. Tomorrow he's my enemy. He would have prevented it if he could, but he was in no position to deny José Luís anything. Weeks earlier, Kingie had executed two youths who were disrupting business in the Marrecos favela. Even before Zequinha could thank him, his partner had already presented the 'bill', which was precisely the OK to establish direct contact with Gavião. I don't like this, Suzana, Zequinha had said. There's a name for this, it's called getting in through the back door, my goddess. It's the famous 'scoot over,' Cleopatra.

How do you invest your money? Gavião asked as soon as José Luís began speaking of 'profit margins'. Real estate and land, those are good investments, in my opinion. José Luís was little interested in his supplier's financial advice. If he were going to talk about money, it would be to ask about the cities of Tabatinga and Leticia, in the Amazon region, which served as midpoints in the distribution of drugs by the Cali and Medellín cartels. He would love to know if their monthly take was really as high as they claimed back in the favela. But the meeting had a different agenda, José Luís was there to get a better price for the drugs he sold. He promised a rapid increase in sales. A lower price, no, replied Gavião, at least not for now. Increase your firepower and I'll give it some thought. At the moment, the best I can do, considering your ties to Zequinha, who's my good buddy, is to let you pay in installments, with all the risks that involves.

José Luís left feeling satisfied. There was still a very complicated matter to be settled in the next few days. He no longer wanted to pay Zequinha a percentage of the profits. He agreed with Reader. They had already given Zequinha a lot of money. Even if the man was his future father-in-law, his motto would now be 'Friends are friends, but business is business.'

Want something to drink? Zequinha Bigode asked Fake, pouring himself a whiskey. Fake asked for his drink straight up. Whiskey this good, he said, doesn't need ice.

They sat facing each other, each with his drink. The television was on, muted, showing images of a program with a studio audience. You know, Fake, this business of loyalty, as I was saying, is very important. Because in our business what you see are con men and scumbags. Of course, I'm not speaking of myself or of you, after all, as you well remember, when Miltão wanted to end your life, I gave you shelter and protection here on my hill. And I've done even more for you. If we analyze it in detail, it was because of you that I killed the pastor.

Fake was surprised at the revelation. He hadn't known that Zequinha was behind the crime. Do you think Miltão would be stupid enough to kill a preacher right after making a bunch of threats? Of course not. Miltão may have been crazy, but he wasn't an idiot. It was me. And I won't even say I suffered a lot, because, you know, I can't stand those Bible-thumpers. The fuckers give me a pain. Miltão was right to kick their asses. When a preacher shows up here in Marrecos, I tell him right off, Friend, if you don't kiss my hand, we have nothing to talk about.

And Zequinha related the details of the murder of the pastor, how his soldiers had set up the ambush in the church and how Walmir had died 'begging for his life'. I killed the pastor because of you, continued Zequinha. You were proposing the alliance, and that was the only way Kingie could take over Berimbau. So, the central question is one of loyalty. I was always loyal to you. And you, let's face it, weren't such a great thing in those days. Today I see you like this, well dressed, a shirt that matches your pants, but in those days you were just a black guy with braided hair who liked rap, that and nothing more, protected by Noble, who was always crazy about that kind of music. Am I exaggerating? All right then. I'm loyal, and with me there are no maybes.

I'm loyal and I learn that Kingie is out there making deals with Gavião. Just look at it. Bad, isn't it? But OK, it's just business. What I can't accept, Fake, are these rumors about Marta and Kingie. That kills me. You swore to me he was going to marry that Kelly, and I don't see anything like a marriage happening. Marta lies. Marta disappears, Marta makes up stories, and I'm not stupid. So I'm going to talk to you. I want the truth. Is Kingie carrying on with Marta?

Fake looked at his glass of whiskey, avoiding Zequinha's gaze.

How do you want it, Fake? To tell me and walk away with dough or to have it beaten out of you? It's your choice. I'll wait while you decide.

25

BOOZE FESTIVAL. SATURDAY THE 20th. Music. Fun. Don't miss it. The poster, illustrated with a drawing of a red bottle, had been hung on the wall of Onofre's bar beside the image of Our Lady of Aparecida. If anyone had asked Onofre, it would have been hard to explain what type of festival that was, for in actuality, except for the poster, as Reader commented, there's nothing new in all that. A scam, scoffed Zino, the butcher. And, in fact, the various brands of booze displayed on the counter were the same as those routinely for sale, at identical prices, everything the same. What about the music? said Onofre, doesn't that count? Onofre had asked the samba band from Unidos do Berimbau to send over a group and was offering customers the first round on the house, he explained, that's the festival.

From the tables placed outside the bar one could watch a good part of the favela, the bus stop, the congested Avenida Epitácio Pessoa, and the countless commercial stalls set up along it, which sold souvenirs of Rio de Janeiro, cigarettes, shoes, music tapes, T-shirts, dried beef, plastic bowls, eggs, dolls, and odds and ends of every kind. In the late afternoon it was pleasant to sit there, watching the residents arrive from work, the children, freshly showered and playing in front of the houses, and the booze made all this even more pleasant, especially on the days when a clear sky turned sunset into a true spectacle.

Everything was ready for a night of fun, and it was horrible, Onofre later told his wife Maria. José Luís had reacted violently when he discovered his father drunk at the counter. What's my father doing here? I almost said, Getting soused, Zé. But I'm no fool, I kept my mouth shut. Every other day the old man gets plastered and then starts yelling when it's time to pay, I'm the father of the man, you looking for trouble? Worse yet, I've seen Francisco, completely smashed, get behind the wheel of his van and drive around committing atrocities in traffic. Zino told me the old man doesn't know what a red light means. He runs them all. And, on Avenida Brasil, the man's like a chicken with its head cut off. Nobody has the courage to say anything to Kingie, you know how it is.

José Luís was in fact quite attentive and concerned about his father. For two months he had gone with him to Alcoholics Anonymous meetings, encouraging him to give up drinking. How many days, Father? he asked every time he met Francisco. Sixteen days without drinking, the man replied. Seventeen. Nineteen. Twenty days? Shit, let's have some Coca-Cola to celebrate. Let's get something to eat to mark the occasion. What's important, they said at the meetings, is not to drink today, each day without drinking is a victory, and José Luís enjoyed celebrating the triumphs with his father.

Weeks earlier, he had bought Francisco new clothes, helped him bathe, taken him to the barber, and when his father was virtually unrecognizable with his new look, told him the news: You're going to meet my girlfriend. Marta had been wanting to meet Francisco for some time. Is your father still married to that secretary? Pop. José Luís had made up so many fabulous stories about Francisco, had created such an exceptional man in Marta's imagination that there was no way to set things right except by telling even more lies. Actually, José Luís had said, my father was let go by the firm, they shafted him, at the firm, shit, pop, Really? It was the secretary who did it. The woman's a whore, shit, it's better not to bring up the subject, José Luís had advised her. Father, this is Marta. Pop. Francisco almost thanked José Luís when he called him father, he felt so good there, father, my son, he said, What a pretty girl, he was so proud of his son, a winner, my son, he told Marta, You're a very lucky girl.

Sometimes, José Luís would take Alas to play with his grand-father, and at such moments Francisco would burst into tears.

Shit, Father, stop that. Every time I bring the boy here you get like that, shit. What happened was that Francisco was remembering Carolaine, so pretty, his daughter. You think, Zé the day will come that she'll speak to me? Every time he met his daughter, in the street, he felt sadness in his heart. Maybe, he thought, that's why I can't stop drinking. I'm going to stop. Yes, he went around drunk. Every day. And swearing that he wasn't drinking. Not a drop, José Luís. Nothing at all. And he did actually want to stop. I want to and I will. This is the last one, he would say before getting drunk. If Carolaine would at least say hello to him it would be easier. Now he had the impression of seeing Alzira wherever he went. Hello, Alzira, he'd said once. When the Devil appears, she replied, he comes in disguise. Deliver me.

As he was leaving, carrying Francisco over his shoulder, José Luís shouted to Onofre, You're forbidden to sell my father anything to drink, he said, it's forbidden.

That was not the only unpleasant episode of the night. Kingie had already come back from taking Francisco home and was no longer angry at Onofre, when Negaço ran up to say that Lobo and Valtinho were in a police van on Avenida Brasil. It was a setup, Negaço said. Couldn't be anything else. We'd just left here with a delivery for the sites in Sambacuim when suddenly the worms pull us over and yell: Everybody out. And they started hassling us and shit. Negaço related that the police had come straight to the point. Five hundred, they said, and none of this ever happened.

Let's pay it, Reader said. We pay, José Luís agreed, but we're going to teach those guys a lesson. I don't think it's a good idea, Reader went on, to stir things up over this, they're just some sons of bitches out to make a little dough, let's pay and forget about it.

Fifteen minutes later, they were all in the car, Fake driving, Negaço giving directions, Turn right, now left. José Luís remained silent during the trip. Put a sock in it, he told Negaço when he tried to tell a joke.

When they arrived at the scene, Fake flashed his headlights

and slowed down. Negaço got out, taking the money with him.

José Luís, from the front seat, watched the cops talking. Lobo and Valtinho had been removed from the patrol wagon and an air of pleasantry prevailed. Everyone was laughing at one of Negaço's jokes. The policemen waved, got into the wagon, and left.

Catch up with them, José Luís ordered when they were back in the car. Reader tried to say something but José Luís wouldn't listen to anyone. Catch up with them, goddamn it.

When the two vehicles were side by side, José Luís hurled a grenade that went in through the patrol wagon's left window. Fake accelerated at full speed. Seconds later they heard the explosion, fleeing without seeing the flame that consumed the policemen.

Something's amiss in paradise, sang the singer on Marta's Walkman, *it's much more than a contradiction,/ I'm falling into the abyss*, Marta removed the earphones, jumped out of bed, *You, flying away in a plane*, she hummed, 11:20 p.m., but she was wide awake and famished.

The box of chocolates on the dresser was empty, and in the drawers was nothing but a few sticks of gum.

In T-shirt and panties, she went downstairs to the kitchen. She took the toaster from under the sink and made a cheese, tomato and ham sandwich, exactly like those her father used to make for her when she was a child. Sitting alone at the table, she savored the sandwich, listlessly leafing through a magazine about plastic surgery that Priscilla had forgotten in her room. Before-and-after photos. Before, fallen buttocks full of cellulite, after, hmm, it does look better. Priscilla wanted to have lipo done on her thighs, and had asked for the operation as a birthday present. Yeah, it really does come out nice.

Still up? asked Suzana, coming into the kitchen in a robe. Marta didn't lift her eyes from the magazine. Uh-huh. It was really something how Suzana managed to be so bothersome, thought Marta. She couldn't sit down anywhere in the house without her stepmother popping up with her famous inane remarks. Don't put your feet on the sofa. Wash the dishes afterwards. Your room's a mess. Straighten up the pillows you threw on the floor. A real drag. Giving orders in the house, in the kitchen, bossing her father around, monopolizing the bathroom, it had been so nice when they lived without that woman around, just the four of them, Marta, Priscilla, their father, and their grandmother, so nice, they would remain at the table after lunch, talking, their father was so devoted, so loving, on Sundays they would all go to the beach or to a movie, to the steakhouse, how long since they'd gone to a steakhouse? Trillions of years. Now Zequinha only went out with Suzana. We want to be alone for a bit, he'd say, come, my night-blooming flower, my blossom of vanilla, goddess of my life. Suzana never let their father talk to them, and even their grandmother agreed. Suzana's jealous, their grandmother had explained. The woman's a real pain. I want to have three children with your father, Suzana had said. Three boys, because there are already too many women here. The bitch. Marta had put a curse on her, she'd told José Luís, that whore isn't going to get pregnant. And hadn't the spell been working? Now she's talking about getting fertility treatment. I told your father, Suzana said, that what Priscilla's asking is crazy, liposuction is very dangerous. Show your smile, the magazine said. Disgusting, those photos of wide-open mouths with false teeth. A modern odontological treatment. Priscilla's too young, continued Suzana, don't you agree? Marta had an excellent technique for escaping Suzana's 'life lessons', simply turning on her automatic 'uh-huh' response, leafing through the magazine in her hand, the cost of vanity, six thousand for a nose job, eight thousand for a face lift. Suzana didn't notice and went on talking. I have a friend, she said, who died on the operating table. Marta had heard the story a thousand times, but Suzana was like that. I keep wondering, Marta once told José Luís, how the mind of a nutty woman like that works. You wonder if she's senile and doesn't know she's already told that story, or does she say to herself, I've told the story before, but fuck 'em, they'll just have to put up with it. It has to be that. She's too young to be senile. It's like a joke, before she leaves for the hairdresser, she wanders around the house, tormenting everybody, I'm going to the hairdresser, my cellphone's turned on. Don't go to bed too late, Suzana concluded, you have to get up early tomorrow. Mommy-style, Marta said sarcastically. She's not my mother, she told José Luís.

After Suzana left the kitchen, Marta peeled a tangerine and ate it.

As she climbed the stairs, she heard voices from the front bedroom, where her father had put on a DVD, she thought that Zequinha and Suzana were arguing. She tiptoed down the steps and approached the door. Tomorrow night, she heard someone say, he's going to the Vasco game, maybe that's a good time. Whose voice was that? I'm not up for killing half the stadium, said Zequinha, it has to be somewhere quiet. But he's going in a car, the voice said, a voice that Marta thought she knew. The parking lot could be a good opportunity. He usually goes to the game without bodyguards. That's the place, brother.

Marta recognized it, it was Fake's voice. She listened to the conversation for a few more seconds, shaking from head to foot when she realized what they were talking about: killing José Luís. Fake was giving her father information about José Luís. I just don't want to be around when it happens, Fake continued.

Marta ran up the stairs, into her bedroom, put on jeans, threw a few clothes, the Walkman, some CDs, and chewing gum into a backpack, taking several minutes to figure out how best to elude the guards who stood watch over the house at night.

Before she left, she called José Luís on her cellphone and asked him to meet her in Copacabana, at the home of her friend the manicurist. In one hour, she said. It's very important.

No, said Rick Molzer, it's no good. Translate, Dunga, quick. Spray water on her face, he told the make-up artist. It was two in the afternoon, and the girl taking part in the filming didn't seem to mind Rick Molzer's exaggerations, poorly translated at full speed by the producer Dunga. That's the advantage of working with beginners, Rick had said when he cast the roles. They don't bust your balls. Professionals and extras don't do anything but complain about salary and the food. Action, he shouted, *Ação*, echoed Dunga. Communication on the set wasn't easy, everyone had to shout to be heard over the noise of buses passing nearby. Besides which, Dunga's simultaneous translation kept the scene lively. C'mon, he told the actress, walk, woman, be sensual, swing your hips, that's it, camera two, that's right, Karina, now stop, you're thirsty, he said, show that to the viewers, thirst, internalize your thirst. Now look at your hands. Bam! A bottle appeared in your hands, it's magic, that's right, smile, you've been saved by a soft drink. Now drink it, that's right.

Carolaine, sitting next to Reader in a chair beside the video monitor, was in ecstasy. What a pretty thing. What wonderful work. What interesting people. And all of it in English, on top of everything else. That's what she wanted to do. Be an actress. She had never imagined that making a commercial was so much work. She knew from gossip magazines that actresses spent hours in the studio but supposed that wasn't tiring for the stars. Paula Mendonça of the soap *Sweet Vengeance*, for example, who only had to kiss André Vilares (what a handsome man!), every episode was like that, kissing and kissing André, the two of them holding hands on the beach, riding a motorcycle, and rolling in the sand, how could anyone with work like that get tired?

The entire street had been blocked off for the filming, and the residents crowded into the windows and doorways of their houses to see the soda girl. This gave Carolaine a sensation of importance, after all, she was there among the artists, and Rick Molzer always said something to her. Enjoying it, Carolaine? Dunga translated. Take a look here in the monitor. I'm going to redo this take. Action. And Reader, at her side, how much he understood about television, Reader, explaining it all. I didn't know, said Carolaine, that everything was written down on paper. They took each other's hands. Every last word. Reader assured her, they do the script with the speeches of each one, for example, they write: Pretty girl descends the stairs, thirsty, and then she says: This is life! You think she's pretty? Carolaine asked, pinching Reader's leg. They both laughed. She's not ugly, he replied, but she's not my type, too thin. Carolaine loved the answer. She had lost only six pounds since Junior was born, and, you know, I don't think it's good to be too skinny myself.

Arf, arf, arf, Reader and Carolaine were holding hands when José Luís arrived with his dogs, causing tumult on the set, the dogs took over the street. Cut, cut, ordered Rick Molzer, welcoming José Luís effusively. I wanted to thank you, the crew is loving it, translated Dunga. This country is sensational. What a wonderful people. Thank you, thank you very much. José Luís didn't feel like talking to the American that afternoon. Distressed and disconcerted, he signaled to Reader.

OK, thought Reader, I get it, and prepared himself to speak about Carolaine. I like her a lot, he'd say, yes, we're going out together, you know how it is, there's chemistry between us, and if you don't mind, I want to go on seeing her, just remember that we're still getting to know each other, understand?

Zequinha wants to kill me, José Luís said abruptly as soon as they moved away from the set. José Luís told him everything, his meeting with Marta the night before in Copacabana, the conversation she had overheard in her father's house, Zequinha's plan to assassinate him after the Vasco game at Maracanã stadium, and Fake's betrayal. Marta's staying with me now, José Luís told him, she's not going back to her father's place. We're getting married. Jesus, said Reader, Jesus, what a story.

José Luís wanted his friend to go to Zequinha immediately on a peace mission. Explain to him, he said, explain to him that I love Marta, I'm crazy about her. We're going to pretend we don't know anything, that Marta heard nothing, we're going to act like everything's normal. Go there and say to him: Here's the situation, the two of them are getting married, they want to do it right, veil, white gown, the works. You don't understand, argued Reader, that none of it will do any good? Shut up and listen, Reader. You're going to go there and say we want his blessing. I'm even willing to pay something, if that's what he wants. I don't know if I'm the one to speak to Zequinha, Reader insisted, he's not my biggest fan. Shit, I can't send Negaço, he's thick as a brick, you're the one who's going, for shit's sake. What about Fake, Reader asked, what do we do about Judas?

Just take care of the problem with Zequinha, replied José Luís. Leave Fake to me.

Hi, brother, said Fake, getting into José Luís's car. Where we going? The meeting had been set up fifteen minutes earlier, by phone. A shipment of good dope is coming in, a parallel deal that's got nothing to do with Gavião, explained José Luís, we're going to pick it up. Just the two of us? asked Fake, looking in the vanity mirror on the visor, isn't that taking a chance? Zequinha's in on it too, answered José Luís. Fake, showing no reaction at the mention of Zequinha's name, went on smoothing his hair and talking nonsense, turned on the radio. He doesn't have the tiniest hint of guilt, thought José Luís, he handed over his friend and there he is, shit, like nothing happened, shit, these goddamn ungrateful pieces of shit don't give a fuck about anything, shit. Reader had said it all: there's no greater lack of consideration. Fake rattled on about a new way of removing tattoos by using lasers. José Luís heard only scattered words, radical, pile of garbage, got tired of my look, I've moved on, something prevented him from carrying on a normal conversation, he felt like cursing Fake, beating him, smashing his face in, kicking him, shit. He recalled when he had met Fake, rap, funk all the time, all those great afternoons, the two of them getting stoned and roaming around, going to dances, music the best thing in their lives, they'd even thought about putting together a band. On examination, thought José Luís, it wasn't good at all, shit. In fact, he thought, it was the crappiest period in my life. Fake had never agreed to include him in the rap band, always spoke about 'my band,' 'my demo tape,' 'my fans.' Of course, shit, José Luís remembered perfectly how he'd been excluded from Fake's plans. Fake, he asked suddenly, you remember when you wanted to have a rap band? What was I going to do in that band? Fake laughed. I never thought you'd be part of it, answered Fake, laughing, why're you asking that now? Shit, he doesn't even realize it, shit. No reason, said José

Luís, I was just thinking about those times. Good times, replied Fake, changing the station on the radio, but now is better, and you know why it's better? We have money, brother. The long green. And it's goddamn good to have money, isn't that right? Look at my watch. Look at my new shoes. Look at my belt. Look at the make of my shirt. I'm worth a small fortune just for my clothes. He laughed. He doesn't realize it, thought José Luís. Shit.

The sun had already set when José Luís parked the car at the trash pickup station in Caju. Two trucks were leaving the scene. Is he coming by trolley? Fake asked, wanting to know if the drugs would arrive in the municipal garbage trucks. Yeah, said José Luís, getting out of the car. Don't tell me we're going have to go through that pile of shit, said Fake, getting out of the car and walking carefully so as not to get his new pants dirty.

They stood side by side, looking at the mountains of garbage before them.

You know, said José Luís, unfortunately things are real shit, Fake. What are you talking about, brother? At that moment, José Luís lost the desire to talk. To deliver a lecture. You did this, you did that, just thinking about the words made him give up.

José Luís, years later, would still remember Fake's behavior. Don't go down on your knees, he ordered, enraged, I'll blow your brains out right here, man. Get up and run. Shit. Fake begged, Brother, don't do this, I'm clean, man. Run, I told you.

Fake ran, looking back. José Luís waited for a few seconds before he began to fire. Three shots. On the fourth shot, Fake fell.

Kingie advanced a few yards, took Fake's wrist to check for a pulse. Nothing. Shit.

26

YES, THE PEOPLE ARE from Mato Grosso, said Gavião on the telephone. Gavião had closeted himself in his office but was talking so loud that Reader, waiting for him in the living room, could understand that he was discussing a shipment of drugs from Bolivia. The odd thing was that the trafficker, however he tried to communicate in code, couldn't avoid certain telltale slips like 'Are the sneakers pure?' or 'Fourteen kilos of sneakers isn't for just anybody.' Even a fifth-rate detective overhearing the conversation could tell they were talking about cocaine, thought Reader.

Gavião hung up the phone and came into the living room wearing a satiny greenish-gray robe. Hi, Marilza, he said to the young woman also waiting on the sofa, curled up like a frightened animal. Reader had barely glanced at the frail, pallid, awkward girl. Isn't she pretty? commented Gavião, sitting on the sofa and placing his hand on Marilza's lap. Now then, what's the problem? Reader was reluctant to talk about the matter in the manicurist's presence. Spit it out, said Gavião, Marilza here can keep a secret like a dead man, isn't that right, Marilza?

While he related the drama of José Luís and Marta, Reader had the impression that Gavião wasn't wearing undershorts beneath his robe and that he opened his legs on purpose so the manicurist could see his penis. The girl shyly drew back further and further to file the trafficker's nails. I can try, Gavião said, but I'll tell you right now, it's a very serious matter. You know why? Zequinha has an obsession with college degrees. He even tried to buy an engineering degree, I found out. He laughed loudly. To Zequinha, there are two types of

236

people: those who went to college and those who didn't. The guy practically falls all over himself when he sees a diploma on the wall. I've been hearing the same litany for some ten years now: my daughter's going to marry a lawyer. I get a laugh out of that lawyer business. The only lawyers he knows are jailhouse lawyers, real low-rent shysters on the edge of starvation, but he treats those pieces of crap like they were somebody important. What can you do? Everybody's got their hang-ups. Tell Kingie I can't promise anything, but I'm going to try.

Reader's mission was a failure. Marry my daughter? said Zequinha, totally indignant, who does that little bastard think he is? That piece of goat shit. That pissant. That cow-dung. Up to now, I was only thinking of putting a bullet between his eyes, that's all, Gavião, but now I'll have to gouge out the fucker's eyes, tear his head off, and grind up the ingrate's tongue, that's what I'm going to do. Poor Marta, falling into the hands of that tenth-generation illiterate, that reprobate (Zequinha pronounced it 'reeprobate') is going to die.

Flower of my life, he said, every time Suzana tried to intervene on behalf of José Luís, daisy of my existence, do your king a favor and don't get mixed up in this story, my little rose-colored angel. You can ask your saint here for anything, just ask, goddess of love, daddy's little girl, ask for money, whims, extravagances, whatever you want, but don't mention the name of that piece of crap, my sweet.

Twenty men were protecting José Luís. Those were tense days, but Kingie and Marta didn't complain about being locked in at home, completely by themselves. I thought about going to a place like this for our honeymoon, he said, showing her a magazine picture of a pair of TV personalities in brightly colored outfits, skiing in the snow, or like this one, he said, turning the page, pop, a couple in a dune buggy on the beaches in Natal. Disneyland would be the greatest, pop, but I have to admit it's nice here, she said. They spent an enormous amount of time in bed, saying dumb things, laughing, making love. Do you really love me? Yes. You're not going to dump me for somebody prettier? Never. What if it's some tall, gorgeous blonde with green eyes? Fuck blondes, replied José Luís. You promised, she said. You made a vow and so did I.

And when they got hungry, they would go to the kitchen and Marta would make some sensational spaghetti. The recipe's simple, pop, a can opener, a can of tomato sauce, grated cheese, and that's it. They played with the dogs, ate chocolate cake with Coca-Cola, watched television, talked about the children they would have. The first one will be named Tiffany, I think that's a pretty name, said Marta. And she'll wear stylish clothes, miniskirts, nice sandals, no lace and ruffles, you'll see, pop, I'm going to be a supermom, and I'm not going to die young like my mother, pop, I'm going to see our children grow up, pop, get married, and I want to be a grandmother too.

What José Luís liked most about his new life was waking up and seeing his home functioning, Marta taking care of everything, of the dogs, running things, giving orders, the house wasn't the same, not that it was more organized or better, it was a different house, more comfortable, pleasant, fragrant. A house with a woman in it, said Reader, is always a palace. I made a list of things we need, said Marta, see to everything for me, Negaço: a broom, soap, cleansing powder, chocolate, yogurt, and frozen pizza. Sweep the living room, Zenaide. We're going to move these pieces of furniture out of here, Reader. I'm going to change all the curtains, help me up on this ladder. Marta frequently turned on the stereo, donned a bikini, and cleaned the house, humming and dancing. I'm great at cleaning, she said, there's nobody in the favela who scrubs a floor better than me. Look at my muscles, you like 'em?

There was one night in those days of 'imprisonment' that was very special. That was when the American Rick Molzer, accompanied by his interpreter Dunga, came to show José Luís the film he'd made in the favela. Actually, what brought Rick there again was the quality of the powder given to him by Dunga. I've never had such a powerful drug. Absolutely fantastic. You take a snort and you think you're the president of Microsoft, the power goes straight to your brain, you know what that's like? I adore Brazil. Brazilian powder is very good stuff. Too bad I'm leaving tomorrow. I'm heading to Guatemala, tomorrow. And then I'm shooting in the Australian Outback.

José Luís got excited at the commercial, watching it eight times at maximum volume. Very good, he said enthusiastically, the music's great, who's the music by? It's our jingle, answered Molzer, translated by Dunga. You wrote that music? José Luís asked, not understanding. No, the people at the production company. José Luís wanted to know if you could buy a CD with that music on it. No, replied Rick, but I can get it for you.

José Luís did in fact love the commercial, the image of the girl descending the favela, wiggling her hips, the happy, rhythmic music, everything about it was quite good, but what really imparted a special color to the night was being able to show off for Marta, shit, Marta seeing all that, him and Rick Molzer, chatting excitedly like old friends, Rick Molzer the foreigner, thanking him, saying how cinematic the hillside was, telling him about his future projects, the credit card commercial he was going to make in Haiti. More whiskey, Rick? I've ended up specializing in exotic locales, said Molzer. I only do publicity that involves that concept. When they want something different, mine is the first name they think of. I've filmed in Bosnia, the Amazon, Africa, India. I've been around the world. And I can guarantee you, powder like this I've never seen. This is sensational powder. You got any more?

José Luís looked at Marta, shit, those big eyes of hers glued on him, smiling, in love, Haiti, American ad agencies, commercials, cigarettes, Martinis, English. I was dying for Rick to leave, dying to fuck you, he would say later in bed while they made love. Shit, it's so good to fuck a foxy woman like you.

The two were inseparable. Even when José Luís took care of matters with Reader, Marta would remain beside him, participating in everything, giving opinions, especially when the subject was her father.

Despite his best efforts, Zequinha could not get within reach of José Luís, but he was nevertheless able to cause him numerous headaches.

One Wednesday morning, the police, acting on an anonymous tip, raided the favela, looking for the cache of arms belonging to José Luís's gang. There's no doubt it was Zequinha, said Reader, who had friends on the police force. But José Luís had moved quickly and, as a security measure, changed all the strategic centers of the traffic.

That same week, the access tunnel to Nova Barra was closed twice by robberies, and Zequinha was also behind it. In this way he achieved what he wanted, to gain media attention and bring the police into Berimbau. We're not about to take this lying down, the mayor said.

Overnight, José Luís, who had never been in the newspapers, was transformed into a recognized name. Journalists began roaming the area in search of information, and many articles were published. American publicist asks Cocaine Kingie's permission to film in the favela. The articles, besides being riddled with errors, especially in relation to the profits from the drug trade, depicted a violent and unpopular trafficker. Goddamn, what shit, said José Luís when Reader read the material to him. Didn't they say anything about the day-care center? Huh? Or the sewage system?

What most upset José Luís was the statement by Paulo Fernando, director of the Drug Suppression Division. We have a plan in place for his capture, he'd said. It's just a matter of time. Shit. Zequinha is complicating things.

You're not going to do anything to my father, Zé, Marta said. Don't even think about it. You're not even sure he was the one who did it. It wasn't my father. Promise me, Zé.

That night, lying side by side in bed, their eyes open, after having a good time, Marta asked if it wouldn't be better for her to return home. No, said José Luís, you're not going back, your place is here. José Luís, though aware of the danger he was in, didn't even consider living without Marta. He was happy, married, Shit, what are we going to do about Zequinha? he asked Reader, concerned.

Deep down, Reader said, this isn't about Marta. He's been suspicious of you two for some time now. The problem for

Zequinha is our independence. That story about percentages, he never swallowed it. The guy sees our operations expanding, sees us growing, and it drives him crazy.

The only way, suggested Marta, for us to solve this business is this: I'm going to call my father. Daughter, said Zequinha on the phone, I love you very much, and the house is very sad without you here. We're suffering, all of us, your grandmother, Priscilla, Suzana, and me. Come home, don't make your father suffer. There were seven long conversations, and in the last one, Zequinha realized there was little that could be done. His daughter wasn't ever coming back. Tell Kingie to meet me at the Boiada steakhouse, on Rua Pitanga, tonight at nine, he said. Promise, father, that you – Click. Zequinha hung up the phone before hearing his daughter's pleas.

You have two options, Reader advised him: you can negotiate or you can kill the guy and take over Marrecos.

José Luís was inclined to come to an agreement. Even if it cost him money. I'll give him up to five sites, if that's what it takes. Ten, if that'll settle the matter once and for all. I might even consider going back to paying him a percentage, what do you think? I'm willing to do a partnership.

You have to go in there laying down conditions, Reader stated, if the guy sees we're trying to avoid a war, we're fucked in spades. Go there and complicate things, say: This won't work, that won't work, and then, when the guy's good and dissatisfied, we make an offer, real low-ball at first. One site. We'll go slow.

Saturday afternoon, Reader prepped the men who would be José Luís's bodyguards and sent Negaço to the Boiada at three p.m., with two other soldiers. Let me know everything that's going on, he said.

At nine that night, on the dot, the car with José Luís parked in front of the restaurant. Minutes before, Marta had placed her St George's medal around José Luís's neck. Wear this, she said, it belonged to my mother.

Only a few tables were occupied at the restaurant. José Luís, always with Reader and two more soldiers at his side, sat down in the corner, allowing him to watch the entrance. The TV was on, a football game, Palmeiras and São Paulo. They remained alert, from time to time one of them made some comment on the progress of the game. It's a trap, said José Luís, after waiting fifteen minutes. I've never seen Zequinha late for anything.

When they left the restaurant, everything seemed calm. Negaço gave the sign guaranteeing cover.

As they got in the car, the firing began. I'm going to die, thought José Luís, throwing himself to the floor.

The hydrogen peroxide spread through the wound on Alzira's leg, whitening the lesion. Carolaine, from habit, was applying the treatment to her mother's leg almost automatically, spreading on the ointments and taping the gauze without taking her eyes from the eight o'clock soap. Ernesto had left Rita at the altar in the last episode. I want to see his face when he finds out that Rita is the illegitimate daughter of the magnate Pedro Henrique, who's filthy rich. Careful, Carolaine, where you put the bandage. Rita is going to inherit her father's companies, Mother, I saw it in the paper. Is she really? Serves Ernesto right, all he thinks about is money. And Ana Paula is going to catch Roberto with Teresa at the movies. Who? Alzira couldn't keep track of the soap operas because she always fell asleep during them. Roberto demanded an explanation from Teresa, remember? In the last episode. Because of the stock in the 'textile factory', Mother. Alzira didn't answer. She'd dozed off again. Alzira liked to sleep in front of the TV, it gave her a sense of well-being, that it was still early and lots of free time remained. Also, sleep was better on the sofa, sometimes she would open her eyes and see the couples kissing, fighting, margarine commercials, such pretty women, and then go back to sleep, waking, sleeping, until she noticed the television had been turned off and Carolaine was no longer there, or Alas, or Junior, everything calm and silent, only then would Alzira go to bed. And each morning, upon waking up sleepy, feeling the throbbing in her leg, she promised herself to go to bed early that evening. Even during the weeks that Dona Juliana had been away with her husband and the children and she had hardly any work to do, even then Alzira tired very easily.

What's happening, Carolaine? Alzira asked, waking up and seeing Heloísa kissing Henrique. Isn't Henrique engaged to Elisa? Shh, Mother, listen.

Carolaine had the cellphone in her lap, hoping that Reader would call at any moment. They were going to meet at his house that evening. Alzira had given Junior his bottle in case he woke up during the night, and Alas was already asleep. It hadn't been difficult to convince her mother. Alzira, in the first days of Junior's life, had taken over caring for the baby. Carolaine doesn't know how to bathe the child, she said. Carolaine doesn't know how to change a diaper. That's not the way, here, let me do it. And, little by little, Alzira had taken over responsibility for Junior the same way she had with Alas, doing everything, even while experiencing sharp pains in her leg. You mustn't lift anything, or exert yourself, the doctor had said. That wound, Dona Alzira, isn't going to get better unless you rest. A varicose ulcer. Each time she saw the doctor, Alzira promised to take his advice seriously.

When the phone rang, Carolaine answered happily, Hello, Carolaine, it's Negaço. Alzira saw her daughter's expression change suddenly. Where? she said. Near the reservoir? While she dashed about the house, grabbing her purse and putting on shoes, she told her mother that Reader had been shot in a gun battle. Carolaine, come back here and explain it to me, said Alzira, at the door, watching her daughter rapidly disappear.

Is he going to die? asked Carolaine, minutes later, in a clinic hastily set up by the traffickers. When anyone was wounded, a doctor was brought to the shack and did what he could to keep the victim from going to the hospital. Reader had been the only one struck in the gun battle with Zequinha's men. They were only after him, said Negaço, I was unprotected, my back wide open, they were just after Reader.

They spent the rest of the night waiting. Now and then José Luís would come into the room, anguished, trying to pressure the doctor. He's lost a lot of blood, the doctor explained. Reader's condition was critical.

* * *

Early the next morning, José Luís returned home, found Marta awake in the bedroom, her eyes bloodshot from crying. The remote control in her hand, she went on flipping channels, paying no attention to the images being shown.

José Luís turned off the TV, lay down beside her, they took each other's hand and remained silent, looking at the ceiling. Marta had already been told about Reader, José Luís himself had called to tell her, some hours earlier.

I didn't want this to happen, she said, the words catching in her throat. Now you're going to kill my father, aren't you?

José Luís thought about saying that he wished things were different, shit, that he could act some other way, shit, that he were free to forgive, that he didn't have to kill Fake, shit, but it had nothing to do with friendship, they were drug dealers, shit, there was a lot of money at stake, shit, and lots of danger too, people died, they killed traitors, informers, all of them died, shit, he'd killed Fake, his best friend. Shit. Business plans, as Reader himself liked to say, had to be taken extremely seriously.

Before locking himself in the bathroom, the only thing he managed to say to Marta was that now one of the two, him or Zequinha, had to die.

Under the shower, as he washed the bloodstains from his body, he heard Marta sobbing in the bedroom. The reddish water ran down his legs and formed a puddle at his feet. However he tried, he couldn't stop thinking about Reader, lying in the street after the shooting. I'm fucked this time, Reader had said. And in the car, while Negaço phoned the doctor to say someone was on their way to pick him up for an emergency, Reader, his head in José Luís lap, had said he couldn't feel his legs. Goddamn it. What shit.

At that time, José Luís considered himself experienced in invading favelas, and he owed that to Zequinha. It had been Marta's father who'd taught him how to put together a team, choose weapons and ammunition, study the enemy. Nothing beats the element of surprise, Zequinha had said. Always look for the best way of catching the adversary with his pants down.

Therefore, the invasion of Marrecos, contrary to everyone's expectations, took place in broad daylight, when families were sitting down to Sunday lunch.

Access points to the favela were occupied by forty five men led by José Luís, and the order was to go in making lots of noise. The artillery fire was so heavy that the residents themselves appealed to the 15th Military Police battalion for help. The hill was surrounded, but the commander of the operation held off on going in, for fear that civilians would be killed in the ensuing combat.

Zequinha was killed in his living room, in front of the television, with twenty-seven bullets in his head and abdomen.

There were many stories about the final moments of the boss of the Marrecos favela, and all of them were recounted exhaustively at Zequinha's funeral. He had allowed himself to be killed, some said. Before dying, others claimed, he had resisted and killed three, eight, ten of José Luís's men. Still others said it was Marta herself who had arranged her father's ambush. Some of the residents swore they had seen Zequinha's head impaled on a fence across from the bakery.

It was not true that José Luís had decapitated his enemy. That Sunday, immediately following Zequinha's execution, there was a moment in which the two warring gangs stopped fighting to discuss what to do if the police, at the foot of the hill, decided to invade. Kingie explained the situation to Zequinha's right-hand man, Osvair, known as Vavá. I'm giving the orders here now. You can swallow that with saliva or with lead. I'll accept anybody who wants to join my group. But it has to be right now, shit. Come over now, or never. The new alliance was forged. The gunfight resumed and the police were kept away.

When it got dark, José Luís eluded the police encirclement by using the narrow, labyrinthine streets that led to Berimbau. Many were arrested that day when the police finally broke through to Marrecos, but Kingie's group suffered no casualties. Ten trusted men stayed behind to handle the occupation.

When he returned, José Luís thought about looking for Kelly

and Yolanda, he missed them, but he thought it best to go home. I want very much for you to stay, he told Marta as soon as he entered the living room. But if you want to you can leave. I just killed your father.

27

THE SCENERY WAS MAGNIFICENT. From there one could view the sea reflecting the lights of the Rio-Niterói bridge, the planes taking off and landing at the international airport. I can't even talk, said Alzira, standing in front of the Fortune of God church, whose doors were opening that night for the first time. It was her forty-seventh birthday, and José Luís had just picked her up at her house. It's your present, Mother, he'd said, and Alzira was moved to tears. José Luís, she said, this work is yours, now open your heart and accept Jesus. José Luís was happy too, but his mother's excesses bothered him, and he especially hated it when she wanted to hug him, kiss him, he didn't like that.

Mother and son went into the worship service hand in hand and sat in the first row, where Kelly was waiting for him, along with Yolanda, Onofre, Cândida, and his closest friends. Alzira looks like a bride, Onofre said good-naturedly to Yolanda.

The shed, whose construction had cost a lot more money than José Luís was willing to spend on the church, could house four hundred worshippers. That night, not a single seat was empty. Not only residents of Berimbau but also many from Marrecos were present.

The 'incendiary' sermon by Pastor Ângelo, who was responsible for the inaugural ceremony of the Fortune of God church, bore not the slightest resemblance to the rituals of the late Pastor Walmir. Ângelo had made a point of inviting the funk rockers from the favela to help him with the hymns of praise and had made use of the melodies. We're going to change the lyrics, he had said, our business is God and love in our hearts. Funk was fundamental to the success of worship in other parishes. It made the faithful jump around and raise their hands to heaven, stamp their feet, and that, along with the 'punches in the Devil's face,' as well as his experiences as a sufferer in the years he had worked collecting garbage, as shoeshine boy, and lemon vendor in the streets, transformed him into an effective leader of his flock.

There was a climate of brotherhood that night. Although Kingie had issued some warnings, Ângelo did not feel pressured by the traffickers. One hand washes the other, José Luís had told him weeks earlier when he was selecting a pastor to run the church. Let's understand each other. You don't get nosy, you don't trash the business, shit, don't overdo the list of sins, and in exchange you get dough and protection.

I wanted, said the pastor, in this our first meeting, to prove, not only to the faithful, because they need no proof, I wanted to demonstrate to the reluctant, to those who have not embraced Christ, that God exists. What you're about to see, brethren, is proof of the existence of the all-powerful, the almighty God the Father Our Lord.

Ângelo gave the signal and the funk musicians, equipped with electric guitars, drums, and electronic keyboard, played music similar to that heard in rock concerts, before announcing the next attraction. He's coming, brethren, shouted the pastor, pointing to the door and directing the audience's attention there.

The entrance of Reader, in a wheelchair pushed by Carolaine, was spectacular.

While Reader was taken toward the altar, the excited crowd cried, applauded, and sang a hymn of thanks, *O thank You, Lord, thank You so much*. José Luís tried to locate Marta in the rear seats, but she wasn't there. Now that he was boss of the Marrecos favela too, he wanted the residents to see them together. You have to come, Marta, he'd said, as he was getting ready, before going to pick up Alzira. Lying in bed, without taking her eyes off the TV, she hadn't even answered, although she felt like shouting that she'd gone by herself to her father's funeral and to the seventh-day Mass as well, pop, and there was nothing but sadness in her heart and therefore she wasn't going to any crappy inauguration of some church, pop. Marta, José Luís had said on the day of Zequinha's funeral, tell me any way I can show up at the cemetery. No chance. And don't think I'm not suffering, shit, it hurts like hell, don't cry, damn it. Marta hadn't really heard him, she'd felt like responding Fuck you, you kill my father and then you come to me saying you're suffering because I'm crying? Fuck you. Pop. Murderer, she said between sobs, her face buried in the pillow. She phoned her sister Priscilla daily, confused. How can I go on living here? But if Priscilla or anyone else accused José Luís, she came to his defense. He's not to blame for anything, she said.

Marta couldn't forget what had happened at her father's wake. As she kneeled beside the coffin, Suzana came up to her and said, softly at first then yelling hysterically, that it was all Marta's fault, that if Marta hadn't been so selfish, so spoiled, none of it would have happened. Shut up, Marta answered, but neither of the two shut up, furiously trading accusations and then launching themselves at each other, causing great difficulty for the people around them who tried to separate the two women. That same day, Marta asked José Luís to take measures to see that Suzana left her father's house and moved far away from Berimbau.

What had hurt her most had been José Luís's lukewarm reaction. He'd done absolutely nothing to prevent Suzana from installing herself in a house not far from them, though she was aware that the bitch, the whore, pop, was already talking to lawyers trying to squeeze money out of her family. And she also knew why José Luís had acted as he had. He was too busy, too successful, making plans for the future, to think about other people, pop. Thanks to her father, since the bulk of the money, pop, came from Marrecos. The same day that Suzana moved to Berimbau, José Luís was honored by the samba school. In red pants and stylish glasses, proud as a peacock, thinking he knew it all, pop. She remembered perfectly because it had been the week after the seventh-day Mass for her father. Pop. Marta was 'dying of unhappiness', and everything would have been different if José Luís had only kicked Suzana out of there. Nothing else. Pop, but no, I can't talk now, José

Luís had replied, a container of yogurt in his hand. We're in a meeting, love.

Since Zequinha's death, José Luís had become inaccessible. Always on the telephone, shouting, busy, difficult. Not now, Marta, he said, we're in the middle of getting rid of the president of the Marrecos Residents Association, shit. It was unpleasant to leave the house, pop. José Luís, with Gavião's help, had recruited sixty armed men who controlled every access point to the favelas, around the clock. Everyone was stopped and searched. Cars were forbidden to use the streets leading to the interior of the two favelas. Local businesses had no way to restock their merchandise, as not even trucks were authorized to come up the hillside. Precautionary measures, José Luís said.

Gavião, who for years had been her father's great friend, practically lived in José Luís's house. You have to have complete control of the traffic, and it's important to show force till things calm down. Dominate it completely and kill as many as necessary. Zequinha furnished the drugs for Padre Moraes prison. And he was the one who set up the escape plans, you have to take over all that, Kingie. Gavião hadn't even offered her his condolences. Marta, dear, can you give us a moment alone? José Luís said, holding back any show of irritation. But she does nothing but cry, he complained to Kelly now and then, when he stopped by his friend's house for coffee. What'd she want me to do, wait for her father to kill me? She cries all day long, she won't answer my questions, shit, and she complains, always has a sour look on her face, crying, I can't take it any more, shit. It was her decision to come live with me. I know I've got to be patient, it was her father, I know all that, shit, but can't she at least stop crying? Damn it, I don't know, damn it all, what shit. It gets to me. Shit.

Reader's going to be there, José Luís had said that night, in one last effort to convince Marta to go to the opening of the church. So what? Fuck Reader, Marta had thought. She'd rather he had died instead of her father.

This man, continued the pastor, referring to Reader, is proof that God exists. At Ângelo's side, many pounds thinner, Reader sat at the altar, distant from what was happening around him, as if he understood nothing. Yes, he is the proof that God exists. Do you know how many bullets this man took? Thirteen, my loved ones. Life is unbelievable, Onofre whispered to Yolanda, one day the man is a genius with total power, the next day he's shitting in disposable diapers. Thirteen shots, brethren, continued the pastor. And one bullet is still lodged in his head. With the amount of blood the man lost, only a miracle could save him. And here is the miracle. Reader can't walk. He's a quadriplegic. He can't talk or write. Maybe he doesn't even understand what we're saying about him.

Sounds to me, Negaço commented to Lobo, like this preacher's doing a number on Reader.

But the miracle of life is here before us, said the pastor, touching the audience's emotions. Reader is alive, and life is the great miracle of God. God wanted Reader to remain among us.

Carolaine couldn't stop crying. Not that she was upset. She was thinking about what she would have to do the next day, find an abortionist and solve the problem as quickly as possible. What if she died? José Luís hadn't thought of that possibility. She'd heard that Madeusa had died from an abortion. And Dirce's cousin also. She regretted having told her brother about the pregnancy. She thought she would have José Luís's support. What are you telling me, her brother had said angrily, that you're pregnant by Reader? Is that it? You're the stupidest woman I've ever seen in my life, and you're not going to have that kid, for shit's sake. Goddamn. You're getting an abortion. And just shut up, I'm not interested in what you have to say, getting pregnant by a vegetable, shit. Stupid. That was what had hurt most of all, calling Reader a vegetable, Reader of all people, who had almost died for José Luís. Here's the money, Carolaine. Go to one of those butchers and take care of it right away, shit. And it doesn't do any good to cry or bitch and moan, it's over, you're not having another kid. What a stupid woman. Shit.

Alzira, despite seeing her daughter crying at the altar and Reader in a wheelchair, wasn't paying attention to the pastor's words, so enchanted was she with all that was going on, her son, imagine, giving her the church as a present, O thank you, God. What a pretty church. She had heard comments about its being built, but she had never had the energy to climb to the top of the hill. Everything was so pretty, clean, organized. The altar, so white. Thank you, she whispered in José Luís's ear, feeling her heart swell with love for her son.

That was a special day, thought Alzira, recalling the kindness of Dona Juliana, that very day, she had told Carolaine, she gave me the day off just because it was my birthday. She's a different person, Alzira had told Carolaine countless times. A different woman. Calmer, more polite. Much nicer.

Juliana had come back from Europe ten days ago. Going through the newspapers that had piled up during her trip, she found something that caught her eye: Drug boss decrees curfew in Marrecos favela, read the headline. She immediately recognized the photo accompanying the article. Rodrigo, she said to her husband in the bathroom, showing him the paper, isn't that Alzira's son? Putting down his razor, Rodrigo looked at the photograph with curiosity. Yes, it's him, he replied. Leader of the drug traffic in Marrecos. And in Berimbau. How awful. We have to get rid of that woman, Rodrigo. And fast.

Juliana had gone to Paris 'to save my marriage,' as she had confessed to her new best friend Helena, and had returned determined to change her life. Never again a personal trainer, Helena. You remember what Fernando was like? The guy would say things like 'he don't,' 'I didn't see nothing,' 'the streets is wet,' a real dumbbell. Lesson number one, my dear: as some writer or other said, no good deed goes unpunished. Now I'm a different person, I want the classic, know what I mean? A high-toned fitness center for women, with that blaring noise and women working out in those leotards that go up your ass. That's it. Enough of personal trainers. I don't ever want anything personal again. I'm like the slogan for that bottled water that my father loved: 'Enough experimenting. Drink Caxambu.'

Among the many changes to be made, the most urgent was

firing Alzira. You just can't live with a person who knows everything about you. Helena, and looks at you with those accusing eyes. I have the impression that at any moment she'll start blackmailing me. I want a car, a new stove, I want a small apartment. Like in that British movie *The Servant*, understand? You know what she said to me when I arrived? Mr Fernando didn't call. And I hadn't asked anything. What makes me nervous is that now I can't even reprimand her when I feel like it, call her attention to anything, complain about the dinner or the cleaning, which wouldn't be a problem if Alzira were a good maid. But she happens to be the dumbest person I've ever seen. The other day, I was talking about São Paulo and she told me about somebody she knows, an excellent cook who lives there, and because I had absolutely nothing else to talk about I asked if that friend of hers lived in the north zone or the south zone. In the north, she answered, with that expression people have when they don't know what they're talking about. So I said, Are you sure? She replied, Isn't the north zone right next to the south zone? That's right, dear. You can laugh. Rodrigo said we should send Alzira's brain to some university. I'm letting her go, very soon.

Juliana would in fact have dispensed with Alzira's services that same month if she hadn't come across the article about José Luís. What are we going to do, Rodrigo?

Distant from all that was taking place, Alzira had nothing but praise for her employer. Get me this, get me that, you don't know anything, Alzira, she had never again heard Dona Juliana say these unpleasant things. Thank you, you're an angel. Angel, now it was like that, and Alzirinha. You can't imagine how lovely Paris is, Alzira. I brought this back for you, she'd said, handing her a small bag with several tiny bottles of perfume whose labels read 'Not for sale'.

Alzira, Juliana had commented that morning as she was having breakfast, your leg is more swollen. Isn't it, Rodrigo? Look how it's swelled. Yes. Your leg looks very bad. It's quite dangerous, Alzira. Have you thought what would happen if gangrene sets in? Eh? They'd have to amputate. Know something, Alzira?

Come here. Take this money and go see a doctor. And you don't have to come back to work today. That's right. A day off. You deserve it. See you tomorrow, Alzira.

Even before she traveled, Dona Juliana had changed her behavior, which only reinforced Alzira's theory that Dona Juliana wasn't bad by nature but rather the victim of the Evil One.

And it was precisely the demon that the pastor was speaking of now. We are going to combat the Devil, together. Let us pray.

And Alzira prayed, fervently. She felt very good there, inside the church. She had suffered greatly. Yes, and she deserved a better life.

28

I READ IN THIS great book, said the lawyer who minutes earlier
had opened the door of his Copacabana apartment to Gavião and
José Luís, I read that to the Russians, even Poland is wonderful.
It's become a crazy thing. You know what it's like to have twice
the area of the Amazon region, veritable pools of diamonds, plus
titanium, plutonium, the works, and sell everything dirt cheap?
Not to mention nuclear warheads, incredible weaponry, all of
it just begging to be snapped up, cash and carry. The Russians
are better than we are at fucking the country. They claim they
even have an Anti-Embezzlement Division. Imagine.

As he listened, Gavião watched fire consume a small quantity
of cocaine on a piece of aluminum foil. Slowly, the drug took on
a brownish coloration. Very good, Gavião told the lawyer, who
wouldn't stop talking about the countless ways of getting rich
in Russia. Three more samples of cocaine were set afire, only
one of which left Gavião in doubt. He asked the lawyer for a
new envelope and emptied it into a glass of water to verify its
solubility.

The three remained there for some time, exchanging pleasantries. Contrary to José Luís's expectations, they at no time
discussed drug shipments, quality, transport, prices, nothing.
It was the first time José Luís had gone with his friend to
such a meeting. Shortly before, Gavião had phoned to say he
was nearby. I want you to see an apartment right in front of
the favela, he said. An excellent deal, you have to get it. I'm
coming by. As they were on their way to look at the property,
Gavião said that something unforeseen had arisen, I have to go
to Copacabana, you want to come along?

It was buyers like José Luís who made Gavião virtually the sole distributor of all the drugs that arrived in Rio de Janeiro. He sold him twenty kilos every weekend, and thanks to business schemes of that sort, he enjoyed favorable treatment from the Colombian wholesalers, among them the lawyer who had received them that afternoon.

Despite their friendship, José Luís knew little about Gavião's operations. At first he thought he was a link between some figure in authority, an important politician or someone in the illegal lottery or the Bolivian cartel. And maybe he was, but everything changed so quickly that just when José Luís thought he was beginning to understand the arrangement, there was no longer any arrangement at all, new names emerged while others disappeared, you didn't buy the refined drug but the coca paste, or vice versa, the refining labs weren't in Mato Grosso but in São Paulo or Cascavel. The secret, Gavião said, is to keep changing the secret. José Luís frequently saw him on the phone dealing with the price of acetone, ether, and kerosene, or talking to pilots about drums and gallons. He had had frequent conversations about the arrival of cars in Ponta Porã. The names of cities like Miami and Amsterdam often arose in these conversations, and there was always someone with the title of colonel, general, congressman, or the like. There were also many, many women, the mules, who brought small quantities from the labs in Bolivia. My girls, as Gavião called them.

Gavião spoke of the Cali and Medellín cartels in a way very similar to how Alzira spoke of God. And that made José Luís understand more and more what Reader had meant when he said one day, 'We're small fry.' Now that he was boss of Berimbau, Marrecos, and twelve more drug sites, he thought only of operations on a large scale. The list of his assets was growing rapidly. A two-story apartment in the Mon Amour building in the Barra da Tijuca. Four commercial offices in downtown Curitiba. Two lots in the Inhangá district in Niterói. Gavião was his mentor in these transactions. Buy this. Sell that. Rent it. Transfer it to Marta's name. The truth is that his life had changed greatly, his name was constantly in the papers, almost every week an article appeared about his activities, under headlines such as: The biggest drug trafficker in Rio de Janeiro, Military troops humiliated by Kingie's soldiers, Chief of police Almeida promises to take Marrecos. I feel personally insulted, Almeida declared, when I see in the papers this worthless perpetrator, this dangerous killer talking as if he were some kind of Robin Hood. You journalists help romanticize this scum. It's incredible.

The press had a lot to say about 'efficient strategies to end the traffic', and José Luís was always mentioned in such reports. But, unlike in the past, now José Luís liked being in the spotlight.

Despite no longer being able to move about without body-guards, José Luís saw nothing but pluses in his fame. He enjoyed being loved and feared by women and children, enjoyed the excitement that materialized when he strolled the streets with his well-fed dogs, enjoyed chewing out his men, guffawing, shouting, cursing people, getting plastered, and waking up as late he liked, work or not, buying things at the supermarket without looking at prices, and sleeping with every pretty girl who crossed his path. He also enjoyed going around in boots, of which he'd bought numerous pairs, some with spurs that left the floor in his house scarred and scratched.

After the stop in Copacabana, Gavião took him to the pent-house that a realtor friend had offered him. The owner is up against it, explained Gavião, but that's not the best part. The best part is here, he said, taking him to the kitchen. It was possible to see the entire favela, even though one had to bend down a bit. José Luís had never noticed the tangle of power lines, the result of illegal installations, in front of Zino's butcher shop. A mess. It's perfect, said Gavião, looking at the view. It's like you were right inside it.

It wouldn't be a bad idea to move to that location. Nowadays, said the realtor, who had come with them, the favela is part of the Rio landscape. We have foreign clients who come for a vacation and ask for a favela view. At night, this is my personal opinion, the favelas are quite interesting, that mass of little lights shining, it's different, he said. And the favela residents, from my experience, are very civilized people. You can shut up now, Gavião told the realtor, nobody here needs convincing.

Three bedrooms, including a master bedroom with bath, hardwood floors, the materials were very similar to what José Luís used in his own house.

Do I buy it or not? he asked Reader later, when he got to his office. José Luís had the habit of speaking to his friend, who now and then would emit a kind of moan. Shit, Reader, how am I supposed to understand that? You sound like a cow. Well, is it yes or no? Blink, Reader. The 'blinking' technique was infallible, José Luís believed, pleased at having invented it. Weeks before, while studying strategies for invading a drug site, he had laid out his plan in minute detail to his friend. Blink, he had said, if you agree with this. And Reader had blinked. Shit, take a look at this, Negaço, this is the smartest vegetable in Brazil. It was common for him to refer to Reader in that manner, vegetable, and there was neither malice nor irony in it, just the opposite, it was an affectionate nickname. Shit, Vegetable, what should I do? Do I buy a plane or not? How much does a Cessna 310 cost? Speak, Vegetable. How much does a pilot charge to bring in a shipment? Huh? A hundred grand, two hundred grand? Blink, Reader. Is it worth it? So you understand what I'm thinking? I'm thinking about Tabatinga and Leticia. Vegetable. Is it worth it? Huh? he asked, referring to the cities where it was possible to buy Colombian cocaine wholesale. Those were good times, José Luís said, when you could talk.

It had been some weeks since Carolaine had stopped taking care of Reader. Now, with her pregnancy in its fifth month and having spent the money her brother had given her for the abortion, Carolaine had come to hate 'the cripple'. How could I have slept, Kelly, with that fat turd, stinking of cigarettes and shitting in diapers? The other day, Kelly, I was there, imagine it, wiping that overweight guy's ass, and I thought, What? Me pregnant, fucked over, and here I am, cleaning up shit? Enough. I'm out of here.

Now it was Onofre who took care of Reader. 'Took care of' was a figure of speech; Onofre would lift him out of bed in the morning, stick him under the shower, put a clean diaper on him, and then place him, dressed and his hair combed, back in his wheelchair, complaining about his wife Maria the whole time, 'that wretched fart-factory,' I've never seen anything like it, Reader, it's like all the woman knows how to do is complain, goddamn it to hell, look over there, he said, pushing the wheelchair as they left for José Luís's headquarters, that young girl, you see her? There's so much beauty in this world, he said, pointing to the nannies and maids who were descending the hill on their way to work, really sweet things, and what I ask myself all the time, Reader, is how can such pretty creatures that God made turn into something like my Maria?

Often, when José Luís was very busy or out of the favela, Reader would be left forgotten in the kitchen, or elsewhere in the house, for hours at a time. Marta ignored him completely. Get that out of my sight, she once said, after stubbing her toe on the wheelchair.

At night, José Luís could frequently be seen pushing Reader in the narrow streets and alleyways, and then taking him home. I don't know if it's a good idea to leave Berimbau, he told Reader that afternoon, after visiting the apartment. You're going to make the decision. Let's go there now. Negaço, Cachaça, get me a car.

As they were leaving, two boys brought him a note from Suzana: 'Meet me at Kelly's house, eight o'clock tonight.'

What could she want, Reader? Money, I'll bet.

'My dear Santa Claus, everything's fine here, you can't imagine how happy Dadá's daughter is, she doesn't even seem like the same sly little girl. She and Heinrich talk only in German. Heinrich loves the girl. He's even learned to dance the samba with her.

'As for the rest, everything's the same. My German's gotten worse since Jennifer arrived. I let Augusta, my tutor, go (but now she's my friend and practically lives here), and Heinrich doesn't mind having Jennifer translate the things I say.

'Yesterday I was shocked when I weighed myself. I've put on

over twenty pounds. I think it's the cold weather. Stop sending me candy. My clothes don't fit anymore.

'That's it for now. Kisses to all the gang. Rosa Maria.'

She loves Brazilian candy, Onofre said to Alzira, who was opening a bottle of cheap wine with the corkscrew that Rosa Maria had sent as a gift. Dona Juliana has one just like this, it's a very good one, explained Alzira. You're real good at uncorking, Onofre declared, fascinated at seeing his friend remove the corks from bottles so easily. I'd already asked a bunch of people and nobody knew how to use the gizmo. It's the best they make, he was assured by Alzira, who had been pressed into service as she was passing by the bar on her way home.

Onofre served Alzira a turnover and showed her several photographs that Rosa Maria had sent. Rosa Maria in front of a snow-covered house, Rosa Maria in front of a church whose steeple had been destroyed in the war. I didn't understand that, said Onofre, showing the photo of Rosa Maria standing beside a wall, she said that the wall came down, I don't know what wall she's talking about. There were more recent photos, Jennifer standing between Rosa Maria and Heinrich at an amusement park. How pretty the girl is, commented Alzira. She always was, said Onofre, and if she'd stayed in Brazil she'd be the best standard-bearer in all of Rio.

The two were looking at the photos when they heard the sound of squealing brakes and a collision. Now he's done it, said Onofre, seeing Francisco's van against the tree where José Luís had ordered a placard placed reading 'Do not tie animals here.' He's finally managed to crash the car.

Francisco got out of the van, staggering. He's drunk as a skunk, Onofre told Alzira. Take a look, Alzira, the man doesn't even know where he's going. They both laughed.

Alzira finished her soft drink, pleased. The van was dented everywhere, served him right.

That hadn't been the only good thing to happen that day. In the afternoon, Juliana had called her in and said, I've been thinking, Alzira, you can't go on working with that leg the way it is. We're very grateful for all you've done for us. And here's your reward. A check for thirty-six months' salary. You can go three years without working. So you can take care of your health.

Now, satiated, her stomach full of the sweets that Onofre had offered her, Alzira was going home with the check in her pocket. Carolaine was also very happy when she heard the news. The bank's still open, Mother, let's deposit the money.

Which is exactly what they did. Carolaine suggested opening the account in her name, after all, her mother was illiterate and didn't know how to use a magnetic card. It would be great, thought Carolaine, especially after the argument she'd had that morning with her brother. She had gone to him once again for money, she was going to get the abortion, but it wasn't easy to fool José Luís. She stammered a bit, and that was enough for José Luís to understand the situation completely. You didn't get the abortion, did you, Carolaine? No, she hadn't. She had bought CDs, two pairs of sneakers, and all those clothes, some small teddy bears, but she didn't tell her brother that. She began crying, You don't know, Zé, how hard it is to get an abortion, she explained that many women died in the attempt. Enough, interrupted José Luís. You are really, really stupid. Stupid as they come. No more money from me ever again, Carolaine. The well's dried up. Now you'll just have to take care of yourself.

Carolaine had begged, but there was nothing to be done. Now she was in this situation, having to hide her belly. At least she was fat, which helped things. Fat hides everything, that was the advantage of being obese. Maybe she could still find a doctor to do the abortion. There was always some butcher or other on duty. Maybe she could even use a part of Alzira's money. Let's open the account in my name, Mother, it's better that way. Don't be a fool, Carolaine. Forget it. I want the account in my name. Alzira told the bank manager.

Boyfriend? Suzana couldn't even think about such a thing, and that was the answer she gave when Kelly bombarded her with questions about her new life. It was only two months since Zequinha died and she was very unhappy. I open my eyes in the morning, and the first thing I think is that he doesn't exist anymore. I don't even feel like getting out of bed.

Drawn, many pounds thinner and smoking nonstop, Suzana told her that on the day of her husband's death the two of them had stayed in bed late. I took him his breakfast, we read the papers, we made love. Too bad I didn't know it was a farewell. You don't know, Kelly, what it means to be married to a man who calls you my goddess, queen of my existence, flower of my rainbow, my Cleopatra, a man who has nothing but praise for you, who thinks any crappy thing you do is beautiful, there I go, crying again. It's the worst thing in the world to meet a man like that. After that, Suzana continued, there's nothing else that can interest a woman. Nothing. Everything is too little, after that. He was the best. The most intelligent. The most affectionate. The most interesting. The funniest. The most generous. And he knew he was in danger. He told me once that he had opened an account in my name. If I die, he said, leave this house, go see our lawyer, it's all taken care of for you. And everything happened just the way he'd predicted. What shit.

Yes, it was true that a certain Denilson had been asking her out. Yes, he was the manager of a supermarket. Kind. Honest. I don't know if he's good-looking, Kelly, I don't care. I've dried up, Suzana said, I gave all my love to Zequinha, it's used up, I don't have any left for anyone, ever again.

At eight p.m. they heard the barking of approaching dogs. The pack surrounding José Luís was ever larger, any dog that showed up immediately became part of his band, and José Luís had also bought Rottweilers, which wore collars and frightened pedestrians.

José Luís thought that Suzana wanted to talk about money, which was fair, after all, she was a widow. I have enough money, she replied. I asked you here for two reasons: first, I want you to know that I'm never going to forgive you for killing my husband. Never. If today you go around on top of the world, it's because Miltão and Zequinha helped you. And neither one of them liked you. I protected you. And you repay me by killing my husband. You're just like any other outlaw who sells drugs, you're scum, that's all you are, one more piece of shit. The second thing I have to say to you: it wasn't Fake who betrayed you to Zequinha.

Marta was confused when José Luís got home, pop, late that night, yelling, and it took some time for her to understand what he was talking about, the night she'd fled from Zequinha's house. Remember, he asked, remember that you told me Fake was there talking to your father? Yes, she remembered. Pop. Did you see Fake that night? asked José Luís. Answer, goddamn it. No, she hadn't seen Fake, just heard his voice, but it was him, she was sure of it. It wasn't Fake who betrayed me, shouted José Luís. Calm down, Zé. Marta vaguely recalled someone saying 'brother' in her father's office, it could only be Fake, pop. It was Fake, she said, I knew that way he had of saying 'brother' all the time, it was him. Fuck, shouted José Luís, everybody in this shithole says 'brother', goddamn it. Marta, how could you do that to my best friend?

It was Negaço who betrayed you, Suzana had told him at Kelly's house, hours earlier, that prick who now sucks up to you, Suzana had said. I don't know if you know it, but Fake, before he died, suspected Negaço. And I also don't know if you know Negaço is buddies with Gavião. And on his payroll. You see where that leaves you in this story. Every night, before I go to sleep, Suzana had continued, I think about Fake. They say he was found in the garbage dump. I feel so bad. And when I see you running around with Negaço, the guy fucking you over and the two of you together, friends, I like it, I say to myself, serves him right, he deserves to get fucked. And don't think I'm telling you this because I'm your friend, or to alert you to the danger. To me, Zé, you can die before my very eyes, I swear it, and I couldn't care less. I want you to get fucked. I don't know you anymore. If I'm telling you, it's because I want you to suffer a little longer. You killed your best friend unjustly. And I hope you remember that every minute for the rest of your miserable life. That's all. I've said everything. Ciao.

José Luís remained alone for a few seconds, until Kelly came into the living room and found him lying on the floor. What happened? she asked. My god, get up. José Luís clutched Kelly's

263

legs tightly, he felt so terrible, Get up, Zé. Shit, he said, crying, Kelly helped him to the sofa. And she consoled him, gave him strong coffee, caressed his hair, and that was how it all began again, the old times returned, she would say, after they made love on the living room rug. But it hadn't been how she had imagined it. José Luís smoking, distant, his eyes closed, I'd been hoping all this time, she said affectionately. José Luís couldn't stop thinking about Fake. It's not your fault, she said. Of course it is. He would build a square in Fake's honor, a statue, yes, that's what he'd do.

What took you so long? asked Marta when he came into the bedroom, hours later. And then the argument began. You betrayed me, he screamed, goddamn it, you forced me to kill my best friend. At first Marta tried to understand, explain, but then she too started yelling and accusing, throwing objects at the wall. You kill my father, she said, and then throw this up to me? Go fuck yourself, man.

José Luís locked himself in the bathroom, splash, everything being smashed to pieces on the other side of the door, shit, he called Cachaça on his cellphone, and ordered Negaço's head cut off. Then he removed his clothes and sat under the shower. If not for Marta, Fake would still be alive. Shit. The bitch.

29

THE DOGS' BARKING CREATED a hubbub in the vicinity. Recording, yelled Kingie, a video camera in his hands, its lens focused on the list of prices at Zino's butcher's shop. We have chickens, both live and cleaned. Liver's on sale, cheap. Chicken hearts, wings, tripe.

The barbecue grill on the sidewalk, against the butcher shop wall, where spits of smoking meat rotated, was surrounded by José Luís's restless dogs. That, stated the trafficker in a voiceover accompanying the image of the pack, is pure poison. Kingie, who'd received the camera from Gavião in a negotiation, had been amusing himself the last few days by filming the favela. It was Zino's birthday and José Luís had decided to show up at the butcher shop to say hello to his friend and 'jerk his chain'.

He had collected sensational testimonies there, none of them about the butcher. To me, one of the residents had declared, eating a piece of cake that Zino's wife offered to all comers, Zé Luís is a saint. Next year, said one of the Carnival planners, we're going to make a big splash thanks to Kingie. But the best one was what Onofre had said, explaining that the history of Berimbau was divided into two parts, before Kingie and after Kingie. Sensational. Before and after, he'd never thought of it in those terms. He loved hearing praise, which always acted in his body in a way similar to the drugs he took when he was a child, spreading rapidly through his bloodstream, rising to his head and bringing him a sensation of dynamism, happiness. It stimulated him so much that he had started seeing Kelly more often, especially after he'd gone back to living by himself. He would take Kelly or some other pretty girl from the favela to sleep with him at the penthouse, eager to hear them whisper pleasant things in his ear: brave man, strong man, good man, funny man, Kelly would repeat in bed.

You're overdoing it, Marta had said when she found out that José Luís was filming the weapons deposit and the drug-packaging sector. What's this business of going around record-ing everything? What for? You think you're so cool, such hot shit, Marta had said, you're so full of yourself, pop, that you don't even realize those tapes are going to be used at your trial and put you in prison, pop. Don't hassle me, Marta, you don't know shit. You're out of it. She wants to bring me down, he told Kelly in bed. Marta does nothing but aggravate me.

The camera framed Zino behind the counter, handing out pieces of birthday cake to the ladies. This no-good that's laughing, that's Zino, continued Kingie in a voiceover, this fucker, shit, he cooks spoiled meat and sells it to us. It's good-quality meat, Zino retorted, smiling.

The camera was placed on the counter. To show you, said Kingie, now also in front of the lens, wearing a beige blazer, Ray-Ban sunglasses, new sneakers, and two gold chains around his neck, to show you, the color of this meat when it goes on the rotisserie, is olive green. Laughter. It's fresh as can be, said Zino. Eat it then, in front of me, I want to see it, Zino. More laughter. Take advantage of the fact it's your birthday and show us you're honest. Shit, didn't I tell you? He's laughing so he doesn't have to eat it, the bald-faced thief. The two embraced, I love this man, said José Luís, kissing Zino on the brow.

It was at that joyful moment, with everyone laughing and carefree, that José Luís was arrested by three plainclothes policemen who were mingling with the small crowd celebrating the butcher's birthday. There was no time to react, draw his gun, nothing, it was all so fast, so stupid, as José Luís would tell Marta later by phone. There was so much going on at the butcher shop, lots of people coming and going, eating cake, everything cool, and suddenly, shit, they arrested me, real strange.

An incident like that, in those circumstances, was unaccept-able. First because José Luís hadn't lived in the Berimbau favela since the newspapers, a month earlier, had begun running front-page articles on the investigation of the narcotics trade in Brazil. Kingie had become the leading name in the wanted listed of traffickers. Since then, he had moved, by himself, into his new apartment, the penthouse of an upper-middle-class building overlooking Berimbau and purchased in Marta's name. From there he commanded the business, avoiding exposure. There were five outstanding warrants for his arrest. He had learned through Gavião that the governor had okayed another invasion of the favela. It's only because of things like this, Gavião had commented, that I put up with informers. Sometimes you get good information. Take a look at this, he said, pointing to the day's headline: Governor promises to end police corruption. Another: Secretary of Security declares drug traffic threatens democracy. This is the best one, War on drugs. 'We're going to adopt drastic measures,' the president declared, proposing the involvement of the armed forces in the combat against drug trafficking. Get ready, they've decided to go all out. It's for real this time.

I'd expected, said José Luís to Marta when she finally was able to visit him, on Sunday, I'd expected they would just come by for their cut. Or else, shit, they'd come in with a battalion like always, the usual show, shit, journalists, a night raid, all that confusion, a lightning attack, the whole shebang. But it wasn't like that, I was arrested at eleven in the morning at Zino's butcher shop by three cops. Shit, it's ridiculous.

In the patrol wagon, as he was being taken to the precinct where he would be booked, José Luís tried to negotiate, several times raising the price he was willing to pay to put a rock over the entire matter. If you don't shut up, one of the cops had replied, I'll add attempted bribery to the charges. Look, he told his lawyer later, I'm used to that crap with phony arrests, I spend a lot of money on it, but attempted bribery, shit, that's a new one. Where did those cops come from?

The first week he was in jail, he devoted himself to analyzing each minute leading up to his arrest. Hi, Lucivan. Such a pleasant morning. Hi, Máiquel. His bodyguards had assured him that the atmosphere in the favela was calm. He strolled about easily with his new camera, Hi, Reginaldo, documenting the benefits he had brought about in Berimbau. The new day-care center. Hi, Dona Zilda. A blue sky, a cool morning. Hi, Mr Paulo. I really make things happen in this shed. I sponsor. I pay. I get things done. Resurfacing the sports court, look. Hi, Lurdivan. Hi there, kid. At every moment, someone would come up and shake his hand, thanking him. Children mingled with the pack surrounding him, all of them followed him, noisy, housewives leaning out their windows, Hi, José Luís, to see what was happening. It was part of his work, that contact with the community. It was essential to walk through the favela now and then, distributing clothes, meat, crackers, toys, cans of cooking oil, and attention. A leader, he learned, only stayed in power with the support of the community. That's why he did his best to please them, paid bills, settled disputes, and hired shows with 'hip-swinging women to please the crowd.' Yes, exposing himself to capture like that hadn't been a good idea, he should've listened to Marta, but shit, that was part of his job. Besides which, it was Zino's birthday. How could he not be there for as loyal a friend as Zino? Betrayal, shit.

José Luís had been received respectfully by the other prisoners. He had several friends in that block, he supported the families of Agripino, Paulo Agulha, and Rosbife. And Noble's as well, and therefore his transfer to a more comfortable cell hadn't been a problem, though it did cost him money.

At first he believed that Noble could help him escape. Noble's a slug, he doesn't know anything, he later commented to Marta. I spent that money for nothing. And that friend of your father's, he said, referring to the lawyer Marta had hired to defend him, the guy irritates me. He came here with some bullshit about no trafficker spending more than thirty-eight days in jail if the trial isn't finished, like that was some kind of advantage for me, shit. I think you'd better clarify the situation to him, Marta. There's no way I'm spending thirty-eight days in here. You can stop wasting money on that prick.

What was new for José Luís, now that he was in prison, was

Marta's attitude. The two hadn't lived together since he moved to the penthouse facing Berimbau. Listen, Marta, he'd said at the time, the situation is awful, I can't stay here and I can't take you with me, it's better for you to wait, he'd said, and safer. Marta didn't accept it, That 'we need a break from each other' is so old it stinks, she'd replied, you want to get rid of me so you can sleep with those fifteen-year-olds, no way, José. It hadn't been easy to convince her. José Luís had to assign her a role in 'the business'. Now that I can't count on Reader anymore, he'd insisted, you have to be my right arm, I need your help, Marta. Only on those terms had she accepted. Fine, pop, I'll stay, but I'm no toady or doormat, I've got my own methods and ideas, OK? OK, he'd said. And don't think for a minute that I'm going to allow whores to sleep in our penthouse, stated Marta, I'm putting an end to that shit. I'll cut off your dick and shove it down your throat.

Frankly, José Luís had once told Reader before his arrest, I didn't imagine that marriage was like this, this crap. There was no longer any climate of pleasantness between the two, the fun and games, the long nights of lovemaking, Marta measuring his penis with a ruler, none of that, only arguments, always because of stupid things, trifles, whenever she opens her mouth it's to complain about something. Why is it, Reader, that women become such a pain in the ass after they get married? Even for fucking, it's talk talk talk. Shit. After the meetings with the leadership Marta was even more unbearable. You run right over me, she said, you undermine my authority, pop, I'm Zequinha's daughter, you understand that? Don't raise your voice with me, she said, like I was one of those toothless types you hire to steal cars, I finished the eighth grade, I've got brain power coming out my ears. José Luís hated all that, eighth grade, shit, she irritates me, he told Reader. For all these reasons he never imagined that in such an adverse situation Marta would be, in his own words, so cool a girl. He loved it when he found out she'd ordered the assassination of a manager who'd tried to 'branch out on his own'. He loved it even more when she said 'so *they*'ll know that you're the boss in Berimbau.' The woman's professionalism didn't surprise José Luís. She'd always been great in that respect, from the beginning. The new element was the affectionate way she began treating him in prison. I want you to know, she said on one visit, that in spite of everything bad that's happened to us, I'm still your wife.

The last Sunday in November, Marta took him containers of yogurt, cans of condensed milk, news from his family, letters from friends, and a corn-meal cake that Alzira had made. Marta was excited. I've got great news, she said. You know how the Secretary of Security distributed flyers with your photo, offering thirty thousand for information about you? Thirty grand? asked Kingie, is that all? How much did they offer for Chiclete? I don't know anything about Chiclete, his girlfriend replied. Pop. The fact is that nobody said anything at all, continued Marta, pop, taking a photograph from her purse. This is the good news, she said, placing the photo in José Luís hand. At first he didn't recognize the woman lying in the garbage dump, her bruised, deformed face. It's Suzana, Marta said. She was the one who betrayed you. Only the right foot wore a shoe, her nails were painted sparkle-pink, a yellow dress clinging to her body. Suzana always said that yellow was her favorite color, José Luís remembered, observing the details in the photograph, while Marta told how they'd discovered that Denilson, Suzana's new boyfriend, was a cop, not a supermarket manager, pop, as she had been telling everybody. The guy was an undercover cop, a piece of shit, pop, who disappeared from the favela like that, she said, snapping her fingers. The day after they arrested you, Marta went on, I went by his house and there was a 'For Rent' sign. I got suspicious. I talked to Valdo, at the rental agency, and he told me Denilson paid three months in advance, just listen, and suddenly he 'needed' to move. Quite a coincidence. What supermarket manager does that? I kept after Suzana. Bingo. The whore helped in your capture. Pop. She set everything up. She provided all the information. It was Denilson's team that nabbed you. And what drives me crazy is that she didn't make a peep when she was taken to the dump. Cachaça had gotten the bitch out of bed minutes before. I want to say goodbye to my mother, she told Cachaça, which means she knew she was going to die. When they got to the dump, I did a lot of talking. You still have a chance, I explained. Confess everything and I can even send you off to Bahia, I suggested. And it was the truth. I can't forget that, after all, she was married to my father. I suggested she return my family's money, every cent of it, and I would forgive her. I said, Tell me the truth and I'll let you go away, with the clothes on your back. She just looked at me with a sneer, doing the go-ahead-and-shoot bit. I mentioned Denilson, and she didn't say a word. Nothing. That was when I couldn't take it anymore. You can't believe how much I enjoyed smashing her face. Hitting her felt so good. I thought, pop, too bad my sister Priscilla and my grandmother aren't here to hit her too. It's so good to really give it to somebody like Suzana. Priscilla would've loved it. I hit her again and again, without mercy.

José Luís, holding the photo, remembered Suzana dancing with him, a vague recollection, the two of them whirling around at her house, a samba playing on the stereo, Suzana always was a good dancer. He also remembered Suzana defending him from Alzira, protecting him with her own body, one Sunday when his mother grabbed a belt to give him a whipping.

José Luís felt terrible, he closed his eyes and felt nothingness all around him, melancholy, darkness. He felt sorry for Marta. He had been insensitive when she'd asked him to take a stand against Suzana, just after Zequinha's death. Shit, he hadn't done anything, and now, there they were, the two of them, Suzana had betrayed him, not to mention Zequinha, shit, he had killed Zequinha, so much shit, he thought, he just wanted to go to sleep and not think about anything. Can I give you a hug? Marta asked. They embraced, not the way they had done at the beginning, urgently, each feeling the absence of the other. I miss you so much, Marta said, a sob in her throat, everything's so awful without you. José Luís felt like apologizing, but he wasn't good at that. They hugged in silence, Suzana's photo fallen to the ground.

I've got one more thing I have to say, Marta added before she left. I don't want Kelly coming to visit you anymore. Pop.

I know you've been sleeping with her. It's unpleasant to say, but I'd hate to have to take that fat girl on. Drop her right now.

It was very sad to talk to Kelly that very same day, when she came during visiting hours, bringing an orange cake, smiling, considerate. You're acting strange today, she said. And José Luís explained that he didn't want her to wait for him. It wasn't worth it; he was a married man, and he might not be out of prison all that soon. Kelly was young and deserved someone better. Someone who wasn't in 'that life'. It was all bullshit, Kelly told Carolaine later, crying. A married man, but he's not even living with Marta. It was all one big excuse because he doesn't love me. He doesn't like me. Carolaine, an open can of condensed milk in her hand and the television tuned to the eight o'clock soap, made an effort to pay attention to Kelly's story. Men are all alike, she said, repeating what Alzira had said all her life. Men are no good.

A short thick penis, with a small arrow coming out of the orifice. That's what I call a real dissing, said Fuinha, as he gave the last touch to the inmate's back. The prisoner had been brought by force to be tattooed, done with a sewing needle and paint left over from the cafeteria. It came out real nice, said Fuinha. Now, man, he told the youth, who had arrived that morning, with the jailors informing everyone that he was a child rapist, now everybody's going to know what you are. And be ready for you. Fuinha removed his right sandal and, slap, slap, struck the tattoo powerfully. That's just to set it good, he explained to José Luís.

Fuinha, a famous bank robber, was José Luís's cellmate and, in his words, 'the best tattoo artist in Rio de Janeiro.' I do butterflies, Our Lady, anchors, Chinese dragons, but what I like best is putting a big prick on the backs of rapists. I hate rapists. Ever since I've been here, you can check it out, every one of them's got a huge prick on their backs. It's a sign, so they can get a good cornholing and learn. I can do a Jesus Christ on your chest if you want to. I'm not a thief, answered José Luís, I'm not going around like some billboard for Jesus Christ.

That morning there was an air of tension in the courtyard where the inmates sunbathed. They killed a couple of guys in Block 4, Fuinha said. To empty the cell. And they announced they were going to kill more tonight. José Luís, shirtless, feeling the sun on his body, didn't feel like talking. Take a hike, Fuinha, he said. He closed his eyes, remembering the photo of Suzana, shit, why the hell should he feel guilty? He hadn't killed Suzana. Shit. It was at that moment that a jailor approached and began a conversation. José Luís had never seen him around there. My name is Jonas, the guy said, Noble told me about your situation. I've got a deal for you, a real good deal, it'll cost you money but it'll get you out of here fast. All you have to do is pay. They talked about numbers and after some back-and-forth settled on an amount. Now you're sitting pretty, the jailor assured him. How's it going to happen? José Luís asked. You'll find out, soon, real soon. But do me a favor. Keep a tight lid on it. Not your family, not your wife, or a friend, or a whore, not even your sweet old granny, nobody can know about it. Otherwise, I'm outta here. We understand each other?

30

PLEASE INSERT CARD. ENTER your code. Indicate desired transaction. Carolaine was already accustomed to taking money from her mother's account at the automatic teller on Rua Sete de Abril, the one closest to the Berimbau favela. Although there were never many people waiting, the lines were unbearable, extremely slow. The users, almost all of them residents of the favela, drivers, nannies, maids, salesgirls, didn't know how to use the magnetic card and took a long time at the machine. Faced with the technology, most of them seemed inhibited, hesitant, or wary, and many left without completing the transaction, while others had their cards swallowed up. Carolaine had seen it all as she waited, people who socked the machine, or were startled at the voice that gave directions about its operations. Hicks, thought Carolaine, irritated. Stupid people. To her, it was all quite simple. Ah, how good it was to have a bank account. How easy modern life was. It was no trouble at all, you just pushed a few keys, and presto, the money came out, in bills of ten or fifty, according to your needs. Her friends had been enchanted with the party she'd given at the sports center to celebrate her son's birthday. Five hundred Walt Disney balloons, plates, glasses, tablecloth, all by Walt Disney. She'd been in doubt about the choice of theme for the party, there were so many options: Hercules, Tarzan, Snow White. She ended up choosing the Little Mermaid. Even on the invitations the image of the young woman with her fish's tail appeared, beautiful, blonde, We're Expecting You at Our Party. What pleased Carolaine the most were the hostesses in their miniskirts and knee-high boots, microphone in hand. Let's see, people, who wants a gift? You have to play if you want one. We're going to have a dance contest, kids, everybody get out there and swing your hips, the winner gets these ping-pong paddles. This soccer ball. This box of gum. What a delight! What a party! The children loved imitating famous actors, their bodies swaying to the sound of lively music. It was like a real TV program, one with a live audience of children, the kind Carolaine loved to watch. The entire hillside was there. People came up to her and said: Carolaine, what a lovely party, it must've been a lot of work for you. How could it be work for someone who has a magnetic card? She hadn't done anything, absolutely nothing, except withdraw money from Alzira's account again and again. She adored that card. A television set, car, radio, motorcycle, microwave, freezer, washing machine, nothing in the world beat a simple magnetic card. She kept it in her purse, always handy. It hadn't been easy to convince her mother to let her use it.

At first, Alzira had insisted on withdrawing money herself at the Leblon branch. She preferred the 'personal touch', as she put it, to the ATM. I get dizzy in that little 'cabinet', the former domestic explained. Alzira took advantage of the lines to 'make friends', chatting with the retired people and office boys, showing them the photos of her grandchildren that she carried in her purse and, time permitting, recounted the drama of the lesion on her leg, which had doubled in size since she stopped working. But she didn't talk about José Luís, for she was ashamed of her son being in prison. Just the one girl, she answered when asked about children.

But the fact is that Alzira had worked her entire life, and now, with free time, even the most commonplace things, such as going to the bank or paying the light bill, seemed a pleasurable novelty to her. It was very good to go to the street, walk unhurriedly, chatter away in lines, see the merchandise on display in the stalls, boots, toys, the street vendors, everything was enjoyable. Sometimes, on one of her strolls, or when she was at home on the sofa, crocheting, Dona Juliana's voice would come into her head, shouting her name. She remembered exactly the distress that voice had brought her. Alzira, where's my pink silk dress? Despite everything, she liked Dona Juliana. Poor Dona Juliana. Always trying to lose weight. She nearly killed herself working out so much with Mr Fernando, but she was always the same. Have I lost weight, Alzira? You think I'm any thinner? The bad part was when Dona Juliana let in the demon, yes, that bad humor was the Devil, the woman even snarled around the house, a screaming hurricane, slamming doors, crying in the bathroom, poor Dona Juliana. A wretched sinner. Alzira didn't like remembering the times when her employer's friends would gather in the living room and amuse themselves with the stories she told about Alzira, always in hushed tones that were perfectly audible in the kitchen. I've never seen anything worse, her ex-employer said. It's enough to drive you crazy. She's the dumbest woman I've ever seen in my life. The other day, I came in and she told me: Mr Rodrigo asked you to call him, with or without fail. Why did Dona Juliana say those things? Yes, the Devil. The pastor had explained that the demon changed people's behavior, the Devil got inside human beings' heads, in their blood, and brought about the changes. Alzira knew everything about the Devil. She liked to think that she'd been able to put up with it all, the insults and curses of the Horned One, because finally her reward had come, God had been victorious, and now she had a bank account with a magnetic card, she could live thirty-six months without working, doing nothing but taking care of her health. The lesion did throb and ooze pus, but it was nothing compared to the pain she felt at seeing José Luís in prison. The Dark One had taken possession of her son also. Is the food good here? she'd asked when she'd gone to visit her son. Very good, José Luís had replied. They fell silent, Alzira sweating in her tight polyester dress, José Luís unshaven, neither of them with anything to talk about. How sad it was to lose your son to Satan. It was after her visit to the prison that the lesion 'went wild'. It had doubled in size in a week, and the ankle was so swollen that it was no longer possible to see the foot bones, everything was a round mass, with the lesion larger than ever. Starting today, Carolaine had said, you're not leaving the house. Until that thing gets better. I'll take care of the bills, let me have the card.

Alzira had finally given in, and Carolaine had begun disposing of the money according to her needs. The bank statements came in the mail, and Carolaine tore them up without reading them. Bank statements were real complicated. And, anyway, Alzira couldn't read, why would she want to see the statements? The card brought much happiness to Carolaine, the greatest of which was no longer having to depend on Marta. 'No' was the answer she always got from Marta when she asked for money. No, no, no. Marta paid all the household bills, supermarket, butcher shop, pharmacy. I'm very sorry, Carolaine, Zé doesn't want me to let you have any cash, she would reply. And there'd been that godawful day. Listen to me, Carolaine, you need a reality check, girl. Wake up. Are you saying you want to buy clothes? Toys? Straighten your hair? Dangles for the baby that's going to be born? Simple. Go to work. Get a job. If you want to, you can work for me, I need a secretary. Work, thought Carolaine, irritated. In my seventh month of pregnancy? She hated Marta. Strutting around like she owned the favela. Exercising absolute power, and what had she done with Reader? Onofre had told her about it. Get that out of my sight, Marta supposedly said one morning upon seeing Reader in the packaging sector. I don't want him here listening to what I'm saying, she'd said. But it was José Luís who asked me to bring Reader here every morning, Onofre had replied. This isn't a hospital for cripples, Marta had answered. Onofre had told Carolaine other things as well. I never trusted her type, Onofre had said. I don't trust women who are too thin, he said. How could Kingie trade Kelly for Marta? Kelly was much better, more of a companion, Kelly would never refuse her money. But it paid to be patient. In the soaps the false always got their comeuppance. Like Isadora with that pious face of hers. Like Laura asking Pedro's forgiveness. Like Eneida with the story of the stolen car. All of them false, betraying their men. All of them would be unmasked before the final episode. Why should it be different in real life? Marta would also be unmasked. Good thing she didn't depend on her for anything anymore, she was independent, thanks to Alzira's card. When Carolaine wanted to go dancing with her friends, all she had to do was stop at the ATM and there everything was taken care of. Ah, how simple life could be!

The cell was empty when Onofre entered, pushing Reader. It's really amazing, commented Onofre, how easy it is in this country to grease a cop's palm. I imagine you must spend a fortune on those guys. All I had to do to get in here, without being searched, or even having to answer any questions, was mention your name. Well? asked José Luís anxiously. Everything's set up, replied Onofre. Help me put Reader somewhere, the bar owner said. Reader was lifted from his wheelchair and placed on the lower bunk where José Luís slept. Then Onofre pushed against the sides of the chair to release the seat. In the space now revealed were several stacks of large-denomination bills, wrapped in supermarket bags. How's that? asked Onofre, pleased. You know, that blinking method you invented for Reader is crap. I came up with something much better. Now communication is easy. If Reader blinks once, it means *a*. Twice, *b*, and so on. The alphabetical blinking system, he said, laughing. The problem is, it's very slow. Now listen to this: you know where Reader keeps his money? In the mattress. Even the Portuguese have bank accounts these days, explain that to him, Kingie. The guy was all the time giving lessons about the modern world, computers, all that stuff, and he kept his money in the mattress. Give me a break.

The idea of getting Reader's help for the escape had arisen two weeks earlier. He'd thought of speaking to Marta, but Jonas himself, who had proposed the escape, had told him to avoid involving the woman. The problem with women, Jonas had said, is they like to talk, they just can't keep quiet. And it has nothing to do with wanting to screw you. That's just the way women are. Born to talk. You tell her today and tomorrow everybody in Berimbau will know. And that could screw up our plans, you know, so we take no chances. That was why José Luís had telephoned Onofre's bar, asking him to bring Reader that Sunday. The guy was like a child, Onofre said, when I told him you called. As soon as he was alone with Reader, José Luís had come straight to the point. Pay close attention and answer me, Reader: Do you still have that money stashed away? Reader blinked in confirmation. Great. Now listen: I need ten grand, can you get it for me. Reader blinked again. Very good, shit. Way to go. Another thing: can we trust Onofre? Reader opened and closed his eyes slowly. What the shit does that mean? José Luís asked, is it yes or no? Yes, blinked Reader. Yes. Great.

Now the money was available, thanks to his friends Onofre and Reader, who had been nothing less than sensational, shit. I'll pay back every cent, José Luís assured him.

After getting the money to Jonas, all José Luís could think about in the following days was the escape. He'd heard spectacular stories about prison escapes. Escapes through tunnels that took years to dig, escapes in helicopters stolen from pilots who flew sightseeing excursions for tourists, escapes in rowboats, ambulances, and in laundry carts. But in José Luís's opinion, nothing was better than when the inmate walked calmly out the front gate. Escaping, strolling along the sidewalk, no hassles, free. Shit, that was good. The first thing I want to do when I get out of here is fuck you, he'd told Marta on her last visit. You animal, pop. Fuck all day long till my prick's raw, José Luís had said. Pop, Really? Then I think you ought to get me pregnant, I want to have a child, I'm at that stage, pop, when I can't look at a baby carriage without turning green with envy. Do you want to? she had asked. I want everything. To loaf around. Watch television half the night. Shoot the shit with Onofre. Go to the beach. Not do a goddamn thing. I want to eat the *feijoada* my grandmother makes. And I want to go out to our porch and take a piss, looking at the sky, he said, recalling Fake. What an idiot, Marta had replied, laughing. Fake, José Luís had said, then stopped, changing his mind about telling the rest of the story. What about Fake? Marta asked. Nothing. Tell me, pop, I want to know. Fake liked to piss in the street, José Luís had explained, in a less enthusiastic tone. Pop, how about that. They fell silent for a time, holding hands.

Sometimes, José Luís couldn't stop thinking about Fake. He remembered the time when they were inseparable friends, the two of them smoking grass and having fits of laughter, they would listen to music, fuck it, what shit. It caused him great sorrow to recall Fake on his knees at the garbage dump. Don't go down on your knees, I'll blow your brains out right here, man. Get up and run. Fake begging, Brother, don't do this, I'm clean, man. Fake running, tripping, bang, bang, falling dead. He couldn't close his eyes without the thoughts attacking him, unlike when he was a boy and could spend hour upon hour fantasizing delightful things, going out with his father to modern luncheonettes, in fast cars, swimming at the beach, now, in the cell, he had developed a great knack for imagining bad things. Fake tumbling to the ground, dead. The escape helicopter exploding in midair. Police breaking into his house and arresting him again. Shots in the back. Instant death. Fire, everything coming to an end. He couldn't stop thinking about bad things unless he occupied himself with something, conversing with his cellmates, talking loudly, telling stories, playing football, but all of that left him drained, exhausted. I can't take it anymore, he'd told Jonas. I want out of this shithole, now.

On Wednesday the prisoners were let out of their cells for their sunbathe earlier than usual because of the high temperatures of the last few days. There was no shade. And the inmates put T-shirts or even shorts over their heads to protect themselves from the summer sun. José Luís was half asleep when two policemen came to take him to testify at the 14th precinct, where the investigation was being conducted. It was the first time he'd left the prison. Shit, I don't know anything. I want my lawyer, he said. On the way out, they allowed him one phone call.

It appears, the lawyer said when they met in the hallway of the precinct, on their way to the interrogation room, it seems there's another accusation against you, they're charging you with Miltão's death. I don't know what the chief detective wants, maybe he's planning to start another investigation. Tuck in your shirt, he said, as they entered the room where a recording clerk and the detective were waiting to take the trafficker's statement.

Have a seat, said the detective, indicating the chair opposite him. And that was when it all happened. Not even José Luís expected it to be so easy. Shit. He was still thinking about what he was going to say, when four men armed with machine guns burst into the room, threatening the policemen and announcing the rescue. Quickly, five more men occupied the area, disarming the police, who were taken to the bathroom and handcuffed.

José Luís walked out the front door, protected by the group. He caught a taxi by himself and disappeared into traffic.

31

YOU'RE GETTING FIRST-CLASS material. It's light and can stand up to machine-gun fire, explained the former military policeman, opening the trunk of his metallic-blue Chevrolet to show Marta the bulletproof vests brought specially from Miami. But I'm only selling it as a package, either take the whole thing or no deal. Marta tried on the equipment, which was too large for her small body. It's a different style, lady. The style is not to die, you understand? One size fits all. And it only comes in black. Marta didn't like the comment. Pop. She was sick of you-don't-understand-shit-because-you're-a-woman jokes. Pop. When she negotiated for drugs or weapons, when she met with her men or the leaders of other favelas, there was always somebody or other ready to criticize the fact that she was a woman. I never saw, one of the traffickers had told her, a pretty girl walking around like that with an Israeli-made rifle. Pop. Idiot. She had completely changed her image and attitude as a result of that kind of prejudice. She now dressed like a man, military pants, sneakers, baggy T-shirts, close-cropped hair, and a beret. She made an effort to talk like a man, walk like a man. I'm a fair guy, she would say in negotiations. She dealt with 'those people' by looking them straight in the eye, hardened, menacing, exactly as her father had done. Zequinha was infinitely superior to those nobodies, pop, who came to her house. She treated them like despised beings. You've got to put the guy in his place, Zequinha used to say. Fifth-rate. Rabble. Marta also felt superior to those 'ignoramuses'. A gang of turds, she told Priscilla, that's what they are. Wherever she went, she was always the best. Much better than any leader she'd met.

Even better than José Luís, a thousand times better. Pop. When she'd been forced to take over the operations because José Luís was in prison, she'd found total disorganization, and no lack of wasted money and stupidity. Pop. Let me see that other vest, she said. Pop.

What irritated her most was how people had changed in their treatment of her. In the days when she was just José Luís's wife, everything was different, everything was easy, simple, everybody flattered her, pop, and now that she was the boss of the favela, pop, powerful, she had the feeling they didn't like her. They criticized her. Pop. There's nothing but illiterates in the traffic, stupid people, she told her sister Priscilla. And the problem is that they can't stand taking orders from a woman. They're used to dealing with women in two situations: in the kitchen and in bed. Then I show up, pop, smart, shrewd, and they don't understand anything. They get disoriented. Yes, pop, maybe she had overreacted to José Luís's three 'little girls', his lovers. But she'd become possessed when she found out that he was paying for the food and housing of each of those adolescent 'tapeworms'. She had received an anonymous letter in which the whole 'filthy story' was revealed. Marta kicked out the girls and shaved their heads before expelling them from the favela. For three days, that was the only topic of conversation in Berimbau. But what did they want her to do? Put up with it? What permissive leader is respected? No. She had acted correctly. She regretted not having beaten up the blackest of the three, the one who'd said: You're not as great as you think you are. The bitch. Show up here again, Marta had threatened, and I'll set fire to that steel wool cunt of yours. Not to mention Kelly, the dummy. Everyone in the favela preferred Kelly to Marta. They felt sorry for Kelly. The fat girl, always wearing an unhappy expression. Poor Kelly, they said. The truth was, Marta hated Berimbau. Pop.

Well, lady, you taking them or not? asked the ex-policeman, referring to the vests. Pop, I'm thinking, Marta answered, irritated. She should have moved to Marrecos and commanded the business from there, her father's house. But instead, she'd committed the 'blunder' of bringing her sister and grandmother to live with her in Berimbau. Pop. She couldn't have stood living in her father's house, seeing his things scattered about, objects, it was too sad. Pop. They don't like me, she was always complaining to Priscilla. Well, lady? This is like McDonald's, it has to be fast, insisted the gunrunner. Pop, the imbecile. Any day now she'd have to kill a guy like him, pop, in front of everybody. Put the junk in my car, she told Cachaça. How much does all this cost?

When they were on Avenida Brasil, Cachaça at the wheel, Marta told him to stop at the first service station. She dialed Information. I want the number of the Tips Hotline, please. She then phoned to denounce the gunrunner.

That'll teach him to treat women better, she told Cachaça when she returned to the car. Stuck-up son of a bitch.

Because of the pedestrians, Marta's car slowly made its way up the steep streets of the Berimbau hillside. Long before arriving home, even before she saw José Luís's dogs in front of the kitchen door, barking happily, she guessed the cause of so much excitement.

José Luís was in the shower when Marta came into the bathroom. Take off those clothes and get in here, he said.

This *feijoada*, Onofre explained, skewering the chunks of dried beef, sausage and smoked bacon floating among the black beans, this *feijoada* is authentic. I cooked it myself. And Reader helped me, didn't you, Reader? Reader emitted a curious noise. That whinnying sound, Onofre explained, is a laugh, that's how he laughs now. Oranges, kale, rice, manioc meal, everything here's first class. Onofre was very pleased to have prepared such a 'whale of a party' in a single afternoon. Several tables had been placed in the sports court, where all the residents came to greet their recently-freed leader, who moved happily among the guests, pulling Marta along by the hand. Ângelo, the preacher, was more excited than anyone. Our church needs to put on shows now, even the Catholics know that. The new approach is proactive, he said. What the shit is he talking about?

José Luís whispered in Marta's ear, laughing. Shows, the pastor continued, it's simple, worship services these days have to be constructed like a show, a spectacle. That priest who's making such a hit around here merely confirms my theory that today the faithful want a different kind of liturgy, something more sensory. We have to bring pop music into our services. Rap. The samba. Before the competition starts doing rap in Latin. Is it money you want? José Luís asked. No, no, it's not a question of money, but we have to popularize our activities. Of course, to do that we need money. A reasonable amount. I thought about cutting a CD with the 'Jesus Rap' hymn, have you heard it? The children around here sing it all the time. José Luís hated the kind of person who insisted on serious conversations at parties. A party's for fun, shit. Drinking. Eating. Goddamn. Amusement. Come on, Marta, let's try the *feijoada*. The people from the samba school want you to see the theme samba, said Cândida, taking her grandson away from Marta. Marta tried to go with them but was blocked by the line of wardrobe artists, props people, solo dancers, percussionists, and all the other 'ass-kissers who are here just for José Luís's money.'

Suddenly, she found herself alone in the middle of the court, none of the managers, none of the packagers, the errand boys, no one paid much attention to her, no one treated her like the boss of the favela, yes, the boss, she was still the boss, pop, the fact that José Luís had returned meant nothing. She would continue to be the boss, she had the right, after all, a large number of the sites that José Luís now ran had been Zequinha's. She would have to straighten that out with José Luís. Money. Who would take care of what? The pieces of crap. Pop. Divide up territories. People walked past Marta as if she were one of those little whores the traffickers screw. Hi, they said, dryly, hurrying to flatter José Luís, pop, you're finally back, guy, way to go, they repeated, now Berimbau can move ahead. *Who is he?* sang the chorus of samba dancers, *Ale-Ale-Aleijadinho, the king of mulatto art,/ Ale-Ale-Aleijadinho, the slave Isabel's son,/ he's Antônio Francisco Lisboa,/ your Brazil of art and gold,/ Brazil the perfect treasure.* Marta felt out of place among those people, and her back hurt, when she and José Luís had made love in the shower José Luís had pinned her against the wall forcefully, and the faucet had dug into her skin. And it was aching badly. Pop. She remembered the sense of uneasiness that had prevailed when they were all in the kitchen, Marta, José Luís, her grandmother Noemi, and Priscilla, Shit, I think it's great, José Luís had said, for the family to live here. Priscilla, the place is yours, he'd repeated several times. Shit, that would be too much, for me, your husband, not to want you to bring your grandmother and sister to live with us. I'd have to be some kind of idiot not to agree. You should've told me earlier, shit, right away. Three times in a row José Luís had gotten the name of her grandmother wrong, Dona Eva, he'd said, Emma. Erci. It's Noemi, Marta had corrected, irritated. *Ale-Ale-Aleijadinho*. The dummy, pop. I love Dona Noemi, shit, I think it's great to have the family all living together, he'd said. Maybe I should even bring my father, what do you all think? Noemi and Priscilla remained silent and quickly found an excuse to leave the table. Marta felt very awkward, she had been confused about her feelings for some time, but now, at the party, she'd understood everything perfectly. She was enraged at José Luís. Priscilla had said, I'm never going to forgive that scum for killing our father. You say he's this and he's that, that it's not his fault, maybe that's true, but when I look at him I only see a murderer, said Priscilla. You didn't tell us he'd be coming back here, her grandmother commented. They were both right. Why had it taken her so long to realize it? All that time she had made an effort to believe she loved José Luís, and maybe she still loved him, yes, she did love him, it was good to lie with him in bed, but Priscilla was completely correct. Murderer. Womanizer, keeping three young black girls. Yes, she loved him, but there was always that hatred. Idiot. He thinks he's number one, pop. Even the way he danced was annoying. Besides that, José Luís could perfectly well have thanked Marta for her dedication, but no, there he was, dancing. How long now that there hadn't been even a single invasion of the favela? And why was that? Because she, Marta, had adopted a different policy toward the police, the policy of spending real money on corruption. Yes, because what

José Luís was doing at first, handling out nickels and dimes to small fry, hadn't had any effect. Marta had spent a lot of money buying the right people, detectives, chiefs, and not 'some cop on the beat looking to supplement his salary.' And José Luís, even though he didn't know about the innovations (or that profits had doubled since she'd taken over) ought to be very grateful to her. Very. But no. Since he had arrived he hadn't once said thank you. *Ale-Ale-Aleijadinho*. Marta felt happy at having taken certain stands. *The king of mulatto art*. She had opened an account in her name and hadn't said anything to José Luís. *Ale-Ale-Aleijadinho*. And she'd also bought two pieces of land in her name. *Son of the slave Isabel*. And said nothing. She had acted correctly. And she'd also bought their new allies. *Brazil the perfect treasure*. Everything was going to work out. She would be the boss of Berimbau in much less time than those turds could imagine. Pop.

This monkey wanted. The poster showed a photo of Denilson and offered a reward to anyone who handed him over to the traffickers. Alive. I like the idea, said José Luís after observing the poster. Monkey. They laughed. Look at this, Marta, he said, we're going to plaster all the favelas with this poster, what do you think? Pop, Yeah, cool, she replied. But it isn't going to do any good, Denilson doesn't live in Rio de Janeiro anymore. How do you know? someone asked, which irritated Marta, a zero like him challenging her. I know because I'm informed. Fuck him, said Cachaça. We'll get the guy in Pará. In Bahia. The fucker's going to die, wasn't he the one that put you in prison, Kingie? It's not that simple, said Marta in a severe tone, irritated because Reader wouldn't take his eyes off her. And I don't think, Zé, that the topic should be discussed here, with these people. War with the cops is a very serious thing. *We* have to settle the matter. You'd think she didn't even want to catch Denilson, someone said, a voice Marta couldn't identify. Pop. Fuckers. Better to drop the subject. I'm going to get something to drink, she told José Luís.

Did you see the sour look on Marta's face? Kelly asked, coming up to Caroline, who was sitting at a table, devouring her second plate of *feijoada*. Not that the dish was all that good, she could barely taste its flavor, because when she was nervous she ate compulsively. She had spent the day eating, two boxes of chocolates, a can of condensed milk, two buckets of popcorn. She was shocked at what had happened that afternoon. She'd gone to the ATM to get money and had been horrified to see on the monitor screen: INSUFFICIENT FUNDS. What was that? Balance, less than seven dollars. The machine must be broken. Seven dollars. There was a bundle of money in the account, much more than that, a real bundle. Dona Juliana had donated a large sum so that Alzira wouldn't have to work for years. A lot of money. Yes, but it was all withdrawn, explained the manager when she went to the branch office later. Look at this statement. Withdrawal on the second. Withdrawal on the third. The fourth. Three withdrawals on the seventh. Two more on the ninth. It's gone. Carolaine couldn't believe it. Yes, she'd spent a little money on Christmas presents, but it wasn't possible that the money was gone like that. Precisely that day, when her mother had sent her to get her medicines? Where's my medicine? Alzira had asked upon her return. Mother, she had replied, José Luís is out of prison. There's going to be a party for him today. Alzira felt very happy. They let him go? That's so good, my prayers were answered. God has won. Alzira could no longer walk, the lesion had been too swollen for three days now. What a shame I can't go to the party, you think he'll come see me, Carolaine? Huh? Maybe now, after his suffering in jail, José Luís would finally give himself to God.

I heard, Kelly continued, not noticing Carolaine's distracted manner, I heard that Dirce, Suzana's mother, has something to tell José Luís. I think Marta has a very strange look about her. I wonder if they're fighting?

The party went on all night, his friends not leaving José Luís alone for a single minute. Everyone had something to say to him, to ask, to offer. I'm going to read this letter, Onofre said, and you tell me what you think. 'Onofre you whale, here's a poem that I wrote with Augusta, inspired by a very famous author that Augusta loves. (Did I already say that we ought to introduce Augusta to Reader?) Here's how it goes: "The

Germans and their dainty little cities and their perfect little houses the Germans and their tree-lined boulevards covered with flowers or fluffy snow the Germans and their boots the Germans and their jams and supermarkets and little old ladies and blond blue-eyed children the Germans the Germans the Germans and their smelly asses." A kiss from Rosa Maria.' Do you understand that, Zé? Shit, José Luís laughed loudly. Smelly asses, that's strong stuff. I wonder why Rosa Maria is putting down Germany, Onofre asked, disappointed. And who's this writer she's going out with? Very strange, he said. Famous. I'm worried. How much do you think a phone call to Germany would cost?

When almost all the guests had left the party, Marta called José Luís aside, advising him that it was best for them to leave before daybreak. I'll take you, she said. Take me where? José Luís asked. To the penthouse, she replied, pop, I think it's better for you to go back there. Or to a hotel. I'm staying, José Luís said, I'm going to stay right here. Here? Pop. But every policeman in Rio is after you. Pop. And that's why here nobody'll catch me, said José Luís, kissing Marta. I'm staying.

Onofre asked José Luís to help him take Reader home. The right wheel on this chair is busted, we'll have to carry him.

The night was cool, pleasant. In the steepest spots, Onofre and José Luís carried the chair. Let's buy an electric chair, said José Luís. Electric, Onofre couldn't stop laughing, are we going to electrocute Reader? It won't do any good, an electric chair, with all the holes around here what you need is a chair that won't turn over.

The door to the shack was open. Onofre and José Luís made their way in with difficulty. We need to widen this entrance, commented José Luís. Piles of books scattered everywhere, a sour smell. Doesn't anybody clean this place? the trafficker asked. Shit, what a stench. Nobody in the country is more of a tightwad than Reader, Onofre joked. With the money he's got stashed in that mattress he could have six cleaning ladies a day. Did you see him blink? We communicate very nicely now, he said, referring to the way Reader blinked his eyes. He wants to tell you something. Now you'll see how the blinking-alphabet system works. Go ahead, Reader. Each letter, one blink, pay attention, Kingie. You can start, Reader. Reader blinked slowly, calmly. Slow down, Vegetable, I'm not a calculator. Blink. 3, c, 1, a, ca, 18, r, car, 5, e, 6, 21, 12. Careful. Careful of what? 13, 1, 18, 20, 1. Marta. Careful of Marta.

That's what he said, stated Onofre, embarrassed.

José Luís squatted beside the chair. Marta is betraying me, is that it? Shit, if that's it, blink. Reader blinked. Shit. That's all I need. Is it a man? No, it's not. She's betraying me in the business, is that it? Reader blinked in confirmation. Jesus, Reader, you're going to have to explain everything to me, detail for detail, so start blinking.

32

I DO WHATEVER I feel like, and no man gives me orders. He opened his eyes and saw Marta beside him, her tanned legs, red shorts. Come with me, she said, we're late. Hurry. I'm in command. Pop. Me. There's a meeting, right now, with Gavião, she said. We're going to close a real good deal. Lots of money. Heh heh heh. Whose laugh was that? Big profits for you. He tried to move his arms, but it was as if he were tied to the bed, paralyzed, his legs wouldn't respond, or his hands, his thoughts were confused. Pop, what's the matter with you? asked Marta. Pop. Are you going to just lay there, looking at me with that sly expression? Get up. I'm tired of *flaader giutar futr*. Now Marta's voice seemed slurred and it was impossible to pinpoint the exact cause of her anger. You *guartirmir furncal*, understand? Behind her, near the door, Priscilla and her grandmother were observing the scene, their arms folded. Their watching irritated him. He tried to explain that to Marta, shit, there was no problem with them staying there, eating there, living there, but, shit, they should quit looking. They should get out of there. Shit. That's what he meant to say, but no words came out. Marta started laughing, pop, you're afraid, she said. That's what it is. Afraid of dying, afraid of me, I know it. Afraid I'll put a bullet in your head. Only then did he see the revolver in Marta's hand. You were always telling me you weren't afraid of anything, she continued, but now, pop, there you are, shit-scared. This, she said, pointing the weapon at his head and firing, is for my father. Pop.

José Luís woke from the nightmare at exactly the moment of

the gunshot, abruptly sitting up on the sofa where he had spent the night.

It was two p.m., and although everything was closed in Reader's house, the sun came in through holes and cracks in the roof. He stayed there on the sofa for some minutes, his eyes closed, listening to the shouting of children in the street while he tried to organize his thoughts and decide what to do. Reader had already gone out. I want to know everything, detail for detail, he'd told his friend the night before, everything you know about Marta. Shit. But Reader didn't know anything. And that method of blinking invented by Onofre was 'complete crap'. It's enough to drive you crazy, Onofre had agreed. It had taken an enormous amount of time for Reader to express just the words 'Careful of Marta.' What bothered José Luís was the conversation he'd had later with Onofre. Understand one thing, Onofre had said, nobody has anything concrete on Marta. But there's plenty of suspicion. She and Gavião are always talking in private. We know a bad woman just by the way she chatters nonstop on the telephone. But here's Marta on the phone, he said, adopting an evasive tone: Yeah. No. Uh-huh. I know. I'm going to. Yes. No. It's very strange. Sounds like she's talking to a lover. And then there's what she did to those girls, those sweet little things you were screwing, throwing them out, humiliating them like that, leaving them bald, without a hair on their heads. Pardon the frankness, but Marta's problem is plain old meanness. Go call Paula and Cachaça, the trafficker said. I wouldn't call anybody, replied Onofre. That's my opinion. The truth is we don't know what's going on here. We don't know who's who anymore. Cachaça has taken up Marta's way of speaking on the phone. Yeah, no, yeah, I know, I'm going to, yes, no. You hear the guy talking a blue streak and still can't discover absolutely anything. Nothing at all.

As he removed Reader from the wheelchair and onto the bed, Onofre noticed a blue envelope under the cushion. This is what he was trying to say, the merchant commented, opening the envelope. It's for you, from Suzana's mother. Read it, he asked. 'Come talk to me please it's urgent it's secret I don't want to die like my daughter died don't say anything to Marta. Address: Rua Santa Clara, 254, apartment 7. Dirce.' Is that all? José Luís asked. That's all, answered Onofre, now I understand why Reader was so excited, he wanted to give you this letter.

José Luís recalled the events of the night before. He remembered his conversation with Marta, shortly before his escape from prison. The first thing I want to do when I get out of here is fuck you, he'd said excitedly. You animal, pop. Fuck all day long till my prick's raw, José Luís had said. Pop, Really? Then I think you ought to get me pregnant, I want to have a child, I'm at that stage, pop, when I can't look at a baby carriage without turning green with envy. Do you want to? she asked. A child. How could anyone say that, I want to have your child, and then betray you, like that, calm as anything? Shit. Impossible. Everyone was against Marta. His fear, when Reader had spoken to him of betrayal, was another man in her life. But she'd said, I want to have your child. Shit. The issue, from my point of view, Onofre had said, is this: is Marta on your side or not? If she is, fine. Even if she's stealing from you, fine. She can steal some small change, everybody steals. If she's not on your side, well, that's the real shit, whoever's not with me is against me, as the saying goes. In other words, you're a marked man and can die at any moment, including now, somebody comes barging in here, and it's all over. Isn't that the way we do it? We make alliances, we kill, and we betray, all in the blink of an eye? That's the big question, Onofre had said. I've been with you all this time, I've always supported your group. I don't want anyone from Marrecos in these parts. I'm worried. Very worried.

José Luís didn't like all that crap that Onofre was saying, considering his attitude 'abusive', attacking Marta, his wife, who did he think he was? Sure, Onofre had helped him a lot, thanks to Onofre he'd been able to escape from prison, that was one thing, shit, but another, completely different, was Onofre starting to say, We kill and betray, we this, we that, shit, what kind of idiocy was that? Onofre sold turnovers, nothing more. And Marta wanted to have his child. Shit.

Dirce's note was in his pocket, José Luís reread it. Don't say anything to Marta. Why? What if all that was just a big zero, nothing, insignificant? Maybe Dirce just wanted money. It was very possible. As far back as he could remember, she had lived off Suzana. A child, shit.

As he was leaving the shack, a kid came up to him to say Marta was looking for him.

He went down the streets, his mouth dry. He had an unpleasant feeling, everything was wrong, he thought. He could have returned home, slept with Marta. Nothing had changed, after all. He stopped at the pharmacy, looked for the piece of paper Carolaine had given him the night before, with the names of Alzira's medicines. He'd lost it. Shit.

Christ forbids vanity, and for that reason Alzira wasn't vain. No lipstick, earrings, rings, no costume jewelry of any kind. Alzira wore only a silver crucifix, which Dona Juliana had given her for Christmas. But when she received guests at home or went to Mass, she liked to wear her navy-blue polyester dress, which, despite being hot, made her look 'presentable.' She especially liked going after she'd had her shower, with her hair still wet. Often, before going to church, when she noticed in the mirror that her hair, piled on top of her head, had already dried, she would wet it again, for only then did she feel 'ready to go out.' To Alzira, cleanliness was all. Nothing gave her greater joy than the smell of bleach coming from the sidewalks washed by the maintenance staff of the buildings during her morning walks through Leblon, in the time when she worked. After a day spent cleaning, she loved to get under the shower and wash herself, scrub her nails, put on clean clothes. Which is why she was so annoyed that afternoon when her son showed up unannounced. If she'd known José Luís was coming, she'd have showered. Or at least covered the lesion on her leg with gauze; José Luís was surprised to see how large it was. Shit, Mother, it's grown a lot. And it hurts, Alzira had said, it hurts a lot, the only time it stops plaguing me is when God intervenes, I pray and pray and pray, and the pain disappears. Jesus will take care of it, she explained.

The lunch was noisy because of the children. José Luís ate practically nothing, spending his time making paper airplanes for Junior and showing Alas photos of the Vasco players, teaching him their names. Alzira took advantage of the moment when they went out to buy ice cream and quickly entered the bathroom, patted down her hair with water, so that when José Luís returned she'd be 'more presentable'. They remained in the living room for some time. Alzira spoke of Carolaine, The baby's due before Christmas. His name will be Alex if it's a boy, continued Alzira. Do you like the name Alex? It's the name of a young man on the soap. I wanted it to be Moisés, but she thinks Moisés is an old man's name.

Before leaving, José Luís held out a wad of bills he'd gotten at Reader's house. I brought this for you, he said. Alzira refused to accept it. We don't need it, son. We're all right.

I didn't understand, Alzira said later, intrigued, when Carolaine came from the doctor's office, where she'd gone for prenatal exams, I didn't understand why José Luís came here with that talk. He knows very well that God is against that type of money, I can't accept it, dirty money, money from the drug traffic. But Carolaine wasn't listening to her mother's musings. Nothing could break Carolaine out of her trance when she watched the reruns of *See and See Again*. Especially now that Vitória was marrying Henrique. She had dashed home from the clinic so she wouldn't miss the final episode. She'd already seen Vitória marry Henrique once and wouldn't miss the rerun for anything in the world. Too bad the soaps never showed the afterward. It would be nice to see the day-to-day of the actors, Vitória and Henrique married and settled down. What would they do on a Saturday afternoon? What would they have for lunch? Why didn't television do a soap like that, showing life, the actors taking care of children, cooking, making love. She always felt a bit depressed when the soaps ended, a sensation that things would go well, without her being able to participate in any way. Even with everything turning out well, even with Leleco and Vânia dating, Pedro and Valentina in Venice, even with Mr Alfredo's amnesia, living with his daughter, Carolaine felt sad at the end. She got up from the sofa, the children were asking for things. Shut up, Alas. Alas was big already and kept on hitting Junior. And after the other one was born, it would be worse still. I feel so listless. Where'd José Luís leave the money, Mother?

When she heard Carolaine's question, Alzira understood everything that had happened. So you asked José Luís for money? Did you? Of course not, Mother, she protested, he offered, I accepted, shee. You spent all our money, Alzira continued, going to the bedroom. Now I know why Zé came by with that talk. You squandered it all. Give me the card, I'm going to the bank, she said. Carolaine tried to stop her. But Alzira was furious. Give me the card, she screamed. If you spent all my money, you wretched woman, I'll kill you, Carolaine.

Alzira limped from the house, her leg was very swollen that afternoon. You can't walk with it like that, her daughter said from the gate. Mother, come back. Alzira ignored her. Jeez. Now things were going to get really bad.

Suzana in jeans, smiling with the newborn Alas in her arms. Suzana and Carolaine, in bikinis, at Copacabana beach. Suzana sitting on Miltão's lap. Suzana beside Zequinha at the Marrecos samba school rehearsal. Suzana and Alzira at the baptism of Junior. Suzana at the party for José Luís's tenth birthday, standing in front of the cake. She was just crazy about you, Zé Luís, from the day you were born, commented Dirce. It was Suzana who helped your mother give you your first bath. Alzira sometimes had to shoo my daughter away from there, Suzana only wanted to hold you on her lap. You're spoiling the boy, Alzira used to complain. Suzana really and truly loved you.

Sitting on the sofa at a friend's house, where she'd been living since Suzana's murder, Dirce showed the keepsakes of her daughter and wept. José Luís couldn't take his eyes off the photo he held in his hand: Suzana, pretty in a red ruffled dress, him with his arms around her waist. He remembered that day so clearly that it caused pain to rise in his chest, an immense sadness. It had been Suzana herself who had made the cake and the candy for his tenth birthday, he remembered even the moment when the photograph was taken. Go over by Suzana, his grandmother Cândida had said, and it had filled his heart with happiness. Suzana, goddamn it. What shit.

That day, José Luís found out that Suzana had died because she knew too much, and Dirce had been forced to leave the favela, in light of Marta's threats. Disappear, Marta told her, disappear before I have to turn you into hamburger for my dogs. Dirce also said that during the investigations leading to José Luís's arrest, the undercover policeman Denilson had had the full support of Marta, who had even been responsible for letting Denilson into the community. And it had also been Marta who encouraged the cop to approach Suzana for more information about the drug trade, claiming that Suzana had been the lover of both a boss of Berimbau and Zequinha, who controlled the Marrecos favela. He showed up saying he was a supermarket manager and everyone, including Suzana, believed him, Dirce related. And the problem is that after you were arrested, the man was already in love with my daughter and ended up talking. He told her everything. All the details. It was Marta herself who rented the house for him to move to Berimbau. The bitch. That happened at the time when the two of them were fighting over Zequinha's belongings. Suzana didn't think twice about it, she went straight to Marta, told her she'd go to see you in prison and spill 'the whole dirty story'. That's why Marta killed my daughter. You may not believe a single word, but Marta is the biggest bitch who ever set foot on earth. A real whore, Marta. Denilson suspected that she'd even hired people inside the prison to kill you, Kingie.

The story hadn't taken place exactly the way Dirce presented it, but it had in fact been Marta who'd brought Denilson to the favela. The idea, however, hadn't been hers. Denilson was a longtime partner of Romeu, the police detective who was a partner of Miltão but had been cut out once José Luís became boss of the favela. Shortly after Zequinha's death, Denilson sought out Marta. I was a friend of your father's, he said, a long way back, when your father did odd jobs. We did a lot of business together. I'll tell you what we're going to do with

José Luís: we're going to wipe him out. I thought you might like the chance to settle accounts for your father's death. You might want to set up your own business, I've heard you're good at it. As for me, it would be good for my career if I caught Kingie. My promotion depends on that sort of thing, you know how it is. We can work in that direction. Together. At that time, Marta wasn't thinking about killing José Luís, she merely wanted him to go to jail, wanted to demonstrate that he wasn't as great as he thought he was, pop, that he was vulnerable, but afterward, with José Luís's imprisonment, things got worse, pop, and she also began 'enjoying the business' and making money. Her feelings toward José Luís grew more confused as her dealings with Gavião became more complex.

Do you love Zé? More or less, she said that night to Priscilla as she waited for the trafficker's arrival. She was worried about the delay. He'd said he would return after taking Reader and would sleep at home. She had already sent messages to Reader and Onofre. Maybe, suggested Priscilla, he's fucking some woman out there. Or else he suspects you. That was what worried Marta, she wasn't prepared for what had happened, if she'd known of Kingie's escape she would have spoken more with Gavião. In this business of ours, Gavião had told her when informed of José Luís's escape, in this business of ours there's no such thing as 'wasting time'. Gavião, weeks earlier, had offered to lend her men to take over the favela. It was in his interest to help Marta because later it would be a simple task to remove her from there, at his convenience. In the drug trade, my dear, there can be no hesitation. You should've already taken a position. Do you want Berimbau or not? If you want it, there's only one way. Kill the guy. The only way. What time is it? Marta asked, concerned. A quarter of five. Go get Kingie, she told one of her men, and bring him here.

It was almost five o'clock when José Luís left the building on Santa Clara. A situation like that was easily resolved, that he knew. Simple. Simple. All he had to do was rent some soldiers from another trafficker, weapons, and go into the favela. That's all. Take all of them, the traitors, Marta, Gavião, and the others whose identities he was yet to learn, to an empty lot. Simple. Shoot them. Shit. He hated that sensation of vulnerability and of being pursued. Shit. Hidden things. Someone waiting in ambush, watching. He hated it. Enemies, dying, having to kill. Shit. He had had such good plans for when he got out of prison, and now everything was really lousy, much worse than before, it was like being in hell, an infernal heat, the city and its sewers, the stores full of 'Christmas crap'. Shit. What most irritated José Luís were 'those idiots dressed like Santa Claus'. He knew several of them in Berimbau. Drug dealing all year, stealing cars, con men, bank robbers, and December arrives and all of a sudden they come up with that story of changing their lives. Better than going to jail, they said. Clowns. Very simple to resolve the situation. But the problem was that suddenly he felt a great urge not to resolve any fucking thing at all. Shit, what about Marta? And the child they would never have? I swore, we swore. Shit. José Luís wandered through the streets for a long time, his head felt hot, he didn't know what to do. Very simple. Kill all the traitors. Or go away, far away, he didn't need that shit, fuck it. He could live very well without it. Kill them all, including Marta. Don't come back here. Onofre said when he called, later, from a pay phone. Things are strange as shit around here. Really strange.

Hello? Marta said as she answered the phone, José Luís? Is that you? I know it's you, José Luís, listen to what I have to say to you. Listen, for God's sake. Come home. José Luís? Gavião made a gesture for Marta to take it easy. Click. José Luís hung up. He wanted to curse Marta for a whore, a bitch, a cunt, but upon hearing her voice, imploring, he thought he was foolish to have called. Fuck Marta. Better for her not to be sure of anything, let her consume herself with doubts. After hanging up the telephone, he walked rapidly toward platform 14, where the Vôo Azul bus had just pulled in.

Kelly was nervously waiting for him. You took a long time, she said, where's my Coca-Cola? José Luís had forgotten to buy it, I'll go back and get it. No, Kelly said anxiously, go into the bathroom on the bus, in the rear, she said, it's better, it's safer. I've seen several policemen here in the bus station. It was a horrible sensation. For three days, ever since José Luís had come to tell her of developments, Kelly had been unable to sleep. She expected men to burst into her house at any moment, guns drawn, and take them into the woods, as they'd done with Suzana. She felt she was being watched in the favela. She had decided what she would do from the first moment José Luís had explained everything to her. Yes, I'm going, she'd replied. And José Luís had given her a list of things to be done, most of them relating to money. Do this, do that, it was horrible. She was fearful that they were following her, that she'd be taken prisoner. Thanks to her mother's support, it had all gone well. In the final analysis, it was Yolanda who had taken care of everything. And now it was almost over, in a few minutes they would be leaving the bus station for a new life. Her only regret was her mother, oh how Yolanda had cried. Get in the bathroom, please, José Luís, Kelly insisted, stop being stubborn for once in your life.

José Luís went into the bus's bathroom, sat on the toilet, and wondered if he'd acted in the best fashion, if he'd done the right thing in taking Kelly with him. Yes. Yes, he had. After all, he liked her. Everything was being handled in the best way possible, that was the truth.

He waited for the bus to pull out, and only when he sensed they were moving freely, no longer stopping for traffic lights in the city, did he return to his seat, beside Kelly.

33

'DONA JULIANA I'M WRITING because my situation is very difficult I need 300 urgent to buy medicine for my leg you know they cut off my leg because of the gangrene the sore grew a lot and got into the blood stream and they had to cut it off and now I can't work anymore because I'm a cripple nobody will help me please you're the only one I can turn to because the rich only use us and then when we're no use to them they throw us away help me please for the love of God, signed Alzira.' Now, said Carolaine, handing the letter to her mother, whose left leg had recently been amputated, just sign here, write your name, that's all. But I don't want you to say that about using and throwing away, commented Alzira, referring to what Carolaine had written against her wishes. Dona Juliana is very good to me.

Alex, Carolaine's third child, born three days after José Luís's flight and now six months old, began to cry. Good? If that bitch is good, Carolaine retorted, lifting her son from the crib, I'm Saint Carolaine of Rio de Janeiro. Irritated, she changed the infant's diaper. Shut up, you little pest. She had no luck with her kids. Nothing but crybabies. Alas, Junior, and now this 'cross to bear', a very fat baby, heavy, colicky and whining. A real pain, having kids. And alone, without a father, without a grandmother. Since Alzira's operation, Carolaine had been doing everything, without help from anyone, washing, ironing, and cooking, which is why she was harboring such negative feelings about Dona Juliana. She considered her responsible for her pitiful condition. After all, if the woman were reasonable, she wouldn't have stopped helping them 'just like that, from one minute to the next.' For six months, Carolaine regularly called her mother's ex-employer, asking for 'money for medicine', money that was used for everything in the house except the medicine for Alzira's varicose ulcer. That was how the two had managed to survive in the previous months, when the money from the sale of small appliances and 'junk' that her brother José Luís had left behind was no longer enough. The last time Carolaine had phoned her, Dona Juliana had been rude. I think, she'd said, I think you should get a job. Isn't the baby six months old now? Well, put him in day-care and go to work. Oh, how Carolaine hated to hear that, work? What day-care? What job? Has the woman gone crazy? Three kids, a cripple for a mother, how could she work? And that hadn't been the worst part. Juliana always gave in when Carolaine insinuated that if she didn't 'cooperate', Carolaine would go have a talk with Mr Rodrigo. On those occasions, Juliana would quickly get out her checkbook. Yes, yes, here's the money, three hundred, tell your mother I said hello. Juliana feared that Carolaine and Alzira could 'put ideas' in her husband's head by telling things from the past, about her affair with Fernando, her onetime personal trainer. You had to be there, Alicinha, she said, now that Alicinha had broken up 'definitively' with Fernando, more than enough reason for them to reconcile and go back to being what they proudly called 'inseparable girlfriends', you should hear the insolent tone of voice she uses to threaten me. That girl from the slums is blackmailing me. Alzira didn't know that Carolaine talked to Dona Juliana in those terms. The idea didn't enter her head of making problems for her old employer, after all, she was very grateful to her, Juliana had been the only one who had given her anything in life, she said, referring to the bank account opened with the money donated by her employer.

What are you saying, Carolaine? Juliana had asked in the last phone call. Are you by any chance threatening me? Is that it? Yes, it was a threat. Juliana had told the whole story to her current lover, Ricardo, her daughter's computer instructor, and, encouraged by the young man's advice, was categorical: Listen, little girl, she said, I want you to know I recorded this blackmail threat, the entire conversation was recorded, and if you ever call me again, for any reason at all, I'm going to go to the police and have you put in jail for attempted extortion. Caroline had become quite frightened. Attempted extortion must be something very important. The bitch, imagine, putting her in jail. Attempted extortion. With three children. If she found herself in that situation, it was because of Dona Juliana. If Alzira hadn't worked so hard, her leg wouldn't have rotted off. Now, begging was all that remained, and perhaps the letter would help. Maybe Dona Juliana would be moved by it. Caroline even thought of enclosing a photo of Alzira without one leg. Who knows? Dona Juliana, the whore. Every time Caroline went to pick up the money at her house she felt enormous hatred. Juliana was always on the telephone. Wait a minute, Caroline, she would say, always glued to a manicurist, a masseuse, always enjoying the good life, while she, she and her mother and the children lived in that hell. Yet, Caroline admitted, there was a good side. It was because of Dona Juliana that she'd found a new boyfriend, Edson, the doorman at the bitch's building. Even if Edson was a piece of crap. At first, he spoke all the time about leaving his wife. And now, nothing but stringing her along. Why couldn't she meet a nice romantic young man like Rick in the six o'clock soap? Compared to Rick, Edson was dog droppings on the sidewalk. And married, on top of everything else. And he wasn't about to leave his wife, no way, but 'let it go,' Caroline was more interested in Zino anyway. You know Zino, the butcher? she'd asked Yolanda. Well, Zino's been asking me out. Actually, the relationship between the two was well advanced, and Caroline even suspected an undesired pregnancy, her period was more than a month late, but she wasn't certain of anything. Edson could be the father, it was true. And she had also been with a young man, just the one night, so if she really was pregnant she couldn't say for sure who the father was. And she wasn't at all concerned, she'd get an abortion in any case. Yes, she'd get rid of the baby. Alex had definitely taught her a lesson: she hated kids. It was boring to be trapped in the house because of brats. For all these reasons she had Alzira sign the letter. Or would you rather starve to death? Our situation couldn't be worse, Mother.

Carolaine was leaving to deliver the letter to Dona Juliana in Leblon when Onofre arrived, panting, to say that José Luís was on the phone in the bar. Praise God, shouted Alzira, go, daughter, go and bring me the news of my little boy. The two women had had no news of José Luís and Kelly since the couple had fled six months earlier. Yolanda, Kelly's mother, received telegrams from her daughter now and again. We're fine, they said, and that was all. Many stories circulated about the former boss of Berimbau: that José Luís had become rich. That he was living in Paraguay and commanded the drug traffic from there. That he would return to reclaim his place, taken over by Volnei, an ally of Gavião. That Volnei was actually his right-hand man. But it was all rumor, and in actuality no one knew the details of José Luís's new life.

Carolaine, who had lost only fifteen of the sixty pounds she had put on during her most recent pregnancy, climbed the hillside with difficulty, panting. Let's go, Carolaine, it's long-distance, said Onofre, that's expensive, hurry.

Hi, Zé, she said. When she heard her brother's voice she burst into tears. Glad to hear you're alive. Oh Zé, she said, everything is so hard.

Much had changed since her brother's flight. And what had changed most in the life of Berimbau had been the tragic death of Marta, machine-gunned in the main street of the favela by Volnei's men. It had occurred exactly two weeks after José Luís left. Marta had received a phone call from Gavião asking for men for an urgent operation. Not suspecting an ambush, Marta provided the soldiers, thus opening the doors of Berimbau to the enemy. Priscilla and her grandmother were expelled from the favela. But Volnei had been 'great' with José Luís's family, Carolaine related. He allowed her to take whatever was in her brother's house, television, refrigerator, microwave, and Carolaine had sold everything. We spent everything, she told her brother on the telephone, 'cause Mother had to have her leg cut off, and I've got a new baby, since Christmas. His name is

Alex. And now Mother's a cripple. Shit. José Luís was devastated by the news. Buy her a wheelchair, he suggested, ask Reader about the store where we bought his, it's a very good place, they only sell stuff for cripples. Reader? Carolaine said, you don't know? Reader died.

Although many insisted that Reader's death was Volnei's doing, the truth is that he had died in a fire caused by a candle left in his shack by his friend Onofre. That night, a storm had knocked out the power in all of Berimbau. In the early hours, a strong gust blew the candle onto a pile of books. Reader was still awake and, long before the flames reached him, knew he was going to die. Contrary to what his friends imagined, his end was a moment not of terror but of peace and relief. He saw the candle topple and hoped the fire would spread before anyone could come to save him. Imprisoned in the wheelchair for over a year, without being able to do what he considered the two best things in the world, 'reading and fucking,' defecating in diapers, and, what was worse, understanding everything, for some time he had been nursing the idea of suicide. Therefore, when he saw the flames approaching the bed he was overcome by such euphoria that he succeeded in emitting sonorous laughter.

José Luís was depressed at the news of his friend's death. But there was more, additional tragedies. Their father had disappeared, Carolaine said. But not before causing a lot of problems. He had 'drunk away' both minivans and had created numerous headaches in the favela. He'd had countless arguments with his neighbors. And run up a pile of debts. He started coming by the house, Carolaine said, asking Mother for money, leaning into the window, begging. Now he's disappeared, Carolaine continued. Just as well. Somebody saw him in Praça Argentina, sprawled in a corner among the garbage.

And there was other news. Rosa Maria was back from Germany. It was Onofre who told that story. On vacation? José Luís asked. No, for good. Rosa Maria had caught her husband with Jennifer. Remember Jennifer? That little dark girl that Rosa Maria took to be her maid in Germany? Well then. The girl came out on top. Rosa Maria caught the two of them bare-ass naked, fucking in the garage. Before I could say a word, Onofre, Rosa Maria had told him, Jennifer started screaming at me to pack my things and get the hell out of there. She wouldn't even let Heinrich explain. She yelled and cussed me and my no-good German just stood there with his ass-white face, that damned sausage-eater, and didn't even say gutentag. After all the potatoes, all the sauerkraut I made for the ingrate. And you know what, Onofre? Fuck 'em both. Every night, before I go to sleep, I close my eyes and concentrate. Cancer in the girl's asshole, that's what I picture. I'm casting a voodoo spell on their lives, I'm certain they're going to end up getting fucked. If they have a child it'll be born retarded, with an oversized head, because my saint is powerful. It's going to be a mongoloid mulatto, which'll make them crazy as hell. Even better. It's going to be black, a big crippled black baby, so they'll stop thinking they're better than other people. How I helped that girl. She was going to be a whore like Dadá. I took her to Germany, gave her room and board, the best of everything Germany had to offer, but God will hear my prayers. Every day I wake up expecting news. By then I'm going to know enough German to tell Heinrich, Go fuck yourself, go to hell. Take your potatoes and go fuck yourself. Oh Onofre, it's so awful to hate the one you love. What can you do? Onofre said on the phone. If she'd at least learned German, she'd have known she was being deceived. Now, Rosa Maria was back in 'the life'. She had tried at first to find work as a salesgirl. But a black woman's job here is as a hooker, she had explained to Onofre. I hate having people order me around. I hate bosses. Shit, how about that, Rosa Maria, huh? said José Luís. Those whores are something else. And what about that Volnei guy? Caroline mentioned a Volnei, who is he? Onofre was very enthusiastic about the new boss. He's cool. He only killed Marta, Cachaça, and Mário Paula. The rest are all still here. The same crap as always. And what about my grandmother? Any news there?

At that moment, the connection dropped.

José Luís, who was at a public phone near his house, thought about buying another phone card, but to do so he would have to go to the post office and speak to that Zulmira woman. He couldn't stand Zulmira.

In Depósito Novo, a small town in the northern part of the state of Roraima, almost on the Venezuelan border, life was very dull. No one had a good time. Everything was 'very slow', only television or a bunch of old people playing dominoes in the square, really boring, shit.

At first he and Kelly thought it was going to be good. After all, no one there knew them, it was like living abroad. It doesn't even seem like Brazil here, Zé. He couldn't say what the place *did* seem like. It seemed like the end of the world. They had bought a bar near the river, but José Luís never imagined it would be so hard to run a bar. A lot of work. Very boring, shit. Frying turnovers. Cleaning, buying things, selling, and no profit, only losses. He'd never been good at dealing with money. And that pitiful life was killing him. No one there knew him. He would go for a walk and not even the cops knew who he was, of course, shit, that was good. But no one paid him the slightest mind, and that was a total change from being leader of the Berimbau favela. Shit.

That afternoon, discouraged, he returned to the bar, knowing that Marta and Reader had died, that his mother was missing a leg, and that his father had gone back to living in the street, drunk again, all of it stabbed him in the heart. And Volnei. He vaguely recalled the name. Volnei. Maybe he'd met him in the drug trade, that sort of thing happened a lot, in fact it was a golden rule not to mistreat some nobody because the guy you diss today, Reader used to say in their glory days, may be calling the shots tomorrow.

He saw Kelly sitting at the bar with a sullen look on her face. The turnovers had shriveled up, and a smell of old grease hung heavy in the air. Hi, Kelly. For days now, Kelly had been acting that way, strange, absent, weepy. I phoned Onofre, he said. Sometimes, she got all dolled up to go to the post office and would come back happy, only to become sad again after a few hours, crying in the bathroom. I miss my mother, she said.

José Luís began relating the news, and Kelly burst into tears, a convulsive sobbing. Oh God, she said, the sadness I feel in my heart. Shit, calm down. José Luís said, we'll go back to Rio one day, we'll visit your mother. Shit. It's not that, Kelly answered. I don't miss anything. And I'm not crying because of Reader. Then what is it? José Luís asked. I've been lying to you. I'm going to leave you. I'm going away, she said.

It was all just too ridiculous, thought José Luís later. I'm really a piece of shit, she'd said, I'm crying because I waited for you my whole life, you would go by my house with your men, your dogs, the only thing I didn't do was fall on the ground for you to walk over me, that was how much I wanted to be your wife. And now that we're here, now that everything's good, we have our bar, and even if this isn't the prettiest city in the world we're here, at peace, you have a decent life, we're losing money but so be it, now that everything's fine, this tragedy happens. And then the tragedy came to the surface. Kelly was in love with a man from Bahia, a very nice young man who owned a luncheonette in Salvador and also sang in steakhouses, who two months earlier had come to Depósito Novo to visit his grandmother. What can I do? He left and has been back three times. I want you to know I've never slept with Anderson, he hasn't laid a hand on me, just one kiss and nothing else, but I happen to be in love with Anderson, I adore him, love him, passionately. I told him, Anderson, I live with someone, disappear from my life, for the love of God, don't come back to my bar, but he did come back, yesterday he came here and told me, I'm going to talk with Zé Luís, explain our situation to him. I think of nothing but Anderson all day long, Zé. I made a vow, if I can forget that man. I'll go a whole year without eating condensed milk, but I can't, I think about him, only him, it's like some kind of sickness. Even with you it wasn't like this. I liked you, but it wasn't like this. I admired you, she said, as José Luís noticed the verb tense she was using: liked, loved, admired. I love Anderson. And he loves me. And everything happened, it came down. And if you plan to kill Anderson, it's better to kill me too.

Kelly left that same afternoon. José Luís helped her pack her bags, helped her put her suitcases in the other man's car, and unlike what she imagined, he wasn't sad, or upset. He felt only indifference to it all. He felt empty, with nothing inside, no filling, as if he were nothing but a handful of muscles, and weary, very weary. He liked Kelly, but he didn't care if she left. Let her go, shit. Let everything end, for good. The young man, Anderson, had said, You can be sure I'll take care of her. Ridiculous, shit. Ciao.

An old man came into the bar just as José Luís made his decision. We're closed, he told the man, we're closed. Closed? When do you reopen? asked the man. Never. Never again, answered José Luís. Move along. Shit.

José Luís opened his eyes and only then saw he was at the bus station in Rio de Janeiro. He leaped up, grabbing his backpack, the only baggage he'd brought, and sleepily got off the bus, his body aching. The smell of Rio de Janeiro, shit, how good that sea-smell was, rotten fish and exhaust fumes. He still felt groggy from the long trip, he had changed buses three times, spent four days traveling.

He went to the bar and ordered a drink and buttered bread, but he couldn't eat, Rio de Janeiro had taken away his hunger. Shit, it's good to be back. He went to the bus stop, happy to see the crowds, the city's confusion, how good it was. A cop right in front of him. He walked past him, maybe they'd already forgotten about all that business.

When he got off the bus at Berimbau, in front of Zino's butcher's shop, he saw Rosa Maria arriving from a night's work. In a minuscule pink miniskirt, she made her way up the hillside, hips swaying, in her high heels. He also noticed the movement of the new errand boys for the traffic, he knew none of them, but they were surely letting Volnei know of his arrival in the favela. Nothing had changed after all. By now, a laser-equipped machine gun might be trained on him.

Two of his dogs were there, sniffing around the butcher shop garbage. Thin, famished, Jaboti, Gulliver, José Luís shouted.

The dogs came to him, barking, taking a few seconds to recognize their old owner.

There wasn't a cloud in the sky, and the sun made everything glow and burn. The forecast that day was that the temperature would rise to 107 degrees, abnormal for that time of year, the fare collector on the bus had commented. Shit. José Luís slowly climbed the hillside, not knowing exactly what he would do, the dogs ahead of him, barking.

A NOTE ON THE AUTHOR

Patrícia Melo is a novelist, scriptwriter and playwright. Her novels *The Killer* and *In Praise of Lies* are both published by Bloomsbury. In 1999, *Time* magazine included her among the fifty 'Latin American Leaders for the New Millennium'.

Clifford E. Landers is professor of Political Science at New Jersey City University. His translations include novels by Rubem Fonseca, Jorge Amado, João Ubaldo Ribeiro, and José de Alencar among others. His *Literary Translation: A Practical Guide* was published in 2001 by Multilingual Matters Ltd.

A NOTE ON THE TYPE

The text of this book is set in Linotype Janson. The original types were cut in about 1690 by Nicholas Kis, a Hungarian working in Amsterdam. The face was misnamed after Anton Janson, a Dutchman who worked at the Ehrhardt Foundry in Leipzig, where the original Kis types were kept in the early eighteenth century. Monotype Ehrhardt is based on Janson. The original matrices survived in Germany and were acquired in 1919 by the Stempel Foundry. Herman Zapf used these originals to redesign some of the weights and sizes for Stempel. This Linotype version was designed to follow the original types under the direction of C. H. Griffith.